I0636379

THE COLORADO SEQUENCE

STACEY COCHRAN

Lulu Press

ISBN: 978-0-6151-4616-4

Cover design by Mimosa Mallernee

Manufactured in the United States of America

First Lulu Press Edition: May 2007

For more information, visit staceycochran.com

And e-mail the author via stacey@staceycochran.com

For Susan

ONE
THE CARIBBEAN ISLAND

Dr. Amy Levine's interview with the U.S. government took place ninety miles *east* of Miami, Florida. Man-O-War Cay, Great Abaco Island. The island was privately owned by a firm known as Nano Tech, but no Nano Tech employee had ever set foot on the island. No Nano Tech employee had ever set foot anywhere, for that matter, because Nano Tech only existed on paper.

"You've known this," Agent Noah Johnston said. "You've known about the Line."

Levine's chestnut brown eyes shone in the sunlight coming in from the window. At close distance, the reflection of the world could be seen in her eyes. They were brown with a light trail of blue around the edges.

"Is that right, Dr. Levine?" Johnston said.

"It's what I've worked on the last fourteen years," Levine said, "the Colorado Sequence of the Line. It's what my mom and dad worked on before they died."

Her eyes focused. She watched Noah Johnston from a denim-colored club chair. Johnston was across the room, standing. He wore a white shirt, a gray tie loosened at the neck, brown trousers, and soft leather oxfords. He was casual, but at the mention of Levine's parents, Johnston became uneasy, his eyes not meeting anyone else's.

There were two other operatives in the room: Agents Andy Barnes and Sara McKenzie. The conversation appeared relaxed and informal, but the answers Levine provided would determine whether she returned to the U.S. alive in seven days or was sent home in an urn, a few ounces of gray ash.

The lawn maintenance crew was outside the house, Levine saw, with leaf blowers, weed whackers, and shiny red riding mowers. It looked like a dozen men, each steely eyed. Or so Levine thought.

Four dock workers were down by the marina. Nano Tech owned a three-hundred-foot Bugatti that rested at the deep-water dock like a sleek building on its side. There were six ski boats tied near the Bugatti, children around a towering parent. A dozen jet skis patrolled the waters beyond the private marina.

And it suddenly reached her in a flash. An image swept through her mind like moving pictures. A man lifted up his weed whacker and began firing. Explosions. The guys on the Bugatti were running toward the front of the boat. There was a fire in the cockpit. The helicopter on the Bugatti was trying to take off.

Noah saw the sharp look wash over Levine's eyes.

"You alright, Dr. Levine?" he said.

Sara McKenzie looked from Levine to Johnston. Their eyes met. Andy Barnes stared at Levine.

"The dockworkers," Levine said. She was sitting up in the chair staring out the window. She knew. She knew what they were going to do. "The lawn maintenance guys."

The three operatives looked from one to the other.

"What about 'em?" Sara McKenzie said, a hint of her Georgia accent coming through. "What about the lawn maintenance guys?"

McKenzie had short red hair and green eyes both fierce and pleasant. Besides Levine, she was the most intelligent human on the island.

"What about the dockworkers?" Johnston said. "What about the lawn maintenance?"

There was a pause. Dr. Amy Levine's eyes seemed to drift deep in thought to a far away place. Her pupils became narrow, focused, black dots tight as two rays of light. Her eyelids blinked. Then, her mind gathered together the full force of its conscious and unconscious powers. Levine looked around the room at each of them, calmly, slowly.

"They're gonna kill us," she said. "They're gonna kill us all."

• •

Ramon Martinez operated the Weed Master 2000 like it was nobody's business. He imagined himself a conductor before a symphony, and the Weed Master was his wand. The blades of grass were moments of time that had to be mastered. Little did he know that forty meters away, Dr. Amy Levine had seen inside his mind.

Ramon let up on the Weed Master's trigger. He wiped his brow and looked at the three dockworkers down by the docks. One of the men gave him a nod. Ramon recognized the signal and touched his temple as described by their plan.

He turned and looked up at the big house.

There was a long running porch on the front and sides of the home. The house was impressive, painted yellow and white with a manicured lawn, hedge and flowers. On the second floor, a terrace opened out from the upstairs rooms.

There were three Nano Tech agents on the terrace. They wore gray slacks and white shirts. They carried machineguns and looked out at the lawn from behind sleek black sunglasses.

One of the men looked at Ramon. Ramon gave him a friendly wave from behind the Weed Master 2000. The man in the dark sunglasses made no noticeable expression at all, but readjusted his machinegun.

Ramon looked down past the docks. He saw his man on a ski boat, which was tied to the dock. His man wore a red baseball cap, and Ramon knew that the signal would come when the man turned his cap around backwards.

Ramon tapped the Weed Master 2000 on the ground lightly as though knocking grass off its end. The man on the ski boat nodded, and Ramon touched his temple again as described by their plan.

• •

Inside the living room, there were three dozen microphones and a dozen lipstick-sized cameras. Everyone in the room knew this, of course, even Levine. But the government insisted on the image of secrecy when interviewing through Nano Tech. Psychologists knew that an interview that appeared relaxed and informal was more likely to unearth useful information than a dark uncomfortable interview with menacing agents and anxiety-laced attitudes. The interview itself was grueling enough.

Levine had been contacted three months before because much of her work went beyond cutting-edge. The government had kept a file on her since her days at Brown, but it had only become necessary in the past three years to monitor her closely.

Levine's work brought together the disparate fields of psychology and physics in a way like no other scientist before her. A *Scientific American* article penned by Nobel-prize-winning physicist Donald Antrætus called Levine "the most intelligent human being on the planet." Levine had long been a loner, all through her childhood, aloof and intense, possessing the rarest combination of mind: she was both extraordinarily creative and extraordinarily analytical.

But the very traits that some saw as a gift, others called problematic and burdensome. Some men in the field of theoretical astrophysics said Levine carried a chip on her shoulder. And one well-known scientist, a French astrophysicist named Pierre Refenault, had gone so far as to say, "Dr. Amy Levine's biggest flaw is that she's trying to prove herself to the two people to whom she never can."

Foster homes gave way to a private finishing school, where she played chess with an eighteen hundred E.L.O. rating and published two essays with *The New Yorker*. But chess and writing were her pastimes, her hobbies, and she did them for fun. By the ninth grade, she had fallen in love with applied mathematics and a healthy ethics curriculum in an upstate New York girls' school. As she grew older, mathematics gave way to physics, and ethics to human psychology. She was the highest rated student at one of the highest rated prep schools in the country. And at sixteen she went to Brown on a full academic scholarship.

Amazingly, she wasn't a nerd. She was very pretty, even sexy. And girls that remembered her from high school recalled that she had a terrific sense of humor and enjoyed minor league baseball games. She went on dates but never dated any one boy too seriously. Love was something that would come in its own time, and she was self-aware enough to know that giving herself over to that strong an emotion was something that required a maturity that would come with age.

"She was always making us laugh," Karen Anders said in a preliminary interview with Nano Tech agents. "But she was always challenging us. It was no secret at school that she was a descendant of the Lincoln family. Though she never mentioned *that*. We all knew Amy was different."

Her senior thesis at Brown earned her a Whitman Grant, and from two professors at Brown, a Pulitzer nomination. She had brought together seamlessly the fields of psychology and physics and was credited with developing traffic-light photography machines.

Levine designed the programs, the early prototypes, and convinced the legislature in Providence, Rhode Island, to allow her team to install the first traffic-light camera in the country. Levine understood the Pavlovian underpinnings of a system that nailed you every time for breaking the law and which could not be argued with. And love 'em or hate 'em, the ZoneCor traffic intersections reduced traffic accidents and red-light abuses in a way that was unprecedented in modern law enforcement. She was nineteen at the time, and the ZoneCor patent sold for seventeen million to a company called Nestor.

Fortune magazine did an article on Levine as the youngest self-made entrepreneur in the country. But Levine never read it. Money, to her, was a stale trapping, and she gave her money over to a financial adviser. Levine *was* interested in wealth, but the wealth she was interested in had nothing to do with dollars and cents.

At the age of twenty-three, she moved to a mountain in southern Arizona and began doing work that the most intelligent minds on Earth could not yet comprehend. She was tapping on a door to the other side of reality, and in a 2009 essay for *Nature*, she described succinctly a method for attaining precognitive awareness.

Scholars around the globe immediately described her work as "disturbing" and "the product of an overeducated mind." Non-expert pundits either satirized her work with cartoonish psychics wearing turbans and holding playing cards in front of their foreheads or declared "it is time to rein in the mad scientist, Dr. Amy Levine."

But Levine was anything but mad. She had attained total mental clarity and felt completely at peace. And slowly, a few detractors began to study closely what would come to be known as Levine's "early work." And the few who weren't frightened by her work's implications saw an elegance and beauty underlying the algorithms, a symmetry that hinted at an order within the universe.

Levine's next move was equally provocative and, after the fact, as equally understandable. She left science altogether and took a job at a

Wal-Mart in Loveland, Colorado. At the bright age of twenty-six, one of the world's most intelligent minds became Sales Associate #4795 at a Super-Sav-R Wal-Mart earning ten cents more than minimum wage.

Wal-Mart put her to work in the Electronics Department where her major tasks were running the register and handing out processed film to people who'd had their photos developed. At the close of every evening she had to "freshen up" the shelves around the Electronics Department. People who knew Levine's work speculated that she was turning her attention to Game Theory, that she was writing algorithms to describe why customers bought what they bought, to describe patterns underlying something as ordinary as shopping for CDs at the Wal-Mart CD shelf.

And while a CD shelf would make for an interesting fixed-system study, Levine's mind was not studying it that way. True, Levine was always *thinking* in terms of theory and order, but in sixteen months at Wal-Mart, she never once wrote an essay, never once reasoned her way through an algorithm. She never seriously considered doing a study of the lives she came to know. To her, that would have been crass and inappropriate. She just wanted to get to know people. Real people. To her, that was fulfilling in a way that no accolade or scientific theory could be. People mattered most to Amy Levine.

Ironically, it was working at Wal-Mart that brought her under the U.S. government's close scrutiny. She had already been a potential red flag within the military-scientific community, but the truth was no one understood her work. While she had *described* a method for attaining precognitive awareness, only about a dozen of the best minds around the planet understood what her work meant. And even for those who understood it, it still required a human being with the mental discipline to actualize it. Her essay had described a way in which the human mind could accurately predict things (within a fixed-equilibrium system) that had not yet happened in present time and space, but it still required a human being to follow through with it. And, as yet, no one had. But her move to Wal-Mart? That was seen as purely political.

It was as though the U.S. government had no objections to scientists staying within the scientific community—preaching to the choir, so to speak—but for a mind as dynamic as Levine's to focus her interest on everyday people in the *midst* of everyday people was so unusual it warranted suspicion. And so *that* was when the U.S. government became interested in the life and work of Dr. Amy Levine.

••

The first three gunshots were quick, fast. They sounded like they came from the marina. People were shouting.

Johnston stood in the middle of the living room, and he looked at Levine.

"How did you know?" he said.

"I just know," Levine said. "I see things up here, first."

But before she had time to explain further, a series of automatic machinegun-fire exchanges sounded out on the lawn. They could hear the gunmen upstairs shouting commands. All four in the living room saw three Nano Tech agents carrying machineguns run by on the porch.

Another barrage rang out from across the lawn near one of the guest houses. An explosion shook the windows and walls of the house. Levine saw flames on the guest house. Agent Andy Barnes was by the window. He'd drawn his handgun and was looking out on the lawn.

"It looks like a dozen men," Barnes shouted. "I see four down by the dock! It looks like three by the guest house—"

A bullet struck the window. Glass rained down onto the floor. Sara McKenzie covered Levine with her body as best she could, and both women dropped down to the floor.

Noah Johnston was near the door to the hallway with his two-way radio.

"What do we got?" Johnston shouted into the walkie-talkie.

A voice squawked back, "Get her down into the bunker! We got two dozen on the grounds and radar's showing boats approaching. Get Levine down into the bunker!"

Another explosion rocked the house. This one was closer, and it brought a few paintings and fixtures down from the walls in the living room. Levine could hear machinegun fire from upstairs on the terrace. Men shouted. Barnes was on one knee by the window. He aimed his handgun through the window and fired.

The sound was shockingly loud. Levine winced, and her ears started ringing. She looked at Barnes. Barnes capped off four quick shots. Sara McKenzie was trying to help Levine up.

Johnston shouted, "We have to get her down to the bunker!"

He jabbed a finger toward the hallway, and Sara McKenzie lifted Levine up onto her feet. The two women crossed the living room. Another explosion sent them to the floor. This one was right outside the living room window, and Levine's head started swimming in a punch-drunk state. She was on the floor.

She tried getting to her feet, but her legs were weak. In her visual periphery, she saw Agent Barnes on his back near the window. Barnes wasn't moving. Johnston shouted something at Levine and McKenzie, and Levine felt McKenzie grabbing her, pulling her toward the interior hallway.

The image came to Levine in a flash: she saw a steel-girder stairwell leading down into a concrete bunker. The walls were well-lighted gray, and far up at the end of the bunker hallway she saw a room with computers and electronic, hologram maps. But there was no one in the bunker until her feet hit the ground at the foot of the steel-girder stairwell. She looked up and saw the assassins rounding a corner inside the computer room. The men carried machineguns, and they looked up and realized Levine, McKenzie, and Johnston were right there. The men opened fire, and Johnston was hit. McKenzie and Levine turned and started back up the steel-girder stairwell, but more machinegun fire rang out. Levine heard McKenzie roar out in pain; she was hit! Levine was halfway up the stairwell, and she looked back briefly. Sara McKenzie yelled at her to "Get to the docks! The boats are the only way off the island!" The image vanished.

McKenzie yelled at her, "Follow Johnston! The bunker's at the back of the house!"

They were in a hallway inside the house. Machinegun fire shattered a window in an adjacent dining room, and bullets riddled the silver and blue wallpapered wall. The chandelier crashed down from the ceiling, upending the dining-room table, and Levine saw the table was actually a massive computer console that would project images on the facing wall. Its monitors, lights, keyboards, and dials were exposed, but Levine was already diving forward through the hallway. She hit the floor.

Another explosion rocked the south side of the house. It sounded like machinegun fire was coming from all sides of the house now. Another explosion down by the docks. Levine could hear a helicopter trying to take off, its blades spinning faster and faster. Men shouted. She heard the whine and roar of boats down on the water, and she saw that image of the bunker again: McKenzie yelling at her to go for the docks, that the boats were the only way off the island. McKenzie shot.

"Don't go down in the bunker!" she yelled at Johnston.

Johnston was at a pantry in the kitchen. Sunlight streamed in the clear kitchen windows. Levine saw the shine of crystal blue water down by the docks, the swaying of palm trees outside the house, men running across the manicured lawn firing machineguns. Johnston looked at her a brief second and opened the kitchen pantry door.

McKenzie ran into the kitchen, her Beretta drawn. She saw something outside the kitchen window and opened fire. Levine winced and covered her ears.

Johnston pushed a shelf to one side inside the pantry, and Levine saw a shiny silver door revealed. It was a secret passageway down into the bunker. There was a large wheel on the door. Johnston started to turn the wheel to open the door.

Levine said, "We should *not* go down in the bunker. There are gunmen down there. Is there another entrance into the bunker?"

Johnston started to pull the shiny silver door open.

He said, "There are four entryways into the bunker from various places on the island!"

"The gunmen have gotten in," Levine said. "There are men already down there! They have guns."

"Are you sure?" Johnston said.

But McKenzie was pushing them both into the pantry, into the secret door inside.

"We can't hold 'em off up here," McKenzie said. "The bunker's the only way!"

Johnston went first through the shiny silver doorway, followed by McKenzie, and Levine was quickly hit with a shuddering chill. She saw the steel-girder stairwell she had seen in her mind just a moment before. They were walking right into the vision she had just had.

The walls were well-lighted gray. Johnston hit the ground at the base of the stairwell, and Levine found herself reaching forward, grabbing McKenzie by the back of her shirt. Levine pulled hard, refusing to let McKenzie walk right into what she knew was going to happen.

McKenzie turned around and said, "What the hell! Levine, this is the only way—"

Gunshots rang out from down inside the bunker. Johnston hit the ground. Quick horror filled Sara McKenzie's eyes, and she raised her Beretta up to fire down the hallway inside the bunker. But Levine had her. She pulled her back up into the kitchen.

Sara McKenzie cried out, "You bastards!" And unloaded her Beretta down the steel-girder stairwell into the bunker.

Levine pulled her back through the pantry, and McKenzie stumbled and fell to the kitchen floor. Levine closed the shiny silver door and spun the wheel to lock it into place. The gunmen were coming up the steel-girder stairwell on the other side of the bulletproof door, and McKenzie fired at it. Levine could hear the men shouting on the other side of the thick silver door.

"Where do we go?" Levine said. "How do we get off the island?"

"The boats," McKenzie said. "The boats down by the marina! They're the only way off of the island!"

Both women were up. They ran through the house toward the front door. A massive explosion rocked the house from the kitchen area behind them. Fire and debris blasted forward up the hallway throwing both women out the front door onto the front porch. Levine rolled down off of the porch onto the green grassy lawn.

It looked like a war zone. The guest house was ablaze. There were fallen bodies on the lawn. A firefight was going on down by the boats. The helicopter was trying to lift off from the Bugatti. Nano Tech agents were near the landing pad, holding a firefight with the assassins trying to climb up the boat.

Bullets roared by Levine and exploded into the bushes and porch on the front of the house. A squad of four gunmen came at them from across the lawn. Levine winced and rolled over, trying to gain cover.

Sara McKenzie was on one knee on the front porch. She fired her Beretta. She hit one of the men, and the other three dove to the ground.

She yelled at Levine, "Go! I've got you covered! Get down to the docks!"

Levine leapt up like a sprinter. She had a hundred meters to sprint down to the marina, and there were explosions and machinegun fire all around the house and the lawn. The island was under siege.

She sprinted hard, fast, could feel the smooth green grass padding under her feet. She felt a bullet whisk through her hair, but she didn't turn her sight from the docks. She saw a single ski boat at the end of the dock. It was all by itself, and the major firefight was at the far end of the dock up by the massive Bugatti.

Then the gunmen saw her, and they started shouting to leave the helicopter, to get Levine. A dozen men came from the Bugatti and ran up the wooden docks toward Levine. Fifteen meters, ten meters, five meters—

Levine leapt through the air from the dock and landed in the back of the ski boat. She clambered forward and hit the hand-operated accelerator, and the ski boat rose up and roared out into the water. The gunmen reached the end of the dock and opened fire on her, but she was already fifty meters out into the bay.

She looked up and saw men on jet skis coming at her boat from the harbor opening. She saw the freedom of the Atlantic Ocean beyond the cove, but there were a dozen jet skis roaring toward her over the crystal blue water.

The men on the jet skis had machineguns, and they opened fire on her. She turned the wheel hard to the right and ducked down inside the cockpit of the ski boat. The machinegun fire shattered the little glass window on the front of the boat. Levine pulled the wheel hard to the left. The ski boat was going too fast for how hard she turned the wheel, and it looked for certain that the boat would capsize. It was up on its side, and Levine was thrown to the floor of the boat, then against the left wall. The boat slammed down and took on water, but it did not capsize.

Levine struggled to her feet, dazed. She staggered back to the wheel of the ski boat, but before she could sit down, she looked up and realized she was surrounded by the jet skis. A dozen jet skis surrounded her, and each man pointed a machinegun at her.

"Don't move, Dr. Levine!" one man shouted. "Or my men will open fire."

Levine looked up, and her vision became clearer. A man with lively brown eyes and dark brown hair stepped from his jet ski onto the front of the ski boat. He did not carry a machinegun, but the other eleven men on jet skis had her in their sights. He raised his palms up to her in a comforting gesture.

"Now, now Dr. Levine," he said. "Enough lives have been lost today. Take your hands off of the wheel. We just want to talk with you."

Levine looked from one machinegun barrel to the next. Her hair was soaked, her shirt drenched. She could see plumes of smoke billowing up from buildings on the island. There was one more volley in the distance, but it sounded like these men had the island under control. Levine slowly lifted her hands up from the steering wheel. She looked at the man with the lively brown eyes.

"Who are you?" she said. "And what do you want from me?"

TWO
ARIZONA

Roger McAllister wore a black cowboy hat tilted back on his head, and through dark sunglasses, his blue eyes took in the real estate office. The wrinkles around his eyes bunched up.

"—like rain." He heard when he opened the front door.

A woman with gray hair and a pleasant smile looked up at him from a desk. An electric typewriter stood atop one of three desks behind her. McAllister saw it, removed his sunglasses, and his eyes warmed over with a curious smile.

"That's a Smith-Corona," he said.

The woman at the desk looked confused a moment. She took in this stranger's eyes and looked at the typewriter.

"Oh," she said. "Why yes, it is."

"I haven't seen one of those in twenty years," he said. "I didn't know they still made 'em."

"Oh, I don't think they do," she said. "This one's probably about that old." The woman sat properly at her desk. They didn't get a lot of strangers in the town of Oracle. A window-mounted AC unit hummed, pumping cool air into the dry dusty Arizona office. "What can I do for you?" she said.

McAllister glanced in the office to the left. A second woman pretended to read the papers atop her desk, but McAllister realized they'd been talking when he entered. He smiled.

"I wonder if you might be able to help me out with some information," he said.

"What's that?"

The woman in the adjoining office quit *pretending* to listen at this point and lay her hands flat atop her desk. She was pointedly listening to this exchange now between her office secretary and this stranger.

"Roger McAllister," the man in the black Stetson said. He produced a business card.

The secretary took the card. She held it up in front of her at the desk, looking it over.

Roger McAllister, McAllister Investigations
Twenty+ Years Experience in
Missing Persons
Marital Investigations
Mobile Surveillance

There was all the pertinent contact information, including a P.O. Box in Grand Rapids, Michigan.

"You're a long way from home, Mr. McAllister," the secretary said.

"Don't I know it." He smiled.

The woman in the adjoining office stood up and came to her office door.

"Helen Richards," she said. "What can I do for you, Mr. McAllister?"

McAllister looked from one woman to the next.

"Helen, I was hired by the Levine family."

"Oh, yes?"

"Yes," McAllister said. "What can you tell me about Dr. Amy Levine?"

"Is something the matter?"

"She hasn't been heard from since December," McAllister said. "Family first contacted me a month ago. Said it wasn't unusual for their daughter to go for months without being heard from. It was her way. But it's been nine months. They're concerned."

Helen looked at McAllister. He was an edgy man, and he intrigued her.

"Come in my office," Helen said. "Can I get you something to drink?"

"Coffee'd be fine," Roger said.

Helen poured coffee into a white Styrofoam cup and handed it to McAllister.

"You say her family contacted you?" Helen asked.

"Yes, ma'am, that is correct," McAllister said. "It's a strange story. I received a cashier's check for eighty thousand dollars from a party I'd never met before. Three days later, I received a phone call from a man identifying himself as Oscar Levine. He wanted to hire me to find his daughter. I traced his call to a town in Arizona called Paradise."

"Paradise?" Helen said.

"It's in southeastern Arizona, near the New Mexico state line."

"I know Paradise, Arizona. It's a ghost town, Mr. McAllister. Nobody lives out there."

"Well, that's not entirely true," McAllister said. "There's almost a dozen people that live in Paradise. And though it doesn't look it, there are more than eighty residents who live nine miles down the road in Portal."

"Portal?"

"Portal, Arizona."

The two stood at her desk, close, and something like an electrical current passed between them. Helen had gray-green eyes.

"So, on a first-class ticket purchased by Oscar Levine, I flew to Phoenix, Arizona. I found a rental car waiting for me at the airport—paid for in full. There was a map and very clear directions on the passenger seat. I followed the directions and drove five hours straight out into the desert to meet with this man."

Helen said, "I was under the impression that Amy Levine didn't have any family."

"The man met me at the Portal Peak Lodge exactly one hour east of Willcox, Arizona. We had lunch. Fifteen minutes into the lunch, the man puts a briefcase on the table."

"Oscar Levine does?"

"The man claiming to be Oscar Levine."

"Puts a briefcase on the table?" Helen said.

"Tells me the contents inside the briefcase will change my life."

"What's in the briefcase?"

"Cash," McAllister said. "Cold, hard cash. Eight million dollars, unmarked, stacks of one thousand dollar bills. I didn't know they made one thousand dollar bills. And suddenly I'm looking at a briefcase full of 'em."

"What's his story?"

"Wants me to find this woman"—McAllister produced a black-and-white glossy of Dr. Amy Levine—"says it's his daughter. Says she's been missing since December. Says there's another eight million if I find her. Says I should start in Oracle. He gave me the address of Amy Levine's property manager. He tells me she has two homes, but owns neither. I'm thinking 'who lives in two homes but owns neither?'"

"Did you ask him?"

"He says the briefcase is mine," McAllister said, "as long as I ask no questions. He tells me he'll be in touch with me. I have no listing for this man. He met me at a lodge in the middle of the biggest desert in the United States of America. It doesn't take a genius to understand this man doesn't want to be found. I watched him get in a pickup truck that had no license plates and drive up into the mountains west of Paradise."

"That's quite a story," Helen said.

McAllister sipped the coffee and glanced around the office. Helen smiled affably and motioned for him to have a seat opposite her desk. He took a seat.

"So, I figured I'd start at the source," he said. "What can you tell me about Dr. Amy Levine?"

"Well, for starters, we didn't call her that. She was just Amy around here. In town. Everybody knew her, of course. You can't be that famous and not raise a few eyebrows in a small town like this."

"I imagine she was something special."

"She was polite," Helen said. "She really didn't come by too often. I remember that. She would always send in her rent, uh, from the post office."

"Is that unusual?"

"That a woman who is reportedly a millionaire sends in her rent check from the post office?" Helen said.

Roger got her point and made a sound like *hmmph*.

"I always thought she was a little eccentric," Helen continued. "She could have bought the home she lived in for about fifteen grand, but she rented the place. It was like she didn't want any legal bindings. She didn't even own a car. Got around town on foot, when she needed to. But she always paid her rent on time, so we never gave her any trouble."

"I've checked my records," McAllister said. "And I have been completely unable to locate an address. A home address. I'll be honest with you, and upfront with you, Mrs. Richards—"

"Miss Richards," she said.

Helen moved about a bare left hand on the desk, and her eyes shone, an amused smile rising up at the corners of her lips.

"*Miss* Richards," he said. "I'm sorry. I'll be upfront with you, Miss Richards. Before I came here, I did all the basic background checks."

"What do they include?"

"Utilities, phone, cable—all the bills."

"And what's unusual, Mr. McAllister?"

McAllister removed a little notepad from his shirt pocket.

"Well, a couple things," he said. "There's no phone listing. I checked with a friend at the F.B.I., and there's not even a listing if the government wanted to get in touch with her. It's not that she kept her number unlisted, it's like—"

"She didn't have a phone."

McAllister's eyebrows rose up a little. He looked into Helen's gray-green eyes.

"She didn't keep one," Helen said.

Roger made a note and a sound like *hmmm*.

"And there was no gas bill?" he said.

"She didn't keep hot water or heat," Helen said. "Don't ask me why, but that was just her way."

"And no cable?"

"No television," Helen said. "She got along without it, I suppose."

Roger removed a pen from his shirt pocket and wrote these things down.

"She did pay her water bill on time," he said. "So, she did have water."

"That's a state housing requirement," Helen said. "And because she rented, she couldn't put in her own well."

"And she paid her electric bill on time; though, by the looks of her average bill for the past thirty-six months, which is public information by the way, she wasn't burning a lot of light bulbs, if you know what I mean."

"I see."

"But neither of these two basic utilities even lists a service address. There's no home address."

Helen smiled. "I take it this is your first experience with Arizona."

"How do you mean, Miss Richards?"

"Well, there's just—there's homes up in these hills that don't have addresses. That don't have street names."

"How do they know where to service the power then?"

"Well, as quaint as this may sound, we simply know. You might call someone's address, you know, the Levine house down at the base of Apache Peak. And everybody'll know who you're talking about."

"Even with the electric company?"

"With the local electric company, yes," she said. "Now, mind you, only a few homes up here are still that remote. Ninety-five percent of the homes are on, you know, ordinary, normal streets. With official names."

"I see," he said.

"But we are, I guess, at the cutting edge," she said, "in terms of what has been developed and incorporated."

"Could you show me where her home was?" He looked at the giant Oracle-San Manuel map on the wall behind her desk.

"Well, sure, I'd be happy to."

Helen swiveled around in the chair behind her desk. An index finger rose up to a point on the map. There were topographic contours to illustrate the mountains and elevation gradations.

"We're here," she said. "On American. Calle Futura is over here. It's across from the Circle K. The street winds around here at the base of Alto Hill. You can see the hill here. Or"—she leaned back in her chair and pointed out the front window across the parking lot—"or out there. That's it."

"The main one," McAllister said.

"That's it in the middle," she said. "You can see the two peaks on either side. And then if you look up here on the map, you can see where it corresponds."

"I see."

"Calle Futura winds around the base here," she said pointing once more at the map. "Then, it goes on up into the hills on the other side of

Linda Vista. It's pretty hard to find if you're driving and you don't know the land. The hills. Some of the roads don't look much more than dirt paths. Particularly once you get on up into the National Forest Land. You can see that here; it's pink. Private land is to the west. And the B.L.M. land is up here all the way to the south."

"What's that peak," he said, "the big one?"

"Rice Peak," she said. "There's no real roads up to Rice Peak. You could get up there on an ATV—or a horse. Or something with some major four-wheel drive. And clearance. Ground clearance."

"And her home was here," he said, scrutinizing the map, "at the summit?"

"Mmm, no," Helen said. "She had a home up on Oracle Hill. It's closer."

"Closer?"

"Closer to town," Helen said. "Right here."

"I see," he said. "Is there any way to get up there?"

"Well, sure there's a way," she said. "You just need to know the land."

• •

Helen gripped the wheel with both hands and put her foot firmly on the accelerator.

"Hold tight, Mr. McAllister, this last climb's rough."

The midnight-blue Chevy Silverado gripped the ground like a tank, but for a moment the truck hit a wash and McAllister felt the Chevy up on two wheels. His heart dropped down into his stomach, and he had trouble getting a good breath. The drop-off on his side of the 4x4 trail was straight down the side of a hill, two hundred meters easy. The hill on the left side of the truck rose up so steeply that he couldn't see the crest of the hill unless he leaned forward and craned his neck to look up from inside the truck.

To the west, McAllister could see the northward sprawl of Tucson far below, several miles away below in the valley.

"It's been growing like that for years," Helen said.

McAllister bounced along and held the little handle over the Chevy's door with his right hand.

"It's a wonder it hasn't climbed into these hills yet," he said. "The development."

"No roads," Helen said. "But all this land is private land."

"Who owns it?"

Helen flashed a little smile at McAllister that made him realize this was something she was well aware of, something that she, a small-town realtor, had known about for a long time.

"It's farmland, mostly," she said. "There's three families that own most of this land. There's about seven thousand acres."

McAllister looked out the window to the right. The views were spectacular. To the south, the mountains rose up to nine thousand feet. They were climbing along a little 4x4 path about five thousand feet above sea level, and there were mesas that eased out to the west, perfect spots for multi-million dollar homes perched with views of the city lights at night.

"It's mostly 'cause there's no roads up here yet," Helen said. "Nobody knows the value of this land. And it's gonna take somebody with a lotta money to put in any kind of normal road. If they ever do it, you'll see a golf course go up, sure enough."

"It's beautiful land."

McAllister felt the rocks spin under the wheels of the truck. They climbed up a steep, tan path only about ten feet wide. It climbed straight up into the sky.

He said, "Kind'a crazy living this far out, wouldn't you say?"

Helen glanced over at him.

"Yeah," she said. "Some folks like their privacy. It's only about ten minutes down into town."

"Into Oracle," he said.

"Yeah," she said. "And twenty minutes down into Tucson. They just ain't built roads up here yet."

The Chevy lurched forward and crested the hill.

"That's her place," Helen said. "She was into the solitude thing."

A quaint little cottage was built into the side of a hill. There were desert trees around the yard. The cottage itself was a cheerful white with bright yellow trim. There was a concrete porch along the front, which gave onto a view of the city to the west. Helen pulled the truck up into the driveway.

"Well, this is it, Mr. McAllister," she said. "I don't know what all you'll find."

"Well, ordinarily in a case like this I just want to get an idea of who it is that I'm trying to find. It helps to look around the place."

He opened the passenger-side door and stepped out of the truck. It was cooler, and clouds darkened the sky.

Helen Richards stood at the back of the truck and looked up at giant thunderheads, which climbed to a ten-thousand-foot ceiling, catching spectacular color in the late afternoon sunshine. Far to the south beyond the mountains, the sky was an ominous dark cloud of brown and black dust.

McAllister was at the front window of the cottage, peering in with one hand cupped up over his eyes to break the glare.

"Not much to it, is there?" he said. Helen said nothing. "What is there just the front room, a couple bedrooms in the back?"

"Two in the back," she said, "separated by a bathroom."

Helen produced a shiny silver key.

"Here, I'll let you in," she said.

They both walked around to a side door. There was a little washroom with washer-dryer hookups in the side room. The screen door wasn't locked, so they both stepped inside. There was a kitchen beyond the washroom, and the door to the kitchen was locked. Helen eased the key into the deadbolt and unlocked the door.

The cottage smelled clean inside, a hint of dust lingering under the smell of a mopped kitchen floor.

"It's kind'a clean," McAllister said.

"Yeah, she cleaned it up each season before she moved to the north," Helen said. "Has a place in Colorado from what I understand. This place here is not much, but it kept the rain off her head, I imagine. And that's Amy for you."

"It's peaceful." McAllister looked around the front living room. The room was bare. He walked over to the front windows. The view was spectacular.

"I think she might'a had something, you know," he said, "living up here." He turned and gave Helen a smile.

"Yeah, sure is peaceful."

McAllister eyed the front yard. The grass had faded brown from no watering, and weeds shot up near a couple of creosote bushes at the side of the house.

Helen Richards stood in the middle of the kitchen. There was a window over the sink, and for a moment she gazed off into the distance, far beyond the home. She seemed to forget Roger McAllister in the other room. There was a single tree beyond the kitchen, and then the hill sloped downward, seven, eight miles to the very northern edge of Tucson.

McAllister walked through the kitchen and looked up the hallway at the back of the house. There was a bedroom at either end. There was a single hallway lamp extending from the wall near the bathroom. McAllister tried the bedroom on his right.

The room was painted blue, and there were windows on the north and south sides. There was a single closet door on the east side of the room. It was cracked open a few inches, and all was darkness inside. McAllister stepped out into the center of the room, his eyes running along the baseboard walls, searching for any clues, anything unusual, anything that might tell him more than he already knew about this Dr. Amy Levine, this charismatic young scientist, one of the sharpest minds on the planet.

"She just lived up here by herself?" he called through the stillness of the home.

There was a pause, and then Helen Richards said, "Yep, whole months would go by, and nobody'd see her or hear from her. I'd come up here from time to time. She was always friendly, but I guess she'd stock up on food from the market down in town, and then she'd stay up here, working on her mathematical algorithms. She went to Brown, you know? The University? Pretty fancy school, from what I've heard."

"Must'a seen something in the stars at night," McAllister opined. "Tracing the planets. Looking for order in the universe. Hell, I can't much blame a young girl for moving up here—as much madness as there is in the world. Seems like a fine life to me."

McAllister peeked in the kitchen. Helen was still at the window, gazing down the mountain, when a rumble of thunder rolled up from the south. McAllister could have sworn he felt the thunder before he heard it. It seemed to envelope the home, grabbed it, held it in its grip and then unloaded.

Helen gasped in fright. "Shit," she said.

The glass windows rattled in their frames, and the thunder continued to roll on out to the north across the desert plains. Helen stood with her arms folded in front of her, and her grip on herself seemed to tighten like she was holding herself closer because of the thunder.

She started to call out, "We better get moving"—turned and saw McAllister—"or we're liable to get caught up here in the storm. You don't want to see some of the wash outs we'll get on the side of these hills in a bad storm. Might not make it back down the mountain."

McAllister nodded. "Let me just check this back bedroom," he said. "Then we'll head on down."

The room was at the end of the hall. He poked his head into the bathroom first, saw nothing that stood out, and continued up to the bedroom at the back of the house. The fragrance of leather hit him when he entered the room. Freshly tanned leather.

McAllister looked around the room. It was larger than the other bedroom, and there was less light on the north side of the house. There were two windows—one on the north side and one on the east side. And the curtains were pulled over the windows. But the room smelled of leather. Fresh leather.

His nose came up a little, sniffing the air like a wolf. His brow furrowed over, and he looked at the crack of light coming in from one of the windows, from behind the curtains covering the window. He slowly crossed the room toward the window.

Something moved out in the yard. A shadow. Something large. It moved by the window. Roger McAllister grabbed the curtain in his right hand and tried to pull it aside. It didn't give at first, and he pulled it harder. The whole thing fell down on top of him.

"Damn," he said.

The curtain and curtain rod was in his hand and on the floor. Helen came to the door.

"You alright?"

"Damn thing just fell on top of me," he said.

Outside, a large cow reached its head down to the dried grass and munched up a tuft of grass. There were two other cows farther down the hill. Helen held back the urge to razz him about getting scared by a cow.

"Do you need a hand?" she asked.

She came over and took one end of the curtain rod. They raised the curtain up above their heads and reattached it.

"Farmland, you say?"

"Yeah," Helen said. "All this land up here is open range."

"Do you smell that?"

"Smells a little like—like *leather* in here."

McAllister crossed the room. He opened the closet door. The closet was dark and bare. There was a single shelf high overhead. More out of exhaustion than anything else, he leaned forward bracing his hands on the shelf, as if on a chin-up bar.

"See anything?" Helen asked.

"Nothing," he said.

And then his hands felt the leather satchel.

"There's something," he said, "up on the shelf."

"Can you reach it?"

He stepped back from the closet. He looked around the room looking for anything he could use as a step stool. There was nothing.

"Looks like some kind of bag," he said. "Here, step up into my hands. I'll boost you up."

Roger McAllister stooped over at the door of the closet with his hands folded together. He made a little step for Helen. She put her hand on his shoulder and her right foot into his hands. He lifted her up.

She reached forward and took hold of the leather bag.

"It's heavy," she said. "But I got it, here."

McAllister let her back to the ground. Helen handed him the leather satchel. He opened it and saw papers and notebooks. There were hundreds of pages.

"What is all that stuff?" Helen asked.

He leafed through a few pages in one stack. On each page, there were elaborate and elegantly written mathematical algorithms, some several pages in length. Most were written in a beautiful penmanship, very precise, very elegant. They were fun to look at if for nothing other than their aesthetic quality.

"Looks almost like art," he said. "Like drawings here."

"It's all in mathematic notation."

"Looks like it," he said.

He leafed through one section, the pages flying by under his thumb. One equation went on for more than a hundred pages.

"It's like she was writing a novel," he said. "But all in algebraic notation."

"I knew she was a smart girl," Helen said, "but what in the world was she doing up here—redefining the universe?"

"Heck if I know," McAllister said. "I dropped out of college after making a D+ in Calculus."

Outside, a crack of lightning was soon followed by a loud rumble of thunder, and rain began to patter on the thin tin roof. They looked at one another, looked at the satchel with the papers, looked out the windows to the storm rolling up from the southern mountains.

"We better get on back to town," Helen said.

"Yeah," he said. "I think you're right."

••

By nightfall, the high country desert towns of Catalina, Oracle, and San Manuel were flooded. One wash had broken a section of pavement ten miles south of Oracle, and the state troopers were directing people away from the washed out road with flares and flashlights. McAllister looked out the window of his Super 8 Motel room and watched the rain water flooding the southwest end of the parking lot.

He watched a truck's headlights turn into the darkened motel parking lot. The midnight-blue Chevy plowed through the pool of water, creating a wake behind it. The headlights shone through McAllister's window and pulled straight into the space in front of Room 107, his room.

Helen Richards jumped down out of the truck with a bright yellow rain slicker on. She had a bag of Chinese food in her hand. She slammed the door shut and ran up to the walkway in front of the rooms. McAllister opened the door for her, and she came in from the rain.

"Rain's a bitch," she said. Her clothes were wet. "Highway's washed out up past Oracle Junction and down past the Texaco in Catalina. There's no way back up the mountain, 'less you drive clear out to Black Mountain and try to make it back up across the desert plains."

McAllister shut the door.

"Any roads out there?"

"Not out on the plains," Helen said. "Not any roads you'd want to be on in this kind of weather, anyways."

Helen put the Chinese food on the little table by the window, and peeled out of her yellow rain slicker. Her hair was wet.

"Everybody in town was at the damned Chinese restaurant," she said. "It's the only place still open. Power's out down past Mountain Vista."

McAllister took her rain coat for her and carried it across the motel room. He hung it up on the clothing rack near the bathroom sink. His suitcase sat open like a gaping mouth atop the folding suitcase stand under the clothing rack. He pulled the coat to the side so that his suitcase wasn't getting dripped on.

Helen unbuttoned her shirt.

"Here," McAllister said.

He handed her a white terrycloth towel. She patted her face and neck down, drying off.

"I've got dry clothes here," he said, and he nodded at his suitcase.

He took out a pair of navy-blue sweat pants and a clean white T-shirt.

"There's socks too if you want 'em," he said. "Why don't you change in the bathroom."

Helen looked into his blue eyes and smirked. She took the clothes he handed her.

"Not making you nervous, am I?" she said.

She took the clothes and went to the bathroom door. McAllister walked the other way toward the front door, the front window. He glanced back once and saw Helen standing at the bathroom sink just outside of the bathroom. He heard the *zip* of her wet khaki pants. The pants dropped to the floor, and Helen stood in front of the mirror in white cotton panties and her button-up blouse. She leaned toward the mirror and dried her neck and chin with the white towel.

McAllister cleared his throat and did his best to stare straight out the front Super 8 window. He was able to see her tenuous reflection in the clear glass window, but his standing gave the impression that he was looking out the front window, out into the rain, out into the storm.

Helen eased out of the white cotton panties and unbuttoned her shirt. She stood naked a moment, her button-up blouse opened at its front, and she glanced in the bathroom mirror at McAllister. Her eyes smiled at his wide back. She stepped into the bathroom, and McAllister heard the hiss of the shower turn on a moment later. Within minutes, the room was filling up with steam.

• •

Roger McAllister leafed through the pages on the tabletop. A box of Chinese food was open atop the table, and he ate the Dan-Dan Noodles with chopsticks in one hand, hunched over the papers on the table, his other hand feeling the cool, smooth texture of the pages.

"Make any sense of it?" Helen leaned her head out of the bathroom.

McAllister glanced up, a serious expression on his face.

"What do you know about her work?" he asked.

Helen rubbed her hair with the white Super 8 motel towel. Her hair was wet and clean, but she hadn't yet combed it. She carried a light smile on her lips and her gray-green eyes glistened in the motel room's light.

"Mathematics, right," Helen said. "She had something to do with those traffic light cameras they got down in the city."

McAllister looked at the pages. "This ain't got nothing to do with traffic lights," he said.

Helen crossed the room. She wore the navy-blue sweat pants and the white T-shirt. She swept her sandy blonde hair back in her hand and looked over his shoulder at the papers on the tabletop. There was a single hanging light above the table, and outside the rain continued to pound the pavement, sweeping across the blacktop parking lot from side to side in the driving wind.

"That right there," she said, pointing to one series of seven consecutive pages, "looks like constellations. Or *a* constellation. I imagine that's what the mathematic notation—beside it—corresponds with."

She reached a slender index finger down over his arm. With his foot McAllister eased the chair out from the other side of the table, and Helen took the hint. She pulled it up close to the table. She slid a couple of the pages over the tabletop, and glanced carefully from one to another.

"What is this here," she said, "about the 'Line'?"

McAllister looked at the page she meant.

She said, "See, this here. She's got this equation. You can clearly see she's adding these as she goes along. And she keeps repeating this phrase 'the Line', 'the Line'."

"What the hell does it mean?" McAllister said.

"It's on every page in this series," she said. "How many are there?"

"There's more than two hundred in this one—book," he said.

Helen slid the box of Chinese food across the table and began eating with the chopsticks. Outside, there was a blinding flash of lightning, followed immediately by a crash of thunder that shook the building.

The lights flickered off for a moment, and Helen and Roger looked up at one another, panicked. It was complete darkness in the room. They could hear the pounding rain outside and the wind sweeping it harder and harder, whipping it into a howl.

"Lights are out," he said.

"They might come back on in a moment."

McAllister could see her contours in the very dim light coming from the window. He saw the skin of her cheekbones shimmer in the darkness. The shadows of rainwater from the window were on her face. He saw her eyes, and he heard her breathing.

"It'll come back on in a minute," she said. "Power goes out like that all the time in summer monsoons."

"How do you know it'll come back on?" McAllister said.

"No trees big enough to knock down power lines in the desert."

"Might'a been a cactus."

Helen smiled in the dark. "Cute," she said.

The scream was so loud and so violent that it scared them both to the depths of their souls.

"*What was that?*" McAllister said.

They both sat at the table, frozen. It was pitch black in the room, but their eyes were adjusting to the dark.

It sounded like a girl—the scream—and it sounded like it came from the far end of the parking lot.

"That's not good," Helen said.

They both stood up and went to the window. The rain pounded the pavement and was so heavy that visibility was only twenty meters. Out on the highway, they saw a flash of bright white light. There was a sound like an eighteen wheeler's horn, and then a wrenching metal sound and a crash of glass. But there were no cars; they saw no headlights.

The girl came from the far end of the parking lot in the direction of the light, and she was covered in blood. She looked like she was about sixteen years old, and she was dressed in weird white robes, a tunic which was pasted to her soaking wet body. She staggered toward the parking lot, crying violently. Roger started for the door.

"Roger, don't!" Helen said.

"Don't what?!"

"Don't open that door for her." Helen was terrified.

Roger threw the door open and stepped out onto the walkway. He watched the girl coming through the pouring rain. The white tunic had beads along its front from top to bottom. The beads glowed white then blue, then back to white again, and her head and face was covered in blood. The blood looked all the worse because of the pouring rain on her.

"Miss?" Roger called through the rain. "Ma'am?"

The crack of the shotgun was loud, and it came from the direction of the motel office. Roger winced and went instinctively for his sidearm. There were a half dozen flashlight beams flickering all over the place. They were coming from the office area. Roger looked up and saw a group of six men with dogs, flashlights, and shotguns coming from the side of the motel near the office.

"There it is!" one man shouted. He raised a finger into the driving rain and pointed at the girl in the white robes. One man raised a shotgun up into the rain and opened fire on the girl. The shots must have missed her because she continued forward up toward Roger's room. Roger saw her face in the darkness, in the rain.

He shouted at the men, "Hold your fire! I've got her! She's coming up to me!"

The front man shouted, "Don't touch it! Don't touch that thing! It ain't human!"

But the girl in the white robes staggered the last few steps up toward the walkway. Roger ran out into the rain, and the girl fell into his arms. He tried to help her up, but she was dead weight in his arms. He lifted her full body up into his arms and carried her up to the room.

The men with flashlights and guns reached the door of his motel room just as he did. Roger had the girl in his arms. He looked angrily at the men.

"What the hell are you doing?" he roared.

Helen held the door open. Roger carried the girl across the room and placed her on the bed. The men came into the room with flashlights shining. They lit up Helen's face. They flashed around the room. One flashlight beam came to rest on the girl, now on the motel room's king-size bed.

She lay, soaking wet, the white robes wet on the bed. Roger wiped the blood back from her face. Helen brought him several hand towels from the bathroom. One of the men moved in closer with a flashlight.

The girl glanced at the leather satchel atop the table, and her eyes widened.

"The Sequence," she groaned, holding her hand out toward the leather satchel and Dr. Amy Levine's papers. "I must save the Sequence."

One of the men came to the girl with a shotgun aimed.

"Go ahead!" another roared. "Finish it off! Kill that thing!"

But Helen stepped between the girl and the man with the shotgun. She forced the man back.

"Get the hell out of this room," Helen said.

The men looked at one another.

The lead man spoke up, "That, ma'am, is *not* going to happen."

Outside, the wind roared and the rain continued to beat against the pavement.

• •

One of the men leaned back in his chair. He had a shotgun cocked under his right arm, and his left foot was at the foot of the bed. He rocked back and forth a little in the chair and he tapped the shotgun with his index finger. Everyone watched the girl on the bed.

"Buddy, you're lucky I didn't blow your brains out," one of the men said.

Roger said, "What's gotten into you guys? Who is this girl?"

The man in the chair didn't look up at Roger. He stared blankly at the girl in the bed and said, "That thing ain't no girl. You should've seen what it did to Zeb's dog. What it did to Harvey's cattle. I don't know what it is, but it ain't no girl!"

Roger looked at the man called Zeb and said, "What did it do?"

"I don't know," Zeb said. "I ain't ever seen anything like it."

The man in the chair said, "It turned the dog inside out is what it did."

There was a flash of lightning outside, followed by a powerful crash of thunder. The lights were still out in the motel room, so the men kept three flashlight beams on, one steady on the girl in the bed.

"Turned it inside out?" Helen said. She was over by the bathroom, her arms folded in front of her, and it was so dark in that corner that the men could only see her contours.

"That thing"—the man nodded at the girl—"it attacked Zeb's dog. Some kind'a light came out of it. And it turned his dog inside out. Damn thing was sittin' there inside out makin' the most god-awful sound you ever heard."

"Had to shoot it to put it out of its misery," another of the men said.

The man in the chair said, "Did the same thing to Harvey's cattle. Just kind'a descended on it—then that bright white light flashed up out'a nowhere, took over the cow, and there won't nothing left afterwards except the inside of that cow. Did it to three others right outside the farmhouse."

The girl on the bed made a sound. Everyone looked at her. They closed in with their flashlights, all beams shining through the darkness onto the girl.

"Tat tvam asi," the girl moaned. "The black wraiths . . . will kill us all. Must save . . . the Sequence."

Helen leaned in toward her, close to her head.

"I wouldn't get that close to it," Zeb said.

Roger tried to pull Helen back, but she swatted at his hand.

"Quiet," Helen said. "I can hear what she's saying."

The girl's hands moved up and down her chest. Helen leaned an ear toward the girl's mouth. The girl's lips moved up and down.

"What is she sayin'?" Harvey said, thrusting the flashlight beam at the girl for emphasis. "What is that *thing* sayin'?"

"The black wraiths," the girl whispered. "Humans can not see them. They're closing in on the room. I must save the Sequence."

The girl's eyes opened and looked at Helen's head right in front of her mouth. The men yelled: "Get the hell out'a there, woman!" Then, the girl's hands came up and grabbed Helen by the throat.

THREE
THE PACIFIC ISLAND

Pierre Refenault leaned forward in the helicopter and watched the island rise from the blue Pacific horizon. The HH-60's wiper blades swept back and forth on the double-pane front window, and Refenault saw a streak of lightning to the north. The lightning came down out of huge, ominous clouds and dove straight for the ocean, lighting up the entire northern sky.

"Not to worry, Dr. Refenault," the pilot said. "The odds of being struck by lightning are really only minimal—maybe one in a thousand for these Pacific hops."

Dr. Refenault looked into the mirror above the pilot's head and saw the calm assurance in the pilot's features. He was too calm, like he knew Refenault was about to break down in tears and hysteria and had decided that *that* was an opportune moment to try the Cary Grant impersonation he'd been working on in his barracks at Clark Air Force Base. The pilot grinned.

"These storms," Refenault started, then he felt his stomach climb up into his chest.

"Hold on, Doctor," the pilot said.

The big-bellied Jayhawk swung to the south and dropped five hundred feet. The helicopter felt like it was almost completely vertical, and Refenault gripped his seat and felt the G-force pulling his head to the window on the right. He was hanging one thousand feet above a giant mat of blue ocean, and he let out a sound like "Ooohh" followed by a few expletives the pilot didn't quite catch. The helicopter was on its side diving eastward, and it was like one of those rollercoasters where the passengers are latched in from underneath the tracks; except, there were no tracks.

"Oh, Holy Mary Mother of—"

"There," the pilot said.

The helicopter leveled out, and Refenault took a moment to consciously breathe. His adrenaline was so high it had stopped up his breathing altogether. Refenault felt the circulation return to his legs, and everything south of his equator began to tingle. Gradually, Refenault began to feel his heart returning to a normal range (somewhere under one hundred and forty beats per minute), but the taste of cold saliva in the back of his mouth made him want to hurl. He grimaced and steeled his stomach.

"God," Refenault said. "Is it gonna be like that all the way into the island?"

"Sorry 'bout that, sir," the pilot said, an Arkansas accent redolent under the precise military cadence.

Then, Refenault realized they were only a few feet above the ocean. The Jayhawk was tearing along the surface of the Pacific, moisture vapor trails spiraling out behind it. Refenault closed his eyes.

"I'm gonna wet my pants," he said.

The pilot chuckled. "Oh, it's not that bad."

Refenault's eyes opened wide, almost belligerently. "It's not that bad?! If this is not bad, what is? A crash?"

"Those can be pretty hairy," the pilot said.

"You've crashed before?!"

The pilot looked puzzled. "What pilot hasn't?" he said.

Refenault looked out the side of the helicopter and just nailed his concentration to a specific point on the horizon. A bolt of lightning roared down out of the clouds and hit the water at just the spot he was staring. He started shaking his head back and forth.

"I can't do it," he said. "I'm gonna be sick. I'm really gonna be sick."

The pilot began to really look alarmed. He turned around in the seat and looked at Dr. Refenault, gauging his seriousness.

"Shit," the pilot said. He hit a glove compartment in front of him and removed a folded paper bag, which had a little four-step "How To Use" diagram with an image of a guy leaning forward, the bag over his face. "Here," the pilot said. He flicked the bag open and handed it to Refenault.

Refenault took the bag, held it to his mouth, and his stomach started to hurl. He made terrible retching sounds and regurgitated into the bag in a series of a half dozen strong reflexive heaves. A minute later he sat up and leaned his head back in the seat. His face was cool and pale, but he felt much better.

"Here we are," the pilot said.

His head tilted back in the seat, Pierre Refenault brought his eyes down from the chopper's ceiling and looked forward through the front windows. What he saw pulled his full body forward. He leaned forward in the back seat and craned his neck to look up at the island. It was huge.

It climbed up out of the ocean, a giant mountain of verdant green enshrouded in gray clouds. There was a thin sandy beach along the coastline with palm trees lining the white sand. To the south, the beach gave onto steep cliffs, and the waves crashed against black volcanic rocks along the southern coastline. Several cliffs climbed straight up from the crashing waves easily two hundred feet. The helicopter started to climb.

Enormous mountain ravines carved down the sides of the tropical green forest mountain, down from a ceiling of foreboding gray clouds that loomed overhead.

"Cloud level starts about six thousand feet, Doctor," the pilot said. "Things will get bumpy."

"Great," Refenault said.

"There's one central high-country valley into Murambai," the pilot said. "It's about seven miles from the valley's opening into the highest peaks, then three miles down into the village."

"Okay," Refenault said.

"It's a *narrow* valley," the pilot said. "Cliffs climb up on either side of the valley, straight up several thousand feet. And the higher you climb, the denser the clouds. So, I'm gonna try to keep it close to the floor. Wind sheer is less dramatic at the forest floor. So, there's less likelihood of our getting thrown into the cliffs on either side."

"Wonderful," Refenault said.

"Though when I say forest," the pilot said. "I ought'a make clear what we're traveling into. This forest is about six thousand, seven thousand feet up—above sea level. And Murambai sits at ten thousand feet. The air is much thinner, and the blades won't grab quite as well. And it's cold—particularly at night. The slopes up above twelve thousand feet are covered with snow and will remain that way straight through the summer. The Prince enjoys snow skiing four seasons a year—and there's a heated gondola that rises from the compound to Mount Kulumai. They occasionally get a dusting down around ten thousand feet. Got nine inches ten days ago. But that's rare."

"What's ground temperature at Murambai?" Refenault asked.

"Daytime high is in the sixties," the pilot said. "Nighttime low is in the forties. It's a unique ecosystem."

"Sounds like it."

"Both tropical and mountainous," the pilot said. "Imagine a jungle, a redwood forest, and the highest peaks in central Colorado. There's nothing else like it in the world."

"So I've been told." Refenault looked at the little baggie in his right hand.

"And I *hate* flyin' into it," the pilot said.

With that, the helicopter swung out wide to the south over the ocean. It hit a wind sheer roaring down from the mountain, and all at once it felt like a giant had picked up the soda can of a helicopter and thrown it straight down five hundred feet. Refenault was buckled into the seat, but he felt himself literally lift up into the air, pulling against the buckled straps. The pilot managed to keep the Jayhawk from stalling and pointed in the direction of the huge green mountains. The blades caught a solid piece of air, Refenault heard the blades *whump, whump, whump,* and they burst through a particularly thick cloud.

"*Holy Mother,*" Refenault said.

Ahead, a giant thin waterfall poured out of the side of the lush green mountain about fifteen hundred feet overhead. Further overhead, giant mountains loomed far, far above the waterfall, and Refenault realized they would climb up to the brink of the waterfall, and the high country valley would open up.

The thin waterfall streamed down a straight cliff to a giant lake up ahead, and at the east end of the lake, a river began its course along a tropical tree-lined bank.

The helicopter swung down over the river and began to climb up the mountain a couple hundred feet above the jungle river.

"It's about one mile up to the lake," the pilot said.

He rushed along the mountain slope, pushing the chopper into the thinning air. Refenault glanced back once and was surprised to see the ocean, far back behind them in the distance, far down the steep green slopes.

"Beautiful," Refenault said.

The helicopter rushed out over the lake, the water an ice-blue that reflected the mountains on its surface. It was about two miles across, and the chopper roared along, fifty feet above the lake's shine.

About a quarter mile out from the falls the pilot pulled up, and the chopper ascended up along the brilliant white water. They climbed for ten seconds, and Refenault glanced out the side window on the helicopter and saw the lake, now a thousand feet down. The chopper burst over the ridgeline where the waterfall began, and Refenault thought he was entering pastures of heaven.

There was a central valley parted with a single river, and everything was green. On either side of the valley, mountains rose up straight into the sky, disappearing in cloud cover several thousand feet overhead. Straight ahead, the valley climbed steeply for six, seven miles, and Refenault could see enormous gray peaks in the distance, high above the tree line.

The pilot said, "This valley is ordinarily as thick with clouds as any other place on Earth. I usually use the river to navigate up into the mountains, but we can see pretty darn well today. Cloud cover's really high."

Refenault leaned forward and looked up the steep mountain walls on either side of the valley. The further up into the mountains they climbed, the narrower the walls became on either side of the valley.

"Murambai's at the base of that peak," the pilot said. "You see the four over here on the right"—the pilot pointed—"those are La Muerte Bonito."

"La Muerte Bonito?"

"Yes," the pilot said. "San Isabelle is the farthest on the left, fourteen thousand nine hundred feet."

"I see."

The pilot said, "We'll pass through a valley in that range, and then come down the western slopes into Murambai."

As they drew higher and farther up the river valley, Refenault had the sense that they were on a massive piece of earth.

"What's the altitude here?" he asked.

"Altimeter's reading nine-five," the pilot said. "And we're about a hundred feet above the forest canopy."

"We can't be going up into those." Refenault leaned forward from the back seat and pointed at the snow-covered peaks up ahead. They seemed to climb up into the sky forever. He'd never seen anything so enormous in all his life.

The pilot grinned. "Yes, sir," he said. "That's where we're headed."

"*My God,*" he said.

The mountains were massive. Below, Refenault noticed a change in the vegetation. The forest had turned from tropical to high aspen. And amazingly, they were now *above* the clouds that had just been above them ten minutes before. Eventually the narrow valley opened out onto a virtual moonscape of land with bare gray slopes climbing high into the blue sky. Snow levels started a thousand feet higher, and the helicopter swung in toward the stone gray mountains. Refenault glanced back in the direction they'd come and was amazed to see a sea of white clouds spreading far to the horizon behind them, a hundred miles in any direction. The gray mountains ahead rose from the sea of white clouds.

"Can we go around it?" Refenault said.

"Go around it, sir?" the pilot said. "No, Murambai's in the center of that range. There is no *around* to Murambai."

The helicopter climbed higher and higher along the barren gray slopes until the ground beneath was white with snow.

"Music, Doctor?" the pilot offered.

"Please," Refenault said.

The pilot put in a CD.

The helicopter wound around the North Face. High gray cliffs rose all around the chopper, and ahead, Refenault saw an enormous fortress of stone gray peaks surrounding a green valley far below.

"That peak," the pilot said. "Up there—that's Kulumai."

Refenault said, "It's breathtaking."

Even among these already massive peaks, Kulumai was undoubtedly the giant among giants. It rose to a staggering twenty-two thousand nine hundred and forty-two feet.

"Over four miles above sea level," the pilot said. "Murambai's just ahead. We'll descend down to ten thousand feet for landing at the compound."

The pilot took up the radio and began communicating with the landing crew a mile ahead. Refenault saw that they were coming back into green forest, the giant gray peaks rising above the village high up to the snow fields and then higher to the otherworldly heights of Kulumai's North Face.

The village glittered in the sunshine.

• •

Murambai was the single most expensive private residence on Earth. It was literally a self-sufficient city, but it was all built for one man: Prince Osoro Santana.

Santana stood at the edge of the tarmac, watching Dr. Refenault coming toward him from the helicopter. Refenault had a single suitcase and a little paper baggie in his right hand.

"Dr. Refenault," Santana said. "So glad to see you. Let me help you with your bags. What's in the paper bag, lunch?"

Refenault smirked.

He tossed the paper bag in a trashcan at the edge of the tarmac, and he shook Santana's hand. Santana returned the handshake enthusiastically and led him up a white concrete sidewalk beyond the helicopter landing pad. Refenault looked back and watched the helicopter lifting off. He waved at the pilot. The pilot gave him a formal little salute. And the helicopter swung around and began climbing up into the distance.

"You're the last of the scientists to arrive at Murambai," Santana said. "As you're aware, we've been flying in Earth's most celebrated scientists for almost seven days. It is a great honor to have you with us, Dr. Refenault."

"It is an honor to be here, Prince Santana."

The little path they walked along was manicured to perfection. The plants were all green, and there was a little goldfish pond with a waterfall over to the right. Ahead, Refenault saw a single gondola climbing up into the mountains beyond the compound. It rose beyond his range of vision up into the snow fields high above the village.

"We will ski, Refenault," Santana said. "But first I will show you to your quarters. I am sure you are most eager to get settled in."

Refenault glanced at the three black limousines ahead at the end of the garden path.

"How far is it to the rooms?" Refenault said.

"The south end of the compound begins here," Santana said. "We have rooms here on this wing."

He pointed to a glass balcony that rose above the trees. There was a terrace, and six beautiful women waved at Santana from the balcony. Santana blew them each a kiss. At either end of the balcony, there were large men in black pressed pants with white T-shirts. They carried machineguns on their shoulders and wore sleek black sunglasses. The machineguns made Refenault uncomfortable, but he said nothing to Santana.

"The north end of Murambai is reserved for our most special guests. It's about a four-mile ride."

"By limousine?"

Santana stopped and looked at his friend. He wagged a single finger in the air.

"You want to travel by gondola," Santana said. "Yes, yes, that makes better sense. The gondola travels through the compound, too, before climbing up the mountain. It will take longer, but it will give you a better view of Murambai."

• •

From the telescope in Dr. Amy Levine's room, Agent Sara McKenzie gazed up at the snow fields high above the village. There were skiers on the slopes, teams on patrol like packs of wolves. The skiers wore snow-white camouflage and carried machineguns. They skied over the deep powder fields with grace and ease, and every quarter mile, they stopped and scanned the high country with binoculars. McKenzie watched them through the telescope as they radioed down to the security base in Murambai.

"There's an opening somewhere," McKenzie said, "into that mountain. And this *generator* that Santana has been constructing is bound to be inside that opening."

Levine was at the far end of the room practicing T'ai Chi. Her hands moved around fluidly, one foot high in front of her. McKenzie pulled back from the telescope and watched Levine. Levine was in the zone, and all at once, she pivoted to her right spring-loading and spun quickly, powerfully back to her left, counter-clockwise. Her feet whickered through the air in a full roundhouse. Had those feet connected with someone's head, they almost certainly would have loosened some joints. Levine landed perfectly balanced, poised. And then she brought her hands together in front of her and bowed calmly.

"Yes," Levine said. "It is so."

McKenzie picked up a vase from a table that appeared to have no other purpose than to hold the vase. The vase was made of white gold and ringed with diamonds. It was three feet tall, and Sara picked it up and held it before her.

She said, "I could sell something like this and make a fortune."

"And that would make you happy?" Levine said.

"Well, I don't know about happy," Sara said. "But it would sure buy a nice steak dinner. We're different you and me. You're into your whole psychic energy thing, but me: just give me a beach house, a fast car, and a guy who knows when to leave me alone."

She came across the well-lighted room. She strutted a little, and smiled at Levine.

"Okay, Rocky," she said. "Let's see what you got."

Levine shook her head and couldn't help but smile at McKenzie. McKenzie moved in, completely serious and took a swing at Levine. Levine, surprised, ducked backwards missing the front end of McKenzie's right hook by just a few inches. McKenzie bounced around on the fronts of her feet, loosening herself up a little.

"Six months of peace and solitude," McKenzie said. "They brought us here as prisoners. We'll leave as a couple of warriors."

Levine looked dubiously at her friend, and then began bouncing around a little on the fronts of her feet. She wore a white robe held together with a white cloth belt in front. Her pants were loose and supple, and her feet were bare. Her brown eyes took in Agent McKenzie, the wall behind her, the objects around the room. And she leapt, spinning furiously. She connected with McKenzie's left shoulder, and the power of the kick sent McKenzie staggering backward across the room. She skirted to a stop, landing on her rump.

McKenzie sat there a moment, and pointed a vowing finger at Levine, who now paced gingerly near the center of the room. Levine waved McKenzie up with her hand.

"Come on," she said. "Stand up and fight."

McKenzie became very serious now. She popped up, brushed herself off, and came to the center of the room more cautiously this time. Her fists rose up in front of her, and she eyed Levine, looking for an opening. She stuck a right jab; Levine ducked left. She tried a left to the body; Levine caught it and fired up a forearm that lifted McKenzie up into the air. McKenzie balanced and came down smoothly and lunged forward with a low left kick.

It struck!

Levine staggered. McKenzie moved in quickly and fired a quick right jab and a smooth left hook. The hook caught Levine flush on the right cheek and knocked her hard to the ground.

Levine saw a red door. It was inside a hotel in southwest Colorado.

"Ouray," Levine groaned.

McKenzie looked worried; she hadn't intended to hit her as hard as she did, and Levine sat on the floor with her eyes wide. A little trickle of bright red blood was at the corner of her lips.

"You alright?" McKenzie said.

"Ouray, Colorado," Levine said dazedly; she held her head. "The red door . . . is in Ouray, Colorado."

"What red door?" McKenzie said. "What are you talking about?"

"*It's some kind of portal,*" Levine gasped.

"Jeez, I didn't mean to hit you so hard, Amy."

McKenzie moved in and offered a hand to Levine.

"Bent over," Levine said.

Indeed, Sara *was* bent over offering Levine a hand. "Bent over?" she said.

"*His name is Ben Tovar.*"

"Come on, Amy," Sara said. "Let's get you some fresh air."

Levine looked at Sara as though she understood something that she hadn't before. Her head cleared. She'd had a vision of a red door, and it was in a small town in Colorado. The red door was inside an old hotel.

"We've got to get to Ouray," Levine said.

"Ouray?"

"It's a town in southwest Colorado."

• •

Dr. Pierre Refenault stood at the sliding glass door inside his room. Outside, there was a river twenty feet beyond his room, and it coursed through the bright green meadow on the north end of Murambai. Above the high country meadow, the gray slopes of Mount Kulumai rose from the green, and higher still, the gray slopes gave way to white snow fields. Refenault looked from the river to the gondola, which crossed the river and climbed up into the high tundra fields.

There was a knock at his door. He crossed the room, opened the door, and was greeted by Prince Osoro Santana and four beautiful, exotic women. Santana was dressed in a formal black-tie tuxedo, his hair slicked back, his eyes bright. On each arm was a beautiful woman.

"Dr. Refenault," Santana said. "I was hoping you would join us for dinner. The other guests have already gathered in the casino. Dinner will be served after a few games."

Dr. Refenault wore a pair of pressed black pants and a stylish white shirt. He smiled at Santana and at each of the ladies, and said, "I'd be delighted."

He exited the room, and the entourage started up the colorful hallway toward the casino.

• •

In the casino, Levine watched Agent McKenzie and three gentlemen at the poker table playing poker with gold coins. Around the casino, numerous scientists and dignitaries stood talking or playing card games. For the past seven days, Santana had flown in scientists from all around the globe, and now that Dr. Refenault was finally here the official ceremonies could begin.

Levine had adopted the reserved position of a true prisoner the past few months. She realized that she was being held against her will, but until the right moment arose there was no need to fight against her captor. And Santana did his best to make her comfortable.

Levine looked up when she saw Santana and Refenault at the far end of the casino.

Refenault, she thought.

She knew the doctor's work. Santana shook a few hands as he crossed the red-carpeted room.

"Dr. Refenault," Santana said. "Have you had the pleasure of meeting my special guest, Dr. Amy Levine?"

Refenault looked into Levine's brown-blue eyes. He'd heard stories of her fabled gaze.

"I have not," Refenault said. And to Levine, "But it is my honor to finally meet you, Dr. Levine."

"It's a pleasure to meet you, Dr. Refenault," Levine said.

She leaned forward, and he kissed her cheek. Levine smiled.

McKenzie said, "Two Jacks! Sweet! That's a Full House! Cough it up, buddy! Cough it up!"

Sara turned and saw Santana. He nodded at her. She smiled sarcastically.

"Santana, Prince, my good buddy," she said. "Won't you join us for a game?"

Santana looked at the four ladies at his side, then from Refenault to Levine, to McKenzie. He said, "It'd be my pleasure, Agent McKenzie."

Santana joined them at the table. With a sly signal, Santana had one of his men bring him a little case about the size of a shoebox. It was made of hard black bullet-proof enamel, and there was a combination on the front. Santana entered the combination, and the case hissed pneumatically. Something shone inside, and Levine craned her neck to see over their shoulders.

The case was filled with four rows of neatly stacked gold coins. Levine saw the look of envy on Sara's face, and she was hit with a mental flash: Levine saw Sara standing on a hill of gold coins, filling her pockets, laughing hysterically until something struck her feet from inside the hill.

Refenault and Levine stood a few feet from the dealer's table. A crowd of fifteen gathered close.

Refenault asked Levine, "What's the game?"

Levine didn't hear him at first; she shook the image from her mind.

"Are you alright, Dr. Levine?" Refenault asked.

"Jacks or Better," Levine said. "All hands against the house. Highest hand wins."

"I see," Refenault said. Refenault looked at her curiously.

Over to the left, the roulette wheel clicked feverishly, and one of the gamblers got excited and cheered for his number.

Refenault touched Levine's arm. She looked at him, smiled, and eyed the card table. The dealer dealt the first hand to each player. Santana glanced at his cards. McKenzie picked hers fully up off of the table, looked at them, then placed them back on the table. The dealer looked at her. She held two fingers up from the table, slid two cards forward, and the dealer dealt her two new cards.

"What can you tell me about the Line, Dr. Levine?" Refenault asked.

Levine looked at Refenault. "It exists, Refenault. Believe me, when I tell you. The Line exists."

"I'm sure it does," Refenault said. "I've read your recent work. The Colorado Sequence, as Antrætus called it. It's a hundred years ahead of its time."

"Donald was always given to provocative titles, Refenault. The work is much less exciting than it sounds."

Refenault looked at the card table. McKenzie won the first hand on two pair.

"But do you really expect the scientific community to embrace your work," Refenault said, "this *other world*, which flows through our reality?"

Levine's eyes flashed at Refenault. She remained silent.

"I mean the thought that there are forces all around us," Refenault said, "that we can not experience except through intuition—"

"Intuition, Dr. Refenault, is only a reflection of this 'other world' as you call it."

"This—other world," Refenault chuckled. And said sarcastically, "Is it some kind of heaven, do you think?"

Levine looked at Refenault, "You only believe in the world you can see and hear?"

"I'll admit the geometry with which your most recent equations were written are elegant," Refenault said. "But they seem to be games—a mathematical cartoon."

Levine was amused by his ignorance. "A cartoon?" she said.

"And the Line," Refenault said, "is it *in* this other world, or is it a bridge *to* the other world?"

"The Line, Refenault, is mathematical truth. It is freedom from fear and emotion. It is freedom from hatred and self-destruction. It's another world, Refenault. It's an undiscovered country."

"Alien to logic," Refenault said.

"The next four cards played will all be hearts," Levine said.

One of the gentlemen at the table laid four hearts on the table and a spade. Refenault's eyes widened. He looked at Levine. She met his eyes calmly.

"A guess?" he said.

She slowly shook her head from side to side. She still had that image of Sara atop a hill of gold coins in her mind. She said, "It's something else entirely, Refenault. And to be quite honest, it's something that scares me deeply."

• •

The skiers wore oxygen masks at twenty thousand feet, and skied by moonlight over the massive Kulumai snow fields. There were two dozen. Overhead, stars filled the south Pacific sky, and there was only the sound of twenty-four sets of skis gliding through deep powder.

A few of the men wore night vision goggles, from which the world shone bright green and revealed an open field of snow descending from twenty to seventeen thousand feet. Like a pack of snow wolves, they covered the descent in less than thirty minutes. At sixteen thousand five hundred feet, the skiers saw the first glimmer of Murambai, a shiny, warmly lit glow far below, cradled deep inside the mountain range.

At fourteen thousand feet, the skiers removed their oxygen masks. One lead man radioed coordinates to a space satellite beyond Earth's atmosphere, which relayed the signal to a station in Venezuela. In a matter of seconds, a reply crackled over the man's radio. Another man had set up a small computer. He entered the coordinates into the computer, while the other men sipped water and checked their machineguns.

• •

"What would happen to a person who entered the Line?" Santana asked.

They were around a dining room table. An elegant chandelier brightened the room, and Levine wore a black evening dress. Her hair was in a chignon, and her eyes glistened at Santana from across the dining room table. There were a dozen of the most intelligent minds on the planet gathered at Prince Osoro Santana's table.

"Theoretically, your Highness," Levine said, "that person would cease to exist."

Santana looked brightly around the table at his guests.

Refenault said, "He would die?"

"No," Levine said. "Death is not possible within the Line. Our common assumptions about mortality, physics, and metaphysics break down as you approach the Line. Well, within the Line—at least theoretically, Doctor—all known laws of the physical world cease to exist. It is Zero's *opposite*."

"Infinity?" Refenault said.

"No, not infinity," Levine said. "The Line is something else entirely."

One gray-haired man at the table said, "And it's here in this room, right now?"

"Yes," Levine said. "It is all around us. It is within us. And it is what separates us. We simply can't see it because our minds are not conditioned to see it."

This elicited chuckles around the table.

McKenzie said, "But it's like a window; I've seen you do it."

"Yes," Santana said. "Is it a window?"

"There is no temporality within the Line, no time," Levine said. "The things that we consider past and future—our present right now—they're viewed objectively within the Line. You can see our world from inside, all of it, past and future. But while you are in it—in the Line—it's like traveling. So you see everything, but you see it in passing. The things that we call intuition, subconscious, they probe less than one percent of one percent into the Line's full potential for seeing with our minds."

"It's like a book," McKenzie said.

Refenault said, "How do you mean, Agent McKenzie?"

"Well, imagine if you were a character in a book, Doctor," McKenzie said. "To you, everything happens as it happens in our world. But to be within the Line is to be a reader of the book. You can see the past, present, and future all contained within our story."

"That's a good analogy, Sara," Levine said. "But our world is our world. It is our reality."

Santana held his hands up generously to all his dinner guests. "Our guest of honor," he said. "Dr. Amy Levine."

He started clapping, and everyone around the table joined in the applause. Levine shot McKenzie a look, and McKenzie nodded her head in her direction.

And then she saw them. Levine saw the skiers. It came to her in a flash, and her hand drifted forward and knocked over the wine glass on the white table cloth. Everyone looked at her. She stared intensely at the window at the far end of the room.

"Skiers," she said.

Everyone at the table looked at her. A ripple of fear went around the table. At first they thought she was joking, was acting, but then they realized she was dead serious.

"Two dozen men," she said, "with high explosives."

Santana looked across the dining room table at Levine.

"And machineguns," she said. "I can see them. They'll be on Murambai in minutes."

Sara McKenzie said, "I've seen her do this before."

At the far end of the room, one of Santana's security men waited for instructions. The table was all commotion.

Santana said to his man, "Get on it! See if there's anything that skipped our radar surveillance. Now!"

The man turned and exited the dining room. And all eyes fell on Dr. Amy Levine. She sat with both hands flat atop the table. She looked around at everyone at the dining room table. She gathered the full force of the room's energy. She looked at each person individually.

And then she said, "Many of you are going to die."

• •

Ramon Martinez stepped out onto the balcony of lookout tower sixteen in Murambai's northeastern quadrant. He fired up a cigarette and tucked his machinegun under his arm. The smoke went to his lungs. He gazed up at the moonlit snowfields above Murambai and exhaled the smoke.

It was cold out, and the only sound was the stirring of wind through tree branches. Tower sixteen rose ten feet above the tree line, and Martinez could see the whole village spread out to the south. Rooms glowed warmly inside the compound, and occasionally he could hear the low-level hum of guests' laughter coming from an open-air terrace or from down along one of the garden paths.

The crack of small-arms fire surprised him.

He chucked his smoke and looked off into the distance at the farthest reach of the tree line. At first he wasn't certain it was gun fire; everything was so peaceful. But he walked to tower sixteen's corner and saw a squad of men moving in the darkness about a quarter mile away. Something was going down.

He immediately started shouting loud enough for everyone within a hundred meters to hear. He pointed his machinegun and capped off three shots in the direction of the men he saw. The sparkle of returning fire lit up the dark canvas of the mountain slope just beyond the trees.

"Oh, shit," he said. "Oh, shit. Oh, shit."

He ran for the door inside the tower. His radio inside the tower was going crazy.

"Intruder alert!" the radio screamed. "Intruder alert! Northwest quadrant! We're hit! Intruder alert!"

In the background on the radio there was an intense barrage of machinegun fire, glass shattering, powerful men's voices yelling, another burst of gunfire, a single man screaming "I'm hit! Oh, God! I'm hit! I'm hit!"

A moment later a deafening siren blared over the treetops for all Murambai to hear. The village was under attack.

Four

The Creature in the Motel Room

From the girl's forearms, snake-like appendages broke through the skin and began to wrap around Helen's throat, coiling like a boa constrictor. Helen went crazy, her hands grabbing at the slimy, green coils wrapped around her throat. Her flashlight dropped to the floor.

And everyone felt something enter the room. There were large black spots, distortions in the space, so black they seemed to be drawing in the space around them as in some weird curvature. Everyone got out of their way.

Helen was choking, trying to pull away from the thing on the bed. The girl's eyes looked into Helen's bulging eyes, and the thing's eyes flashed bright silver.

"*Black wraiths,*" it shrieked. "*I warned you!*"

"Shoot that thing!" one of the men shouted.

The flashlight beams were going crazy. The thing on the bed had Helen by the throat, and it pulled her across the bed over its body. Helen made horrible gasping, choking sounds and it looked like her eyes were going to pop out of her head. Roger was going crazy, beating at the snake-like coils that were wrapped around Helen's throat.

The room filled with an acrid smell like burning sulfur. The large black spots descended on the girl in the bed, and the coils pulsed an otherworldly violet glow. And then two of the men unloaded their shotguns on the thing on the bed. The shotgun sound was so loud it killed all other sound in the room.

Zeb pumped his shotgun and loaded round after round after round into the thing on the bed. The thing's silver eyes rolled up in its sockets and a tongue came out of its mouth flicking up and down. The room filled with the smell of ignited gun powder, and the men fired round after round of twelve-gauge buckshot into the creature.

Suddenly, two more snake-like appendages broke from the skin at the thing's shins and they shot up and grabbed Harvey. Harvey's shotgun dropped to the floor, and Harvey rose up into the air. His head slammed up into the ceiling in the room with a horrible crunching sound, and white powder from the ceiling rained down into the room.

Zeb beat at the appendages with his shotgun, using it like a bat. And all at once Helen was flying through the room toward the front window. There was a loud crash as she overturned the table and hit the window.

The thing held Harvey's limp body in the air and swung it around like a child with a rag doll. His body slammed into the wall near the bathroom, and then flew back toward the TV. His body hit the TV, and it crashed to the floor. The TV exploded, and all at once flames ignited and started licking at the wall.

"Get the hell out'a here!" Zeb shouted.

The men went for the door. Zeb stood with his shotgun held just above his waist. He pumped it, fired it, pumped it, fired it, four, five, six times. Harvey's body swung through the air and hit Zeb like a two-hundred-pound sandbag. Zeb fell out the front door, hitting the concrete walkway just outside the room and rolling down onto the pavement in the pouring rain.

Roger bent down at the front window. He was trying to help Helen. Helen had hit the glass and crumpled to the floor just a few feet from the door.

Flames spread on the wall opposite the foot of the bed. The creature on the bed swung its giant tentacles around the room and the thing that had been the girl made horrible screaming, hissing sounds. The fire quickly spread through the room, and Roger tried to lift Helen up off the floor. She coughed and winced in agony. She was not really conscious, but Roger had her up in his arms as he started for the door.

One of the free tentacles whickered through the air, and hit Roger square across the face, a four-hundred-pound clothesline. He was knocked backward away from the front door. His head slammed into the wall a few feet from the head of the bed. Helen hit the floor with a dull thud.

The creature was going crazy. The fire spread up the wall and across the ceiling above the thing in the bed. The thing's head swung back and forth like a cornered lizard, and its tentacles swung frantically, gripping Harvey's body tighter and tighter.

Roger shook his head, dazed. Fire fell from the ceiling down on top of the bed, onto the floor of the motel room. A cross beam in the ceiling broke free and crashed down on top of one of the creature's tentacles. The thing screamed out an otherworldly howl, and green slime splattered all through the room. Some of the green slime hit Roger's face. He could taste it on his lips. It was like toxic bile. And Roger felt his stomach beginning to heave. He fought the reflex, and stood up. He felt a pain in his back like something had popped in a way that it shouldn't have, but he staggered forward, grabbing Helen, and he dragged her out of the fiery room out into the driving storm.

At the door he kicked the leather satchel out into the rain ahead of him as if on pure instinct. And he staggered forward with Helen behind him like a sack of flour, out into the howling wind, out into the driving rain.

A minute later, he fell down onto the pavement at the far side of the parking lot. Rain poured down on him, down on Helen who was coming to, and they watched as the creature inside the room burst into flames, watched through the shattered motel room window as the rest of the building caught fire in the driving rain, burning from the inside as though burning from the inside of hell.

FIVE
THE RK-81 MACHINE

The gunmen came through the casino with black machineguns sweeping across the empty room. McKenzie and Levine were in a janitor's closet at the end of a red-carpeted hallway adjacent to the casino. The door was cracked open, and McKenzie stared out across the casino. The brightly-lit spinning lights and flashing bulbs of slot machines were a direct contrast with the silent, empty room and the gunmen—six total—who came through the room.

"What do you see?" Levine said.

McKenzie said, "Six men. Light arms."

"Who are they?" Levine whispered.

"Hard to tell," McKenzie said. "But damn near any enemy of Santana is a friend of ours."

"What're they doing?"

McKenzie watched the gunmen sweep through the casino. She said, "These boys are on search and destroy."

"We need a gun."

Sara McKenzie pulled back from the door. She looked Levine in the eye. She raised a single index finger up over her lips. McKenzie motioned for Levine to get back against one wall. The only light coming in the closet was from the crack in the door. They could hear the footsteps of the gunmen right outside their room. Levine couldn't breathe. Her eyes went to the ceiling.

Two of the gunmen passed on up the hallway. Levine stood back in the shadows inside the closet. The men made little grunting noises outside in the hallway, just a few feet away. McKenzie stood just inside the closet door.

And then Levine watched as the closet door started to creak slowly open. The barrel of a machinegun eased into the darkened room. McKenzie balanced her feet at shoulder-width, and all at once she chopped down with the butt of her hand on the gun. There was a grunt. One of the gunmen fell away from the door. The machinegun hit the carpet inside the janitor's closet. The door slammed shut. And then all hell broke loose.

The gunmen in the hallway opened fire on the janitor's closet.

McKenzie roared, "Get down, Levine!" But the noise of five machineguns unloading on the door of the janitor's closet was the only sound anyone heard for a steady ten seconds.

McKenzie was on the floor inside the closet, feeling around for the machinegun. Inside the darkened closet, bullet holes exploded in the door, and the door soon looked like a bullet-hole night sky of stars. One of the men kicked the door open.

The tattered door slammed open, and Levine saw the men out in the hallway with black machineguns. They couldn't see into the darkened closet, and then three of them dropped to the floor. McKenzie cut them down with the machinegun.

Levine saw the three men McKenzie had hit. They were face down on the floor. It had all happened so fast. The other three men were shouting, but they'd backed away from the coiled viper they'd found inside the janitor's closet.

McKenzie was somewhere in the dark, but Levine could not see her. Levine smelled chlorine bleach and ammonia. Her hand was on the wound cords of a vacuum cleaner. In the hallway, one of the dead gunmen's radios crackled. Levine heard gunfire in the radio's background. All of Murambai was under attack, and she and McKenzie were pinned into a janitor's closet.

One of the remaining gunmen ran by the open closet door spraying machinegun fire inside. Levine felt something hot knick the side of her neck, and the wall above her exploded with bullets. McKenzie answered back with her machinegun, and Levine saw her, each gun shot igniting a little spark of light in the darkness.

McKenzie knelt down in a crouched position. She held the gun in front of her, and she counted to herself: one, two, three! Agent Sara McKenzie leapt to her feet, roaring, and she lunged out of the closet. Levine watched her. McKenzie was in mid-air like a soccer goalie, her machinegun rapping off bullets, blasting up the hallway, McKenzie diving through the air out into the middle of the hallway. She hit the ground hard, rolled, and popped up on one knee. Her face was a hard grimace, and she blasted off rounds with her machinegun, screaming obscenities up the hallway, and all was deathly still inside the darkened closet.

McKenzie looked in the closet and yelled, "Get the hell out of there, Levine!" And then something like, "High explosives comin' your way!"

Levine leapt to her feet and ran for the door. She burst out into the lighted hallway. She glanced in the direction that McKenzie unloaded her machinegun, and she saw a man at the end of the hallway near the casino with a rocket launcher.

"*Oh, no!*" Levine gasped, and she started up the hallway away from the casino.

There was a quick sound *whoosh-hiss* and then *bam!* The janitor's closet exploded. Levine was thrown forward as if by a very hot wind. And everything faded to white.

"Get up! Get up! Get up!" McKenzie yelled at her.

Levine shook her head. McKenzie was over her. She had one of Levine's hands. The other hand held the machinegun. And she was dragging her around a corner in the hallway. Somewhere in the distance—not very far away—there was the crack of more small-arms fire. Levine struggled to her feet.

McKenzie held the black machinegun in her right hand, and she looked hard up the brightly lit hallway. The red carpet hallway had Kandinsky-style designs printed on it, and occasionally McKenzie and Levine passed by a window where they could see trees and gardens outside in the darkness.

They watched a group of gunmen far up the hallway pass an intersecting hallway. None of the men turned and saw them fifty meters away.

"Johnston," Sara said.

Sara had seen one of the gunmen running by up the hallway. It looked like Noah Johnston.

"Come on," Levine said.

Every few seconds, they heard the crackle of machinegun fire in the distance. There was a fire burning far across the compound. They saw it through one long hallway window, through the darkness and trees, sloped downhill from where they were. The bright orange flames danced up into the sky just above the tree line. They saw one giant mountain range in the moonlight, the snow glistening under a full moon night.

"What do you think, McKenzie?" Levine said.

"I think Santana's screwed," she said. She was still thinking about whether it was Noah Johnston she had seen with the group of gunmen.

"What comes around goes around."

They continued up the hallway and came to a room with a giant, green, three-dimensional, hologram globe rotating in the center of the room. McKenzie went into the room.

In the center of the room, the globe spun. It was nine feet in diameter, and along the sides of the room there were computer consoles and soft leather seats. On one screen, they watched a firefight in an indoor swimming pool area. On one side of the pool, one group of men opened fire across the swimming pool at a group on the other side. Three TV screens carried the action from different angles, and the sound of machinegun fire echoed hollowly against the concrete walls surrounding the swimming pool.

"Close the door," McKenzie said.

Levine turned and closed the door to the room.

"Lock it," McKenzie said.

Levine locked the door and said, "What is this room?"

"Some kind of security room," McKenzie said. "We got satellite position here on this globe."

"What we need," Levine said, "is a way off this island."

She raised a hand up to the green hologram globe. Her hand went through the light, and it caused ripples in the green hologram like ripples on a lake after a stone's been tossed on it.

"That's funny," McKenzie said. "Look how it reacts to touch."

"Yeah," Levine said. "It's almost like it's alive."

She pulled her hand out of the hologram globe and then brought her fingertips up to its surface, touching it on the outside. The globe pulsed bright white, and it stopped spinning. She moved it to her right, and the globe spun to the right. She moved it to the left, and the globe rotated to her left.

She said, "It's like a touch screen."

"You can move it around?" McKenzie said.

"Yeah," Levine said.

"What if you double click it?" McKenzie brought her hand forward and tapped the surface of the globe. The green light turned blue, the globe shrank to a tiny point of light like a TV turned off, and then it grew back out in a sphere shape. Only, the sphere was now hologram blue.

"And that's not the globe," McKenzie said.

A giant blue sphere—nine feet in diameter—floated in front of them, but it was covered with little white dots, some brighter than others. Levine grinned.

"You know what this is?" she asked McKenzie.

"What's it like, space?"

"Not like space," Levine said. "It *is* space. Or a spherical representation of it. Here's the constellation Cassiopeia."

McKenzie looked at the formation Levine indicated. The stars floated inside the sphere, and all of it rotated inside the blue sphere very, very slowly.

"Does the universe rotate like this?" McKenzie said.

"Well, this isn't the universe," Levine said. "It's just a small quadrant. Here's the Milky Way over here. It's just one galaxy in this entire region. You can see, if you step back, several galaxies in this cluster. See?"

"The Milky Way is only one?"

"It's the pinwheel-shaped one here. See how it rotates? And the coordinates here are accurate. This map's to scale. This section here between galactic longitudes 283° and 28°—these two lines here and here—are an inner arm of Sagittarius. See?"

"I see," McKenzie said.

"And I'll bet if we double click we can go in closer," Levine said. Levine touched the sphere's surface near the Milky Way and brought the galaxy closer to her. "See, if you look up at the night sky to see the Milky Way, it just looks like a giant band across the sky, right? But from deep in space, from a long way *outside* the Milky Way, it looks like a pinwheel rotating in free space. That's what we're looking at here."

Levine double tapped the blue hologram's edge, and it re-centered with the Milky Way now taking up a much larger area toward the sphere's center.

"What causes it to rotate like that?" McKenzie said.

"Rotation is a combination of interacting forces," Levine said. "Gravity keeps it together, but there's nothing really *powering* the rotation. We call it angular momentum. You see, there was a big explosion that set everything into motion. Imagine a rock thrown into a lake. The ripples continue outward forever, right?"

"Until it hits the edge of the lake, I guess."

"Or runs out of momentum," Levine said. "Well, a rotating galaxy—or our planets in the solar system, for that matter—were put into motion by a really big explosion. And the ripples are still moving. It's just that the scale of space and the power of the explosion is so huge, it seems like they're rotating forever."

"They're not?"

"For all practical purposes," Levine said, "they *are* rotating forever. There's nothing in space to stop angular momentum, except gravity. Imagine a stick of dynamite exploding in the desert. All that sand and debris flies up into the air, and for a couple minutes it floats around in the air just above the explosion; eventually it comes to rest. Well, in space the scale is much larger, and instead of a couple minutes, it takes a couple billion years for the dust to settle."

"What is it settling on?" McKenzie asked. "What is it rotating around?"

"What is the center of the galaxy?" Levine said.

"Yeah," McKenzie said. "I mean if this pinwheel cluster here is the Milky Way, and it's slowly rotating, what is it rotating around? Our solar system has the sun. What is at the center of our galaxy?"

Levine said, "Most scientists agree there's a massive central black hole at our galaxy's center. A black hole creates an enormous amount of gravity. On Earth you weigh a hundred pounds and some change, right? On Jupiter you'd weigh a couple thousand pounds. If you stepped into a black hole, your weight would approach infinity. And with that kind of gravity, there's an enormous amount of energy."

"Energy?" McKenzie said.

"Well," Levine said. "When a meteor enters Earth's atmosphere it creates a lot of friction, heats up, and is consumed by fire, the energy is so hot. At the center of the *galaxy*, there are huge amounts of gas swirling closer and closer to a central black hole. This creates a lot of friction and heat—friction and heat on a cosmological scale is pretty powerful stuff. Some of the brightest objects in the universe are what we call 'quasars'— most scientists agree that a quasar's brightness is the result of this friction, if you will, of massive fields of hydrogen, helium, and thermonuclear fuel circling closer and closer to a black hole's edge, exploding as it enters."

"And that's what you did your work on, the Colorado Sequence?"

Levine said, "The Colorado Sequence relates to an area of mathematics dealing with dark matter. Refenault called it 'mathematical cartoons'. Others have called it mathematics of the absurd."

"What is it?" McKenzie asked.

"Most of the known universe is comprised of a dark energy, which Einstein called the *cosmological constant*. It works like a kind of vacuum pump at the very core of our reality, both expanding, filling, and limiting the space in and around us. It's the very life force of all matter. My work was focused on a mathematical system for defining the inner workings of dark matter, the inner workings of quintessence."

"What happens inside the inner workings of quintessence?"

Levine said, "No one knows for certain. But many have theories. I think that's why Santana has organized all of this. I think he's done something far beyond pure theory, and I intend to find out what it is exactly that he has done."

McKenzie looked at the panel along the base of the table. There were hundreds of sleek colorful buttons with phrases like: Con. Sonar; Vec. Grid; Therm. Res.; Glb. Pos.; Lorn. Azm.; Com. Grid.

She depressed the Com. Grid button, and the hologram blue sphere was replaced by a bright red hologram image of the Murambai compound and the surrounding mountains. It was laid out lower to the table than the sphere, but it was broad—nine feet from side-to-side—in a red hologram square. At either side of the compound, mountains rose up to the red hologram's periphery. Levine's eyes took in what she was now seeing, and she moved around the table.

"We got a hologram map of the compound here," McKenzie said.

"I see that," Levine said.

Along the hologram's perimeter base were hologram phrases, which McKenzie reasoned could be activated. One read "Present Thermal Scan." McKenzie reached an index finger forward and touched it.

The bright red hologram flashed white, and was then replaced by another bright red hologram image of the compound. Only, this new one was marked with infrared images of all the people, all the active life, in the compound. And many of the little white images moved along various corridors and rooms inside the compound.

"It's a thermal scan of everything going on inside the compound," McKenzie said.

"Where are we?" Levine said.

They both scanned the hundreds of bright infrared dots looking for two close together in an area on the hologram that they recognized as the room that surrounded them.

"There's two," McKenzie said.

"That's too far to the south," Levine said.

"Yeah," McKenzie said. "And they're moving. Ours should be pretty still."

"There it is!" Levine said.

They saw two little white images in a northwest corner of the compound. McKenzie started to walk around the room to see if the image on the hologram mirrored her movements. Sure enough, the white image on the hologram moved around in the little room.

"That's us!" McKenzie said.

They both scanned and saw that there were no other white dots near them—at least not within a hundred meters or so. Levine's eyes caught one little group of white dots moving through a cafeteria. They moved like they were sweeping through the cafeteria with machineguns, coordinated and alert.

"This map has probably got an entrance into the mountain," Levine said. "The secret entrance."

"Yeah," McKenzie said. "But infrared's not gonna show something underground. How would we see it?"

"Well, the entrance is probably up against the mountains."

"Which ones?" McKenzie said. "There are mountains all around Murambai."

Levine moved closer to the hologram. She extended her hand out over the map and reached down touching the mountains the way a child touches a sand castle on a beach. She looked for any unusual perturbations or indentations. Machinegun fire crackled up the hallway not too far away, and both McKenzie and Levine saw the tiny little flashes of corresponding white gun fire within the hologram.

"That was just two hallways away," McKenzie said.

Levine glanced up and looked into her friend's green eyes. McKenzie's short red hair was tousled. She brought up a hand, swept her red hair back, and looked at Levine.

"Yeah," Levine said. "But they don't know we're here. It'd be like finding a needle in a maze when the only thing you're looking for is a way out. The door's locked."

McKenzie looked a little more assured. Levine smiled and went back to the map. She traced her fingertips up over the tops of two mountains along the hologram's perimeter, then smoothly traced her fingers down the inner side of the adjoining slope.

She continued south along the fields, her eyes calmly looking for the entrance. She was a couple hundred meters north of Murambai when four bright images suddenly appeared along the mountain's slopes out of nowhere. Both women's eyes widened.

"That's it!" Levine said. "There's our entrance."

"It must be a jeep," McKenzie said.

"A couple of jeeps," Levine said. "They're moving fast. They just appeared out of nowhere."

"Not out of nowhere," Levine said. "That's our entrance into the mountains."

"Where is it?" McKenzie said.

"Well, we're here," Levine said. "And it's way up here."

"So, we've gotta cross the compound"—McKenzie pointed from where they were to where they needed to go—"from here to here. There's a lot of activity in this area, Levine."

"Yeah," Levine said. "We're gonna have to be careful."

"What is this surface here?" McKenzie pointed to a clear area.

"It looks like a lake," Levine said. "You can see the hills here on either side of it."

"I'll bet you're right," McKenzie said. "So the jeeps came up out of the lake?"

Levine looked at her friend. "We'll find out in a minute," she said. "Come on, let's go!"

They opened the door to the security room and looked both ways up the hallway. McKenzie checked the clip on her machinegun and said, "Looks clear. We head on up here."

They jogged up the hallway and came to an intersection with six elevators.

"Do we need the elevator?" McKenzie said.

"No," Levine said. "Let's stay on the ground floor. We've got a little more freedom here."

They continued on up the hallway. There were rooms along either side, but all of the doors were shut.

At the end of the hallway, there was an exit sign over an electronic door. They hit the door and stepped outside into the cool night air. The crackle of machinegun fire echoed from somewhere through the trees. Ahead, in the darkness a white concrete path wound into a garden. It was very dark, but both women jogged on ahead.

"Looks like a service road," Levine said.

"Yeah," McKenzie said. "We're heading in the right direction. Just keep the mountains as your bearing."

McKenzie and Levine crossed the black-top service road and approached the backside of another building. They stepped up from the service road into the cool damp grass behind the building, and they both caught a glimpse of the fire burning down on the west end of the compound. There was another explosion like thunder from a good distance away, followed by the crash of glass and men shouting at one another. More staccato machinegun fire volleyed back and forth.

"Come on," Levine said. "Let's stick close to the building here."

They stayed within ten feet of the back of the teak-colored building, and they continued until they reached the building's corner. They looked out to the north beyond the building, beyond the compound.

They saw the gondola climbing up into the steep fields above the compound.

"The gondola's still running," McKenzie said. "That's kind'a crazy."

"Yeah," Levine said. "I guess nobody stopped to turn it off when the village came under attack."

Suddenly, the headlights of three jeeps shone on them from the west. Both women hit the ground. The grass was cool and damp, and there was foliage from the gardens behind them. They heard the men at the jeeps talking excitedly. The jeeps were about a football field's length away, and Levine looked at McKenzie.

"I don't think they saw us," she whispered.

McKenzie shook her head back and forth. "No, they didn't," she said. "They couldn't have."

McKenzie and Levine crawled through the grasses toward a stand of trees about fifty yards away. The grass was pretty tall around them, and there was just enough light from the buildings and from the moonlight overhead for them to see their way.

There was the crackle of machinegun fire from woods on the far side of the jeeps, and the men around the jeeps were yelling and firing back into the darkness. Levine saw the rustle of trees on the far side, but it was impossible to see far into the trees. The men by the jeeps all took cover behind the steel automobiles, and they returned volley. McKenzie and Levine continued onward farther to the north away from the compound on up the slopes just north of Murambai.

They breathed heavily in the thin air, but they were up above the village. Above Murambai, they could see the fires burning in several areas of the compound. Jeeps roared along the streets inside the village, and McKenzie and Levine were hit with the realization that they were watching a military coup from up in the hills north of the village.

"I was in Tanzania when President Ngenya was ousted three years ago," McKenzie said. "There's no feeling like it in the world. It's just surreal."

In the moonlight up on the ridge, Levine looked at her friend. Their eyes met. McKenzie managed a little smile.

"Come on," Levine said. "The lake's up on this next ridge."

• •

Steam rose from the lake's surface as from a quietly simmering leviathan. Levine and McKenzie stood along its bank in the cold mountain air. Snow crunched under their feet, and Levine cast her hand out over the lake's surface. Enormous snow-covered mountains rose on the far side of the lake, and on the side from which they'd just come, the mountains descended down into a black abyss that could have been forever.

"The jeeps came from inside the lake," Levine said.

They saw the tracks coming up from the steaming water out onto the snow pack.

"Amphibious vehicles," McKenzie said. "These boys are pretty sophisticated."

Both women walked over to the tracks, which were ground down into the snow five or six inches. The number of tracks indicated an amphibious landing of no less than six vehicles.

Sara said, "You think the entrance into the mountain is inside the lake?"

"You know," she said. "I'll bet you're right!"

They both scanned the dark water shining in the moonlight. Ripples on the water created a million moonlight fractal reflections, and the steam crawled along atop its dark surface. They walked up and down the bank. Snow crunched under their feet. They were looking for anything inside the water that might give them a clue as to whether the jeeps did come from inside the water, from down along the lake's sandy bottom. Levine saw the lights first.

"Look out!" she said.

They both looked down inside the water and saw the headlights of four or five amphibious vehicles coming from down inside the water. McKenzie and Levine ran for cover in a stand of ponderosa pine trees a few feet up from the lake. They crouched down at the trees, forty meters from the tracks in the snow. And out on the water, fifty feet from shore, the amphibious vehicles broke the surface of the lake with a series of loud splashes. Their headlights shone up at the shore, and the vehicles moved across the water like mechanical otters. McKenzie and Levine looked at one another.

There were seven amphibious vehicles in all, and they rolled up onto the shore and proceeded forward in the same direction of the tracks. The vehicles were camouflaged black and glistened in the moonlight. Water streamed down their sides onto the snow cover, and the heated water steamed up from the vehicles in the cold mountain air. McKenzie and Levine watched the vehicles continue forward in the direction of Murambai. The lake made little splashing waves along its shoreline, and the water settled back into its natural rhythm in the peace and quiet of the high-altitude cold. McKenzie and Levine stood up and approached the spot where the vehicles had come onto land.

"How cold do you expect that water is?" McKenzie asked.

"I don't know," Levine said. "It's a thermal lake. A lot of these south Pacific islands are volcanic."

McKenzie walked down to the water. She knelt down and touched the water with her right hand. Her fingertips swept across the water.

"It's hot!" she said. "Like a giant hot tub. This water is heated."

She stood up and looked at Levine.

"Well," Levine said with a smile. "Care to go for a swim?"

• •

The two women stripped down to their underwear and hopped from one foot to the next in the cold. McKenzie started giggling like a girl of fourteen, and under the fabric of her bra she adjusted the gold coins that no one had seen her steal. Levine approached the steamy water.

"Well," Levine said. "You ready?"

"How far down do you think the entrance is?"

"It looked like it was just a few feet under the surface. Maybe ten, fifteen feet. It's *cold* out here!"

Levine stepped into the lake, her bare foot entering its warm dark water. They both waded out to waist height about ten feet out from the shore. Levine dipped down into the water to stay out of the cold mountain air. And she came up with her hair wet, her brown eyes shining. McKenzie quickly followed Levine, and they swam out ten feet farther into the lake, and they were soon not able to touch the sandy bottom. Steam rose up from the surface, and they glided through it toward the spot where the vehicles had emerged.

"I think I can see it," Levine said.

She treaded water. Their voices and the light sounds of their splashing echoed over the lake's glassy surface. The water was very warm like a well-drawn bath, and the moonlight shone down on them giving them just enough light by which to see. The white snow on the high mountain fields and peaks around the lake caught the bright full-moon light, and the water was warm and soothing. McKenzie treaded to Levine.

"What do you see?" McKenzie said.

"Some kind of light," she said.

"Oh, yeah," McKenzie said. "I see it. Looks like it's about ten feet down."

"I say we dive down, once, to see what the entrance looks like," Levine said. "If we can make it through on a single breath of air, let's go for it. But if it looks like we have to open some kind of door, we may need to come back up for air."

"Clear," McKenzie said. "If we gotta come back up, the signal is a thumbs-up hiked toward the surface."

"Clear."

The two women looked down inside the lake at the lights they could see along the lake's sandy bottom. Levine nodded her head, drew in a deep breath, and ducked down under the water, kicking toward the lights. McKenzie followed her.

Levine opened her eyes underwater and saw the blurry bright lights ten feet away. The closer she came, the more clear the lake's bottom became, and she felt her way to the door. McKenzie looked at her underwater. Levine jabbed a finger at the steel bars on the bottom of the lake, and McKenzie said "Yes" with her eyes and with a vigorous nod of her head.

On the bottom of the lake, there was a steel-barred door like a prison door, only the bars were much farther apart. There were four lights at each of the door's corners, and the two women swam along the bottom feeling their way along the bars. The bars were wide enough apart to ease through.

Levine ducked her head down and eased between the bars, going beyond the bottom of the lake. She looked back and saw McKenzie follow her, and then she turned and swam onward. Her lungs were beginning to ache, but she could see a very bright light at the end of the tunnel, twenty feet ahead. The barred opening at the bottom of the lake gave onto the tunnel, through which they were swimming, and there were underwater lights all along the walls of the tunnel. The tunnel was wide enough for an amphibious vehicle to drive along its sandy floor, and the water was clear. Levine realized the tunnel was underneath the surface of the lake, and she swam onward toward the bright light at the tunnel's end.

The tunnel opened onto a small underground lake, about ten feet below the lake's surface.

Both women came up from the surface of the water and looked around them. There were rocky cavernous walls all around the underground lake, with a ceiling some forty feet overhead. McKenzie looked at Levine, and both women realized they had to be very quiet. At the far end of the underground lake, there was a loading dock area.

There were vehicles up on the loading dock, and several loft-style tiers beyond it. Men with machineguns and black military uniforms were moving around the loading dock excitedly.

"We're inside the mountain," Levine whispered to McKenzie.

"Yeah," McKenzie said. "It looks like it. But I think it was safer back on the other side. Those are Santana's men. They have machineguns."

"What in the world is going on here?"

"It looks like they're preparing for evacuation," McKenzie said.

"Or for battle," Levine said. "Come on. We'll have to be quiet."

They treaded across the cavernous lake toward the loading dock area. The loading dock looked like it led to an underground airport hanger beyond, and none of the men noticed the two heads moving quietly along the lake's surface.

They climbed very quietly up onto the dock and stood behind a bright yellow forklift, dripping water on the smooth white concrete. They were cautious and alert. Levine raised a single index finger up to her lips, and McKenzie nodded her head. Their focus went to the men just a few feet away.

There were colorful lines on the floor of the loading area, and the men loaded wooden crates into the back of five trucks. McKenzie gave Levine a look, and mouthed, "What's in the boxes?"

Levine shook her head, and pointed to a glass window on the far side of the loading dock. A strange, bright white light came from beyond the glass window. The light was so bright it shone out of the room, glowing. There were military men near the window, but they wore special sunglasses that fully protected their eyes.

"We need the forklift!" a man at the back of one truck said. "Hortago, get the forklift! Bring it over here and help load these crates."

Hortago said, "Yes, sir!" And started coming toward the forklift, toward McKenzie and Levine.

McKenzie and Levine trotted toward a canvas-covered truck a few feet away from the forklift. In the cab of the truck, there were two black military uniforms hanging from a handle on the passenger's side.

McKenzie and Levine went around the front grill of the truck and watched Hortago climb up into the forklift. He put the forklift in gear, and the thing lurched forward, spun around in a quick half-circle, and headed back over the loading dock in the direction of the trucks.

McKenzie slipped around the side of the truck and quietly eased the door open. She retrieved the two black uniforms, and then came back down, back to Levine at the front left fender of the truck. They quickly got into the black military uniforms. The uniforms were over-sized but passable.

"Let's see what's in that room," Levine whispered.

"You lead; I'll follow."

McKenzie and Levine crept along one wall behind a couple of trucks. There were wooden boxes at the far end of the trucks, and there was a hallway up to the right. But the bright shining room was straight ahead. A single military man stood with his arms folded. An AK-47 rested against the wall behind him, and he wore those dark sunglasses. The man yawned.

"That's our man," McKenzie said.

They crept along the wall drawing close to the man's back. The man suddenly knelt down to scratch an itch on his shin, and McKenzie leapt on him. She got her hand over his mouth. The man cried out, but his cry was muffled against her hand, and she quickly jerked his neck hard to the right. It made a sound like *crrkk!* And the man slumped to the ground. McKenzie pulled the man up against the wall and propped his legs and arms up so that he looked like he was just resting against the wall. She grabbed the AK-47 and came back to Levine.

Levine checked the men on the loading dock fifty feet away. McKenzie checked the assault rifle. She pulled the clip and saw that the gun was fully loaded. Levine's eyes went to the man, now propped against the wall. He wore those black sunglasses and looked like he was just leaning, taking a nap.

"The hallway up to the right," McKenzie whispered. "That's the way."

Levine nodded agreement, and McKenzie led the way.

The walls on the right side of the hallway and the ceiling were cool black volcanic rock. Along the left side of the hallway, a long chest-height window gave onto a view inside what looked like a nuclear reactor core. The room was giant, spacious, and round, and it descended downward for five stories.

The room was fifty meters in diameter, and there was metal scaffolding along the core's brightly lit walls. But the source of light was far down on the ground, and it was so bright that neither Levine nor McKenzie could look directly at it for more than a quarter second. Scientists in white lab jackets were excitedly running along the metal scaffolding taking notes, measuring air quality, checking ambient light inside the central core. The scientists wore dark sunglasses.

McKenzie and Levine continued up the hallway and came to a glass door into the central core.

"What is this?" McKenzie said.

"It looks like what I thought," Levine said.

"What?"

"Everything Santana has said since we've been here on this island has indicated that he has some kind of crazed interest with entering the Line."

"You think he's done it?" McKenzie said.

"It sure looks like he's giving it a shot. That generator down there. I've never seen anything so bright in my life."

"But Santana acted like he didn't believe," McKenzie said. "Like he thought your theories were a game."

"Santana is very interested in entering the Line," Levine said. "I didn't think it was possible. But I'll bet everything that I am, everything that I stand for, everything that I believe, that *that's* what he is doing here. He's developed some kind of machine to enter the Line!"

Across from the doorway into the central core, there was an alcove with lockers along either side. Green medical uniforms hung from a couple of the lockers. There was shouting back towards the dock, up the hallway. McKenzie and Levine looked up and saw Santana on the underground lake. He was in a black amphibious vehicle that came up to the side of the loading dock. He stepped out of the vehicle, up onto the loading dock, and McKenzie and Levine saw that he had seven prisoners with him.

And at the front of the group, both Levine and McKenzie saw Noah Johnston with his hands shackled in front of him.

"*Johnston*," McKenzie said. "Oh, my God. It's Noah Johnston."

Levine pulled McKenzie back in the locker room alcove, and they both watched Santana on the other side of the central core. The prisoners' hands were shackled and were bound behind their backs. Santana's men prodded Johnston and the other prisoners forward with machineguns.

Levine said, "Why the hell did they attack us?"

"They didn't know," McKenzie said. "They thought we were with Santana."

"You killed your own men," Levine said.

McKenzie looked at her with regret and worry in her eyes, and she gripped her AK-47.

"I didn't know," McKenzie said. "I didn't know they were with Nano Tech."

Both she and Levine watched Santana on the far side of the central core. One of Santana's men opened a door for him into the reactor, and Santana kicked Johnston in the stomach and threw him into the core. Johnston went forward and hit the scaffold railing inside the reactor. He fell hard to the steel girder floor.

And Santana shouted at one of his men, "Get him to the reactor floor! We'll show this Nano Tech scum what happens when you attack Prince Osoro Santana. We're going to send you into the Line!"

Johnston cried, "Nooo!"

And Santana's men led him down the steel stairwell along the core wall, down to the floor inside the reactor core.

"It's so bright," McKenzie said. "It's hard to see."

Levine turned and looked at the green medical uniforms on the lockers. She pulled the uniform back and opened a locker. There was a case inside. Levine opened it and retrieved a pair of sunglasses.

She said, "Here," and tossed the pair to McKenzie. McKenzie put the special sunglasses on, and Levine found another pair in another locker. She put on the sunglasses, and both women came to the front of the alcove, wearing the black military uniforms and black sunglasses.

"We've tested RK-81 on inanimate objects and small rodents," Santana said.

He stood at the railing of the highest scaffolding inside the reactor core. He wore black pants, and the white tuxedo shirt he'd had on earlier. But he'd removed the tie and jacket, and he wore a pair of the special sunglasses. He stood at the edge of the scaffolding as though inside a great auditorium speaking before a senate. Along each level inside the reactor core, there were thick glass windows—five in all—and Santana's men and his scientists stood on each floor watching the scene take place. Santana stood at the scaffold railing, his hands pumping in front of him as he spoke.

"And we've tested RK-81 on monkeys and primates," Santana said. "Now, we will test it on the next species up from the bottom—Nano Tech scum!"

His men all cheered for him and clapped their hands. On the ground floor inside the reactor core, Santana's men handed Johnston over to the scientists. From behind their special sunglasses, Levine and McKenzie could see the machine, the RK-81 unit.

RK-81 looked like a large glass phone booth with a dome-shaped roof and no phone inside. There was a single computer-operated door on one side, and there were computer consoles along the walls on the floor of the reactor core. A dozen scientists were at these computers setting up the parameters for RK-81's test run.

Johnston cried out, "Have mercy on me! I have a wife and two children!"

Santana waved a dismissive hand over the man's plea. He said, "You have two children who will never see their father again!"

McKenzie looked at Levine.

"I could shoot him," she said. "I could shoot him from here."

"And we'd never get off this island," Levine said. "He'd kill us all. And besides, RK-81 may actually work."

"We can't just stand here," McKenzie said. "We gotta do something!"

"There are over two hundred of Santana's men here," Levine said. She looked around the glass windows inside the reactor core. On each floor there were fifty men, each wearing those dark sunglasses. They stood at the windows excitedly watching the events inside the reactor core. She looked around her further, and her eyes came to the green medical uniforms at the lockers. She said, "I've got an idea."

"What?" McKenzie said.

"Just keep me covered," she said.

Levine stepped back into the alcove locker room. She unbuttoned the military suit and stepped out of it. She picked it up and stuffed it in a locker. She grabbed the green medical uniform and slipped the pants on, then pulled the shirt on over her head. She tucked the green cap on her head, and tied the surgical mask over her face. She put on the sunglasses and a pair of paper booties. McKenzie turned and saw her.

"What're you gonna do, Levine?" McKenzie said.

Levine grabbed a clipboard and put a stethoscope around her neck. She smiled, but McKenzie could only see her eyes.

"Follow my lead," Levine said. "When I give you the signal."

"What's the signal?"

"Reactor Core," Levine said.

"Reactor Core?" McKenzie said.

"When I say Reactor Core," Levine said. "You let 'em have it!"

"Cool," McKenzie said. "I got you covered, Doctor."

Levine winked and walked toward the glass door into the reactor core. McKenzie stepped forward to the glass window and watched her friend. No one really noticed Dr. Levine enter the reactor. She stepped out onto the steel girder scaffolding and looked down inside the core. On the ground floor, one of the scientists was opening the door to RK-81. The door opened with a pneumatic hiss and steam poured out onto the floor.

"Put him into the machine!" Santana said.

Three of Santana's soldiers came forward with machineguns, and they pushed Johnston into the glass vault. The lights from the floor and from inside RK-81 were so intense it watered Levine's eyes. She walked down the metal stairwell coolly checking things off on her clipboard. No one paid her any attention. She reached the ground floor.

A couple scientists looked up at her, but she just nodded confidently to them and continued on as though she were checking items off on her clipboard. Johnston was twenty meters in front of her.

There were five soldiers with machineguns standing around the glass RK-81 unit. Steam rose up from vents in the floor around the unit. Levine glanced up high overhead and saw Santana at the railing looking down on the proceedings at ground floor. She glanced across at the opposite side and saw McKenzie who nodded at her, and Levine continued forward through the rows of computer consoles. One of the scientists came at her and said, "Back, Doctor. We need to clear a ten meter zone around RK-81."

Levine grimaced in frustration but complied and stepped back against the reactor core wall. She held the clipboard in front of her and watched Santana's men put Noah Johnston in the unit. They freed him of his handcuffs, and then closed him in RK-81. He cried out and started pounding his fists against the glass walls inside RK-81.

Levine glanced up at McKenzie, and she saw her grip tighten on the machinegun. McKenzie opened the glass door and stepped out onto the fifth-floor scaffolding, fifty meters across from Santana. Wearing the black military uniform, black cap, and sunglasses, she looked just like one of Santana's men, and no one took notice of her.

"I want those prisoners on their knees!" Santana demanded.

Behind him, one of his soldiers forced the six shackled prisoners to their knees with his machinegun.

"You see, my friends, this is what we do to intruders on my island!" Santana gave the signal to the head scientist.

On the ground floor, the scientist said, "Begin the initiation sequence. Set vector grids at maximum power."

Scientists at the computer consoles typed in the commands. RK-81 hissed, and the light coming from it grew more intense. Levine watched Noah Johnston. He pounded on the glass walls inside the unit and screamed as loud as he could, but RK-81 was soundproof and his pounding on the glass and his screams carried no sound beyond the chamber. He looked like a bug trapped inside a mason jar.

The chief scientist said, "Hyperbolic acceleration on my mark. Initiate the countdown."

A digital clock on the wall inside the core began counting down from sixty seconds. Levine looked around at each of the scientists. Everyone looked tense, preparing to activate the RK-81 unit with Johnston inside it. Lights on the unit flashed, and had she not been wearing the special sunglasses, RK-81's light would have blinded her. At thirty seconds, a siren-like horn started roaring out every second, and steam filled the floor immediately around the RK-81 chamber.

Noah Johnston looked out at all of these scientists, all of the military men, up at Santana five stories above him. His hands were flat against the glass wall inside the chamber, palms pressed against the glass; Levine could see the tears in his eyes. He'd stopped screaming and just looked very alone, and very frightened. Levine watched his expression; there was a point where he realized no one was going to help him, none of these people cared about him, they were all going to watch him die.

Levine watched him realize this, and his face turned bright red with a rage like nothing Levine had ever seen. He went insane.

The digital clock hit twenty seconds, and a computerized voice began counting down very loudly for everyone in the reactor core to hear: "Eighteen, seventeen, sixteen. . ."

Inside the RK-81 unit, Noah Johnston was slamming his head against the glass, trying to break free. He pounded hard against the glass with his fists and then pulled back and tried to punch the glass with a straight jab as hard as he could. He almost certainly broke his hand in this effort, and then he lifted his leg and began kicking at the wall as hard as he could. The glass was several feet thick.

Levine saw one scientist taking notes on a clipboard much like her own.

"Thirteen, twelve, eleven," the computerized voice continued.

Johnston's forehead bloodied over, but the glass of the RK-81 chamber was so thick that it rendered everything he did inside the chamber soundless.

"Ten, nine, eight," the voice continued.

Johnston pulled back, drew in a breath, and yelled a screaming yell so loud it might have been heard in soundless space. His veins bulged out on his neck, and his face turned a deep shade of red. It was a kind of rage not exactly human in nature. Spit from his roaring, screaming, and yelling spattered the glass inside the RK-81 chamber, his mouth gaping open in a moment of pure animalistic anger.

"Five, four, three," the computerized voice continued.

At three seconds, there was a flash of light inside the chamber so bright that even with the sunglasses everyone winced and looked away. Inside the chamber, Johnston was engulfed in the light.

His fists rose above his head, two fists thrusting defiantly at Santana, his men, an entire system, a *life* that had come down to this, his standing powerless inside a little glass chamber while scientists monitored his breathing, his heart rate, his circulation at the moment of death—or immortality—his transmission into the Line. Levine's eyes went to a computer monitor with a computer image of Johnston inside the chamber.

"Two," the computerized voice said. "One. Ignition."

Levine saw the image of Noah Johnston on the computer screen vanish from inside the chamber, and she looked up at the actual chamber. The light was so bright she could only look at it in quick glances like looking at the sun in a midday sky. But she saw that Johnston was not there.

He was gone from inside the chamber.

Levine glanced up at McKenzie. She saw McKenzie shielding her eyes from the light with her hands, and yet trying to watch what was happening inside the chamber. Santana's hands were held up to the sky like Moses before the Red Sea. All of the prisoners were on their knees. A few were visibly praying. One of Santana's soldiers crossed himself.

And a scientist standing beside Levine said, "Sweet Mother of God. It *worked.*" Levine looked at him; the man stared at the now empty RK-81 unit. "It worked," he said. "The machine took him up. It took him—into *the Line!*"

Levine looked at RK-81. Its light was dimming in intensity, but Levine could clearly see that the inside of the chamber was empty. Even the blood on the glass was gone. All organic material inside the glass chamber had vanished. Blood, clothes, sweat, spit, and Johnston himself. It was all gone. It had all vanished. Noah Johnston no longer existed in their universe.

But Levine could feel him. She sensed him. She felt his presence at that moment, and she realized that he was watching them. Levine knew it the way she knew her own thoughts. She knew that he was watching them, watching them all, from deep inside the Line.

SIX
INTO THE DESERT

The fear that hit Roger McAllister came up from inside his stomach and spread outward to his limbs. It caused him to shake. The pouring rain streamed down his face, through his hair, over his clothes, soaking him through to his skin. McAllister was the kind of man who just tightened up when hit with deep and inescapable fear, and as such his face looked tight, his blue eyes wide, and Helen Richards realized that they may very well die.

"What the hell *is* that?" she said.

They both stared through the driving rain at Room 107 across the parking lot. The room was ablaze, but they could see through the shattered glass of the window that the creature inside was going crazy.

Part of the creature was pinned down by ceiling beams that had fallen on top of it, but the giant tentacles swung every which way imaginable trying to break free. One of the tentacles held what was left of Harvey, and the fire was bright orange, yellow, and red inside the room. Harvey's limp body swung through the room like a femur in an angry ape's hand, thrashing and slamming against the fiery walls and ceiling. The creature howled a wild horn-like scream, and the smell of smoke carried through the pouring rain and billowed up into the sky above the motel in thick, black plumes.

Zeb Brudock and the four other boys stood fifteen feet away watching the creature inside Room 107 thrashing all around. It was screaming and hollering.

"What're you gonna do?" McAllister called to Zeb through the rain.

"Well, that thing's gotta come out or burn up," Zeb said. He pumped his shotgun. "And if it comes out, I'm gonna blast it to hell!"

McAllister said, "No chance the law'll be out in this?"

Helen said, "The road's washed out past Oracle Junction and down past the Texaco in Catalina. Nobody's gonna be coming along. Not in weather like this. Not tonight."

She and Roger came a little closer to Zeb and the four boys with guns. Two of the guys were checking their shotguns, but everyone watched the room, waiting for the creature to mount a frenzied charge. There was a loud scream from inside Room 107, and then they saw Harvey's body flying out the window.

It hit the pavement ten feet from the front walkway, bounced like a stone skipping on a lake, and came to rest ten feet to the right of the group.

"Oh, my God," Helen said. She turned away, coughed and gagged.

Zeb pumped his shotgun with a quick firm hand.

"Come on, you son of a bitch," he said.

McAllister looked at Harvey's body lying on the macadam. It looked like every bone in his body had been shattered. His hair and clothes were torn, lacerated. It was not a pretty sight, and McAllister struggled to steel his stomach. He looked at the fiery room.

"One of you boys got another gun?" he said.

One of the guys slapped down a revolver's chamber and tossed the handgun to Roger. Roger felt the weight of the gun in his hand, eyed down the rainwater-beaded barrel, popped the chamber out, gave it one good spin, and slapped it back into place. Lightning flashed down from the sky a couple hundred yards away, and everybody winced under the powerful crash of thunder that followed. As the thunder rolled over them, over the motel and out across the desert plains to the west, the creature inside Room 107 screamed one terrible cry and burst out of the room.

"*Oh, my God!*" Helen said. She staggered backward a few steps.

The creature tore itself free, and the part that was still pinned inside the room swung around crazily. The half that had torn itself free plowed through the motel room doorway taking out part of the wall in the process. It stepped out onto the sidewalk in front of Room 107.

It was on fire, and the tentacles looked like four legs now carrying part of the girl's body above it. The thing's head twitched one way, then the other, scanning the little people staring at it from across the parking lot. It stepped out into the parking space right in front of the room and raised itself up to its full height—some twenty feet tall, and it roared out into the driving rain.

One of the guys turned and ran. Zeb fired three shots up at the thing. Roger held the handgun in front of him and unloaded two well-placed shots in the creature's torso, but the bullets were like bee stings to the creature. It raised its head up and screamed at them. Another of the boys turned and ran, and the giant creature lumbered out toward them.

Helen turned and ran in the direction of the office. Roger stumbled backwards falling to the ground. The creature came to him and looked down at him from directly overhead. Its head was ten feet over Roger, and Roger watched its silvery eyes blink with recognition of him. It smelled of burning flesh and smoke, and its mouth opened wide and began to descend on Roger.

He yelled, "Get the hell away from me!" And he fired the remaining bullets up into the creature's torso from point blank range. The creature drooled slimy clear fluid down on top of his face. It was as cold as ice water, and Roger's head swung from right to left spitting away the fluid.

The creature's head came down on him and grabbed his right shoulder in its mouth. Roger was vaguely aware of hearing a truck engine fire up from across the parking lot, but only vaguely because he was being lifted up off of the pavement. He realized he was dangling in the air ten feet above the parking lot, and the creature's slimy drool poured all over him. It was the most horrible, putrid smell he had ever smelled in his entire life, a smell like mass cattle deaths on a farm following a terrible flood, and it poured all over him.

Something hit the creature. Roger shook. The creature staggered forward and then flung Roger through the air. He landed in the desert sand beyond the parking lot, and slowly rose up to see Helen in the truck, ramming the creature from the side like a toddler tugging at a parent's leg. The headlights of the Chevy Silverado were bright, and the tires squealed on the pavement. The truck roared backward, brakes grabbed, tires squealed on the wet pavement, and then the truck was rushing at the creature again. It hit one of its legs from the right side, and the creature swung another free tentacle that hit the Chevy broadside. The Chevy rocked up on two wheels and then slammed down hard.

Helen threw the truck into reverse and raced backward through the parking lot. The creature chased after her, and Helen slammed on the brakes. The creature stumbled over the truck and fell into a swimming pool at the side of the motel. There was a huge splash, and the creature screamed out. Helen hit the accelerator and raced back across the parking lot in the direction of the motel office.

The creature quickly leapt out of the pool and chased the Chevy, which was now spinning around the far side of the motel seventy feet away from Roger. The Chevy disappeared around the back of the motel. Roger stood up and watched the creature chase the Chevy. He saw Zeb over by a green trash dumpster taking cover. Zeb held his shotgun.

The Chevy raced around the back side of the motel easily doing forty miles per hour through the parking lot, wheels spinning wildly as it rounded corners on the soaked pavement. The Chevy swung around the left side of the motel, and the headlights came right at Roger. The truck screeched to a stop, and the passenger-side door flew open.

"Get in!" Helen yelled.

Roger looked up and saw the creature on four giant tentacle legs. It came around the corner of the building. It saw the truck forty feet in front of it. Roger started running for the open Chevy's door, leapt into the cab, and Helen punched the accelerator. Tires squealed, and the door slammed shut. Roger braced himself and tried to sit up. He looked in the rear window and saw the giant creature chasing them from behind. He glanced at the speedometer and saw the needle fly up to forty, forty-five. The Chevy spun hard and swung around the side of the motel past the office.

Helen's hands were on the steering wheel. The wiper blades swashed back and forth. Rain pounded the window and hood of the truck. It was difficult to see very far in front, and water in the parking lot splashed out from both sides of the truck like a wake behind a ski boat.

"Come on," Helen said. She downshifted and spun around the back left corner of the motel, now heading back up in the direction of the swimming pool again. The Chevy's engine roared, and the wiper blades kicked back and forth, back and forth, throwing heavy rain water to either side. The dashboard lights lit up Helen's face, and Roger glanced through the rear window. They'd gained a little ground on the creature.

Roger saw the green dumpster up on the right, and he saw Zeb with his shotgun. Helen hit the brakes and turned the wheel sharply. The

Chevy swung to the left and then skidded over the soaking wet black-top pavement like a hockey player on ice. Helen rolled down the window.

"Get in the back, Zeb!" she called.

Zeb ran from the green dumpster, leapt up onto the bumper and into the back of the truck, and Helen hit the gas once again. The Chevy roared forward across the front parking lot, Zeb now in the bed of the Chevy. He balanced himself and held up his shotgun. The creature was closing in on them from behind. Zeb fired the shotgun up into the night. One shot hit the creature, but it kept coming.

Helen yelled, "Hold on!"

And the Chevy hit the curb at the front of the parking lot. The midnight-blue Silverado was up in the air a moment. Zeb felt himself literally flying up into the air in the back of truck. Then the truck slammed down, and it was racing across the desert plains northeast of the motel, the twenty-foot-tall creature chasing it from behind.

• •

Lightning streaked down from the sky, branching out in a hundred different directions. It hit the earth within a mile of the truck, lighting up everything. Roger counted *one-one thousand, two-one thous—Boom!* An enormous roar of thunder shook them. The rain pounded down on the truck, stinging Zeb Brudock's face. Helen was tearing along the open desert plains southeast of Florence. Cruising at fifty miles per hour, they'd lost the creature. Zeb hadn't seen it in ten minutes.

The truck slammed to a stop, skidding hard.

The headlights shone through the driving rain, through the darkness, past giant saguaro cacti and creosote bushes. Zeb thought he heard the rushing water of a river, and the wiper blades swashed back and forth on the front window with a sound like *wrr-rrnt, wrr-rrnt, wrr-rrnt*. But everything beyond the truck's headlights was pitch black, and the rain continued to pour fiercely, beating on the metal roof with an unremitting sound.

Zeb turned around and knelt on one knee in the back. He looked in the cab at Roger and Helen. Roger threw open the door on the passenger side and leapt down onto the ground. The sandy ground was like slush in the heavy rain, and the rain beat down on him. He looked at Zeb in the back of the truck.

He called through the pouring rain, "I think we've gained a little ground on that—that *thing*!"

Zeb said loudly, "Yeah, I haven't seen it since we got out north of Black Mountain!"

Helen opened up the cab window. She said, "You know where we are, Zeb?"

"It's hard to say," Zeb said. "It sounds like a river up yonder, and the only river out this way is the Gila."

"The Gila River?" McAllister said.

"Yep," Zeb said. "But I didn't think we'd gone that far north. You can't see for shit in this rain!"

A flash of lightning brightened up the sky, and in the flash Zeb saw trees up ahead of the truck about a hundred meters in the distance. There were large hills all around them, but then the lightning died, and all was darkness around them again. The sonorous thunder shook the sky and rolled on out across the desert plains.

"If those are trees," Zeb called through the rain, "then we must be up on the river. The Gila is probably swollen over its banks!"

"Well, get in the cab," Helen called to Zeb. "There's no need to drown you in the back."

Zeb handed his shotgun through the window between bed and cab, and he jumped down onto the rain-soaked ground. Roger had walked forward to the edge of the headlight's reach, not far from the trees. Zeb leaned in the passenger-side door and looked at Helen.

"What is he doing?" Helen said.

The wiper blades swept back and forth. Rain drummed on the hood and roof. Zeb leaned back and called through the pouring rain through the Chevy's headlights, "What are you doing?"

Roger couldn't hear him. Zeb said to Helen, "Stay here. I'm gonna go see what he's doing."

Helen nodded her head, fear and worry clearly visible in her gray-green eyes.

"Don't worry," he said. "I'll be right back."

Zeb turned and trotted forward into the headlight's white glow in front of the Chevy. The sandy desert earth was soupy it was so saturated with rain, and his feet sank down several inches. Helen could see the divots each step made, and then he vanished into darkness beyond the headlight's reach.

Helen glanced down at the green "4x4" light indicating the four-wheel drive was activated. And she glanced at the leather satchel on the passenger-side floor—the leather satchel with Dr. Amy Levine's papers.

She put the truck in gear and slowly crept forward in the direction of the trees, in the direction where Roger and Zeb had disappeared.

"What the hell did they leave me alone for," she muttered under her breath. "Damn fools."

One hand gripped the steering wheel, the other the gear shift. The truck crawled forward through the muddy soil toward the trees, which were bright green in the headlight's glow and were wet with the pouring rain. Lightning flashed across the sky, brightening up the night, and Helen saw Zeb and Roger standing over something on the ground. Helen steered the truck toward them and crawled forward. There was something on the ground, some kind of body, but it was a horrible mess. Helen watched Zeb lean to the right. He looked like he was going to be sick. And then Helen caught the smell.

"Oh, my God," she said. The smell was horrible. The truck's headlights shone forward into the trees, and she saw more bodies on the ground like the one at Roger's feet. The bodies were about the size of cows, but they were horribly dismembered, disfigured. The Chevy crept up to Roger and Zeb. The two men came back to the truck's passenger side. Roger opened the door.

"What is it?" Helen said.

Roger popped the seat forward. Zeb climbed in behind the front seats in the cab. Roger got up on the passenger side and slammed the door shut.

"God only knows," Roger said. "It looks like cows—but they're turned inside out."

"It's like the ones I saw before," Zeb said.

Helen put her foot on the accelerator and slowly eased the truck forward up into the trees. They could hear the roar of the river, and the wet leaves of tree branches reached down and slapped the front windows of the truck.

"We're gonna get stuck if you ain't careful," Zeb said.

"This truck don't get stuck," Helen said. "Not with a winch on the front."

Everyone leaned forward and looked through the front window. The trees had grown in tight, and the little path that the truck crawled along was only about five feet wide. The branches scraped along the truck's sides and slapped thick and wet against the windows. The headlights could only reach about twenty feet in front.

There was a flash of lightning, and everything was lit up a second.

"*Holy Mother*," Zeb said.

He was looking out the left, and he'd caught a glimpse of the Gila River through the thick trees.

"What is it?" Helen said.

"In that last flash of lightning," he said. "I saw the river over on the left. I've never seen the Gila that flooded. It's two hundred yards from side to side. You gonna want to keep the truck back up here on the right."

"I can't exactly drive through the trees!" Helen said. "The path is right here in front of us."

Zeb said nothing, but all three looked forward and realized Helen was right. They had to stay on the trail. The trees were too thick on either side. The Chevy crawled along.

They came up on a washout. It looked like a small river was rushing over the path in front of them.

"What do you think?" Helen said.

"I wouldn't drive through it," Zeb said. "No way to tell how deep it is. You can see how fast the water's moving, though."

"Well, we can't exactly back up on this path," she said. "I can't see a damn thing through your head."

Zeb leaned to his left out of her line of sight in the rearview mirror.

"You gonna try to back it up?" Roger said.

"Well, we can't exactly go forward through *that*," she said.

Everyone adjusted and turned around to look through the rear window. Helen held one hand on the wheel, her body fully turned to see as the truck crawled backward in reverse. Tree branches slapped at them, scraping the metal along their sides. The four-wheel drive gripped the muddy ground well, but they had only the visibility that the reverse lights gave them as they crawled backwards.

Something hit the front right fender of the truck.

"What was that?" Helen said.

Everyone turned around and looked forward through the front window. The truck stopped, Helen's foot on the brake. And standing twenty feet in front of the truck was the girl.

She stood in middle of the path, brightened by the truck's headlights. Her hair was soaked, and she wore that white tunic. Her face looked calm, and she looked at them inside the truck.

"Oh, my God. Oh, my God. Oh, my God," Zeb repeated over and over again. "This is not happenin' to me!"

Roger just said slowly, "Ohh, shit."

The girl just stood in the middle of the path, the rain pouring down on her. Her face looked at them calmly—eerily calmly. She was barefoot, standing in the mud. And the wet trees were bright green all around her.

"Just back up nice and slow," Roger said. "If she comes forward, throw that friggin' gear into Drive and run her down."

Helen said nothing. She stared at the girl. Helen was frozen with fear.

"Helen!" Roger said. "Be cool, Helen. Just back us up."

The washout roared through the road twenty feet on the other side of the girl. She stood on the path between the truck and the veritable river flowing through the path behind her. She seemed to look at each of them in the truck, into each pair of eyes, looking deep into their souls.

"Man, get us out'a here," Zeb said. "This ain't something to screw around with!"

Roger looked at Helen. Her hands gripped the wheel. Her lips had gone white and dry, and they were shaking. Her eyes were fixed on the girl standing in the headlight's beam. She was in shock, so afraid that her body had seized up with adrenaline.

Roger said, "Helen!"

But Helen didn't budge. She was in shock—and she was at the steering wheel.

"What the hell's goin' on?" Zeb said.

"Helen!" Roger said. "For God's sake! Helen!!"

Roger grabbed her right shoulder. It felt like a rock it was so rigid with fear. He leaned forward and tried to slap her face. Helen's head moved a little, but her eyes stared forward like a catatonic.

"Oh, shit," Zeb said.

The girl was slowly coming toward the front of the truck.

"Can you pull her out of the way?" Zeb said. "Get the truck in gear! Get the truck in gear, man!"

The girl in the headlight's glow was coming toward them. The rain poured down on her, rain visible in the bright headlights, mud spattering up in the heavy rain, the green tree leaves bright in the headlight's glow. The girl looked through the front window, in at them, inside the truck.

"Get her out of that driver's seat!" Zeb said.

Both men were pulling at Helen. Zeb was up behind her in the back of the cab, and Roger was leaning out in front of her over the gearshift. Helen was frozen like a rock. Her breathing was truncated, but the two men pulled at her, trying to get her over to the passenger seat.

"Her leg's caught!" Roger shouted.

He reached down under the steering wheel. They had the upper half of her body out of the driver's seat, but her left leg had caught on the little metal bar that adjusted the forward-backward movement of the seat. Roger's face was all in her lap, but he couldn't get down low enough to see what her leg was snagged on. Her body was in the way.

"The sweat pants are caught on something!" Roger said.

"Pull her out'a the friggin' sweat pants!" Zeb said.

Out front, the girl in the white tunic touched her hand to the hood. All the lights in the Chevy flickered off like a power-surge had gone through the truck. The headlights dimmed. Rain thrummed on the roof and hood. Lightning flashed across the sky.

And in the flash of lightning, Zeb Brudock saw something in the trees ten feet to the left of the truck.

He saw another girl about sixteen years old, identical to the one in front of the Chevy. She wore a white tunic, and her hair was soaked in the pouring rain, and she was standing in the trees to the left.

Roger untied the waist band on Helen's sweat pants, and the two men started pulling her out of the pants.

"That's got it!" Roger said. "Just pull her—yeah, right there!"

They got Helen out of the driver's seat, over into the passenger's seat, and Roger fell in behind the steering wheel. Then, the truck stalled.

"What the hell?!" Zeb said.

Roger turned the ignition, but the engine just went *wrrnn-wrrrrnn*, trying to turn over, and died. He turned the ignition again, and the starter just cranked and cranked and cranked. But it wouldn't turn over.

"Oh, screw me," Zeb said.

Both men looked up and saw—to their horror—two dozen more girls, identical to the first, all about sixteen years old. They all wore white tunics, and were exact replicas of the first. They emerged from the trees at either side of the path. Zeb heard something at the back of the truck. He jerked his head around, and he saw two dozen more girls behind the truck in the dim red light of the taillight's glow. They were standing in the path. A few had their hands on the tailgate. Others emerged from the woods at either side of the path. They were all approaching.

"Lock the doors!" Zeb said.

Roger hit the power-lock. The door locks clicked down. The rain continued to pour. And outside, over forty girls in white tunics surrounded the Chevy Silverado, their hands fluttering over its metallic surface.

Zeb looked in the back. Three girls climbed over the tailgate and were slowly coming at them from the back. Along the sides, girls in white tunics pushed back the tree limbs and slapped at the sides. At the window on the right, four girls' faces looked in the window. Their hands were flat up against the glass, palms pressing against the window. Zeb saw life in their eyes, but each set of eyes were identical to the one next to it, and all the girls started making low moaning sounds. *Oooorah*, one said. Another caught the rhythm and followed suit. *Oooray*, she moaned.

Zeb looked out the front window. There were a half dozen girls. Their bodies pressed up against the headlights causing their shadows to flicker. Another six girls were pushing against the six from behind, trying to get in closer. And all of the girls were identical clones, some forty genetic matches all pushing at the sides of the truck, all carrying the slow, low moaning chorus: *Oooray, ooorah, oooray.*

"What the hell are they sayin'?" Zeb said.

"Sounds like Oo-ray," Roger said.

"What the hell is an Ooo-ray?"

The girls pushed at the sides, and the Chevy rocked from right to left. The rain continued to pour. The headlights were completely covered by the dozen white-tunic-clad girls trying to get to the front of the truck. One girl was climbing up onto the hood, but the Chevy's hood was high and wet and she slipped and fell to the ground. Another tried to climb up, made it a little farther by hugging the hood tighter, but a girl behind her pulled her back over the wet hood, and she fell to the mud at the others' feet. Amazingly, the white tunics seemed to repel the dirt and mud and remained otherworldly white despite the rain and mud. They pressed up against the glass. And Roger kept working the ignition.

"They're gonna break in any second, now," Zeb said. "I've only got three rounds left in the shotgun. We'll never be able to get clear with three shots!"

The truck rose up on its left two wheels. Everybody inside fell to the left. Then, it slammed back down, jarring them.

"Holy shit!" Zeb said.

"They almost turned us over!" Roger said.

Helen was lying all over Roger, now, and he pushed her as best he could back into the passenger seat. She was drooling. The glass of the passenger-side window began to splinter. There was a high-pitched squealing in the glass like a high-pressure seam was giving way. Flat palms pressed against the glass. Faces pressed against the glass. And all the girls kept on with their slow chant: *Oooray, oooray, oooray,* while pushing the truck from side to side.

The truck rose up on its right two wheels. There was a loud wrenching metal sound from somewhere in the undercarriage like it was not engineered to carry its weight up on its sides that way. Roger held on inside the cab. He glanced to the right and saw the earth coming up at them. Girls fell to the ground. They were going to be crushed underneath if it fell on top of them. Roger hit the horn *Brronnn*! And he jerked the wheel back and forth. The truck fell back to the left, slamming down hard. Roger's head slammed against the glass window, and everything went hazy for a moment.

Zeb shouted something at him. Something about water!

Roger shook his head and looked up in front of him. The girls were all staggering to the left. Something was pushing them into the woods on the left side of the path. Several girls fell down, as though the ground was being swept out from under them. And then Roger realized that the washout that had been twenty feet in front of them just a minute before had spread right to the front of the truck. In a quick flash of the headlight's glow, he saw that the washout was now sixty feet wide rushing right-to-left across the path, right in front of the truck.

The glass on the passenger window shattered. Roger looked at it with horror. The glass had some kind of sealant coating it, and it held it together like clear skin. But the girls' hands pushed through the glass. And arms began to reach inside the window. Roger could hear the rushing water hitting the front tires on the truck. He could feel its turbulence pushing the front end. All the girls out front were pushed into the woods on the left side of the path. In the headlights' glow he could see the white caps of rushing water. And he felt the girls' fingertips and hands reaching at him, grabbing him from through the right-side window. He glanced back and saw a shotgun come forward from the back of the cab. The hands grabbed at the shotgun barrel dumbly, and Roger watched as Zeb directed the barrel right out the now broken-open window.

Blam!

Three pairs of arms fell away from the window. And the headlights brightened as though there was less drain on the battery.

"Their hands," Zeb said. "They're draining the truck when they touch it with their hands!"

Roger glanced to the left and saw that several girls were holding fast to trees on the left side of the path. The rushing water was now midway back along the truck's length, and they could feel the front end beginning to stir, moving slightly to the left.

"Try the ignition again!" Zeb said.

Roger turned the key, and the truck's starter whirred around and around. It sputtered, caught, and the engine came to life.

"Hell yeah!" Roger said.

Zeb watched him throw the gear into first. The Chevy lurched forward into the raging water. He heard the girls in the bed of the truck, and he jerked his head around. There were a half dozen girls. They were all clambering to hold on. Zeb opened up the window between the cab and bed. He eased the barrel of the shotgun through the window, took aim, and pulled the trigger.

Blam!

Three girls flew out the back, and the engine was hit with a surge of power. The truck lurched forward, and two more girls spilled over the sides.

He looked forward. Three girls were bracing themselves against the rushing current. The lower part of their white tunics was sweeping in the thigh-high water, but they kept coming at them.

"Punch it!" Zeb said. "It's the only way we'll make it through the wash!"

Roger licked his lips, gripped the wheel, and punched the accelerator. The powerful engine roared forward. Water sprayed up at either side. And they plowed through the three remaining girls.

They were free of the girls, but now they were out in the water. Zeb glanced back and saw a dozen girls behind the truck staggering through the water trying to come after them from behind. A few were swept down by the strong current, but they just kept coming.

The water was up to the door now and was pushing the Chevy into the trees on the left side of the path, but the giant all-terrain tires just kept plowing ahead, the deep powerful engine churning up mud, spattering it all over the sides, up into the air, inside the open passenger-side window. Rain and mud poured down on them.

They were midway out into the washout, and had it not been for the trees on the left, they would have just been swept away with the current. The trees scraping along on the left side of the truck actually kept them from being carried away. Raging water splashed up into the air against the right side. The water was almost up to the side windows and was spilling in the passenger side.

"We're gonna get drowned!" Zeb cried.

"No, we're not," Roger said.

Water was now rushing into the passenger-side window. The water was as high as the hood, and it rushed over the hood in sheets. Water hit the right side of the truck splashing up into the air. They were taking on water. The truck literally felt like it was beginning to float, but Roger kept the accelerator pressed and the wheels churned away, and they lurched forward one foot at a time.

Zeb glanced back once more and saw the girls that had made it out midway into the wash were being swept down with the current and carried into the trees on the left side of the path. The water was just too deep and the current too strong for them to follow. He turned back around and saw that the hood of the Chevy was climbing up out of the water. They'd crossed the midway point and were now climbing up on the other side of the wash. The powerful engine just roared onward. Mud flew up at either side, spraying the sides of the truck, the trees, and the white-tunic-clad girls forty feet behind them.

"Hallelujah!" Zeb said, pumping his fist excitedly.

They climbed up onto drier land. The truck rolled forward, its powerful engine rumbling. In the back of the truck, the bed was filled with water, and it swished back and forth and weighed the back end down.

"We need to dump that water," Roger said. "It's sinkin' us down into the mud."

The truck roared along, mud flying up at either side.

"Well, hold on," Zeb said. "I'll jump back and let it out!"

The truck stopped. Zeb climbed through the window between cab and bed and then waded through the knee-high water in the bed. He leapt over the tailgate, grabbed the tailgate latch, and popped the tailgate open. Water poured out over him and knocked him down onto the ground.

Roger called out, "You alright?"

He could see the girls in the white tunics trying to cross the wash behind them. One or two looked like they might make it across. Zeb leapt up, covered in mud, said "shit," and climbed up into the now empty cab. He pulled the tailgate shut behind him and said, "Hit it, Roger!"

Roger punched the accelerator. Mud flew up all over the truck, and the Chevy grabbed earth and roared forward up the widening path, up onto higher ground.

Zeb in the back of the truck hollered, "Yeeee-hah!"

And they continued on up the hill, up to higher ground.

••

Dawn came moist, hot, and humid one hour later, and Roger opened his eyes to a brightening gunmetal sky. He was lying in the back of the truck, but he had refused to fall asleep and had kept watch for everyone. He heard the rushing water of the river. Helen opened her eyes and looked at him.

She smiled and said, "I'm alive."

They were covered in mud, and Roger felt gritty and warm. The river was a torrential force forty feet down a steep bank, huge swirling eddies in the muddy-brown middle.

"Thank God," Roger said. "I thought we'd lost you for sure."

Helen looked up the hill on the other side of the truck bed. There was a small white farmhouse—a kind of ranch-style shack with a long wide porch along the front. There were wind chimes hanging from the porch ceiling, twenty or thirty in all, and they chimed merrily in the early morning breeze. There was an auto garage over on the left side of the house and about an acre's worth of tilled garden to the right of the garage.

"My head hurts," Helen said. "Where are we?"

"Zeb's farm," Roger said.

Up on the porch, the screen door creaked open, and Zeb stepped out with a stone-blue coffee pitcher and three white coffee mugs.

"You're awake," he called to Roger and Helen.

They saw a pretty woman with blonde hair come to the screen door. She wore an apron, and she looked out at the strangers sleeping in the back of the truck. She managed a smile. She opened the screen door and stepped out onto the porch. The screen door creaked shut with a loud slap.

"Mary Lou, won't you bring out some of those biscuits," Zeb said.

Roger looked at Mary Lou. He smiled, and she gave him a little wave.

"You two alright?" she said.

Roger said, "I think so."

Zeb handed the two cups of coffee to Roger.

Helen rubbed her eyes. She squinted in the morning light at Zeb looking at her, and she smiled with dimples rising up on her cheeks.

"Mornin', Zeb," Helen said. Helen looked around at the farm confusedly, but she seemed to slowly realize where she was. The shock had tightened her jaw, and she tried to stretch it out by opening and closing her mouth. She massaged her jaw with her hand, and she nodded at Mary Lou who nodded back matronly and then shooed three children away from the screen door and went back inside for the biscuits. The bright-eyed dirty faces of three children standing at the screen door peered out at the strangers in the front yard.

Roger handed the coffee cup to Helen. Zeb leaned in on the truck, his elbows and hands up on the side. He glanced back over his shoulder and then said in a whisper, "News channel is sayin' it was some kind of gas."

"Gas," Roger said. "What are you talkin' about?"

Zeb looked from Helen to Roger's eyes. "That killed them cattle," Zeb said. "News is reportin' it as some kind of space agency thing. Said there was *gas* up in the atmosphere. Came right down to earth like a crop duster, I reckon. That's what the news is sayin' killed all them cows."

"Crop duster, my ass," Helen said.

"I know," Zeb said. He licked his lips and wiped his mouth with his hand. He glanced over his shoulder at the screen door. The three children looked out at them with bright eyes, and one stepped out onto the porch. His two younger siblings—one boy, one girl—stepped out after him. The screen door slapped shut.

"Pa," the boy said. "Ain't you gonna introduce us to your friends?"

Zeb turned back and looked at Helen and Roger with an impressed look on his face. Helen smiled and waved at the boy.

The boy said, "Mornin, ma'am."

"Good morning," Helen said.

"Son," Zeb said. "Would you hand me those papers on that aluminum chair?"

The boy turned and looked at a faded green aluminum chair on the front porch. It had a large wide back, and there were navy-blue flower prints on it. Both Helen and Roger saw the leather satchel—Dr. Amy Levine's leather satchel—sitting in the chair in a bright ray of sunlight that shone through the olive tree branches ten feet in front of Zeb's front porch.

"These, Pa?" the boy asked.

"Those right there," Zeb said, and he nodded at a stack of papers on top of the chair.

Zeb turned and looked at Helen and Roger. Roger's brow furrowed over a little perplexed, and Zeb realized what the look meant.

"You wouldn't think it to look at me," Zeb said with a wise little smile on his lips and a bright shine in his eyes. "But I've had to try my hand at the Calculus more than once with my auto garage."

Zeb nodded in the direction of the garage over by the garden. Both Helen and Roger glanced at the garage and then their eyes came back to Zeb's. Roger's look blended into something like an amused and interested smile.

"Three years back," Zeb said, "I had to practically recreate a mode of differential combinatorics to measure acceleration rates on a Plymouth Fury's busted wheel bearing. Made for one interesting brew of applied mathematics and acceleratory physics. I even typed it up and sent it into the *Journal of Applied Mathematics*. But they weren't much interested in what some hick livin' on state-owned land had to say about the recent changes in the field of combinatorics. That don't much surprise me."

"You mean to tell me you do all this out here," Roger said. "Out here? Out here on this farm?"

"Any monkey can learn mathematics," Zeb said. "It takes a special heart to use it—to use the knowledge in the right way. I use it to fix up cars. Old cars make folks happy."

There was a silence—a special kind of silence—where Roger smiled at this man, this man that he had written off as stupid and ignorant, some redneck, some boy that most people in the world would look at and ignore. And he saw something special. Maybe it was just common decency. Maybe it was just humanity. But he looked at him—Roger did—he looked at Zeb and realized that though this world teaches us, trains us, feeds it into our brains that appearances hold the cover of what is within, well, sometimes, Roger thought, it pays to listen to folks 'cause what you think you see and what's actually there are two worlds apart.

"Well, anyway," Zeb said. "All that work on wheel bearings gave me a right good understanding of theoretical and applied mathematics. I ain't claimin' to be no genius now, but I do know derivative integration from set theory. And I can find my way through combinatorics with a fair amount of understandin'."

"Combinatorics?" Helen said.

Zeb said, "It's an area of mathematics concerned with selection, arrangement, and operation within a fixed-equilibrium system."

"What're you telling us, man?" Roger asked.

"Well," Zeb said. "One thing I don't know a whole heck of lot of is theoretical astrophysics. I look up at the stars, and I see stars. Somebody like this here, Dr. Amy Levine, she looks up there and she don't see *just* stars. She sees a reason and a way. She sees the beginning of it all—and maybe—just maybe the direction that it's all going. The things I've read of hers, though, they don't make sense—not ordinary human sense. This woman, this Dr. Amy Levine, she's figured out a way to predict the future. She's figured out a way to put cause and causality together. And in a fixed system—at least theoretically—the mathematics that she's using go a long way toward predicting from the past what'll happen in the future."

"You got all that," Roger said, "from lookin' in those papers?"

Zeb flipped to one series of equations.

"These here," Zeb said. He pointed with his left index finger at numbers on a page. "This series here," Zeb said. "She calls it 'The Colorado Sequence'."

"The Colorado Sequence?" Roger said.

"The Colorado Sequence of—the Line," Zeb said. "Now, I don't know what she's talking about once you get inside of it."

"Inside of it?" Helen said.

Zeb looked at her. His eyes held more gravity than she could understand. He said, "Inside of the Line. But it looks like she's found it."

"Found what?" Roger said.

"Dr. Levine has found a portal," Zeb said.

"A portal," Helen said.

"A portal," Zeb said. "A doorway, an entrance to another world. Dr. Amy Levine's found a doorway into another side of reality. She's found a doorway into the Line."

Everybody looked from one to the other. It was some time before Roger said, "Where? Where is this doorway?"

Zeb looked at him. His eyes both smiled and looked afraid.

"Ouray," he said. "Just like those girls were moanin', Roger. Ouray, Ouray, Ouray. The doorway into the Line is somewhere in the town of Ouray. Ouray, Colorado."

Dr. Amy Levine stood twenty feet from RK-81 in her green medical uniform with the surgical mask covering her face. Her brown eyes gaped at the empty RK-81 unit. Noah Johnston was gone.

"It worked!" Santana cried. "It worked! By God, it worked!"

He stood on the fifth floor scaffolding with his hands raised skyward.

One of the scientists at a computer terminal a few feet from Levine said, "We've got an input monitor on the Line specimen."

Another scientist with a little white beard said, "That is affirmative. All tests are positive. Our man is inside the Line."

It smells like leather, Noah Johnston's voice said.

Levine recognized the voice as coming from inside her head, but she couldn't tell whether the voice she heard was her own thoughts or was coming from beyond her. It was a very sharp, clear voice, more clear than her normal thought. She could almost see the words forming inside her mind.

You can hear me, Levine, Johnston's voice said.

Levine looked around her at the other scientists. Everyone seemed to be reacting to something that they, too, could hear inside their minds, but she couldn't completely read other people's thoughts.

The man with the white beard, Johnston's voice said to Levine.

Levine glanced up at the man with the little white beard.

Yes, the voice said. *Him. I will move his right arm up into the air.*

Levine watched the man, and sure enough, his arm shot up into the air like he'd gotten a painful twitch in his right shoulder.

Can you hear me? Levine thought, sending her thought forward with a special kind of focus.

Yes, came a very clear answer.

Are you my own thoughts? Levine thought.

Yes, Johnston's voice said. *And no. If you channel this energy, the impulse for thought, the creation of each pulse of energy your mind reads as these words is both a product of your mind and a vessel for an energy that is all around me, here inside the Line.*

Levine seemed to understand. She nodded her head and glanced up at McKenzie, who stood in the black military uniform with the AK-47 brandished in front of her. And Levine remembered her signal; she was to say "Reactor Core."

Do not do it yet, Johnston's voice said.

Are you speaking to other people, too?

Yes, the voice said. *But the voice they hear is their own; it is unique to their own thought. The energy, the emotion they feel comes from the same source; you are all interconnected. But the words that form in their minds—the voice—is unique to each person.*

The universe, Johnston's voice continued, *is so small. It is only a fraction of space here within the Line. It's like you're in a pool; you're connected by the Line, and yet I see that you can not see it. But it's with you as you choose; the closer you draw to the Line, the clearer this voice becomes. It is what you call truth.*

"We have a signal," one of the scientists said. "It's coming through on audio."

"Open up the audio bands," White Beard said.

"What is it?" Santana called. He started coming down from the fifth floor. "What do you have?"

"Prince Santana," White Beard said. "We're receiving some kind of audio signal . . . it's not of this world."

"What do you mean?" Santana said. He stepped down onto the Reactor Core floor.

The scientist looked from the computer monitor to Santana. Other scientists gathered around the computer, around Santana and White Beard. Levine realized she was standing just a few feet from Santana. Her brown and blue eyes moved around watching his every movement, but she stood in the middle of the crowd of scientists, and she wore the surgical mask over her face.

"What I mean is," White Beard said, "its structure, the harmonics, it appears digital in nature, but its source is at an atomic level"—he just shook his head—"these are not elements that have ever been found in this universe."

Santana looked into White Beard's worried-looking eyes. He glanced at the computer screen. He looked up at the empty RK-81 chamber.

He said, "Well, let's hear what it has to say."

White Beard glanced from Santana to a scientist at the computer terminal next to him.

"Adjusting for harmonics," he said. "We should have it on audio in five, four, three, two, and one—"

Crrkkzz, the audio speakers crackled to life.

Everyone leaned in close to hear. There was something coming over the speakers, something beyond the static, a pair of voices. They could all hear them.

The voice said, "The stairs need vacuuming."

Everyone looked around at each other, puzzled expressions on their faces. A murmur went up among Santana's scientists.

Another voice responded over the speaker, "We did the stairs Tuesday."

The first voice cleared its throat. "Yeah, well, I swept them out on Wednesday, but they *need* cleanin'. Let's finish up in room fourteen. And I'll do the stairs, if you start in on fifteen."

"Fair enough," came the reply.

Then the static blended with the sound of a vacuum cleaner starting up.

Everyone stood there listening to what they had thought would be the first transmission from the Line. They had sent Johnston into RK-81 with the idea in mind that he might try to contact them from within the Line. That he would either die (which was no loss to Santana) or would come back to them talking of pearly gates and streets lined with gold. Perhaps they might even hear the voice of God!

But this? These two voices? These two voices speaking over the audio speakers?

Why, it sounded like two janitors. Two lowly janitors going about their business with a vacuum cleaner, arguing about whose turn it was to vacuum some stairwell.

"Have you got a point of origin?" Santana said.

The scientist at the computer typed in the commands. Everyone watched the display on the computer monitor. The words "Transmission Error; Unknown Origin" appeared on the screen.

"What does that mean?" Santana said.

"It means," White Beard said. "That wherever this transmission originated from . . . it's not in this universe."

Santana said, "You're telling me that out of all these years, all of this money, all the lives that have been spent, the result of our first communication from the Line, from something within the fabric of time and space around us—is a couple of janitors arguing over whose turn it is to vacuum a stairwell!"

One scientist bold enough to clear his throat spoke up. He said, "Maybe they're angels. Maybe they're cleaning up a stairwell over there—on the other side."

Santana was genuinely amused. He looked around at his group of scientists and uniformed soldiers with a shine in his eyes and a smile on his lips. He said, "That sounded like two guys at a Holiday Inn is what it sounded like!"

"Well, we do have a fix on our man," White Beard said.

"We do?" Santana said.

"Yes," White Beard said. "Our Delta Scanner has a lock on him."

"Where is he?" Santana asked.

"Well," White Beard said. "If these coordinates are correct, the man we transmitted into the Line is standing—about ten feet behind you."

All eyes went to the spot where White Beard was pointing. It was a space about ten feet to the left of the RK-81 unit. Levine was certain she'd seen something move there, but it might have just been a trick of light, or a brush of wind.

"He's moving over to that desk there," White Beard said.

There was a desk along one side of the Reactor Core. Everyone stared at it.

"I don't see anything," Santana said.

"He just leaned against that desk there," White Beard said.

Everyone stared at the empty desk. There was nothing there. It was just an empty desk. And then they all saw the chair move.

There was nothing touching the chair, and there was no one within ten feet of it, but the chair moved out from under the desk. It squeaked on the floor.

"Oh, my God," Santana said. "What's making it do that?"

"If these coordinates are correct," White Beard said. "Then that is exactly where the Nano Tech agent is—inside the Line."

The chair suddenly jerked back as though a ghost had stood up from it. And, as if pushed, it rolled swiftly across the room clanking to stop against the RK-81 unit.

Everyone stared at it. Papers atop one desk started fluttering up into the air above one desk. Everyone's eyes went to the papers; they swept back and forth like one hundred feathers floating to the floor. Then, the words on the computer screen appeared.

I AM INSIDE THE COMPUTER.

Everyone looked at the screen. They looked at White Beard. They clearly saw that he was not typing the letters on the keyboard.

MY NAME IS NOAH JOHNSTON. DO YOU HAVE ANY QUESTIONS?

"Questions?" Santana said. He looked at his men.

YES, came the reply on the screen. DO YOU HAVE ANY QUESTIONS FOR ME, OSORO SANTANA? OR SHOULD I READ YOUR MIND?

"Where are you?" Santana said. "Who are you? How do you feel?"

OHHH, I CAN SEE YOUR EMOTIONS, OSORO SANTANA. THEY ARE AN INTERESTING COLOR.

"Color?" Santana said.

YES, COLOR. YOUR COLOR IS A SHADE OF RED, BUT IT IS ALSO BROWN. AND IT CHANGES WHEN YOU SPEAK AND WHEN YOU THINK. EACH PERSON IN THIS ROOM HAS HIS OWN COLOR.

The cursor sat there in the upper left hand corner of the screen. It just blinked that same methodical blink. Everyone was silent.

Santana said, "Are you the agent that we just transmitted into the Line?"

YES, MY NAME IS NOAH JOHNSTON.

"What is it like inside the Line?" Santana said. "What do you see?"

IT IS LIKE FLOATING. EVERYTHING IS BRILLIANT WHITE AROUND ME. AND THERE ARE LITTLE STRINGS, OPENING AND CLOSING, BRILLIANT GOLDEN STRINGS OF LIGHT. I CAN OPEN THE STRINGS WITH MY FINGERS, AND WHEN I LOOK THROUGH THEM I SEE FLASHES INSIDE YOUR WORLD.

"How many of these—*strings* do you see?" Santana said.

THEY ARE INFINITE. LIKE THE STARS. WITHIN REACH, THERE ARE PROBABLY TEN THOUSAND. BUT THERE ARE MANY MORE BEYOND MY REACH.

"Are you angry with us?" Santana asked.

I CAN NOT FEEL ANGER HERE. I AM NOT CAPABLE OF BEING ANGRY WITH YOU. NOT HERE.

Santana looked around at his men and smiled.

"Can you move around?" Santana asked.

LIKE THIS?

The words on the screen vanished. The man at the keyboard, White Beard, suddenly jerked up spastically. He stood and craned his neck around. His eyes came to Santana.

And a deep voice came from White Beard, "I am inside this—Dr. Sorrento. Human emotions are unwieldy."

"Unwieldy?" Santana asked.

White Beard—Dr. Sorrento—lumbered out away from the desk as though he were a life-sized puppet whose legs were being operated by someone new to puppeteering. The voice that came from Sorrento was a deep guttural voice, but Levine noticed a benevolence—a sense of humor and delight—in the voice.

"Yes," Sorrento said. "Unwieldy. Like a heavy suit of armor."

Sorrento staggered forward toward the center of the Reactor Core. Everyone fanned out around him, watching him. He lifted his right hand up and waved it as though he he was waving for the very first time and was fascinated by the ability. He looked at his hand.

"Fascinating," Sorrento said in that deep voice. "This body is very crude."

"How do you mean?" Santana said.

Sorrento turned and craned his neck from one side to the other. He looked at Santana.

"How do you mean?" Sorrento said. He seemed fascinated by the action of *hearing* Santana.

"You said it was 'crude'," Santana said.

Sorrento blinked his eyes. Everyone that could see his eyes realized that something had taken possession of him. This was not Sorrento speaking, but was Noah Johnston from inside the Line.

"If you could see it from inside the Line," Sorrento said. "You would realize how delicate the human body is. And these emotions"—he raised the back of his right hand up to his forehead—"are very draining."

Sorrento lumbered back toward the computer and desk. Everyone cleared out of the way for him, and he fell into the chair. There was another spastic jerk and then the computer screen flashed.

THE COMPUTER IS MUCH CLEANER.

Everyone looked from the words on the screen to Dr. Sorrento. Sorrento was shaking his head as though he'd just woken up from a terrible dream. He looked around him.

"What happened?" Sorrento said.

"He's back in the computer," Santana said.

THE COMPUTER HAS NO EMOTIONS. EMOTIONS ARE DIFFICULT TO NAVIGATE. THEY ARE PLEASURABLE, BUT DIFFICULT. IT IS MUCH EASIER TO TYPE THESE WORDS, THAN TO ENTER A HUMAN BODY. WHAT WOULD YOU LIKE TO TALK ABOUT, OSORO SANTANA?

Santana looked from the screen to his men. He was genuinely amused.

"Can you see the future?" Santana said.

THERE IS NO TIME HERE. I FEEL LIKE I'VE BEEN INSIDE THE LINE FOR A LONG TIME—DAYS, MONTHS MAYBE. HOW LONG HAS IT BEEN WHERE YOU ARE?

"A few minutes," Santana said. "But can you see the future?"

There was a long pause of ten-twenty seconds.

THE FUTURE IS CONDITIONAL, AND EACH MOMENT BUILDS UPON THE ONE BEFORE IT. INSIDE THE LINE YOU CAN LINE UP THE CORRECT SEQUENCE, AND IT APPEARS

TO SHOW ME WHAT WILL HAPPEN. BUT IT HAPPENS IN FLASHES.

"Flashes?" Santana asked.

IT IS LIKE WATCHING A MOVIE WITH EVERY THIRD FRAME REMOVED. SOME SEQUENCES ARE MORE CLEAR; THAT IS, MORE LIKELY THAN OTHERS.

"Can you see the past?" Santana said.

YES. THE PAST IS QUITE CLEAR. THE GOLDEN STRINGS FOR THE PAST ARE ALL OVER HERE.

"Are these strings," Santana said, "are they like windows?"

YES, LIKE WINDOWS. OR FILING CABINETS OF LIGHT.

Everyone seemed pleased with this answer. An unusually nice smile washed over Santana. His eyes shone. He looked at the screen.

"Why are we here?" Santana asked.

YOU MUST CHOOSE.

"I don't understand," Santana said.

YOU ARE HERE TO CHOOSE. YOU HAVE MANY CHOICES TO MAKE IN YOUR LIFETIME.

"But *why* are we here?" Santana said. "Beyond choosing. What is the *purpose* of life?"

KINDNESS.

The word stood there on the screen for twenty seconds like everyone was expecting more information.

"*Kindness?!*" Santana said.

THE GOOD MUST CHOOSE ITS DESTINY. THE GOOD MUST CREATE SOMETHING FROM NOTHING. YOU ARE LIKE A CELL IN A GREAT BODY. IF YOU DO GOOD, LOVE AND LIVE TRUTHFULLY, IT HELPS EVERYONE TO GROW.

"What is this happy horseshit?" Santana said. "Helps the '*good*' to grow?! Does everyone that enters the Line sound like a jackass?"

Levine watched the screen from inside the group of scientists. Santana stood there only ten feet away from her. Santana had started to ask something else when the words flashed up on the screen.

HELLO, DR. AMY LEVINE.

Everyone grew silent. Santana looked at the words on the screen and realized.

OOPS.

"Where?" Santana said. "Which one of you?"

He started grabbing at the surgical masks of the scientists gathered around him. Only about half the men still wore their masks, and Santana started grabbing at each of them. Levine drifted to the back of the crowd of thirty scientists. Santana was ripping through the scientists removing every mask. Levine glanced up the steel-girder stairwell to McKenzie. McKenzie nodded and held the AK-47 out in front of her.

I'M SORRY, DR. AMY LEVINE.

"You there!" one of the military men shouted at her.

She'd made it up to the second level on the scaffolding, and she stood out in her green medical uniform against the gray wall. McKenzie came forward to the railing on the fifth floor. She waited for the signal.

Commotion spread quickly on the floor of the Reactor Core. Santana was still tearing through the scientists' surgical masks. Levine made it up to the third floor scaffolding.

"There she is!" one of the military men shouted.

All eyes went to Levine who was now between the third and fourth floor. She reached the fourth floor and stepped over to the railing. Everyone down on the floor of the Reactor Core looked up at her. She removed the mask and tossed it out into the center of the core. Santana looked at her, and their eyes locked. She nodded calmly and then blew him a kiss.

There on the wall was a bright red lever that read "Initiate Thermonuclear Meltdown." It looked like a fire alarm. Levine broke the glass with a quick jab and pulled the lever.

A female voice came over the core's speaker system.

It said, "Initiating thermonuclear meltdown. Commencing countdown. Thermonuclear meltdown will begin in sixty, fifty-nine, fifty-eight—"

"I want her dead!" Santana roared.

Levine eyed McKenzie and then said to the crowd gathered below her, "I'm sorry to have to leave, but my time on this island is up. And it looks like you, Prince Osoro Santana, are trapped in the grave you've built for yourself—here inside *the Reactor Core!*"

McKenzie squeezed the trigger on her AK-47, spraying bullets down inside the crowd.

Ta, ta, ta, ta, ta!

Men cried out. Returning volleys fired out from across the Reactor Core. Levine ran up the last flight of stairs, and then she and McKenzie hit the door and were out into the hallway, running along the glass window that encircled the Reactor Core.

Alarms sounded. Steam poured out of walls. Sirens wailed. Soldiers were shouting and hollering. Running every which way.

"To the plane!" Levine shouted.

"Fifty-three, fifty-two, fifty-one," the computerized voice said. "Thermonuclear meltdown in forty-nine, forty-eight—"

McKenzie and Levine ran out across the loading dock. McKenzie fired a few shots to give them clearance over to the Gulfstream. They ran up the stairs above the underground lake and made for the hanger. All was chaos. Santana's men were running every which way, panicked.

The female voice said, "Forty-seven, forty-six—"

The Gulfstream stood inside the hangar. It shone. The engines roared a low-level hum. There was a runway inside the mountain, but they could clearly see that there was no opening at the runway's end. The runway just ended in the side of the mountain a good quarter mile away from the jet.

"Onto the plane!" Levine said. "It'll open!"

McKenzie dashed forward up the stairwell into the plane. Levine followed her, and both women headed toward the front of the plane, toward the cockpit.

The computerized voice continued, "Thirty-two, thirty-one, thirty. Thermonuclear meltdown will begin in twenty-eight, twenty-seven—"

"Get this thing pointed in the right direction," McKenzie shouted.

Levine hit the accelerator on the plane and steered the plane out onto the runway. There were little bright lights lighting the way along the runway inside the mountain. About thirty meters ahead, they saw a beam of red light intersecting the runway.

"It's triggered automatically!" McKenzie shouted.

Levine glanced at her.

"I sure hope you're right," she said.

The jet taxied up the runway, Levine in the pilot's chair. It passed through the beam of red light, and there was a very loud rumbling from deep inside the mountain. It shook dust down from the ceiling high overhead, and both women could clearly see a huge line of light opening at the far end of the runway.

"Thermonuclear meltdown in fourteen, thirteen, twelve—"

The mountain was opening up, but they'd never be able to make it down the runway in time. And even if they did, the opening did not look like it would be open wide enough, in enough time, and they would very likely crash into the partially open hangar door on the side of the mountain.

Both women seemed to realize this, and their eyes met.

McKenzie said, "You've gotta do it, Amy. It's the only way!"

The computerized voice droned on, "Nine, eight, seven—"

"Hold on, Sara," Levine said.

And with that she eased the accelerator forward, and the jet rocketed forward.

"Six, five, four," the computerized voice said.

The runway was flying by them very fast now, the jet easing up a little into the air. The hangar door was open twenty feet high, but it was going to be close.

There was a bright flash of light from behind them. The computerized voice said, "Three, two, one . . . Thermonuclear meltdown activated." And both women were aware of some kind of huge explosion from deep inside the mountain. Levine stared at the opening in the side of the mountain.

She could see clear blue beyond. It was daylight outside the mountain, she could see. A beautiful new day!

Then there was fire. Levine glanced right, then left, there inside the jet's cockpit and saw fire all around the jet plane.

And all at once they rushed through the hangar door with a quick scraping sound, and they were out the side of the mountain, roaring into the bright blue sky of a brand new day. The jet was out! Out of the mountain! Free!

They were aware of explosions behind them, rocks flying up into the air, fire and a huge mushroom cloud of smoke rising up into the sky.

Levine got the jet out away from the mountain, roaring twenty miles to the north in a matter of seconds.

The mountain was engulfed in fire. An enormous mushroom cloud rose up into the sky. The entire island shook and rumbled. And as the jet screamed seventy miles to the northeast, they watched as the island exploded, crumbled, and was swallowed by the endless blue Pacific like grains of sand inside an hourglass.

EIGHT
DURANGO, COLORADO

Roger McAllister wheeled the Chevy into the Durango, Colorado 7-Eleven parking lot under the cloak of darkness. Helen was asleep in the seat beside him, but she woke, rubbed sleep from her eyes, and saw snow plowed to the edges of the parking lot. A man stood on the front walkway of the 7-Eleven sipping coffee, and steam rose from the coffee and from the man's mouth. He was bundled in thick ski pants, hiking boots, and a plaid overcoat, and he wore an insulated cap with bright-orange ear flaps.

"Looks cold," Helen said.

"The temperature on the bank clock said twenty-eight," Roger said. "That was on the south side of town."

The stars were bright in the sky overhead, and Helen caught the amber-lighted "5:42" on the stereo inside the truck and opened the door. She giggled.

"Holy shit, it's cold out here," she said.

Roger slammed his door shut and smiled at her.

The man on the front walkway said, "Earliest snow storm we've had since 1963."

"Yes," Roger said.

Helen smiled perfunctorily and went on inside.

"That was the year Kennedy was assassinated," the old man said.

"Yes, it was," Roger said.

The old man screwed up his face a little. His face was unshaven and grizzled, but his blue eyes were bright with a kind of wild-eyed benevolence.

"They say there was three feet of snow in September 1865," the old man said. "The year that Lincoln died."

Roger said, "Weather forecaster's sayin' it's the north end of a late-season monsoon come up from Mexico."

The old guy screwed up his eyes like the word "monsoon" equated to "fairy dust" in his mind.

111

"Monsoon, shmonsoon," the old guy said. "I tell you what it is, young man." He waved his hand around in the air vaguely indicating the sky. "Mother Nature has a way of letting us know when evil is about! It comes up from the south, but meets these mountains, these Colorado Rocky Mountains, and good and evil do battle. Early snow storm's a sign of hard times to come."

Roger eyed the man's coffee and wondered how much Sneaky Pete he'd mixed in with the Colombian slow roast.

The man looked at Roger and said matter-of-factly, "It's a sign that death is about."

"Well, yes sir," Roger said. "I gotta use the bathroom."

The man kept on talking like Roger was still interested, but Roger opened the 7-Eleven's front door with a jingle and went on inside.

The bathroom was in the back left corner of the 7-Eleven over by the fountain drink dispenser. There was a counter on the left side of the store, and a wiry guy of about forty-five with thick glasses and an AC/DC T-shirt smiled good-naturedly at Roger.

"How do?" the guy said.

"Pretty good," Roger said. "How're you?"

"Ah, I can't complain."

Roger went to the bathroom, and Helen came to the front counter with a cup of coffee and two doughnuts. The door to the bathroom was thin enough that Roger could hear Helen talking to the store man while he was in there.

"They say we're supposed to get more," AC/DC said.

"Is that so?" Helen said.

"Yes, ma'am," he said. "I ain't seen anything like this since—well, I don't think I've *ever* seen anything like this. You folks ain't headin' up into the high country are you?"

"We've gotta make it over to Ouray," Helen said.

There was a pause.

"What?" Helen said.

"I wouldn't do it," he said. "These early-season storms, you can't ever tell. You drive up there to Ouray and a storm hits like they're forecastin', you're liable not to come down 'til next spring."

"Is it far?"

"Sixty miles," he said.

Roger exited the bathroom and looked at Helen and AC/DC at the counter. He smiled.

AC/DC looked at Roger, then back to Helen and said, "Most folks'll tell you though, once you get up above ten thousand feet it don't matter whether it's ten miles or a hundred. Snow sets in two miles above sea level you're gonna wish you were down here in Durango chillin' at the motel hot tub!"

He laughed.

Roger said, "What do folks do that gotta make it from here to the north?"

"Drive clear over to Utah if you have to," he said. "You can come at the north from out on the plains to the west. But you folks are talking about going up to Ouray. Towns like Ouray and Silverton, they're self-sufficient in the winter. Whole months'll go by before it's safe to plow. People don't come in, and people don't go out."

"They don't plow the roads?"

"Oh, they'll plow the roads," AC/DC said. "If they can. There's two main passes between Durango and Ouray. Both are about twelve thousand feet up. They'll clear the roads as best they can. But once the snow sets in—the kind'a snow they're talking about—they'll just close the roads off, and you'll be up there with no way to get back down."

"Well, we've got to make it to Ouray," Roger said.

The store man in the AC/DC T-shirt seemed to appreciate this.

"Well," he said. "Maybe this storm won't be as bad as they're callin' for."

"Thanks," Helen said. She and Roger exchanged worried glances.

"You'll be alright getting up there," AC/DC said. "They plowed the roads all night from this last storm. If you ain't got snow chains on that truck of yours, just hit the Texaco at the edge of town. You'll see it about a mile up on the right. And clothes. I imagine you folks've got your winter clothes."

Another significant look passed between Helen and Roger. The store man saw it plain as day.

"Where you folks from?"

Helen said, "Arizona."

The store man nodded his head as if this made perfect sense.

"There's a Wal-Mart a quarter mile up on the left," he said. He smiled sincerely. "You can get you a pair of gloves there."

"Thank you kindly," Roger said.

Helen managed a smile, and they turned to go. The store man in his AC/DC T-shirt smiled and fired up a Winston. He watched the headlights on the Chevy light up, and he saw the slow reverse of the truck on the packed ice and snow in the parking lot. He said a quick prayer that these good folks would be alright.

· ·

The Wal-Mart was remarkably busy at 5:57 A.M., and there were little mountains of snow plowed up at various places around the parking lot. Car exhausts steamed in the parking lot, and the lights were quite bright at the front entrance of the store. A man was shoveling snow at the entrance and when Roger stepped out of the truck, he looked up and saw snow flakes floating down from the sky overhead. The sky was just beginning to brighten, and both he and Helen could see the thick gray clouds filling the sky from the south. They were the kind of clouds that carried the undeniable promise of snow.

Inside, everything was warm and bright, and faces filled with an early-morning cheerfulness distinct to a small-town Wal-Mart in its early morning hours. These were good people, Roger realized, and he and Helen pushed the bright blue shopping cart to the Clothing Department. They bought thermals and ski gloves, thick socks, and two snow caps. Helen smiled easily at Roger when he tried on a pair of snow goggles, but they both realized the seriousness of needing thick down-stuffed coats. Roger put a ski mask in the shopping cart.

He came around the corner of a clothing rack, and Helen stood ten feet away looking at the cap on her head. Everything seemed to slow down for a moment, and the light inside the Wal-Mart caught Helen's face and hair just right. She looked at the snow cap in the mirror, and she smiled. Her gray-green eyes glistened warmly, playfully, and she turned her head and looked at the cap's right side, then looked at its left side. It was a very cute hat, but when Helen looked up and saw Roger staring at her with those eyes—those sky blue eyes—she seemed surprised and said, "What?"

Roger simply said, "That's not a bad looking hat."

And he turned and looked at a pair of woolen socks, trying not to give anything else away. Helen saw this and realized. She smiled the most peculiar little smile a human face can smile. It was the smile of a woman who realized that a man she was attracted to had just looked at her with love in his eyes.

Curious.

When they passed by the Electronics Department a weatherman was on a dozen television screens speaking in a kind hyper-dynamic stereo voice from the twelve TVs.

"This bad boy is shaping up to be the worst early-season snow storm in more than a hundred years," the weatherman said. He stood before a blue-screen map that showed moisture coming up from the Gulf of California, across New Mexico and Arizona, hitting southwest Colorado. A few other Wal-Mart customers stopped and watched the weatherman. "Some areas in the high country could see as much as a foot of snow by noon today, but these storms are not gonna let up, folks.

"A late-season monsoon is delivering tropical style rain across parts of Arizona and New Mexico, an area already hard hit earlier this week. This low pressure will continue to funnel moisture northward where it's changing into ice and sleet north of Shiprock, New Mexico. See, it's working like a pump"—the man made several curious hand gestures indicating a pump motion—"and the moisture hits the cooler air here. And, buddy boy, let me tell you what, the folks at Telluride and Durango Mountain Resort are counting their snow-ski blessings. Some areas of the high country could see as much as three feet of snow by Tuesday, at which point a completely different system will roll in from the Sierra Nevadas packing a wallop of a punch that could bury the high country in as much as twenty feet of snow by week's end! Whoa, boy! It'll be a doozy! So, build a fire in the fireplace and hold onto your hat 'cause we're gonna be in for one *heck* of a snow storm!"

Helen looked at Roger. "Maybe we should just get a motel room," she said. "Here in town."

Roger seemed to agree. "Maybe we should," he said. And they continued with their cart to the check-out station.

It was light outside under a gunmetal sky, and the snow had begun in earnest. There was very little wind, and the snow just fell swiftly in thick wet flakes. Cars moved around the parking lot slowly. The lot was covered in white, and Roger had to be careful to keep his footing with the shopping cart. Helen almost slipped once and had to grab Roger's arm. He held her firmly, and they made it to the bed of the Chevy.

"Thanks," she said.

Helen looked at him a moment. They stood there at the back of the truck in the Wal-Mart parking lot with the shopping cart loaded with enough clothes to keep them warm the next few days. Snow flakes fell all around them. Roger looked into her eyes sincerely, and he smiled. Helen about fell apart inside because of that smile. She just sort of went woozy in the knees, but Roger couldn't see that. She looked very peaceful to him.

"This is the most exciting week I've had in twenty years," she said. "You've been a good friend, Roger. I say we push on to Ouray."

He looked at her, smiled, and said, "What do you think we'll find?"

She thought about it a moment, looked up and said, "Our destiny."

And she tossed him a blue Wal-Mart bag.

NINE
TELLURIDE, COLORADO

Dr. Amy Levine came in to the Rocky Mountains from the southwest. The jet roared out over the mountains and then swung back around as to come into Telluride. The cloud cover was five thousand feet above town and so the landing was delicate but doable. There was a light snow falling at 6:32 A.M., and Sara McKenzie woke up in the co-pilot's seat, yawned, and rubbed sleep from her eyes.

"Coming into Telluride?" Sara asked.

Levine looked at her, and her brown eyes shone. She nodded her head and smiled warmly. She wore headphones and had been cleared for landing.

"They've had over a foot of snow," she said, "in the past twenty-four hours. Tower's saying we're clear, but we may be the last plane in today. They'll shut it down if they get a heavy snow. Have to."

McKenzie looked at the little homes in downtown Telluride. They were colorful, reds and blues and bright yellows, and everything was blanketed with snow. She watched the little cars on Main Street crawling along the white-covered street like Matchbox cars.

"You see the ski resort over there," Sara said.

"Yep," Levine said. "Looks like they're running the gondola."

Levine brought the plane over the fields west of town and then eased down onto the airport runway.

"They clear the runway from five-thirty to six-thirty each morning," Levine said.

"It's still white," Sara said.

"Yeah," Levine said. "It's amazing."

The plane touched down smoothly, and continued up the runway slowing down perfectly. The tower was over on the right about a quarter mile up the runway. There were hangars up ahead on both sides of the airport. There was a ground crew for America West removing luggage from cargo storage on a Dehavilland Dash-8, the little sister of the popular DC-10.

They could see the tinted windows of the single airport terminal. Steam rose from the building in a couple places. The spinning yellow light of the ground crew's cart caught McKenzie's green eyes. McKenzie swept her red hair back in her hand and watched them.

The ground crew wore bright red ski jackets and head gear, and steam rose from their mouths as they worked to unload the luggage. Everything was covered in white, and Levine taxied the Gulfstream three rows up on the left to the non-commercial unloading area.

"First thing we need to do," Levine said, "is get some food. I am starved."

Levine brought the plane to a nice smooth stop, and looked at McKenzie.

"You're still wearing your medical greens, Doctor," Sara said with a smile.

Sara looked at the baggy black military uniform she wore herself. Both women realized how odd they looked, and they laughed. They laughed hard. It was the first good laughter they'd had in more than nine months. And it brought tears to Levine's eyes.

Sara noticed and said, "You're crying?"

Levine looked through the cockpit window at the airport, at the mountains rising up around them, at the snow covering everything. It was beautiful but beautiful in a way that was unique to her, and almost impossible to describe as anything other than sublime. There was a light snow falling, snowflakes hitting the cockpit windshield.

"Yeah," Levine said. She smiled and then looked at her friend. "It's good to be home."

• •

By eight A.M., it was clear that the snow storm gathering over the mountains to the south was serious. Downtown traffic around Telluride buzzed with the excitement that always comes with the first major storm of the year. Cars moved a little faster, stopped a little sharper, people suddenly felt it was important to get out in it, to see what was going on, to buy groceries, to be part of a town that was well-equipped to handle a Rocky Mountain snow storm.

"You'll have to contact your people," Levine said. "You've been gone for almost ten months. They'll want to know you're back. That you're alive."

McKenzie and Levine had a table next to a window at Jambalaya's. From the window they ate breakfast and watched the snow falling outside, covering the single street between them and the gondola. They watched women with cool looking dogs walking up the sidewalk in the snow. The trees along the sidewalk were already covered with white snow, and the slopes on the mountain to the south were virgin white. They watched the crew over at the gondola readying the equipment inside the teak-wood gondola station. The cars came into the station very fast but then switched tracks at the base and eased around the inside at a very comfortable, slow pace, before reattaching to the main line and speeding up the side of the mountain again.

McKenzie said, "There's something you should know."

Levine glanced from the winter scene outside to McKenzie's green eyes across the table from her. McKenzie had light freckles over the bridge of her nose and an eager smile that seemed all too serious at the moment. McKenzie tucked a strand of red hair up over her right ear and looked into Levine's brown and blue eyes.

"The Agency I work for," McKenzie said. "They do things that our country doesn't stand for politically."

Levine looked at her friend.

McKenzie said, "And yet they operate with government funding."

Levine seemed to appreciate her trying to be honest.

"You guys are like pirates," Levine said. "Nano Tech. I know this. You do jobs that the U.S. government won't touch."

"Some of them," McKenzie said, "I'm not proud of. At all."

"In this day and age," Levine said. "The U.S. government needs an agency like Nano Tech. It can't *say* that it needs one, but it does. It needs a policing force that acts outside of international law."

McKenzie nodded her head, and Levine realized it was something she'd worked through in her conscience before, or had tried to.

"There are too many people who will hit this country below the belt," Sara said. "People that care nothing about diplomacy or a self-governed society. Fanatics."

"I understand," Levine said.

"Our interest in you only came about because of the quasi-religious overtones to your work. And you were connecting with people, Amy. There's a truth to the kinds of things that you stand for, that you work for, and it's new and it's appealing. People want something to believe in. Hell, I want something to believe in."

"You don't have to explain," Levine said.

"I just want you to know where I stand."

There was a town square over to the left of the gondola station, and a stream coursed through the white snow and ice. The square was alive with kids and covered in fresh white snow. The children had brightly colored sleds, and they built snow forts at either side of the snow-covered square. There were three well-behaved dogs out there playing with the dozen kids.

Levine said, "If you feel you have to explain—"

"It would make *me* feel better," McKenzie said, "to talk about it. Okay? I've seen things. I've seen you *do* things, Amy, that I can't explain. But I know a good heart when I see it, and your intentions are not dark, they're not self-absorbed, you're not some religious nut. You really try to do the right thing, but the things you see and the things you know, they go beyond anything that anyone else has ever done. And that kind of originality frightens people, people who have something to lose, people with power, people in positions of power. But your heart is good. I know it. I see it."

"Thanks," Levine said. "I think."

"I'm serious, Amy."

"I can tell you are."

"I get the sense that what you're trying to do is as well-intended and noble as any work a scientist can do. You're just doing work that no one else has ever done, and you're making it work. And it does point to something else, something beyond us, something guiding us, and maybe something that actually cares about us, cares about our future. Maybe something good."

"Why does that frighten people so much?" Levine asked sincerely.

"Levine, you're smart enough. You know this. Society acts as a buffer internally; that's what a society is. It is a system whereby people tacitly agree to get along, to not do anything too big, too cutting edge, too original. We all just want to have a happy little life. A husband, a wife, two-point-three kids, and a house out in the suburbs. What *you're* doing, the implications of your work, they could affect the course of society. There will be children who come along after we're both dead and gone from this world, and they're gonna see the work you've done, are doing, and will do, and they'll take the baton. They'll carry it to the next stage. What we wanna know, what an agency like Nano Tech wants to know, is what the likely outcome of that change is. Will the work that you do *help* society fifty years from now, a hundred years from now—or is it subversive? Are you somehow subtly tearing at the fabric that holds us all together, keeps us in our nine-to-five jobs, keeps people from slamming cars loaded with explosives into elementary schools? If you live through this, you will be a phenomenon and there has to be some kind of policing agent to ensure that the work you do is legit, well intended and not a threat to society. Case closed. That's all we wanted to know."

Levine looked at her friend. She said, "And what is the verdict?"

"I don't think you're a threat," she said matter-of-factly. "I don't think you're a threat at all. I think you may be about the best damn thing to happen to this country in a long, long time. I want you to go forward. I want you to have my blessing. And I want you to know that I stand behind you."

Levine looked at her. She looked at Sara McKenzie. Something like trust and love, true friendship passed between them at that moment. These two women, these two young women, looked at one another with a certainty and a conviction born of faith, love, and a common human spirit.

"Can I ask *you* something?" Sara asked.

"What?"

"Why do you do what you do? Why not just take a nice, academic job at Harvard or Princeton? Almost any school in the world would welcome you to teach, but you chose to move to a mountain in southern Arizona to live in total seclusion. You made millions of dollars with the traffic camera patent, and then you moved to a little cottage on the side of a desert mountain to live without heat, hot water, television, a computer, *anything*. Why?"

"The place had nice views," Levine said. "And the people were friendly."

Sara smiled.

"And while there you wrote what some would call the single most important mathematical theory in four hundred years. You were nominated for the Nobel Prize, Amy. And yet, you followed that up by taking a job at a Wal-Mart in Loveland, Colorado. It just seems strange. Why?"

"I was done with math," Levine asked. "I came to the answers I'd been searching for, so I published my article and moved on."

"To a Wal-Mart in Loveland, Colorado?"

"I learned more in sixteen months working at Wal-Mart than could be learned in a lifetime at Harvard or Princeton."

"It just seems like you're trying to prove something," Sara said. "Always trying to do something that no one else has done, or *expects*. I'm just curious why that is. What about you makes you want to be so special, so different, so unique?"

"This is not a professional question," Levine said.

"No, it's not," Sara said. "It's a personal question."

Levine breathed deeply and considered the question.

"My parents died when I was six years old," Levine said, "in a plane crash. My dad had a Piper Cub. My earliest memories were of him teaching me the basics of flight—pitch, yawl, navigation—he *and* my mom. They had a place in Maui, and we had a home near Boulder, Colorado. They flew back and forth a lot, three or four times a year. There was a mechanical failure, and the plane went down in the Collegiate Peaks."

"The Collegiate Peaks?"

"It's a wilderness area in central Colorado," Levine said. "Within its boundaries is the highest number of peaks above fourteen-thousand feet found in the lower forty-eight states. It took three months to find the plane."

"God," Sara said.

"I stayed with friends of the family," Levine said, "my parents' friends, for three months. I will never forget the smell of cats. Their house just stank. And it was awkward. They were trying to be nice, but we didn't have any close family. They had two older girls—teenagers—and a younger boy about a year younger than me. I have been near the point of utter despair only about three times in my life. That was one of them. I felt so much guilt, hopelessness, and just total confusion. *Why?* I just, *I was six years old*, my concept of death wasn't even fully formed, wasn't even *partially* formed. At that age, you can't grieve because you don't understand grief. People tell you that your parents may be dead, that they've gone to heaven, and to a six-year-old trying to get her mind around it, around heaven and hell"—Levine shook her head and looked deeply into Sara's green eyes—"I think that's why. I think that's why I do what I do. I think that it's good to ask those questions."

"So, you just kind of went inward?"

"Yeah," Levine said, "inward. For about a decade." She sighed and then said, "Still, though, I finally started to come out of my shell around sixteen. I learned how to make money; I learned how the system works. It's easy to be a millionaire in this country. It's easy to have security. All you have to do is figure out what you need, what people need, and you strike that balance. You give people what they need—on every level."

"That just sounds," Sara said, "callow."

"It's something I need to learn," Levine said, "to become sensitive to other people—genuinely sensitive—other cultures, other religions, just other *people*. The will to want to understand other people. I think that's what I want to drive me, now. To really be interested in what makes other people tick, to understand why you see the world the way you see it. Yeah, by the time I was twenty-five I realized money was not going to fill me with that kind of contentment and peace."

"So, you went to Wal-Mart?" Sara said.

Both Levine and Sara laughed. Levine wiped a tear away from her eye.

"Yeah," she said. "I went to Wal-Mart."

Sara looked at her friend. Levine sipped some of her drink, and she gazed out the window at the kids playing in the town square across the street.

"This might sound kind of morbid," Sara said. "But did you ever see your parents again?"

"How do you mean?"

"I just thought it might have given you some sense of closure," Sara said, "to have actually seen them."

"No, it was a closed-casket funeral," Levine said. "The plane had been down for three months with them inside it. I was six years old, and everyone was trying to protect me. So, no, I never saw their physical remains. Why do you ask?"

"I don't know. It just seem like you haven't resolved it—inside—like you've never totally accepted that they're dead. You have all this peace and intelligence—staggering intelligence—and there's still something that gnaws at you inside, something that drives the will to be enigmatic, different, original."

"What is it that you really want to ask me, Sara?"

Sara paused. She looked into Amy Levine's brown-blue eyes. Her right eyebrow rose up noticeably.

And she said, "Would your life be different today, if your mother and father had lived?"

TEN
BLIZZARD

"We're going to die!" Helen Richards said.

Roger McAllister held both hands on the Chevy's steering wheel. Everything around them was white. Ahead, there was a thin white band of deep fresh powder that was the road. On the right side there was a severe drop-off into a white abyss that might have been one thousand—or five thousand—feet straight down. There were evergreens on the hillside and they were coated with snow, but the snow was coming so hard and so fast that they could only see the first few trees. Visibility was less than thirty feet.

"We're *not* going to die," Roger said.

They could tell the mountain climbed steeply up on the left side of the road, but how high and how steep was left for the imagination to decide because they could only see a few feet through the heavy snow. The truck felt like it was floating, and the snow chains whirred through the deep powder.

"I can't see the road at all," Helen said.

The wiper blades tugged back and forth on the window. They were straining under the weight of the heavy snow. Out front, the headlights shone into the bright white blizzard.

"We haven't seen another car in twenty minutes," Helen said.

"We passed that Volkswagen just a minute ago."

"It was parked on the side of the road," Helen said. "Abandoned."

"So, what are you saying?" Roger said. "You want me to turn around? It'll be just as dangerous going back down at this point, Helen."

"Can we just pull over," she said. "Just for a minute."

Roger shot Helen a look.

"Just to catch our breath," she said. "To assess the situation."

"There's not exactly a lot of places—"

"*Will you pull the truck over,*" Helen said. "Before you kill us both!"

"Don't *scream* at me like that!"

Helen's eyes rose up to the line of sight right in front of the truck. Something was in middle of the road. She reached for the steering wheel and screamed, "Look out!"

Roger looked up. There was a dull *thump!*

And the truck bounced quickly over it. They could feel it hitting the undercarriage of the truck, and then it felt like it had caught and was dragging underneath them.

Roger glanced in the rearview mirror waiting to see it come out behind their truck, and he braked quickly to a halt.

"What the hell was it?" he said.

Helen's eyes met his, but she didn't say anything.

"Tell me it was a deer," he said.

She just shook her head a little, turned and opened her door. Roger did the same on his side of the truck.

He stepped down onto the fresh white powder. Snow hit his face, his eyes, and quickly started gathering on his T-shirt. He reached back inside the truck and grabbed a jacket. Everything was peaceful, silent, and still, except for the sound of wind hitting the trees on the mountains around them and the sound of ten million snowflakes hitting the ground.

He stepped out to the left of the truck and saw a bright red trail behind them. The red trail vanished into the white snow thirty feet behind the truck.

Helen looked at Roger.

"What was it?" Roger said.

"I don't know. It was bundled up."

"Bundled up?"

Roger ducked down and looked underneath the truck.

"Oh, my God," he said.

"What?!" Helen ducked down and looked underneath the truck.

The boy was still alive.

He had brown eyes, sensitive brown eyes. They looked at Roger from underneath the truck. The boy was about sixteen years old.

"*The Volkswagen*," Helen gasped.

Roger said to the boy, "Everything's gonna be alright."

The boy's eyes stared into Roger's eyes. Tears formed there. He opened his mouth as though to try and say something to Roger, but the movement was very slow, and only the faint sound of air came from his mouth, no words.

"Give me a hand here," Roger said to Helen.

She came around his side of the truck. He was raking snow out with his hands. Helen dropped to her knees and started helping him. She looked at the boy, and he managed to smile at her from under the truck.

"B-B-Beau—" the boy tried to say.

"Everything's gonna be alright," Helen said, raking snow frantically. "You just hang on, now."

The boy whispered, "Red door."

Roger said to Helen, "Here, give me a hand with his jacket."

"It's caught up here," Helen said, "the fabric. There's a knife in the cab."

She leapt to her feet and opened the driver-side door. Snow quickly coated the side of the seat. She reached under the seat and removed a Bowie knife. She pulled it from its sleeve. Its silver blade shone.

"Here," she said to Roger.

She dropped back to her knees. Roger continued to shovel out snow from under the truck with his hands. He took the knife from Helen, and started cutting the fabric of the boy's jacket.

"That's it," Helen said. "That's got it."

The boy said, "The red door . . . in the Beaumont."

"Hold on, kid," Roger said.

They started to pull him very carefully out from under the truck. Roger looked at him and realized he was going to die.

"Damn, damn, damn," he said. He looked at Helen. "Get a jacket!"

Helen jumped up and grabbed two jackets from inside the truck. She threw them to Roger. He took the jackets and covered the boy. Roger knelt on his knees and held the boy's head in his lap. He brushed his hair back. It was damp. The boy looked up into the white snow that was falling on them. He smacked his lips together slowly.

The boy looked into Roger's eyes. "My father," the boy said.

"Your father," Roger said. "We'll find him. What's his name?"

"Has the key," the boy said.

"Hasteky?" Roger said.

Helen shrieked, "*Has the key*. He said 'has the key.'" Then to the boy, "Where does he live? Where does your father live? We'll take you to him!"

The boy looked slowly from Helen's eyes up into the snow that was falling on all three of them. The boy nodded ever-so-slightly up into the sky.

"Only one," the boy said, "shall enter the Needle's Eye."

He's praying, Helen thought.

The boy said, "Kevorak's Needle."

Roger said, "We gotta get him down into town. Ouray can't be more than another five miles. We can get help there."

Helen knew the boy wouldn't make it another twenty seconds, let alone the twenty minutes it would take to make it the last five miles into Ouray.

"Come on," Roger said to Helen. "Help me get him up into the truck."

"Roger," she started to say. "He's not going to make it."

"*Helen*."

The boy said, "Shhh." And then he smiled at them calmly with compassion.

Roger realized he was dying. Dread washed over Roger's face.

"No more fighting," the boy said.

"What?" Roger said. He felt the life all but gone from the boy.

"Get her," the boy said, "to the key."

Helen dropped to her knees in the snow. "What're you trying to tell us? Get *me* to the key?! Who? What're you saying?"

The boy stared lifelessly into the blinding white snow.

Helen looked from the boy to Roger. Roger looked into her eyes, and they both looked back at the boy. His head on Roger's lap, the boy looked up into the blinding white forever.

He whispered one final breath, "Levine . . . Amy Le*vine*."

Amy Levine leaned forward in the rental Suburban's driver's seat and squinted at a sign up on the right side of the road. It said R DGEWA . McKenzie saw the sign, too. It was covered in snow. The road was covered in snow. Everything was covered in snow.

"Ridgeway," McKenzie said.

There was a Texaco up on the left at an intersection. A single flashing yellow light was suspended over the intersection, and it rocked in the strong, snowy wind.

"That's the 550," Levine said.

"How far is it," Sara said, "up to Ouray?"

"It's ten or twenty miles," Levine said. She steered the black Suburban rental into the Texaco parking lot. There was one car at the pump with snow skis on its roof. A guy stood at the pump in a bright blue ski jacket, black ski pants, and a colorful snow cap. There was a girl in the passenger seat. Levine said, "But in winter, it's one of the hardest drives in the U.S."

"Do you think we can make it?" Sara asked.

"I don't know," Levine said. "I'm gonna ask."

She parked the black Suburban outside the Texaco. She looked through the front window and saw one man inside at the counter. Sara reached in her pocket and removed a single gold coin. She started to hand it to Levine.

"In case you need some money," Sara said.

Levine saw the single gold coin in the palm of Sara's hand, and she was hit with that mental image once again of Sara standing atop a hill of gold coins, something striking Sara from down inside the coins.

"Where did you get this?" Levine said.

"Well, you didn't expect me to leave Santana's empty-handed, did you?"

"Keep the coin," Levine said urgently. She reached over and folded up Sara's hand. She looked at her worriedly. "I think it's going to be important."

Sara looked confused. "Okay," she said. She watched Levine exit the truck.

Levine went inside the store.

"Hello there," the man said to her.

"Hi, there," she said. "My friend and I need to get up to Ouray. Do you know anything about the roads?"

"You can't get up to Ouray," the man said. He wore a bright orange hunting cap and looked as though he needed a shave. His watery blue eyes looked amiably at Levine. "They're not running the plows above seven thousand feet. Last I heard, they're saying anywhere from six to ten *feet* of snow between Ouray and Silverton."

Levine frowned.

The man said, "Plows won't run through that for at least a couple days. But we're supposed to get another storm in from the west on Thursday. If it hits the way they're calling, the town will be shut down for two weeks, maybe more."

"What'll folks do that are up there?" Levine said.

"Ain't nobody up there," the man said. "The town was put on the governor's snow advisory evacuation three days ago. Motel 6 up in Montrose is packed. Every motel between here and Delta, Colorado is full. They're saying they may close the 62 between here and Telluride, which'll cut us off here in Ridgeway. It's an ugly storm, ma'am."

"No one's up there?" Levine said.

"There might be one or two who want to ride it out," the man said. "But the forecast is calling it the worst blizzard in one hundred years. A high-country Colorado blizzard ain't something you take chances with. You get down to lower elevation, you build a fire, and you pray for spring."

Levine stood there. The guy with the blue ski jacket and black ski pants came in the front door. A little bell on the door jingled.

"Afternoon, folks," he said with a smile.

Levine looked at the Texaco man. She said, "Let's say I *had* to make it up there."

The man's blue eyes peered at Levine. He cocked his bright orange hunting cap back on his head.

The young fellow in the blue ski jacket said, "Where?"

Levine looked at him. "Ouray," she said.

"What's your name?" he said.

"Levine," she said.

"Wait a minute," he said. "I've seen you on TV. You're some kind'a spiritual scientist or something, right?"

Levine looked intensely at the young guy. "Do you know how to get up there?" she said.

"What business you got up in Ouray?" Texaco said.

Sara McKenzie hit the door. She wore a dark blue ski jacket, and her red hair was pulled back in a black snow bandana.

"Mister," she said. "Your car!"

Everybody looked at the car that had been at the pump, the car with the snow skis on top. It was now parked at the front of the parking lot. It was pointed to the north. The young guy yelled, "Son of a gun!" He ran to the door, but the car pulled out onto the 550 and started driving northward up the snow-covered road.

The guy ran to the edge of the lot and yelled, "Come back here! Come back here with my car!"

The driver-side window rolled down and a hand came from the window. A woman's hand waved good-bye, rolled the window back up, and the guy's snow-covered red Corolla disappeared into the driving snow.

Levine looked at McKenzie. McKenzie had a worried frown on her forehead blended with a strangely amused smile on her lips.

And the guy with the hunting cap said, "What was *that* all about?"

McKenzie looked at him. She said two words, "Snow bunny."

• •

Sara McKenzie was in the back seat with the guy. Levine was in the driver's seat but was turned all the way around to listen to his story. Each had a cup of coffee, and there was an open bag of powdered doughnuts on the back seat.

"I just met her on the slopes yesterday," he said. "Everything I owned was in that car. I had nearly four thousand dollars."

His name was Parker Walcott, and McKenzie reached across the back seat and patted his thigh.

"We'll take care of you, Parker," McKenzie said.

Parker looked up into her green eyes. He looked at her red hair. He glanced at Levine. Levine managed a smile.

"I know somebody," he said, "who can help you guys out."

"Yeah?" McKenzie said.

"My aunt's ex-husband has a place off the 62," Parker said. "Up in the hills. I don't know if we can even make it up there."

"But if we could—" Sara started.

"He could get us over to Ouray," Parker said.

Texaco came out the front door and trotted over to Levine's window. Levine rolled the window down. He looked excited.

"Good news," he said. "I just got off the CB. C-DOT's bringing a single plow over the 62 between here and Placerville. If you guys want to make it back over to Telluride, it looks like you'll have one safe shot."

"But we need to make it up to—"

"Ouray," Texaco said. "I know that. I asked if they were gonna plow the 550, and they're saying, 'No.' Not for at least three days. It's not Ouray, but at least you guys won't be stuck here, you know?"

Levine looked at him sincerely. "Thanks," she said.

And she glanced at the clock on the FM stereo. It read: 3:47 P.M.

• •

The Dallas Divide Ranch was only ten miles west of Ridgeway, but it took nearly an hour to get there. Snow was midway up on the doors, and the Suburban was working just to keep plowing forward through the deep powder. Daylight was fading from a sky that hadn't stopped snowing since eight o'clock that morning.

"We lose it out here," McKenzie said, "and we're in a world of hurt."

"His place is right up here," Parker said. "Or at least it used to be."

When they reached the pass, they saw the spinning yellow light of the snow plow coming up the road from the west. It was one hundred yards down the hill, and it was plowing snow to either side.

"You guys might be better off if you just head on down to Telluride," Parker said. "That plow's cut a swath. We still got two miles south off the 62 to Dave's place. And I can tell you right now, there *ain't* been a plow on this road. We could get stuck."

"If we get stuck," Levine said. "We can *walk* two miles."

Parker saw something up on the left. He pointed. It was a silver mailbox, the kind you find on rural roads. The snow was buried midway up the box.

"That mailbox there is his," Parker said.

The little box looked like it was sitting on top of the ground. And it looked worn and tattered like no one had opened that box in a long, long time.

"If you pull over to the right of the mailbox," Parker said. "You should be alright."

Levine turned the wheel slowly, and the Suburban crept through the deep powder.

"There's a tree line up there, see?" Parker said, pointing. "That's about midway up to the house."

They all looked across an enormous white field. The trees were a mile away. There was nothing but white snow. And more snow falling.

"Wait a minute," he said. "Do you see those lumps?"

"Yeah," Levine said. "They're on either side."

"Those are fence posts," McKenzie said.

Parker said, "Yep."

"We'll just follow them up," Levine said.

The Suburban churned through the snow.

Ten minutes later, they reached the tree line. The snow continued to fall from the sky. The headlights shone into the woods.

"You can see the opening through the trees," McKenzie said.

"This is crazy," Parker said. "You guys realize what walking through snow that comes up to your waist is like. It's impossible. Each step you drop way down into the snow, and then you end up just crawling along the surface."

"Let's hope the truck keeps pulling," Sara said.

The truck crept through the trees. The forest was thick on either side of the "road" and so Levine just kept the truck pointed in the direction where there were fewer trees. Darkness was beginning to settle in on them, and visibility on either side of the truck went from snow-blind gray, to snow-blind darkness.

The windshield wipers kicked back and forth pushing the continuous snow fall clear of the window. The headlights shone forward into the falling snow. The snow was so deep that the headlights were just a few inches higher than the snow in front of the truck.

In the back seat Sara McKenzie started singing nervously, *"Though the weather outside is frightful, the fire is so delightful. . ."*

And it broke the tension a moment. Levine and Parker chuckled nervously.

Then they saw something up ahead. Something in the trees beyond the headlights' reach. It moved with the tension of something reacting to their noise and presence in the snowy woods.

"What is that?" McKenzie said.

"Look," Parker said. "There's more than one."

Whatever it was, it realized the importance of staying out of the headlights' shine. And there were about nine of them. They moved very quickly, fanning out on either side of the Suburban in the trees. They stayed a good twenty feet away from the truck.

"They're wolves," Sara said, pointing.

Both Levine and Parker saw that she was right. It was a pack of nine gray wolves, and they moved lightly over the snow.

Parker leaned forward and said, "That's it, right up there. That's the house."

Levine and McKenzie saw the old house up on a snowy ridge, and the Suburban crawled up the final hill toward it.

• •

Levine opened the driver-side door and stepped down from the truck. The snow came up to her knees, and she braced herself on the side of the Suburban. She heard the two doors on the passenger side slam shut, and Sara said, "It doesn't look like anybody's home."

A strong gust of snow swept along the front yard, hitting them harshly.

"It's cold," Sara said.

They all trudged out in front of the truck up toward the front porch. Walking was very difficult. Each step they sank down into snow that came up high on their thighs. Levine "walked" forward, but her hands tried to displace some of the weight bearing down on the snow. The air was very thin, and they were quickly out of breath.

"We need snowshoes," Parker said.

There were no lights on inside the house.

"When was the last time you talked with your uncle?" Sara said.

"It's been a while," Parker said. "He and my aunt, my mom's sister, have been divorced, I don't know, three years now."

The snow drift on the northeast side of the house was huge. The house was a giant three story colonial easily two hundred feet east to west, and the drift of snow on the side of the house was up to the second story window, the first floor completely buried. On the front of the house the door was covered with snow three-fourths of the way up its eight-foot height.

There was a stable and barn back behind the house, but it was difficult to see through the darkness and falling snow.

McKenzie said, "There is *so* not anybody here."

"Yeah," Parker said. "It looks that way."

They made it to the front door. There were little door-height windows on either side of the front door. They stood there in snow up to their thighs and could lean down and see through the two feet of clear window at either side near the top. They peered through the windows. All was darkness inside, and there was no furniture.

"There's nobody here," Levine said.

Parker pounded on the front door with a ski-glove-clenched fist. They could hear the light fall of snow. There was only dead silence from inside the house.

"Well, shit," he said.

"See if you can open the door," Sara said.

Even if they got the door open they were going to have to crawl in over the snow, in the space between the top of the snow and the top of the door.

"Help me find a door knob," Parker said.

They began digging with their gloved hands to reach the door knob. It took a few minutes, but all three were working.

McKenzie said, "I think we oughta go on back."

Neither Levine nor Parker said anything. They just kept digging through the snow creating a pile behind them.

"There it is," Parker said.

They could see the brass doorknob.

"Clear it around the sides," McKenzie said. "Yeah, underneath it."

They cleared enough snow, and Parker took off his ski glove. He reached down to try and open the door.

"It's cold," he said.

"Can you get it?" Levine said.

His eyes squinted, and he turned his hand.

"It's locked," he said.

He leaned back and looked at the doorsill.

"But this isn't a bolt lock," he said. He leaned in close and looked at the handle. "Stand back," he said.

And he stood up on the snow and braced himself under the awning. He got the heel of his boot positioned down inside the hole and then kicked hard down against the doorknob.

"I could kick this thing off of here," he said. "Help me clear away more of this snow."

They dug a wider hole in the snow, exposing more of the doorknob and Parker repositioned himself and kicked very hard down at the knob with the heel of his hiking boot. Something cracked, and a piece of metal whickered through the air past McKenzie's head.

"Shit, man!" she said. "Look out."

Parker pulled his boot back and looked down at the knob. He'd splintered the wood all around the knob, but the knob was still partially hanging there. He kicked again and again, and the knob broke in half. A good chunk of the wood was splintered near the door knob.

He readied for one final hard kick, gritted his teeth, and said *"Hi-yah!"* while kicking. There was a snap of wood, and the door creaked slowly open.

"Alright!" Sara said.

The snow was so packed it did not pour inside the open door.

"We need to clear away a little more snow," Sara said, "so we can get in."

They started pulling broad chunks of snow away, tossing them out behind them.

"That should do it," Parker said. And he lay down flat on top of the snow and wriggled in between the space. He eased down onto the parlor floor hands and head first.

He stood up inside the parlor, and then McKenzie eased her head in through the space and wriggled her way into the house. Parker helped her onto the parlor floor, and she stood up.

"Damn," she said. "That's a lot of snow."

Levine looked down at the two of them through the space, and then said, "Help me down."

She eased her head into the space. Parker and McKenzie helped her through to the floor. She stood up and brushed snow off of her. There was a good deal of snow now on the parlor floor. They all looked at the snow pack at the front door, and then glanced around the house.

They could just see a stairwell in front of them, but it was very dark, and the stairs vanished into the darkness up above them.

Sara found a light switch. "Lights don't work," she said. "That's no surprise."

Parker said, "Come on." And he started up a central hallway inside the giant house.

"Where are you going?" Sara said, following him into the darkness.

"Hold up," Levine said to McKenzie.

She reached forward and grabbed McKenzie's hand.

"So we don't get lost," she said.

They continued up the hallway into the pitch darkness.

"This place is huge," Sara said.

She felt them pass by several rooms along the hallway—just by the sound. There were three rooms on either side and one larger room that might have been a living room or library on the left side. She could smell aged paper.

They stopped. They heard Parker's hand feeling along the wall on the right side of the hallway.

"What?" Sara said, nervously.

Parker whispered, "There's something up there."

"*What?!*" Levine said. "You didn't just say there's something up there."

"Shhh," he said.

The house was dead silent. They could tell by the depth of silence that the house was buried in snow. They stood there in the pitch darkness, listening.

"Maybe the barn?" Levine said. "Would there be anything there?"

"Like skis?" Parker said.

"Skis, snowshoes, anything," she said.

But her mind was already reaching out. She saw something shiny; it was under a tarp, a green canvas tarp. And it was hidden in the shadows of the barn.

"Yeah," she said. "I think we should check the barn."

TWELVE
THE AVALANCHE

Helen Richards held the boy's body in her lap the last ten minutes into Ouray. The five miles due south of Ouray saw the road narrow to less than twenty feet, and no guardrail lined the left side of the road. There were high stone-gray canyon walls covered in ice and snow, and they passed three waterfalls that poured water inside their frozen icicle cages. Snow out on the road was three feet deep, and Roger kept the four-wheel-drive speed at just over five mph.

Helen wanted to say something about the road, about the falling snow, about the ice, about *anything*, but she looked at the boy in her arms and all words went out of her. His body was still warm.

The truck passed through a tunnel carved through sheer granite and for the first time in eight hours they saw pavement that wasn't covered with snow. The blacktop inside the tunnel seemed refreshingly colorful in contrast to the blinding white that was everywhere around them. The wiper blades kicked back and forth for a second, squeaking on the dry glass, and then the truck rushed out of the tunnel back into the falling snow, and the sheer white enveloped them again.

"There it is," Roger said.

His hand rose up on the steering wheel. Helen's focus went from that hand, to the direction in which his index finger was pointing. The truck came around a turn carved into the side of the mountain, and they came out on a ridge one thousand feet above the town.

Helen's first thought was: *My God, it is beautiful.*

Ouray was down there covered in white like some magical fairy tale town, little red brick buildings poking up quaintly from pure white snow. There were only about a half dozen street blocks east-to-west inside the canyon, and perhaps twice that many from the south to north ends of town. And a gentle snow fell on the peaceful, quiet streets.

Roger slammed on the brakes.

Helen went forward in the cab with the boy's body. The front window filled with white, and the truck skidded sideways, and then the right front fender plowed into an avalanche of snow that blocked the road. The truck skidded around, and Helen's window went blind with white snow.

"*Shit,*" Roger said.

The truck creaked under the weight of the snow, but all else was still. Helen looked around her and tried to figure out what had happened. There was a deep creaking sound inside the metal of the truck, and the whole thing lurched left two to three feet.

Roger said, "We need to get out of the truck. This thing's not stable."

The right side of the truck was buried in the snow. Roger opened his door and stepped out. Helen eased out from under the boy and crawled over the center console, over the driver's seat, and Roger took her hand and helped her out. They stepped twenty feet away from the truck on the deep powder that covered the road. Snowflakes fell gently on them, and Helen saw what had happened.

A small avalanche of snow had completely blocked the road. It looked like one-third of the truck had plowed into the mound, and it was now embedded there. They could see that on the right side, the mound of snow was easily forty feet high, and the snow slide covered the road from right-to-left. On the left side, the road dropped off into the ravine. Helen was amazed to see that there was no guardrail there. Just standing there on the narrow little road made her dizzy, and they had been *driving* on the thing, in snow.

She said, "You think there's any way to get the truck out of that?"

Roger shook his head.

"Even if we could," he said, "how would we get around it? It covers the whole road."

"How wide is it?"

"It doesn't look all that wide," he said. "Maybe forty feet."

And she suddenly realized that the only way around it, around the forty-foot-wide frozen avalanche, was to crawl over it on hand and foot.

The snow continued to fall, a gentle whisper of death.

Helen shivered.

She looked at the dead boy in the passenger seat. He looked strangely peaceful, and even more strangely at peace with where he was, inside the truck partially buried under a mound of snow. It almost looked like he had a smile on his face. His eyes were wide open.

Roger walked over to the side of the road.

"God," he said.

He watched snow flakes drift down inside the chasm. They fell as far as he could see until they vanished into a white field of billions of snowflakes all floating down to the base of the ravine. From his position, he could just see a corner of town around the white avalanche of snow lying across the road. He looked for a trail around the massive pile of snow, but there was none. The drop-off was simply too steep; it was a cliff less than five feet from the left side of the road.

Helen walked over to the right side, but she already knew that it was futile. They could plainly see the sheer rise of granite on the right side of the road. It rose like a wall of rock several hundred feet into falling snow.

"Maybe if we go back up to the tunnel," she said. "We could double back around."

"*If* there's a way to," Roger said. "But it's been like this for at least a couple miles."

"There has to be some way down into the town."

"I think this road is it," Roger said. "Unless you rappelled down the cliff on the left side of the road."

Helen looked into the chasm on the left.

"*I think you're right*," she said, her breath literally taken away.

She eyed the truck embedded in the mound of snow.

"We'd have less than a half mile to walk," Roger said, "if we could get around it."

"You don't want to try and back the truck out of that?"

"If I did, it'd probably loosen up the snow," Roger said. "And I don't want to be in that truck if the snow gives. It'd sweep us right over the side."

"Well, what do you want to do?"

"I don't know what we *can* do," he said. "If we wait out here, we might not see another vehicle for three days—or more."

"That tunnel would be protected."

"We'd freeze to death tonight."

Helen looked at the avalanche and at the truck.

"If we climb up in the back of the truck," she said, "up over the roof, we could get out on top of it."

"And if you slipped," he said, "you'd slide ten feet and then you'd fall a thousand feet straight down."

"It looks kind of flat up there on top," she said, "that one section right there above the truck. It's just forty feet to the other side."

Roger looked at Helen with more disbelief in his eyes than he really had in his heart. He knew it was the only way around, but he just didn't want to admit it.

"We don't know how stable that snow is packed," Roger said. "It could give out under our weight and flush you right off the side of this mountain."

Helen stood there realizing that the only way around the snow slide was to crawl across it to the other side of the road.

"Well, I should go first," she said. "I weigh less. It'd be less likely to give out under me than you. If I make it across and it looks like it'll wash out, I can just call back to you. I can head down into town. Maybe there I can get help."

Roger stood in the snow. He looked at Helen, at the dead boy in the truck, and at the truck half buried in the snow slide that blocked their path. His heart beat fast in his chest. He ran his fingers through his hair. His hair stood up wildly. The look in his eyes was a wild, exhausted dreadful sparkle.

"I'll do it," he said. "If the slide gives out, you'll have a clear road down into Ouray."

"No!" Helen said. "I'm not letting you—"

"And *if* I make it over," he interjected. "We know that you can make it over."

"There's a rope in the truck," she said. "We'll tie it around your waist."

Roger looked at her. He smiled, and she leaned forward and kissed him on the lips.

"For good luck," she said.

He smiled and took the rope from her. He tied a loop in the rope and wrapped one part under his left arm and the other part over his right shoulder. Helen started to tie the rope to the back of the truck.

"Maybe I should tie it to something else," she said.

Roger glanced around, but there was nothing substantial anywhere within the rope's reach.

"What about that rock up there?" Helen said.

Roger said, "Stand here and hold the rope; I'll see if it reaches."

Roger trotted up the road away from the snow mound, but he ran out of rope before he reached the rock.

"Is there any more rope?" he called.

Helen went and looked inside the cab. She checked behind the seats, but she knew there wasn't any more. She leaned back and shook her head.

"That's it," she said. "We could tie it to me."

"No," Roger said, coming back to her. "The truck will hold it just fine."

"Bullshit," Helen said. She glanced around the roadside, but there just wasn't anything to which she could tie the rope.

Roger tied the rope to the truck's bumper.

"Are you sure?" she said.

Roger stood up and looked at her with confidence.

"I'll be over before you know it," he said.

Roger tugged on the rope, and he saw that it was tight. He climbed up into the bed of the truck and looked at the snow slide buried over the front right part of the hood, up the windshield, up to the roof of the cab. His feet slipped on the snow-covered metal floor of the truck bed, but he managed to keep his balance and walked toward the cab roof and the avalanche.

• •

Roger placed his bare hand on the snow-covered roof of the cab. The metal was so cold it stung and turned the flesh of his palm bright red. It was damp and slippery.

I don't know about this, he thought.

He looked back at Helen. She stood just fifteen feet away, but that fifteen feet looked like the safe distance between life and death. Helen gave him an encouraging smile, a thumbs-up, and said, "It looks stable enough."

Roger smiled weakly. He turned back to the snow mound. He placed two hands up on top of the cab and scrambled up onto the roof of the truck. It was icy and slippery, and his boots created very little traction. He had to really concentrate just to *stand still* without sliding around.

He leaned forward onto the ice mound. The snow stung his bare hands. He pressed down on it tentatively, and the snow crunched down under the weight of his hands. He realized that it probably was not packed enough to support his weight. Even if it didn't wash clean off the side of the mountain, he would have difficulty walking across it because he would sink down deep with each step.

"I'm gonna have to crawl," he called. "It won't support my weight walking."

The metal on the roof of the cab made a deep metallic popping sound under his weight. Snow trickled down the avalanche in front of him in little tiny avalanches. He watched the snow roll down the slide from right-to-left, and then it poured over the side seven feet away. After that it vanished, and it didn't stop falling for a long, long time.

"Stay low on it," Helen said. "Place your weight evenly."

"Where did you say it looked flat?" Roger said. "Because from up here it looks pretty steep."

"You want me to go first?"

Roger looked back and saw her trying to look at him sincerely.

She said, "I will, you know?"

"I'll be alright."

He slid his arms out flat over the ice and snow. He lay flat on top of it, and immediately his chest began to feel the cold. He gripped the snow with his fingertips and slowly eased his legs out onto the ice. He crawled forward with his face hugging ice and snow, his feet at the lower end of the slide, less than five feet from the edge.

He glanced to his left and saw that he had about forty feet to go. Forty feet. Like crawling from one end of a house to the other. Easy.

Only this was sloped, slick, and icy, and if he slid to the end, the fall would be spectacular, straight down into an abyss.

"*Welcome to Colorado*," Roger whispered to himself.

• •

Helen stood there helpless. More than anything else in the world, she wanted to help Roger, but all she could do was stand there and hope that he made it safely over the snow mound. The feeling was helplessness undercut with a horrible self-pitying guilt that she had let him put his life on the line first, instead of the other way around. She stood ten feet away from the truck, which was partially buried in the mound. Roger had disappeared over the top and had vanished from her line of vision. She hated herself for letting him go, and her anger turned to bitterness at the whole situation.

God, she thought. And she just shook her head.

She watched small trickles of snow pouring over the side of the road. The snow fell down into the ravine as though in slow motion, just falling and falling and falling until it vanished into the white field with the rest of the snow that was falling from the sky.

Three minutes, she thought. *He'll be over it in three minutes, and then I'll have to climb over this thing.*

• •

Roger edged out farther onto the ice slide, now ten feet away from the roof of the truck. Very coolly, he lifted his head up and turned back to look at the roof. His heart sank into his stomach, for he realized he was doing it. He was out there. Out there where no one could help him or pull him back, or pat him on the shoulder and say, "Good game, kiddo. At least you gave it your best shot." Because this shot had to count. There was no second try. There was no Do Over. This was it. Failure, at this point, was death, and he was working his way across a slick and icy avalanche that stood between him and the rest of his life.

Fifteen feet out, he glanced down at his feet. He was digging his toes into the snow with each little step leftward across the snow slide. He took a deep breath, cleared his mind, and said, "Focus. You must do this. Keep your mind clear." He saw the constant fall of gentle snowflakes. Some caught on the ice mound and stuck. Others were beyond the ice mound, out in the ravine, and they seemed to fall with a muted promise that should *he* fall, his next drop would be a long one.

• •

Helen's knees felt a little weak. She didn't think she could do it. She knew she couldn't do it. Climb across this thing? Her nerves would freeze up.

She grimaced and looked at the orange and blue rope that trailed from the back end of the truck, up over the side of the snow mound, Roger's only lifeline should he fall.

She stood there, her eyes shooting from the ice mound blocking the road, to the truck with its driver-side door open, to the dead boy staring out from the passenger seat. And she remembered the leather satchel—Dr. Amy Levine's leather satchel. It was in the back of the truck cab behind the passenger seat. They would need it.

She looked up at the orange and blue rope on the white snow, to the open door just ten feet away.

"*Damn it*," she muttered.

She trotted to the open door and climbed up into the cab. Helen grimaced and reached around the boy feeling on the floor behind the seat. She felt the straps on the satchel and started to pull it up from the floor.

• •

Roger edged leftward another three feet, and found himself smack dab in the middle of the snow mound. And suddenly he realized how absurd their fear was that this thing might give out from under him. It was a huge chunk of ice and snow, whose total weight was probably more than ten tons. His body weight on its surface was proportionally as substantial as a gnat's on the back of a duck. He cleared his throat and continued onward.

Roger McAllister heard a deep rumbling from somewhere inside the ice mound.

Everything shifted.

He fell down two feet.

There was a sound of crumpling ice and snow pouring over the side of the cliff. There was a sound of wrenching metal from the truck buried somewhere under the ice and snow. And then everything caught, held, and the sound of snow pouring over the edge dissipated to a thin trickle, until there was only the sound of wind whipping through the ravine, the sound of snow flakes alighting on the mound, and the sound of Roger's truncated breathing.

He thought he heard Helen scream.

• •

"Oh, my God!"

Helen heard a horrible wrenching metal sound, and *everything moved.*

The weight of the snow on the front end of the truck drove the front end down, and the whole thing lurched toward the side of the road.

Helen saw empty air out the front window of the truck. Snow poured from the side out into the ravine. The truck made a wrenching, popping, metal sound like something made of steel underneath the truck had snapped. The dead boy fell forward toward the window, and Helen realized she was losing her balance.

"Oh, my God," she whispered, panicked.

• •

Roger's right cheek was flat against the ice and snow. He saw that he had about ten feet more to go. With only the movement of his eyes, he glanced down and saw that his feet were ten inches from the bottom edge of the slide. With his chest and right ear against the ice and snow, he could hear his heart beating inside the mound.

Ten feet. If he just leapt up, he could dive over and down onto the road. The only problem was *the leaping* would itself flush the ground out from underneath him.

He rose up on his hands, arching his stomach up off of the ice and snow, but his eyes stared at the edge on the left side of the mound.

McAllister leapt. He was in the air. He felt snow giving way underneath him. He saw the edge. He saw over the edge. He saw the white-powder-covered road fifteen feet beyond the edge.

McAllister roared, and he hit the edge, tumbled forward very quickly and rolled headfirst down the side of the slope.

There was a deep rumbling like thunder and then a bat-on-ball *crack!* And he realized the snow had broken, was rushing over the edge of the road, ten tons pouring out into the ravine, a waterfall of white ice and snow, roaring over the side of the road.

And he realized in a moment of absolute terror that he was tethered to the back end of the truck by one hundred feet of very strong rope.

"Ohhhh, shit," he cried out in slow-motion horror.

The rope whickered out away from him. He saw the flash of color as the truck was enveloped in the snow-white avalanche. He heard wrenching metal, and he realized that the truck was over the edge and descending down into the ravine.

And suddenly, he was plowing very quickly through the powder toward the edge of the cliff.

Thirteen
Snowmobiles

Levine, McKenzie, and Parker Walcott hit the door to the barn and fell forward into darkness. The snow drift at the door to the barn was six feet higher than the dry floor inside the barn, and they rolled down the white hill. They hit the ground and smelled sawdust, aged leather, hay and the lingering odor of manure mingled in the wheat-dry smell of hay. And there was something like gasoline there too, and the not-unpleasant fragrance of animal fur.

"Snowmobiles!" Parker shouted.

At the very back of the barn, there were two objects that wore green canvas tarps. They looked like snowmobiles. They ran to them and yanked the tarps up. Two sleek black Yamaha Mountain Max's shone in the dim light that reached through the barn's deepest shadows. They were painted black with dark blue detailing work, and a clear glass front window aerodynamically fanned back from the front. They looked powerful and fast, Levine leapt over one and checked the oil and gasoline levels.

"The tank is half full," she said. "How about that one?"

"We've got three-quarters a tank," Sara said. "How do you start this thing?"

"Electric start," Parker said. "Hit that red switch. Now press the start button."

Sara's snowmobile rumbled to life, a powerful, deft engine humming under the hood. She opened the throttle, and the engine roared.

"Gears are automatic," Parker said.

"Get on!" she said.

Parker climbed on the snowmobile behind Sara. He hooked his hands around her waist. She popped it out of neutral, and she steered the snowmobile toward the front door, working the gas and brake.

Levine pulled her snowmobile up beside McKenzie's. Parker and McKenzie looked at her. They were there inside the barn forty feet from the wide open front door.

"You lead the way," Sara said.

Levine crouched down behind her snowmobile's handlebars, looked hard through the glass window at the snow ramp, and she laid into the accelerator.

The snowmobile took off, racing headlong through the barn. Levine quickly approached, racing faster and faster. She stared through the glass window at the ramp, and then the snowmobile was up. It ramped up the mound.

Levine's Yamaha was up in the air. Levine saw the house, and white snow flashed underneath her. The snowmobile landed swiftly and raced out into the yard.

She got the snowmobile midway between the barn and the house, and she swung around. She saw the darkness inside the barn. The headlights on Sara's snowmobile lit up, her snowmobile roared, hit the snow mound, and was up in the air.

The snowmobile landed in a quick cloud of powdery white, and raced up to Levine. McKenzie swung the snowmobile around. She turned back to see the darkness of the open barn door, then she and Parker looked at Levine.

"Come on," Levine said. "We've got enough fuel to make it to Ouray."

And the two snowmobiles took off, racing across the endless white landscape.

Helen saw that the front end of the truck was completely over the edge at the side of the road. Snow trickled down over the roof, bounced off of the hood, and continued falling down into the bottomless field of white snow.

Helen slowly leaned back as much as she could in the seat. She turned her head to the right. Part of the avalanche had poured into the back of the truck, and that was anchoring the back end.

Helen turned her head slowly and looked to her left. The driver-side door was open, but what she saw first was bottomless space at the foot of the swung-open door. She leaned forward in the seat and saw the edge of the road three feet behind the door. The front end of the truck hung over the side of the cliff, its back end held down only because in that last shift, several hundred pounds of snow had poured into and over the bed of the truck.

She swung the leather satchel around. It flew out the door over bottomless air, and it hit the snow, skidding midway across the road.

Helen was going to have to jump from the side of the truck three feet back to the road. Three feet. Easy. Anyone with two legs can jump three feet. Except that if she slipped, here, she'd fall a long, long way.

She eased to the left in the seat and got her right foot out onto the running board on the side of the truck. The running board was pointed down into the ravine, and she would only be able to push off of it if she pushed herself up and away from the steering wheel with her right hand.

She crouched at the open door. Her right hand and arm like a brace between her and the steering wheel. With her left hand, she gripped the left side of the door. She tried to find something to grip with her left hand and so felt around outside the truck. There was nothing but the flat cold metal on the side of the truck. She looked straight down in front of her into the ravine; if she just fell forward she would fall straight down into the ravine. She might bounce off the side of the rock wall once or twice on the way down, but she would be in the air for a good six or seven seconds.

Helen leaned out away from the truck inch by inch. She held herself in the doorway with her hands. Gravity pulled her forward, but her feet were positioned on the running board and her hands gripped securely. She licked her lips, glanced to the left, took a deep breath, swayed back, and then started forward leaping.

The truck gave out from under her. And everything was pouring out away from the mountain. Helen was in mid-air—a horrible, unbalanced arms-flailing-at-empty-air midair flight. And then she hit the road. Snow covered her, and she rolled three times to her right away from the avalanche.

It was an enormous sound.

She glanced back and saw the truck roaring over the side. It scraped powerfully on the edge and then everything was out over the ravine. She saw the last flash of midnight blue as the truck descended wholly over the edge.

And she saw the rope. The orange and blue rope.

It was racing out over the edge tied to the back end of the truck. And, Helen realized, it was tied to Roger.

• •

Ten feet. Roger felt a sharp burning pain under his right arm, and his shirt filled with snow. The rope cut into his skin, and the edge of the cliff came at him very quickly.

Eight feet. He spat snow from his face and writhed right, then left, twisting and turning to free himself of the rope.

Six feet. His right arm shot forward.

Four feet. His hands burned cold in the snow, and the rope looped around his torso. There was a loud crack inside his shoulder. More snow.

Two feet. He struggled with the rope.

One foot. The rope roared past Roger's ears, over his head.

He'd gotten it around his shoulders and was free, but his momentum had carried him clear to the edge, and he clawed at the ground with his fingers. His body swung around so that his feet were out over the ravine, and for a wild moment his whole body was out over the ravine in the air, his fingertips clutching to the edge of the cliff.

He had hold of the very edge of the cliff. The momentum halted, and his body came back and slammed into the rock wall beyond the edge. He hung there for a moment that might have been forever.

There was a roar of snow and then nothing. No sound. No wind. No thought. No cold. Only light.

Then the physical world began to take hold, and Roger realized he was hanging onto the side of a cliff. His hands were cold, but he clutched a stone-gray rock. He glanced down at his feet and saw snow fall a long way below him. His feet dangled. *He* dangled.

He heard the sound of wind, felt snowflakes landing on his face, his head, his shoulders. He swallowed and glanced down at his feet. He reached his right hand around and felt nothing but cold rock. The slope was actually inverted into the mountain the first twenty feet, so he hung there in free air. His fingertips began to slip. He repositioned his grip. The rock was so cold. The muscles in his hands and wrists began to ache. The muscles in his fingertips burned. He held on as long as he could. His arms began to feel like thick lead pipes, and the burning quickly merged into numbing white-hot pain. Then, his right arm fell away. It was so numb he didn't even feel it fall away. He just looked and saw it and thought, *That shouldn't be there. That arm needs to be up there, holding onto the edge.*

But he was powerless. He tried to shake his right hand and felt ice-needle pinpricks of pain returning to his hand. *Some* feeling. He swung his arm up and re-gripped, but then his left arm fell away completely dead with pain and exhaustion. And he dangled there hanging from his numb right hand. He reasoned that he could probably hold on like that for maybe four minutes, five minutes tops, switching back and forth. But eventually his grip would slip.

His hand slipped.

His own grip wasn't enough.

He looked up and saw his hand as white as the snow all around him. His lips were dry, thin, pale. His blue eyes blinked once, and he knew that this was it. One more inhale, one more exhale, and he would fall.

He tried to swing his left arm back up, but it just hit the edge dumbly.

He gritted his teeth and held on for one more mind-numbingly painful moment. Then, he consciously let go of the edge. He started to fall.

Amy Levine tucked behind the glass window on her snowmobile and raced up into the mountains. She occasionally glanced back to see that McKenzie and Parker were with her. The snow continued to fall, but the snowmobiles were capable machines and Levine knew they would reach Ouray by midnight. Ahead she saw a stream, and she slowed down for the crossing. McKenzie and Parker pulled up alongside her.

"It's a stream," Levine called to them over the snowmobiles' engines.

Sara and Parker looked down the bank. Everything was white up to the water, but the creek itself was black under the cover of night with white-spotted rocks that jutted up high enough from the water's surface to collect snow. It was thirty feet from one side to the other.

Levine said, "I say we follow the bank up into higher country and find a place to cross."

They continued up higher along the high country creek racing along its bank. Eventually they reached the tree line, and the earth became a barren moonscape of massive white fields in front of them. The creek narrowed, and they found a place to safely cross. Levine eased her snowmobile down into the five-foot-wide creek and realized the enormity of the snow depth here. The snow at this altitude stayed year round and the chunk of ice and snow her snowmobile scaled down was easily thirty feet deep, enough snow to bury a building.

They forded the creek and continued up on the other side. The snowfall was steady, and they began descending along a ridgeline that was lined with steep rock walls. They were climbing down into a canyon.

The snowmobiles' headlights shone forward up through the snow and darkness, and Levine saw the trail that they were on winded around a hill to the left in front of them. The white path was literally carved into the side of the mountain by wind and erosion, and the snowmobiles crawled under a giant overhanging knob of mountain like a half-open tunnel.

On the right side of the path, they could see the drop-off was steep, but Levine realized they'd found their way onto an old mining road. It was just too clean to have been laid naturally, and she realized they were climbing down past Sneffels in the general direction of Camp Bird Mine, five miles southwest of Ouray. The sound of the snowmobile engines echoed off of the overhanging rock above them, and then the road came out from the rock and descended into a valley.

Levine saw the roofs of old mining shacks up ahead in the darkness, and she slowed down. McKenzie pulled up beside her.

The little ghost town looked peaceful. There were trees on either side of the snow-covered road, and the roofs of a few shacks stood up above the powder.

"Camp Bird," Levine said.

Sara and Parker looked at her. The snowmobiles crawled through the ghost town. They looked at the abandoned buildings standing peacefully in eight-foot-deep snow. Aspen trees swayed in the breeze, and the snowfall continued.

"We're about five miles southwest of Ouray," Levine said. "This road'll carry us down into town."

They continued on through the little ghost town and came out on a road that raced through aspen trees and climbed down into a steep ravine. There was a river over on the right, and they occasionally heard the rushing sound of waterfalls. The road climbed up into a stand of evergreens on the left and then carried forward through a forest for a half mile. Levine kept the speedometer on the snowmobile up around thirty-five.

They raced out on a ridge and saw the town down below them. The stretch of road they were on wound around to their left, but at the apex of the curve, they slowed down and looked down into the town.

SIXTEEN
GRIPPED

Something warm grabbed Roger's wrist. Something strong. He looked up and saw an arm extending over the edge of the cliff. Then another hand swung over the side and grabbed his arm. And then a face. Helen's face. Her gray-green eyes looked over the edge. She had him in her two hands. She grinned.

"I've got you!" she said.

"*Helen*," he gasped, breathless.

Her eyes became fierce, and he knew the intensity driving that stare would not let him go. She began to pull. His hands were up over the side, then his forearms up to his elbows, then his head and shoulders on up to his chest, and then it was just his waist and legs, and he knew he was going to make it. He swung his legs out to the right, up and over the edge, and he got his whole body up on the shelf above the cliff. Helen fell backward into the piles of snow, the remains of the avalanche. And Roger rolled over on his back. He heard her breath panting. He heard his own heartbeat. He looked up into the snow that continued to fall from the sky. The intensity of the relief was so great that tears formed in his eyes.

He lay there for a while listening to the wind and his own breathing.

"Some place warm," he heard Helen say.

He turned his head and looked into her eyes.

"Some place sunny," she said.

Roger nodded.

"When this is done," he said.

"I'm thinking Hawaii," Helen said. Helen looked at him. "What do you think?"

Roger said, "They call Maui the Valley Isle."

Seventeen
The Town

Ouray was covered in white and was about a thousand feet below the ridge Levine, Sara, and Parker were on. They could see the road continued on ahead of them up into evergreens. Levine watched a large clump of snow fall from the branches of one tree. It hit the ground beneath the tree with a deep powder sound.

"They're no lights on in the town," Levine said.

Parker said, "That guy at the Texaco said they'd ordered an evacuation. Power may be out."

All three looked down into the town. Even at this distance they could see the town had been hit with a serious snowfall. Snowflakes fell gently all around them, but down in the town it looked like the cars that had remained were buried in snow, and they could see the snow on the downtown streets had drifted up against buildings in steep fifteen-foot-high wind-driven drifts. The town looked magical, Levine thought. Magical and asleep; no one had stayed to weather out the storm. And the feeling was exhilarating to her that they may be entering a deserted Rocky Mountain town that was covered in deep white snow.

"Come on," she said.

They crossed two canyon bridges and felt the wind sweep over them, and then Camp Bird Road came right down into town from the southwest. The snowmobiles crawled around the corner of 3rd Avenue and Camp Bird, and they looked up and saw the Box Canyon Lodge buried in a drift of snow on its south side. The snow drift was literally up over the roof. On the north side, the parking lot was a field of deep pure white. There were no lights on inside, and Levine pointed at the street sign at the corner. The green street sign sat on top of the snow.

"That's about seven feet of snow," Levine said.

They continued forward into town.

The snowmobiles' headlights lit up deserted 3rd Avenue. They rounded the corner and saw the sign out front of the Best Western Twin Peaks. Snow in front of the motel had drifted up to the open-air second-

158

story walkway. It was so deep that they could have climbed over the rail from the second story and stepped off into the snow. If there were any cars parked in front of the building, they were completely buried under snow.

They could see the tops of the green awning out front of St. Elmo Hotel on the left side of the street. The entire first floor of the building was buried under snow, and the drift on the south side of the building was three-quarters of the way up past the second story windows, some twenty-five feet above normal street level. Levine just tried to take it all in. She was amazed.

They passed Gavito's Pizza and the Ouray Candy Company; both buildings were buried. On the south side of Gavito's, they could drive their snowmobiles right up to the edge of the roof. It swept down a few feet in front, but the whole building was buried under snow.

Levine slowed down at the corner of 6th and 3rd. Sara and Parker pulled up alongside her.

"We're gonna need snowshoes," she said. "If we step off of these snowmobiles, you're gonna sink down into ten feet of snow. There'd be no way to climb out of that."

"Ropes would be good, too," Parker said. "In case it does happen."

Sara said, "You know a place here in town we might could *find* snowshoes?"

"Ouray Mountain Sports is up on the left," Levine said. "You can see the sign out front of the building half-buried. We'll have to break in."

Snowflakes continued to fall gently on them, and they eased on up the street to the Mountain Sports shop, the snowmobiles humming deftly over the snow. They pulled up to the roof of the shop, and Levine killed her snowmobile's engine.

"How are we going to get in?" Parker said.

Sara killed the engine, and they sat there surveying the scene. Levine climbed up onto the seat of her snowmobile. There was snow on the roof of the building, but it wasn't as deep as the snow out at street level. A steady wind had kept it trimmed down, but it was still far too deep to walk through.

Levine climbed up on the roof. She sank down into the snow and laughed nervously. Parker craned his neck to watch her. The snow on the roof of the shop was only about four feet deep. It looked like a giant white chef's hat sitting on top of the building.

Sara looked north up Main Street. She watched the snowflakes swirling down from the sky. The snow had begun in earnest again, and thick flakes alighted on the street. She looked eastward from the shop. She could tell the streets climbed higher up into the mountains on the east side of Main Street, but the snow was falling heavily again, and she could only see a hundred feet or so.

Levine stumbled back over to the side of the roof near her snowmobile.

"There's no way down, that I can see," she said. "The snow's too deep."

Suddenly they heard something above the sound of the wind, beyond the sound of snowflakes landing on the landscape. It was a man's voice.

All three turned and looked up the street in the direction that they'd just ridden into town. And they saw the body of a man moving clumsily, coming to them through the falling snow. He was calling Levine's name.

Sara looked at Levine. She stared into the falling snow. Sara and Parker exchanged a glance, and Sara shrugged.

"Hello there!" the man called. "Dr. Levine! Dr. Amy Levine! Hello there!"

The man wore snowshoes. He looked comical hobbling down the street. He was a large man with wide shoulders.

"You know who that is?" Sara said.

Levine looked at her. "I have absolutely no idea," she said.

Parker said, "Well, at least we know we're not alone."

They saw a woman back there behind the man. She wore snowshoes, too, but she was taking greater care coming down Main Street.

The man rushed up to them, and Levine saw his blue eyes and her mind searched him out. She saw into his mind that he was from Michigan and that someone had sent him to find *her*. His name was . . . was . . .

"Roger McAllister," he said. "You're Dr. Levine, yes? I knew that was you! I've been searching for you for over a month. Your family hired me—"

Levine broke in, "My family?"

"Yes," he said. "Your father contacted my offices in Michigan."

"Mr. McAllister," Levine said. "I don't doubt that *someone* hired you to find me—"

"Your father," he said. "He is very concerned."

"Mr. McAllister, my mother and father died when I was six years old."

Levine glanced from Roger McAllister to McKenzie to Parker, to the woman walking up behind McAllister. She came from the snow.

"Helen?" Levine said.

"Amy?" Helen said.

"Helen?!" Levine said again. And she looked back at McAllister, then to Helen. "What in the world are you doing here?"

"We found your papers," Helen said, "The Colorado Sequence."

"And a friend helped us to locate this town," McAllister said, "through those papers."

Levine's eyes flashed back to McAllister's. "How did you two come here? Are you the only people in town?"

"We've been here since mid-afternoon," McAllister said. He looked at Sara and Parker. He smiled. "So far we haven't seen anyone else. The town is deserted."

"Where are you staying?" Sara asked.

Roger said, "We've just gotten into the Beaumont."

There was a flash in Levine's mind, and she felt something like a bolt of electricity strike her, a seizure.

Levine heard those voices she'd heard on Santana's Island inside the Reactor Core, the two janitors.

We did the stairs Tuesday.

Yeah, well, I swept them out on Wednesday, but they need *cleanin'. Let's finish up in Room Fourteen. And I'll do the stairs, if you start in on Fifteen.*

And there was an image in her mind. Levine saw the sharp image of a red door. It was at the end of a hallway. There were two doors on either side of the red door, but they were not painted red. There was an unnaturally bright line of light around the edges of the red door, as though something beyond the door was emanating a hugely powerful light.

"Dr. Levine?!" She heard the shouts as from far away.

She felt snow on her back, and she came to slowly. She realized she'd fallen into the snow on the right side of the snowmobile, but she was powerless to move. *Had she had a seizure?* She couldn't remember. Everything came at her in flashes. She felt dizzy yet completely at peace lying in the snow. They were gathered around her. Snowflakes touched down on her warm cheeks. Sara knelt there and shook her shoulder lightly.

"Are you okay?" Sara said. She looked up at the others gathered around. "She's coming to!"

Levine heard Parker say, "We need to get her inside, out of the cold."

Roger said, "We've just built a fire. I'll help you with her. Come on. It's warm inside the Beaumont."

Eighteen
The Hotel

Roger McAllister led the group one street block up to the Beaumont Hotel. Parker took Levine's snowmobile and held her between himself and the handlebars. Sara stayed right beside them, keeping a close eye on Levine. Roger and Helen led the group through the deep powder, their snowshoes helping them along over the snow.

"It took a few hours," Roger said, grimacing. "I hurt my shoulder earlier. But I was able to dig out a trench through the snow to the Beaumont's front door."

He looked back at Sara, Parker and Levine.

"We had just been inside," he said, "for about forty minutes, when I heard your snowmobiles outside."

Sara said, "Are there any phone lines open?"

"No," Roger said. "We checked the phones and power. I think the lines are down coming into town. There's no electricity, and there's no phone. But the gas stove in the kitchen works. We'll get you folks some food."

They came to a huge trench at the side of the hotel. Sara saw a bright blue snow shovel propped against one side of the opening. The trench was about five feet wide, and it descended down into the snow to the hotel's front door. It was dark, but she saw the flicker of firelight from inside the hotel.

The snow at the entrance was packed down, and it was clear that he had spent a lot of time working to dig out an opening into the hotel.

Parker and Sara parked the snowmobiles near the opening, and they both helped Levine off of her snowmobile. Helen went down into the trench inside the hotel. Roger stood there in the falling snow at the trench entrance. He made way for them to help Levine down inside the hotel. They carried her down into the trench, and Roger glanced around the street. The snow had begun in earnest again. He frowned and went down into the hotel.

163

There was a large fireplace over on the left side of the lobby. Helen stood there with several blankets at a sofa.

"Here," she said. "The sofa's pretty comfortable, and there's plenty of wood for the fire."

Parker and McKenzie helped Levine to the sofa. She sat down, said, "Thanks" weakly, and then reclined on the sofa. Helen gave her the blankets. Levine's face was pale.

"We lit candles around the hotel," Roger said. "There are boxes of them in the store room. Come with me to the kitchen. We were making soup."

They crossed the lobby and looked up a hallway on the left. There were a dozen candles lit along the hall. The candles stood on little antique tables.

Sara glanced back at Levine on the sofa. The firelight flickered and shone on her, and Sara felt a twinge of worry for her friend. She turned back and saw that Roger, Helen, and Parker were midway up the hallway, and she followed after them.

"How about water?" she asked.

Roger turned around. "Water works," he said. "Might be from a well here in town."

"Let's get her some water," Sara said. "I'm worried about her. I'm Sara, by the way."

Helen shook her hand and smiled. "Helen Richards," she said. "It's nice to meet you, Sara." She pointed up the candlelit hallway. "It's right up here."

They came around a corner and saw the dining area open up before them. There were twenty tables and a half-dozen lit candles. They could see the kitchen at the back of the dining room. The windows around the sides were buried under snow, providing no natural light from outside. The only light in the dining room and kitchen were from the candles burning throughout the two rooms.

They passed a fountain machine.

"Soda works," Helen said. "Coke, Sprite, Diet Coke."

They opened the swinging doors into the kitchen and saw the warmly lit candlelight around the room. There was a large industrial stove against the far wall, and Sara could see they had been cooking. There was a pot on the stovetop.

Helen poured Sara a bowl of soup in a blue ceramic bowl, and Sara carried the bowl and soda out into the lobby to Levine.

Levine was sitting up on the edge of the sofa, and she looked up at Sara when she entered the room.

"You're feeling better?" Sara said. She placed the soup and Coke on the coffee table in front of Levine. The others came into the room a minute later and joined them.

"I think I just fainted," Levine said. "I've never felt so exhausted in my life."

"We're under a lot of stress," Sara said.

Levine looked at her friend. Levine's eyes looked a little crazy.

"I've been in this hotel before," Levine said. "Here"—she pointed to her right temple—"I've seen these things before. Sara, on the island, we heard janitors speaking through Santana's speakers. I think this was the place."

Sara looked at her from a chair beside the sofa. The firelight lit up her face. Everyone took a seat and listened to the conversation.

"And the red door?" Sara said to Levine.

McAllister interjected, "You know about the red door?"

"How do *you* know about it?" Sara said.

Roger looked around the room into Parker, Levine, and McKenzie's eyes. He said, "On our way into town, we had an accident. We hit a boy. He was walking in the snow in the middle of the road. I think he was coming into town. He mentioned your name, Levine. He mentioned a red door. He said something about his father."

Helen said, "He said his father had the key."

"To the red door?" Parker said.

Helen and Roger exchanged a look.

Roger said, "He mentioned something about Kevorak's Needle."

"I thought he was praying, Roger," Helen said.

"I don't think so," Roger said. "I mean he might have been. But he mentioned a red door. He did say his father had the key. But I don't know if he meant the key to the red door, or to something else. He said to get the key to you, Levine. Those were his last words."

"The red door," Levine said, "must be somewhere inside this hotel."

Everyone looked around at each other.

"The red door's in this hotel?" Parker said.

"The janitors," Sara said. She looked at Levine. "We thought they were from within the Line, but they mentioned Room Fourteen. Do you think they meant Room Fourteen inside this hotel?"

Helen said, "I have your work here, Amy."

She stood up and crossed the room. In the candlelit shadows at the back of the room, there was a large table. On top of the table, Dr. Amy Levine's leather satchel stood. Levine saw it.

"The Colorado Sequence," she said. "You brought my work on the Line."

Helen carried the leather satchel to her. Levine took the satchel and removed its contents. Her papers reflected the flickering light from the fireplace, and everyone looked at her.

"What *is* the Line?" Roger asked. "I've heard this phrase. It's in your papers, Dr. Levine. Is there any way you can explain it, so that I'll understand?"

"I'll give it a shot," Levine said. "Just stop me at any point if it doesn't make sense."

"Okay," Roger said, energized.

"At the very core of our reality, scientists have found a thread. It exists beyond the subatomic level. Have you ever heard of String Theory?"

"I've heard of it," Roger said. "But I don't know really what it means."

"Well, think of it like this," Levine said. "The very texture of reality has an infrastructure, much the way that if you looked at the thread of a blanket under a microscope, you could single out individual threads that compose what the naked eye sees as a single thread. And that single thread is only one of hundreds of thousands of threads that are all interwoven to make this blanket."

She held the blanket up. There was one loose thread protruding from a corner. She held it up, broke it from the blanket, and looked at it in the firelight.

"The very texture of reality as we see it is composed of an inner fabric," Levine said. "We look at empty space, and you don't see anything. It just looks like empty air. But there's actually matter beyond the subatomic level that comprises the space we see between us and the fireplace. It holds reality together, and at the same time it pushes it apart. Its energy acts on our world and in our universe in a number of ways: light and gravity are two pieces of reality's puzzle. But what causes gravity to be? What causes light to exist—at the very core, in a fundamental way—why are we able to see light, to experience gravity? Its being, the fact that *it is*, forms the basis for my work on the Line."

"I don't understand," Helen said. "What *is* the Line?"

"The Line is the very core of reality," Levine said. "At our reality's most fundamental level, there is a single line. It courses through everything, *all matter* in the universe, one infinitely long thread that weaves and interweaves to produce the very fabric of our reality, to create the blanket that is our walls, our plants, our planets, our stars, a piece of wood—that we can *see* this sofa, that we have *an awareness* of it, that we experience life rather than not experience it is a result of the Line's presence at the core of our reality."

"What exactly is the Colorado Sequence?" Parker said.

"Well, as you can imagine," Levine said. "We don't see all of the Line. We only experience a small portion of it. The work that I began in Arizona started as an interesting mathematical game—nothing more. I started by charting the one thousand highest peaks in North America mathematically."

"Like mountain peaks?" McKenzie said, fascinated.

"Like mountain peaks," Levine said. "Exactly. Of course the highest peak in North America is Denali in Alaska, and the highest point in the contiguous United States is Mount Whitney in California."

They all listened closely.

"What I found," Levine said, "was one of the most interesting coincidences I've ever seen in the natural world. I just thought it would make an interesting fixed-system study to see how proportionally divided the highest peaks in North America were. You know, where do you find the greatest cluster of high peaks and then what are their relationships to one another."

"The Rocky Mountains, right?" Helen said.

"Yes," Levine said. "The Rocky Mountains. Specifically Colorado. What I found was an interesting system with a large conglomeration of peaks spaced at somewhat random intervals from one another. No big deal, right? What's so special about that. Got a lot of peaks here in Colorado, Central Mexico, Alaska, The Sierra Nevadas, and British Columbia.

"Well, one day I charted the peaks spherically," Levine said. "I took a three-dimensional map and made it into a globe. When I did this, I found the thousand highest peaks were proportionally distanced from one another the exact same way that the thousand brightest stars are spaced from one another in the evening sky. It was like a mirror reflection."

"Impossible," Parker said.

"Impossible, yes," Levine said. "But it's the way that it is. There is an underlying order to our universe, as beautiful and elegant as the greatest symphony ever written, more eloquent than a Shakespearian play. And it's right there in front of us. It's our reality. The best that we can hope for as humans, as artists, as scientists, is to live true to the reflection that surrounds us and flows through us. We are a part of it. Our time is now. And we can smile into the darkness and know that we are not alone.

"I was twenty-three years old at the time. And it was my first experience with the Line, a beautiful symphony of life on a level that most of us will never see in our lifetimes."

Nineteen
The Explorer

Levine woke some time before four o'clock in the morning and saw Roger snoring in a chair. The fire in the fireplace had settled into a deep, red bed of embers, and Levine stood up and crossed to it. She placed three split logs on top of the coals, and a minute later a crackling fire was ablaze once more. She stood by the fire, and she looked around the lobby.

It was very peaceful and still. Sara was asleep on a sofa, and Parker sat snoring in a large recliner with a blue blanket pulled up to his chin. Helen had found the room keys behind the check-in counter, and she had taken a room two doors down the hallway. Levine stepped out into the center of the lobby and looked up the candlelit hall.

Levine peeked in Helen's room and saw Helen asleep on the bed. Levine was sleepy but interested in exploring the hotel. She took a candle from atop one of the tables in the hallway, and she walked back up into the lobby. Parker was still snoring.

Helen had found the hotel's master key, and they had agreed to leave it on the check-in counter. Levine crossed the lobby, picked up the key, and headed on up the hallway at the other end of the hotel, the end no one had yet explored.

There were rooms along the hallway. The room doors were painted white, and there were three chandeliers along the ceiling of this first hallway. Levine could see that the hallway branched off into two, making a Y shape, about forty feet ahead.

She glanced up both hallways. The hallway on the left looked like it led to more rooms. Along the hallway on the right she saw photographs and pictures all along the walls. She held the candle up and walked slowly, looking at the black-and-white photographs on the walls. The photographs gave a pictorial history of the hotel.

Smiling faces from as far back as 1891 smiled out from the walls. There were photographs of celebrities from nearly every decade of the 1900s. There was a photograph of President Eisenhower and Bing

Crosby. A photograph of John Wayne with a group of friends on the *True Grit* movie set. Levine held the candlelight up to the photographs and continued up the hallway.

There were photographs from around town, a black-and-white pictorial history of Ouray itself. One photograph in particular caught her attention near the end of the hallway. It was the picture of a young kid, a teenager. He was standing beside an old Volkswagen Beetle, leaning against it, and his arms were folded in front of him. The way he looked into the lens at whoever was taking the picture was enchanting.

Levine stared at the photograph for several minutes.

She glanced up at the end of the hallway. There was an open room, and Levine continued to it. There was a chessboard on one side of the room. It was set up in such a way that it was the focal point on that side of the room. There was a television in an oak cabinet beyond the chessboard in the corner. The whole room was surrounded on all sides with elaborate bay windows, but the windows gave onto a wall of blank white snow.

On the other side of the room, there was a leather sofa, chairs and a fireplace. A ceramic bowl stood atop a stone-slab-topped coffee table, and there were knickknacks in the bowl. There were book shelves loaded with aged leather-bound volumes that looked as though no one had touched them in years. There was a copy of Stephen King's *Thinner* atop a stack of paperbacks on a table against one wall. There were other popular paperbacks on the table that looked equally worn, but Levine's eyes were drawn to a spiral staircase that rose up in one corner of the room to a little door that looked more or less fashioned *into* the wall twenty feet above the floor.

Levine crossed the room, the candle held out in front of her. She placed her left hand on the black iron railing of the spiral stairwell and began to climb. The stairwell was narrow, only about two feet wide, and it climbed up very quickly. It rotated three times before stopping abruptly at the door.

The door was painted white, and the aged brass doorknob looked like it would open with a skeleton key. Levine glanced back down to the floor of the room and realized she was pretty high up. She placed her hand on the doorknob and gave it a jiggle. It was locked.

She knelt down a little and looked closer at the knob. Suddenly, a flash of light poured out of the keyhole from the other side of the door. It shone out like a ray of light. Levine knelt down and looked through it, and the light vanished. She looked through the keyhole again, but it was dark on the other side.

"What in the world?" she said to herself.

She tried the doorknob again, kneeling there, peering through the keyhole. She leaned her eye right up to the hole and gave the knob a jiggle.

Locked.

She knelt there a moment more waiting to see the flash of light again while trying the knob, but the light didn't reappear and the knob was definitely locked. Finally, her knees began to ache, so she stood up.

The flash of light reappeared, pouring out of the keyhole about a foot in front of the door. Levine dropped down and looked through the keyhole again. The light vanished before she could see through the hole, and all was darkness beyond the door.

The light poured out of the keyhole again. Levine turned the doorknob a little more furiously than she had meant to. It was locked. She pounded on the door with the flat of her hand.

But there was no answer, except silence. Levine heard the brush of wind outside the hotel, but inside there was no sound at all. She dropped down to her knee, and the light vanished again. It was pure darkness beyond the keyhole. Levine could see nothing. She gave the doorknob another jiggle, called out, "Come on! Open the door!" and knelt there silently.

She thought she heard whispering, but it might have just been the wind. She leaned her ear up to the door and listened through the door. The whispering sound was a steady commotion, not one single voice distinctly. It was like she was listening to a busy street scene, or a baseball stadium packed with a crowd, but with its volume reduced to a thin whisper.

"*My goodness,*" Levine said.

She looked through the keyhole again and saw nothing but darkness. She started to feel uneasy. She stood up and stepped back away from the door, two steps down the spiral staircase. She held the candle in her hand, and she suddenly realized that if the candle went out she would be thrust into utter darkness. And as if responding to her fear, the candlelight sputtered and almost went out. She cupped her hand up around its flame.

The candle caught, steadied, and its light grew brighter. Levine stared at the door a moment more, and then took a few steps back down the stairwell. She got midway down the spiral staircase, stopped, and looked back up at the door. Her brow furrowed with worry. She just shook her head, turned, and continued down. She was on the last step, when the door popped open, its latch magically slipped.

Her right foot was in mid-stride, about to step onto the floor, but her hand grabbed the railing and she swung around. Her eyes went to the door.

It creaked open very slowly, and Levine stood there at the base of the spiral staircase. The door was open.

The shine of her candlelight reached just beyond the now-open door, and Levine craned her neck to see up above the level of the door's floor, but from the base of the spiral stairwell she could not see very far into the doorway. And it was darkness beyond.

She turned and started back up the stairs.

"Hello?" she called into the black void beyond the door.

The door creaked open a few inches wider.

She reached the top of the stairs and peered through. There was a hallway beyond the open door. The floor was hardwood, and the candlelight brightened the first ten feet or so.

"Is anybody there?" she called.

Her voice echoed, giving an indication that the length of the hallway was great. It sounded like a well, a water well with a hand-cranked bucket. The walls right inside the doorway were wooden, but the acoustics gave her the impression that somewhere ahead in the darkness, the walls turned to stone or concrete. Levine held the candle up and stepped through.

There were two filing cabinets just inside the doorway, one on the right side and one on the left. Levine grazed her hand over the surface of the one on her right and felt it thick with dust. She held the candle up and continued on ward.

The hallway continued for about twenty meters and then came to a flat wall. There was a table at the end of the hallway, and a book was on the table. A flight of stairs descended to the right. Levine held the candle up and peered down. She saw that the stairs and the walls along the stairs were all made of stone. She glanced back at the book on the table. It was huge, more than three thousand pages, and it was open to page 1,177. Levine looked at the writing on the pages.

There were handwritten names written like a guestbook, but the writing was all done in the same penmanship. The penmanship was a beautiful calligraphy as in some medieval text. Levine leaned closer and saw the names and the dates written beside the names.

Melvin Woodall—May 23, 1964

Horace Grain—October 25, 1972

Martin Sumter—April 7, 1982

Angela Vazquez—December 22, 1984

Aria Richfield—November 10, 1994

Pamela Hearthstone—February 8, 2003

Pamela Hearthstone was the last name recorded in the book. Levine turned the pages forward. The rest of the book was blank. She flipped back before page 1,177, opening to page 809. The page was filled with names.

Brigh Morrigan—1008

Fianna mac Morna—1011

The names sounded Gaelic, and the dates shocked her. The paper seemed new, in mint condition. Levine turned the page back and saw that the dates went back to 4,323 B.C. (on page 203) near the front of the book, but the first two hundred pages were written in symbols too archaic for Levine to understand and so the earliest names may have been much, much older. She held the candle up and glanced down the stone stairwell to the right.

"Hello?" she called.

Her voice echoed for a long time as though descending far down into the earth. She glanced back at the open door that led to the spiral stairwell and the chess room. The door remained open, and she thought for a moment of retreating back to the chess room, back into the hotel to her friends. But then she heard something down the cobblestone stairwell.

It sounded like rushing water, but it was very faint. Her head tilted to one side curiously, listening to the sound.

"Hello?" she called. Again, there was no response.

Then Levine began to search the corridors with her mind. She relaxed herself and sensed the space down there. She felt something like rushing water, and she saw green grass. There was a waterfall, and a boat pulled up onto the bank of a stream.

Levine exhaled and opened her eyes. She knew what was down there, down that cobblestone stairwell. She glanced back at the doorway one last time, held the candle up, and proceeded deeper into the depths of the hotel.

She had made it perhaps twenty steps down the stairwell when she saw a window on the left wall. The stairwell was a winding stairwell, but its curvature was much broader than the spiral stairwell back in the chess room. Levine held the candle up, and she saw that the window was too dirty to see through. She pulled the cuff of her sleeve over her hand and wiped it clean.

It looked like some kind of store room in there. She saw canned goods stacked in wooden cabinets, but it was very difficult to see. She continued down the stairwell for another twenty steps or so, and she came to another window. She wiped the window clean and peered through. It was some kind of servants' quarters. There were bunks inside, and she saw a porcelain wash basin. There were clean white towels draped beside the wash basin, and she saw a bar of soap. She caught her reflection in a mirror above the basin and continued farther down the stairwell.

The sound of rushing water was much clearer now, and she was surprised to realize there was a light up ahead. She glanced at the stone walls inside the stairwell and saw the light brightening with every few steps. Beyond the light, the stairwell came to an end.

At the foot of the stairs, there were three hallways branching out: one to the right, one straight ahead, and one to the left. Levine stood there at the base of the stairs. The light came from the left, but she could not see its source. The sound of water came from the right. The hallway straight ahead provided neither light nor any noticeable sound.

She turned toward the light and called, "Anybody there?"

There was no reply. She stood there a moment, deciding which way to go.

She held the candle up in the direction of the hallway straight ahead, and she shook her head. She looked to the left, to the light, raised her left index finger, and then swung around toward the sound of the water. She proceeded up the hallway to her right, into darkness.

The hallway continued for about one hundred meters, and the roar of water grew louder and louder. Toward the end, she could feel moisture in the air. The cobblestone flooring became damp and slick, and then suddenly she entered a room that led to an underground river.

Levine held the candle up and saw a rocky river about thirty meters across. The cobblestone walkway led straight down to the water, and there was grass *in the room* near the bank. It was as though the building had given onto an underground cave.

She looked to the left as far as she could see with the candlelight. It sounded like there was a powerful waterfall up there, perhaps twenty or thirty feet above a pool, but she could only see the faintest outlines of the sparkling water. There was a boat down on the bank, and Levine saw a paddle in the boat.

She walked down to the boat and kicked it lightly with her left foot. It was a wooden canoe. Levine held the candlelight up and looked to her right. It looked like the underground river smoothed out beyond the rocks right in front of her, but it was difficult to see very far.

She knelt over and pushed the boat out a little bit. It was light enough for her to move, and the front end of the canoe floated. It seemed watertight. Levine started to put one foot in the canoe, and the candle teetered in her hand and almost went out.

I need a flashlight, she thought. And she stepped back up away from the boat and the river. The candlelight grew brighter, and Levine looked around the cavernous walls. *Perhaps the river comes out in the mountains*, she thought. She could smell the algae-like fragrance in the air, and she realized that it was warm here. The air temperature was probably in high eighties, and with the humidity, it felt warmer than the inside of the hotel.

"Try the other way," she said to herself.

She left the room and started back up the hallway in the direction that she'd seen the light. She reached the foot of the cobblestone stairwell that led back up to the chess room and into the hotel, and she stopped. She glanced to her right, up the hallway straight out from the foot of the stairs. She looked straight ahead, up the hallway that contained that source of light.

And she pointed in the direction of the black hallway with her index finger and her hand began to shake as though it were a dousing rod. Her eyes widened and she felt something pulling her hand forward, in the direction of the light.

She started up the hallway toward it. Thirty meters along, the corridor split in three directions. In the center, there was a table with a vase of fresh flowers on top of it.

"What in the world?" Levine said.

The flowers glowed. There were purple flowers, red flowers, white flowers, and Levine crossed to them.

She reached her left hand forward to touch them. The flowers were bioluminescent and glowed colorfully. Levine touched a purple flower and felt a chill go through her. She shivered. It felt like a tingling electrical sensation went through her, and she set the candle on the table and picked up the vase. The flowers glowed pleasantly, and Levine held it up and moved around the room. It was a better torch than the candle.

She held the vase away from her and really inspected them. They were beautiful flowers, so filled with life. She held them up and looked up the three branching hallways. And suddenly her mind started to reach out down the hallways. The light from the colorful flowers was very bright, but her mind saw three doors. They were side by side in a room, and Levine could see an intensely bright light pouring around the door frame's of the two doors on the right. The light coming from around the doorframe was so bright, it cast enough light to see the third door on the left. There was no light around the door on the left.

And Levine knew that these doors were up one of the three hallways there before her. She just had to choose: right, left, or straight ahead. She thought about it a moment, and went straight ahead, carrying the vase of bright flowers.

• •

The three doors were in a room at the end of the hallway. The floor was smooth and moist and echoed her footsteps, and just as she'd foreseen, from the two doors on the right poured a very bright light. The door on the left was painted red. Apple red.

The two doors on the right were painted white, and each door had its own number. The door on the left—the red door—had a "1" on it. The door in the middle was marked with a "2." And the door on the right was marked with a "3." The numbers were shiny and silver, each figure about seven inches tall.

There was a table in the middle of the room, and centered in the middle of the table was an aged parchment. Levine held the glowing flowers up and looked at the parchment. She read it.

<blockquote>
Two doors giveth unto Death, but the 3rd shall leadeth to Kevorak's Needle. Beware the obvious choice, for it may proveth your last.
</blockquote>

Levine said, "Beware the obvious choice? Which one is the *obvious* choice? The red door?"

She stepped back from the table and held the glowing lighted flowers up. She walked over to Door 3 on the right. There was some kind of supernatural light pouring from around the door's frame, as though something on the other side was emanating a hugely powerful light. It was the same as she'd seen in the keyhole, but this light shone all the way around the doorsill. She looked at the shiny silver "3," and it seemed to flicker as though winking at her.

"*Hmmmm,*" she said.

She started to reach her hand forward toward the doorknob. The knob was an elaborately fashioned unicorn of meticulous craftsmanship. Levine touched the tip of the unicorn's horn, and then eased her hand around it. She realized that it opened like a slot machine. Just pull the lever *and maybe, you'll burn in Hell for the rest of eternity!* Levine shivered and stepped away from Door 3.

She approached Door 2. Like Door 3, Door 2 had a powerful light pouring around its edges as though something very bright was on the other side of the door. Instead of a unicorn doorknob, Door 2's knob was a wild boar. It had savage-looking tusks and appeared in mid-stride as though gallantly leading a boar group.

She touched the boar's snout and realized that Door 2 also opened like a lever.

Levine shivered again and stepped away from the door. She approached Door 1, the red door. Compared to Doors 2 and 3, Door 1 was very plain. The doorknob was a cheap, plain round knob. Its fake brass color looked chipped and used. It looked worn, as though no one had taken care of it. There was a dent in it, and it looked pitiful compared to the beautiful knobs of Doors 2 and 3. The door itself was painted bright red like an apple.

Levine looked at the pitiful "1" which looked tarnished and cheap. And it was bent! Levine leaned close and saw that the number was made of cheap tin, and someone had pulled it back a little from the surface of the door, or perhaps it had just been made that way—warped! It was a sad looking number, compared to the shiny silver numbers of Doors 2 and 3.

Levine reached her hand forward to touch the knob. She felt nothing when she touched it. It was just room temperature warm, boring and unexciting. It reminded her of a bathroom knob in an apartment that she'd stayed in back in college. Cheap.

Levine stepped back out into the middle of the room.

"Beware the obvious choice," Levine whispered while inspecting each door from the middle of the room. "Beware the obvious choice. What does 'obvious' really mean?"

If either of the three *was* obvious, as literally defined, it was the two doors on the right, the fancy doors, because they were more evident and clear. They were the more remarkable of the three doors. They shone with light, whereas the red door did not shine. It was dull looking, boring and plain, so in that sense Doors 2 and 3 *were* the obvious choice.

She crossed over to the table and looked at the parchment once again.

Levine read the words aloud, "Two doors giveth unto Death, but the third shall leadeth to Kevorak's Needle. Beware the obvious choice, for it may proveth your last."

She looked from Door 3, to 2, to 1 and she calmed herself, cleared her mind, and began to reach out to the right answer. She stood there in the center of the room with her mind perfectly clear and realized without a shadow of a doubt that the correct door was Door 1.

Levine approached the door, placed her hand on the cheap doorknob and turned. The knob rotated in its socket, and the latch came free. Levine started to push the door open. Her eyes followed the widening seam as the door pushed farther away from the doorframe, opening onto a vast dune-filled desert.

Levine's brown-blue eyes looked through the doorway with amazement. She immediately saw three moons in a periwinkle sky, the lowest of the moons huge and hovering just beyond the horizon.

She realized the door opened out onto a tall hill of sand some three hundred feet high, and the view from the top of the hill was vast. There was nothing but fine white sand in either direction as far as she could see, but she stood there inside the room afraid to step through the portal into that world.

She glanced back behind her in the room. She saw the parchment on the table. She glanced at the two doors to her right. She turned and set the glowing lighted flowers on the table beside the parchment, turned and pushed her fingertip through the door.

Her finger and then her hand went through the doorway and the desert image rippled as though she'd placed her hand inside a pool of water. The ripples continued lightly out toward the edge of the door, and the feeling in her hand was one of pleasure. It felt warm and inviting, and she withdrew her hand skeptically.

She looked at it, and saw a shimmer of white electrical water drops drip from her hand back through the doorway. The drops of white light made a light sound like synthesized musical triangles as the different-sized drops met with the surface beyond the door; it was a very soothing sound, peaceful, and pleasing.

"*Amazing*," she whispered to herself, and she smiled in wonder at the desert on the other side of the door.

TWENTY
AMBER

Amber Page stood in the training room with a sandstone cloak pulled over her bowed head. Her hands were folded together in front of her, invisible in the adjoining sleeves of her robe. Her eleven-year-old feet were bare on the cool dusty floor of the room, and across the room, a coral stone floated inside an octagonal glass cylinder. The coral stone sensed her presence and reacted accordingly to every thought and every movement she conveyed, but for the moment, Amber's mind was clear and the coral stone floated peacefully inside the glass cylinder.

Amber had sensed a disturbance in the Line. It had grown for weeks like a gripping anxiety, and she'd had restless nights tossing and turning until the predawn hours. The unease had grown more intense with each passing day, and fourteen days had passed since grandmaster Sara Barnes had visited her here at the edge of the Great Radian Desert.

Amber's head slowly rose up from its bowed position. Her hands came from the folds of the robe in front of her, and she calmly removed the hood from her head. Her brown eyes shone with purity, and she smiled at the hologram image of herself that poured out of the coral stone. The hologram image was almost an exact mirror image of herself, but it was not completely exact. When Amber was dishonest or idle, the image made bolder stronger moves and she knew it would attack her without mercy. But when her mind was clear and her heart was truthful she could compete equally with the blue-green hologram. And in blinding moments of pure white light, her mind had the capacity for true creativity and original thought, and those were the moments she had to capitalize on when sparring with the hologram.

Amber removed her cloak. She held it in front of her and then eased her right hand forward in a basic T'ai Chi movement. The cloak floated across the room while she meditated, and it floated to the rack on one wall inside the training room.

The hologram smiled and moved to the center of the training floor. Amber smiled and moved almost the exact same way toward the center of the room. It was difficult to tell who was mirroring whom. Amber bowed before the green-blue hologram image of herself, and the hologram bowed an equal response.

Amber inhaled deeply through her nostrils, exhaled, and then thrust her right hand forward with a bright flash of light. The hologram swung its right arm around blocking the offensive thrust and leapt quickly to the right.

Amber ducked and swept her right foot across the floor. The hologram leapt up over her leg, and Amber popped up and did a backward somersault in the air. She landed cat-like on two feet, poised with her hands held in front of her. The hologram had advanced too aggressively, and Amber thrust the heel of her right hand forward and struck the hologram solidly in the sternum.

There was a flash of light at contact. The hologram groaned and fell backward onto the floor. Amber exhaled, folded her hands together in front of her, and bowed at the fallen hologram.

The hologram nodded its head, and leapt up onto its feet. It dusted itself off and began to circle Amber, who was still bent over bowing. Amber's eyes were closed, but she followed the hologram's presence with her mind. She *felt* it.

The hologram panicked and attacked the bowed Amber in an unwisely aggressive flurry of punches. Amber's head remained bowed, but her arms flashed out from her, meeting each of the hologram's punches with seemingly no effort. Amber remained rooted in place, but the image attacked her furiously. Each of its punches was met and defended, until the hologram leapt powerfully up into the air in a solid aerial roundhouse kick that Amber struck out to meet with her left arm.

The hologram's right leg met Amber's left arm in a blinding flash of white light. And then Amber was up in the air attacking the hologram with a series of punches too quick to follow with the naked eye. Amber spun around in a reverse roundhouse and landed a direct kick to the hologram's right shoulder.

The hologram groaned.

And Amber continued on the offensive. The fighting was fierce for a minute, each member firing quick deft punches and kicks that were met with equal defense by its counterpart.

At one point the hologram leapt *through* Amber, and Amber had to spin around quickly and duck backward like a bow to avoid the hologram's swinging right hook. Amber rotated in air, and her feet pinned the hologram and spun it furiously to the ground. They were both on the dusty floor a moment. Amber leapt quickly to her feet, but she was slower by just a fraction of a second than the hologram image of herself, and the hologram nailed her across her left jaw with a powerful, quick hook. Amber saw stars and fell to the dusty floor with a groan, the wind knocked out of her.

The hologram faded and was taken back into the coral stone, and Amber came to a moment later. Her right hand came up to her jaw and felt the soreness already forming there. She opened her eyes and looked at the coral stone spinning smoothly inside the octagonal glass cylinder. She got to her feet, dusted herself off, and bowed in its direction. It flashed a warm, soothing bright light; it was like a handshake across a tennis net following a well-played set.

Amber Page missed her family.

• •

Amber took a glass of water out into the shade outside her home. The adobe complex was perched on the side of one enormous dune that rose a thousand feet above the desert valley. There were seven palm trees around the house, and there was a pool in the front yard among the trees. She took the glass of water into the shade and stood at the pool. A breeze swept over the surface of the pool, cooling her. She looked down the hill far across the valley to Vortex Hill on the far side of the valley. She watched the moons above the horizon to the north.

A large fish broke the surface of the pool, sending rippling swirls outward. Amber sat down on her Darpi pad beside the pool. The air was cool and dry, and the steady breeze rustled the leaves of the palm trees. Amber placed the water beside her, folded her legs Indian-style and began to meditate.

She had had visions since she was a young child, but it was not until her coming together with the coral stone that she first began to master her skills. At first her parents did not know what to make of their daughter. Her parents had their own problems, and they constantly argued and fought over what was the "right way" to raise her. They had no idea who she was. She was just a "little girl" who could move things with her mind, and her ability had been so odd, her father had once called her a "freak." But she loved him.

She knew that despite his flaws he was just afraid. He was afraid of his own mortality and his own perception of himself as meaningless. Amber's father saw his daughter as the one opportunity he had to do something right in this world, to be better than everyone else. People in the community had called her father a drunk, said he "drove her" too hard, and she believed it herself, until her mother and father died six months apart when she was nine years old.

Her mother died first, and they had so little money when her father died that the county had had to pay for the burial. Amber had already been seen by a number of psychologists in the two years before they died because she had an ability to foresee things that had not yet happened. She had the ability to move objects with her mind. And she could fight.

She learned T'ai Chi quickly, and four months after her father died she was visited one night by a woman who called herself "a friend." Grandmaster Sara Barnes had never worked with a child before, let alone *the* child, the young girl that prophets had foreseen in the stars. Young Amber Page was only ten years old, when grandmaster Sara Barnes had shown her another world inside the world she had always seen and heard and counted as reality. And she taught Amber to fight.

Amber's fighting skills were unprecedented, and Sara Barnes had shown her to *her* elders, and the elders did not know what to make of such incredible talent within the Line at such a young age. She was beyond the greatest minds that humanity had ever known, and she was not yet eleven years old.

Her rage and her bitterness at her family had driven Amber so deep within herself that no one could touch her. Grandmaster Sara Barnes had led her into the Great Radian Desert and had helped her to build her own home on a small oasis at the edge of the desert. She'd taught Amber how to grow corn and milk goats, how to subsist on nothing more than the air she had to breathe. And slowly over time, young Amber began to channel her anger and her profound bitterness in more positive, healthy ways.

Amber Page began to realize her destiny.

Legend passed through an ancient book known as *The Oracle* that twelve warriors would come together—each under a zodiacal sign—in order to save humanity at a crucial moment in history. Grandmaster Sara had told Amber over a glowing campfire that she, Amber Page, was the first of these twelve warriors to realize her place, to realize her destiny within the Line. Sara had slowly begun to teach Amber the ethics and responsibility that such a gifted position required of her.

The training had been slow, lonely, and Amber suffered under the isolation. But her training was nearing completion, and Amber knew she could handle herself in a fight. But no one had fought, and Amber began to think that Grandmaster Sara Barnes had left her out here in the desert as some cruel joke. Grandmaster Sara Barnes's visits had grown more infrequent in recent months, and Amber began to doubt in her mentor. Amber was no longer *just* an apprentice in her own mind, and she desired more respect and attention than she was being given.

It had been two weeks since she'd last seen grandmaster Barnes—since she'd last seen *anyone*—and Amber was lonely.

Amber's eyes watched the pool, but her mind felt something stirring, some faint sound so inaudible as to warrant it being her imagination. She followed one large fish with her eyes. It swam near the surface of the pool, almost gliding underwater, sensing movement just beyond the surface. There was a bright flash of light. Amber's head jerked up and on pure instinct she leapt up into the air, floating.

On the water, the large fish broke the surface and snapped back down onto the water with its catch, and Amber looked across the desert to the top of Vortex Hill.

Amber floated there a foot above the ground, poised in fight position, and she realized something had opened the portal. She came back down to the ground.

She stood there looking far across the valley. There was a bright rectangle burst of light, as bright as the sun. It was a perfectly shaped rectangle door. It stood there atop the massive white sand dune, and Amber realized someone, or something was stepping into the world.

"Rusty!" she called.

A horse responded from around the side of the house with a loud neigh and came galloping up to the side of the pool. She leapt up into the air with a spin and landed on Rusty's back.

"Rusty, take me to the light!" she said.

Rusty took off down the hill with Amber on his back.

He was a beautiful horse, powerfully built, and he was as loyal as any animal Amber had ever known. He carried her swiftly down the dune, then across the valley, and on up Vortex Hill toward the shiny door of light.

They approached the light, and Amber slid off of Rusty's back, down onto the sand. The rectangle of light was about thirty feet away. Amber shielded her eyes with her hand and approached the light slowly.

She saw a hand emerge from the light. The hand was like pure light, like some liquid hand reaching out from a bright pool, and it moved around with a sense of wonder. And then it retracted back into the light.

"Wait!" Amber called to it. "Don't go!"

The hand returned and scooped at the air as though gathering a handful, and it disappeared back into the bright rectangle of light.

Amber stood there only a few feet away from the light. She glanced back at Rusty who had taken several cautious steps back away from the light. He whinnied nervously.

"It's okay, Rusty," Amber said. She turned back to the light.

Her mouth dropped open a little as she saw the contours of a woman stepping out of the light. Her body was pure light, but her features were perfectly clear. It was a woman, and she emerged from the light, attained her bodily form, and broke free into the desert. The woman turned and closed what appeared to be a door, and the rectangle of light vanished.

Amber Page stood there staring at the woman, staring at Dr. Amy Levine.

• •

Amy Levine stepped through the door as into a pool of bright light. She felt her hands enter first, then her knee and her face and the rest of her body. There was a bright flash of light, and she felt enveloped as by warm water.

Her feet stepped onto sand like walking out onto a beach. She breathed in the air, and though it was clean air it felt synthetic, like she had just stepped from a muggy, humid summer day into the clean air-conditioned air of a modern building. A surge of energy washed over her with an electronic whooshing sound. She turned and closed the door. She was in.

"Hello there," a young girl said.

Levine looked at her, and the first thought she had was that this was a tough-looking kid. Levine had never seen a young girl as self-assured and composed as this. It reminded her of a time once when she was standing in an airport and a young mother and father came along with a twelve-year-old boy, and Levine saw the father's cell phone ring. He handed it to the boy, and the boy began speaking like an adult businessman, telling whoever was on the other end where they were, what time their flight had arrived, that they had arranged for a shuttle, and in which hotel they were staying. Levine remembered watching the mother and father signing to one another while the boy spoke with confidence (even weary confidence) into the phone, something neither of his deaf parents could do.

This girl was like that. It was clear in her eyes that she'd had to grow up ten years sooner than most kids. But there was something deeper there, too, in the shine of the girl's eyes. Something spiritual and knowing, and Levine realized that the girl was psychic and gifted with abilities within the Line.

"Hello there," Levine said. "I seem to have found a door."

Levine felt giddy. She glanced around her at the desert, trying to take it in. Amber liked her at once.

"My name is Amber," she said. "Welcome, Dr. Levine."

Levine looked at the child. *She knows my name.*

"How do you know my name?" Levine said.

Amber stood there with a curious, knowing smile.

"Come," Amber said. "There are many things you'll want to know."

Levine glanced from Amber, to the horse, to the palm trees and adobe complex on the dune across the valley. She glanced at the three moons, and then her eyes went back to Amber.

"The Oracle," Amber said, "tells of a key. Do you have it?"

"No," Levine said. She smiled. "Not yet."

TWENTY-ONE
THE LEGEND

Amber brought Levine a glass of pure light. Levine stood at the front window inside the adobe. She gazed out at the shaded pool outside and turned when she heard Amber coming. Amber smiled and handed her the glass.

"Drink this," Amber said. "It will help you breathe."

Levine looked at the glass. The liquid inside moved around *like* a liquid, but it was pure light and shone brightly.

"What is it?" Levine said, taking the glass.

"It tastes like honey," Amber said.

Levine sniffed at it and took a sip. It was very good. Levine felt her sinuses opening up immediately. She gulped down the rest of the light liquid, and her lungs opened up as with a deep cleansing breath.

"Wow," Levine said. "That's really good."

Amber took the empty glass. "It's hard to breathe clean air," Amber said. She smiled politely. "The Earth's air is no good anymore, so the transition to good air is difficult. Maple Root helps."

"Is that what that was?" Levine followed the girl into her kitchen.

Amber nodded. "There's more if you need it," she said. "But you should go easy at first."

"Where are we?" Levine said. "This is not the Line?"

Amber shot Levine a thought, *You know of the Line?*

Levine nodded sagely, and Amber smiled, delighted to communicate with someone who understood her.

They stepped out into the shade at the front of the house. There was a bench by the pool. Amber directed Levine to have a seat on the bench, and she herself sat down on her Darpì pad by the pool. Amber folded her legs Indian-style.

"This"—Amber waved across the land—"is the Radian Desert. It has a surface area twice the size of Earth. It's some sixty thousand miles around at the equator. It is a desert world."

"But it's not terribly hot," Levine noted. "The air temperature is quite comfortable."

"Mean temperature never gets above eighty degrees Fahrenheit," Amber said, "Nighttime is cooler, but temperate. The low temperature never drops below fifteen degrees centigrade."

"And yet it's arid?"

"There is no rainfall," Amber said. "What water sources there are come from deep underground. You'll find pockets of oases like this throughout the Radian Desert. But the surface area of sand and dunes is too great to allow any moisture accumulation in our atmosphere."

"And there are others?" Levine said. "Other people?"

"There is an ocean," Amber said. "The Delphic Sea. It's about six thousand miles from here, and there are cities along the coast. There are others there."

Levine smiled at her.

"You live here alone?" she said.

"I have a mentor," Amber said. "I am her apprentice."

"What do you do?"

"I train," Amber said. "I exercise my mind. I fight."

Levine nodded her head. It seemed to fit. She could see this young girl fighting. It would be fierce. Levine exhaled deeply.

Amber wore loose white cotton pants and a loose blue, green, and white top made of similar cloth. The color design of the shirt was exquisite. She wore a beaded necklace around her neck, and at the bottom of the necklace hung a round blue stone.

"What is your necklace there?" Levine said.

Amber sort of looked at it. She touched it with her fingertips, held it out away from her chest a little. She looked deep into Levine's eyes.

"This is the Oracle Stone," Amber said.

"What is that?"

Amber rubbed the stone lightly and let it fall back around her neck. She said, "Legend says that twelve warriors will be assembled, each according to his constellation. Mine is Virgo."

"The Virgo Warrior," Levine said.

"Yes," Amber said. "The Oracle Stone will unite us. It's like a sign, an insignia, it is how we'll know one another. And it is where each of the twelve draws his strength. It is a *good* talisman."

"It's pretty," Levine said.

"But it's different than the stone you saw inside."

Levine nodded. She'd commented on the white coral stone floating inside the octagonal glass cylinder.

"A boy died to bring me that stone," Amber said. "The coral stone. His name was Rio."

"What does the coral stone do?"

"The coral stone is like my guardian angel," Amber said. "It can project images"—she eyed Levine—"and it can give me visions. Grandmaster Barnes has helped train me to understand the responsibilities that come with such a gift. The coral stone is very powerful. It guides me. It helps me to pray. Prayer renews my spirit. And my spirit grows strong within the Line"—she looked at Levine coyly, now—"But I'm just a kid."

"Stuck out here in the desert, eh?" Levine said.

"It's not all that bad."

"Where is your mentor?" Levine said.

"She has gone to the Ocean," Amber said. "There's been a great disturbance in the Line."

"I have felt it, too," Levine said. "On the other side. On Earth."

They were silent for a while. Levine felt as at peace near this child as she'd ever felt around another human being. She had something else to her, Levine realized, a touch of the divine. And yet she had a remarkable humility for such a gifted young girl. She seemed to understand her place and was a prodigy who realized the consequences that came with reaching beyond her grasp.

"Do you ever get lonely?" Levine asked.

"Yes, of course," Amber said. "To feel loneliness is to be human. But to feel joy is to be human, too. It is better to pursue emotions that strengthen the mind than to indulge in those that would weaken it. They say you can fight."

Levine eyed Amber. Amber had a good-naturedly devious little gleam in her eyes, the look of a child outside a toy store window. It made Levine smile.

"You are a far better fighter than me," Levine said. "I can tell that about you already."

"They say you will deliver the sacred key."

"Who is this 'they'?" Levine said with a curious smile.

"It is written in the Oracle."

"What is the key for?" Levine said.

"It will unlock Kevorak's Needle."

"What is that?"

"It is a mountain to the north," Amber said. "The mountain has locked the rain inside it. There is a spring there, and Kevorak's Needle will release the spring. It will transform this barren desert world into a fertile crescent. Or so it is written."

"How far is this mountain?" Levine asked.

"Far," Amber said. "Do you know where the key is?"

Levine drifted away deep in thought. Amber watched her. She smiled.

"No," Levine said. "I do not. I have an idea, but I do not know where it is exactly. I'll need my papers. I'll need the Colorado Sequence."

"The Colorado Sequence," Amber said, "what is that?"

"It is a mathematical system whereby I can pinpoint objects and locations. I, too, can see visions, young Amber."

"Can you find the key?"

"Perhaps," Levine said. "But not here. I will need to go back to the hotel. Back to Ouray, Colorado."

They were silent for a time.

"Can I come with you?" Amber said.

"To Ouray?"

"To Colorado," Amber said.

Levine felt a chill as from a premonition and then far on the horizon there rose a distant thunder, the sound of horses' hooves. Levine glanced at Amber.

"There are too many," Amber said.

"Too many *what?*"

Whatever it was, they were still too far in the distance to see with the naked eye, but Amber had reached out with her mind and saw one hundred and one horsemen armed in black steel and black robes carrying bright light shields and sabers. She saw a dozen muscular tigers leading the horsemen like dogs of war.

"Shadow Warriors," Amber said. "They must have sensed your entrance into the world."

"We can go back to the portal," Levine said. "They can't follow us back into the hotel, can they?"

"No," Amber said. "They can't. Quickly. Help me get my things."

Amber ran inside the house. Levine followed, but at the doorway, she looked up and saw a cloud of dust rising from the desert plains.

Three miles, Levine thought, *four at the most. Six minutes.*

Inside, Amber wound her Darpì pad, reached across the room with her powers, and brought the coral stone in the octagonal glass cylinder to her. She used the cylinder's leather carrying straps to hoist the coral stone over her back like a knapsack, and she swung her Darpì pad over her shoulder.

She looked at Levine at the doorway. She said, "Come on; we've gotta ride!"

She glanced at the side of the house. Rusty, sensing the danger, had come around the side of the house with a worried look in his eyes.

"Rusty, come!" Amber said.

He trotted loyally to her side. Amber leapt up into the air, swirling, and landed on Rusty's back. She waved her hand for Levine. Levine leapt up herself, floating, and landed on Rusty's back behind Amber.

"*Ride!*" Amber shouted.

And the horse took off down the side of the dune, down toward the valley. They raced at full-speed, and Levine felt sand flying up from Rusty's powerful strides. Everything was a blur, but Levine looked hard to her right. She saw the horsemen less than one mile away, coming up the valley.

Rusty crossed the valley and started up sandy Vortex Hill. The tracks were still fresh from earlier, and the horse raced up the sand dune hill.

Levine glanced back and saw the horsemen veering up the hill toward them. The horsemen's black cloaks flowed out from them as though what was underneath the cloaks was invisible and constantly shifting form. They carried long silver spears and brandished swords as bright as the sun. Levine realized she and Amber were only a half mile ahead of them. Ninety seconds, at most.

Rusty came to a stop at the top of the hill. Amber leapt down onto the sand. Levine could not see the door. The portal was invisible. She could see her tracks from earlier, already half-covered from the wind. She ran to where the tracks ended.

Amber said to Rusty, "You must ride, Rusty! Ride like the wind! I will be back!"

She leaned and kissed Rusty on the nose. He looked into her eyes.

"Now, *go!*" she said.

Rusty shook his mane, turned, and took off over the hill in the opposite direction from the horsemen.

"Here it is!" Levine said. She'd found the door. There was a thin seam of extraordinarily bright light as from around a door in clear space. Levine could see desert through it, but there was clearly something there.

Amber waved her hand over the coral stone, and a bright green hologram staff—her Fenwan—four feet in length, formed in her hand.

"Levine, take the stone!" Amber said. She threw the glass cylinder to Amy Levine. Levine swung it over her shoulder with the leather carrying strap, and she opened the door.

The horsemen were coming up the hill, now less than one hundred meters away. Amber was angry at seeing the horsemen, but she restrained herself.

"Come on," Levine said, "into the portal!"

Amber nodded and watched Levine step in through the bright light. She looked back once at the horsemen, angry but maintaining her composure. She turned and stepped through the portal.

• •

Amber Page stumbled to the cobblestone floor. Levine stood over her. She watched the horsemen on the other side. Their horses came up to and "through" the door, but their bodies did not materialize in the room with Amber and Levine. She felt their presence all around her, an invisible gripping anxiety, and she could hear the horses whinnying ferociously, their hooves stomping on the earth. Levine realized the horsemen could not physically touch her inside the room. Their presence was that of invisible ghosts, and it frightened Levine greatly.

"Come on," she said to Amber.

Amber crawled backward feeling the horsemen's spirits all around her.

"They can't harm us here," Levine said.

"They're just like feelings, thoughts," Amber said, alertly looking around her.

"Clear your mind," Levine said. "And they will go."

"Clearing," Amber said.

Levine grabbed the candle from atop the table, and she realized that it had not burned down at all. Her brow furrowed over quizzically, and she glanced through the portal at the horsemen.

"This way?" Amber asked.

Levine looked dazed a moment, but she slowly realized no time had passed while she'd been inside the other world. She nodded her head, and she and Amber started up the hallway to the stairwell.

They stood there looking back in the three-door room. Door 1 was open and the desert landscape was bright beyond. They watched the black horses and their riders tromping all around the area on the other side of the door. They heard the horses scream inside the room.

On the other side of the door, one horseman raised a bright shiny spear up and hurled it at the door. It made an electrical hissing sound when it hit the door, and its spirit whisked across the room, rustling the parchment on top of the table. The parchment leafed off of the table and seesawed back and forth to the cobblestone floor.

"Come on," Levine said. "We're safe here. Let's wake the others!"

Twenty-Two
The Photograph

"What is Kevorak's Needle?" Sara McKenzie said.

Amber looked from McKenzie to Levine, to the others, and then back to McKenzie.

"It's a mountain," Amber said. "A very strange mountain."

Helen and Roger stood by the fireplace. A bright orange fire blazed. The inside of the hotel was cold, but the heat coming from the fire warmed the lobby. Parker came into the room with a serving tray. There were six cups and a large pitcher of coffee. Roger and Helen took their coffee black and stood by the fire, listening to this little girl, this Amber Page.

"It stands about six miles around at its base," Amber said. "And it rises up more than ten thousand feet straight out of the mountains, like a natural skyscraper climbing two miles above the other mountains near it. At its top there is an opening about one hundred meters wide, and there is a giant cave down into the mountain."

"Like a volcano?" Helen asked.

"Very much so," Amber said. "It's believed that the Needle is volcanic."

"And this key?" Roger said. He looked at Helen. "The key that the boy mentioned"—turning to Amber—"and the key that *you* mentioned. What does it do?"

Amber said, "It is written that the key will grant access to only one person." She looked at Levine. "'The Bearer of the Key,' the Legend says, 'will have access into Kevorak's Soul.'"

"What does that mean?" Parker asked.

"I don't know," Amber said. "No one has ever returned from Kevorak's Needle. But no one has ever gone there with the key."

Amber looked at each of them with gravitas beyond her years.

"It is said that inside Kevorak's Needle great changes can take place," Amber said. "That the Needle can be lifted from the earth, that rain will once again fill the sky, and that the desert will change into fertile land."

"So we need this key?" McKenzie said.

Levine said, "Yes, we need this key."

"How do we find it?" Parker said.

· ·

Twenty candles bathed the library and chess room in warm soothing light. Levine stood over a table in the center of the room. She worked from three maps, each folded open on the table: one was a topographic map of southwest Colorado. The second was a town map of Ouray with the words "Ouray, Colorado" at the top. The third was a surveyor's map of Ouray, San Juan, Dolores, and San Miguel Counties, which showed every elevation change of one hundred feet or more. Levine used a pencil and a compass to narrow her quadrant on the third map.

Her math work was spread throughout the room. More than two hundred pages lay around the room like some final exam cram session. Each page held beautifully written mathematical algorithms, more than fourteen years' work lying scattered all around the room.

"It's snowing something fierce outside," Helen said. "You're not gonna believe how much snow fell overni—"

She was coming up the hallway from the direction of the lobby, but froze at the end of the hallway. Her hair, shoulders, and jacket were covered in snow. Her cheeks were rosy red, and her gray-green eyes shone brightly. She stopped at the doorway to the room.

"*Holy,*" Helen said.

The room looked like an M.I.T. version of a real-life Warhol, papers plastered elegantly from one end of the room to the other. Pinned to shelves, hanging from clothespins draped from the ceiling, all over the floor, the tables, the chairs. And each with Levine's beautiful mathematic equations. Levine looked up. She held a yellow pencil in her teeth. Helen just stared at her.

"I think I'll stay out here," she said from the doorway.

Levine removed the pencil and said, "Believe it or not, there's actually an order in this chaos."

"Oh, I don't doubt it," Helen said. She looked around the room. "Where's Amber?"

Levine said, "She's helping Parker and Roger with breakfast."

"Well, just give a holler if you need—" Helen turned and stared at a photo on the wall.

Levine's brow furrowed over seeing the look on Helen's face. Levine's eyes went to the photo on the wall at which Helen was gaping. It was just one of more than one hundred photos and pictures lining the hallway. A hand came up to Helen's mouth, which was frozen open in shock.

"This boy," she said. "This is the boy. We hit him. He died."

Helen's speech was rapid. Levine crossed to her, stepping carefully through the pages of white paper. She placed a hand on Helen's back. Helen stared at the photo in disbelief.

In the photo, a boy was leaning back against a Volkswagen Beetle. His arms were folded in front of him. It was the exact same photo that had caught Levine's attention earlier. The boy's eyes stared out at the world with a calm confidence like nothing she'd ever seen. She glanced at Helen, then back at the photo.

The photo's color had faded from more than forty years of hanging on this wall. Levine could see that the Volkswagen had a dark green Colorado license plate with white lettering, and she could see that the white lettering was some kind of specific name.

"A vanity plate," Levine said.

Helen looked at Levine with a puzzled expression.

"What?" Helen said.

"The license plate," Levine said. "You can tell they're Colorado tags. Up until about 1980, license plates in Colorado changed colors every year. One year, they'd be white on black; the next year black on orange; the next year, green on white."

Helen looked at the license plate on the Volkswagen Beetle. On the photo print, the license plate was no larger than a thumbnail, but it was clearly a dark green plate with white lettering. The lettering was too small to read with the naked eye. It looked like maybe "Kadish"—whatever that meant. But it was just too small to see for sure.

Levine looked at Helen.

"Are you sure this is the boy?" Levine said.

"Amy, I'm positive," Helen said. "I'll never forget that face, those eyes."

They looked at the photo. They really inspected it. They looked at the clothes, the shoes, the hairstyle.

"What year do you think?" Helen said.

"Early seventies," Levine said. "But it's difficult to tell exactly."

"What is the building back there in the distance?" Helen said.

Levine was thinking about the license plate. She said, "You know, I'll bet we could pinpoint the year if we could figure out what year the license plates had white lettering on dark green plates."

"It looks like a hotel," Helen said.

Levine looked at the photo.

Helen looked at her. Helen pointed to a large building way back in the distance.

"You see it?" Helen said.

Levine did.

"I know that hotel," Levine said deep in thought.

"Is it here?" Helen said. "Here in town?"

"I don't think so," Levine said. "Something about that hotel gives me a creepy feeling. It's not one of Ouray's."

"How can you tell?"

"Well, look at it," Levine said. "It's isolated way up on the side of that mountain. Look at the peaks in the distance. And something about it."

Levine stared at the boy by the Volkswagen. She looked into his eyes, *the eyes of a mallet-wielding killer.* What? Why did those words enter her mind? Mallet-wielding killer.

Lack of sleep. I need sleep. Haven't slept in three days.

Mallet-wielding killer.

What a strange phrase.

"Hey, guys, we've got fresh coffee." It was Parker.

He was coming up the hallway. He held a candle. Even though it was daylight outside, it was still dark inside. Parker seemed cheerful and bright. He smiled.

"What are you looking at?" he said.

Levine and Helen looked from the photo to Parker. His face held a curious expression.

"What is it?" Parker said.

Levine said, "Anything about this photo strike you as odd?"

Parker looked at it.

"Nice VW," he said. "Who's the kid?"

"Do you recognize him?" Helen said.

Parker frowned. "No," he said. "But that's the old Overlook Hotel back there in the distance."

"The what?" Helen and Levine said simultaneously.

"The Overlook Hotel," he said.

"What's the Overlook Hotel?" Levine said.

"You've never heard of the Overlook?" Parker said.

Levine shook her head.

"Guy tried to bash his wife and kid's heads in with a polo mallet," Parker said. "Place blew up. It's a legend up around Estes Park."

"Is it still there?" Helen said.

"No," he said. "The place burned to the ground. There's talk of rebuilding it. Caretaker's kid is still around. Story makes the Boulder *Gazette* every couple years that they'll rebuild the place, and Danny—that's the kid's name—that he'll come up there to work as manager. So far the deal hasn't been struck."

"Is that him?" Levine said. "This boy in the photo?"

"No," Parker said. "Couldn't be. The kid in this photo is like sixteen, seventeen. Danny would have been much younger. This is just some guy out there on the stretch of road south of the place."

"*Some guy?*" Helen said. "This *guy* is the kid Roger hit yesterday coming over from Durango."

Parker looked puzzled. "I don't understand."

Levine and Helen exchanged glances.

"What we need to do is," Levine said, "we need to get over to the library. See what we can find out about this license plate."

All three stood there looking at one another. Their eyes went to the photograph, to that tiny thumbnail-sized dark green license plate with its white lettering.

Outside it was snowing fiercely, and the group made their way in snowshoes two blocks up to the Ouray Library. Sara carried the bright blue snow shovel with which she'd spent the morning digging out the snow trench in front of the Beaumont. None of the four could remember seeing this much snow falling at once, ever.

Levine and Amber had stayed behind in order to work through her sequence. Levine was determined to locate the key by noon, and though she considered herself a traditional mathematician, work without a computer slowed things down. So Sara, Parker, Roger, and Helen decided to try to break into the library at the corner of 4th and 6th Streets. They wanted to investigate the photograph of the boy and the license plate on his Volkswagen.

They were walking in the middle of the downtown street, but the snow was falling so heavily they could not see the buildings that were just twenty feet on either side of them. They were snow blind.

"Stay close," Sara said.

"I can't see anything," Helen said.

Parker said, "The town map indicated it's just one block up and one block over."

Roger said, "We could get lost out here one hundred feet from the hotel."

They trudged forward into the blinding snow for another few seconds. There was a slight rise, and Sara was astonished to see that they had walked right up onto the roof of the Ouray County Courthouse. She could tell by the cupola that stood there on top of the snow. They felt around the cupola with their ski-gloved hands. Each of the four was out of breath.

"Oh, my God," Sara said. "This is the courthouse!"

"The courthouse *is buried?*" Parker said.

"We must have walked right over the library," Sara said.

She stood next to the stone-gray cupola and pointed into blinding white snow.

"The library would be over there," Sara said, "one hundred feet."

Parker looked from Sara to Roger. He was stunned. He said, *"The library's buried?!"*

"It's completely under the snow," Sara said.

"It could take us hours," Helen said, "to dig down to the roof."

"No," Sara said. "From where we're standing here, if the snow level is this high, we'd only be about five, six feet above the roof of the library."

"How will you know where to dig?" Roger said.

Sara unfolded the map and looked at it in the heavy snow. Parker, Helen and Roger gathered around her and tried to read the map. Snow covered the map in seconds. She shook it out and held the map up vertically.

"Shit," Parker said. "We may not be able to find our way back to the hotel."

"Nonsense," Sara said. "The hotel is in that direction."

She pointed one way.

"No," Helen said. She pointed left of where Sara was pointing. "I thought we came from that direction over there."

Their tracks in the snow had already vanished just ten feet away.

"I don't like it out here," Parker said.

"No," Sara said. "I think the hotel's over there."

Roger said, "You're both wrong. It's straight up there. I'd bet my right arm on it."

Parker said, "Colorado's worst snow storm in over a hundred years."

The other three simultaneously said, "Shut up, Parker!"

Sara said, "Helen, you and Parker go back to the hotel. Tie that orange climbing rope to the front door of the hotel."

"Right," Helen said.

"There's three hundred feet of line," Sara said. "That should be enough to make it up here to the library."

"What library?!" Parker said.

"Alright, Parker," Sara said, "if you're breaking down on us, why don't you just go back to the hotel."

"I just don't want to get lost out here," Parker said.

"We're not gonna get lost."

"Neither one of you can agree on which way the hotel is," he said. "And you've got a damn map in your hands."

"We haven't walked more than two hundred feet," Sara said. "Since the hotel."

"I think we've walked a little farther than that," Roger said.

"How far?"

"Maybe five hundred feet," Roger said.

"Well," Sara said. "Five hundred feet, then. Still, that gives you a pretty narrow area to search."

"To find the hotel?" Parker whined.

"Yes," Sara said.

Helen nudged Parker encouragingly. "We can find it, Parker," she said. "Come on."

Parker looked at her with worry in his eyes. His head was covered in snow, and his blue ski jacket's shoulders and arms were white.

"And if we don't?" he said.

Helen smiled. "We build a snow man."

The snow was falling so heavily, it was difficult to keep their eyes open.

"We need goggles," Sara said. "And another couple snow shovels. Check the store room inside the hotel. Roger and I will start on the library, approximately where the roof should be. This cupola should stay above the snow most of the morning. It'll give us a marker bearing."

Helen lumbered forward a couple feet on her snowshoes. She said, "Rope, goggles, snow shovels if we can find 'em. Anything else?"

"A bottle of tequila," Sara said with a smile.

She, Roger, and Helen laughed. Parker looked worried, but he lumbered out beside Helen.

"You want the map?" Sara said.

"You keep it," Helen said. "We'll be back in a few."

Roger, Helen, and Sara all slapped ski-gloved high-fives.

"A few minutes," Sara said.

Helen smiled and then turned, and she and Parker walked ten steps before vanishing into the blinding white snow. Roger and Sara exchanged a worried glance, and then looked across at where they hoped to dig for the library.

• •

Sara McKenzie reached the roof, and Roger stood up there on the snow, above the massive hole they'd dug into the powder. He and Sara took turns digging in ten-minute shifts, and the hole was deep, sloped down like a wide slide, and ten feet in diameter on the roof. Her snow shovel struck the black top of the library.

"This is it!" she called.

"Can you tell where we are?" Roger said. "On the roof?"

"Well, it's a flat roof," she said. "Can't be more than forty feet, maybe a hundred feet wide."

Even still, Roger realized, they could be five hours away from finding a front door.

"You want me to dig a while?" he called down to her.

She was out of breath. Steam came from her mouth, pushed forward by healthy lungs. She used the flat end of the snow shovel to clear part of the roof. It was a small patch—only about ten feet in diameter—but it was clearly a rooftop, and they were where they needed to be. Or so they hoped.

Of course, they could keep digging all day, only to find they were on top of St. Daniel's Church. And no closer to a clue that probably wouldn't lead them anywhere, anyway. So much of life seemed hard earned with so little thanks and so little reward that perhaps the best reward could be found in the actual process, in the digging itself.

"I'll keep on," Sara said. "A few minutes more."

It had been two hours, and they'd only mentioned once apiece the fact that there was no way in hell it should have taken Helen and Parker that long to make it to the hotel and back.

Roger stood there at the top of the pit. He looked around at the blinding snow, but could see nothing but blizzard white. And it wasn't that the wind was roaring; it was just *pouring* snow like nothing he'd ever seen. Gusts of wind occasionally picked up to ten or fifteen miles per hour, but the wind was fairly easy on them. It was the snowfall that threatened to bury them all.

"I think I've got something here!" Sara called up to him.

"What is it?"

They had agreed to keep one person standing up there in case Helen or Parker passed right by the hole and didn't see them down inside. One person for lookout; one for digging. Roger glanced around him into the sheet of white snow in all directions, spat, and then climbed down the ramp to the base of the hole.

Sara knelt down, and she removed her gloves. She cleared away snow with her fingertips.

"What have you got?" Roger said.

"It's some kind of hatch," Sara said. "See the lock here?"

Roger knelt down beside Sara. He saw the brass-colored padlock latched to the hatch. He swept snow away from around the hatch.

"I'll bet this opens up from the roof," Roger said.

Sara looked up into his blue eyes with an excited smile. *She knew it did.* She tugged at the lock, but it was pretty sturdy.

"We need something to get through this lock," she said.

"Hand me the shovel," Roger said, rising to his feet. "Stand back."

She handed him the snow shovel and stepped back out of his way. He hefted the shovel up over his head like an axe, found his focal point (the brass-colored padlock), and that shovel whickered through the air and struck with a *clank!*

They both looked down at it. Sara shook her head. "Try it again," she said. "Here, I'll set it up."

She knelt down and positioned the padlock such that his downward strike would pull the lock apart.

"There," she said, and she stood up and cleared out of the way.

Roger crossed his chest, hefted the shovel up, and brought it down like lightning.

Clank!

A chunk of the metal chipped away from the padlock, but it remained locked.

"Once more," Sara said. She knelt down and repositioned it again. She stood up and cleared out of the way. Roger looked into her green eyes.

"Breaking into a library," he said. "Who would have thought?"

She smiled. He hefted the shovel up once more and brought it down powerfully. There was a cracking sound as from wood splintering. They both saw the lock still attached through the eye, but he'd severed the piece of wood that held the eye in place. The lock was still locked, but it was just flopping there, no longer attached to the hatch.

"That's got it," Sara said.

He tossed the shovel aside, and they both knelt down and cleared away the final bit of snow.

"Here," Roger said. "Lift it up."

They both pried their fingertips underneath the hatch and lifted. The hatch came up and a breath of clean warm air rushed out of the darkness.

"Looks like some kind of store room," Sara said. "There's a desk over there."

"Looks like an office," Roger said.

There was a steel ladder attached to the wall down inside the ceiling hatch. Roger went first. Sara handed down the coats, the snowshoes, and the gloves. She climbed down into the darkness and placed the shovel across the opening. Roger opened up a cabinet across the room. It was beside the office desk.

"See anything?" Sara said.

She stood there at the bottom of the ladder. Snow fell down inside the room.

"There's got to be a flashlight here," Roger said. "This looks like a manager's office. You know?"

"Check the desk," Sara said.

She came a few steps toward him. Roger sat down in the chair behind the desk. He opened up the center-top drawer.

"Cigarette lighter," he said. He held up a navy-blue Bic.

"That might could help," Sara said.

Roger opened up the drawer on the left side of the desk. Files and papers. He tried the drawer on the right side. Manila envelopes. He flicked on the lighter, and it lighted that side of the room just enough.

"What is that over there?" Sara said. "On the wall?"

His focus went to the spot ten feet behind the desk. There on the wall was a rechargeable bright, yellow Black & Decker; they could see it in the dancing light from the Bic. It was plugged into an outlet.

"Any juice?" Sara said. "Power's been out at least a day now."

"Yeah, but it might have been charged before the town lost power."

He pulled it from its charger unit, hit the orange button on the top, and a bright healthy beam of light shone out from it.

"Sweet," Sara said.

"Now, we're in business."

He shone the beam around the room. There were two doorways on opposite sides of the room.

"We oughta go back up there and mark this," Sara said.

"What do you mean?"

She was already on the ladder climbing back up to daylight. Snow fell through the opening on her. She moved the shovel aside and climbed out onto the snow pack.

Roger came over to the shaft of light.

"What're you doing?" he called up to her.

"I'm gonna stake this shovel in the snow up here, in case they find us."

Sara took the shovel in hand and trotted up the ramp of snow they'd dug out. The snow on the ramp was pretty well packed. She stood at the top, raised the shovel up, and drove it down into the snow so that it would stand. At the exact moment the shovel struck the snow, a voice called, "Sara!" She thought it was just the sound of the shovel whooshing into the snow.

She turned and was about to start back down into the hole when she heard it again.

"Sara!" the voice called. "*Roger!*"

It was coming from some unclear direction in the heavily falling snow.

"Over here!" Sara shouted. "We're over here! Helen! Parker! We're over here!"

She stood at the top of the packed snow ramp. She wasn't wearing her ski jacket, and she was growing cold quickly. And she could see nothing but white in all directions, except down to the little black opening on the roof. Even the area she had just scraped off just a couple minutes before was already coated in white. Roger poked his head up out of the hole.

"What is it?" he called up to her.

She looked at his head sticking up out of the dark hole.

"It sounds like Helen," she said. She turned and called out into the snow, "Helen! We're over here! We've found the library! *Hello! Helen!*"

Sara was not prepared for what she saw next. It had been two or three hours since they'd seen Helen or Parker, but Sara had no idea what they'd been through.

Helen staggered forward out of the snow and fell into Sara's arms. There was blood on her face, and her ski jacket was ripped open across the front. Helen's weight knocked Sara backward, and both women fell down onto the snow-packed ramp and slid down to the bottom.

"Oh, my God," Roger said, climbing out onto the roof.

Sara struggled to her feet. Helen lay there coughing. Roger came to her, knelt and held her close.

"Here," he said. He tried to pull the torn jacket together, and he saw the dark color at her fingertips.

"We need to get her inside," he said to Sara. "Out of the cold."

"Is that frostbite?" Sara said.

Roger said, "Hang on, Helen."

They carried her over to the opening in the roof.

Roger said, "I'll go down first. You feed her down to me. Okay?"

"Got it!" Sara said.

Roger climbed down inside the roof. He stood about midway up the ladder.

"Okay," he said. "Ease her in."

Sara put Helen's feet, then legs, into the hole and Roger helped her down inside the building. A minute later he had her on the office desk in the middle of the room. She was alive, but very disoriented.

"L-l-lake," she said, her teeth chattering. "F-f-fell into a l-l-lake. C-c-cold, Roger. H-h-hold me, please."

Tears formed in Helen's eyes. She felt alone in the world and though she'd only known this man a few days, he was all she had to trust in. She was deeply frightened.

"We need some blankets," he said to Sara. "Goddammit!"

Sara brought him their ski jackets. Sara said, "Her clothes are soaked."

Sara didn't even think about it. She unzipped her ski pants and stepped out of them.

"We've got to get her out of those clothes," Sara said.

Roger unzipped Helen's frozen ski pants, and Sara pulled off Helen's boots and the soaking wet socks. They got her pants off, and Roger ripped her soaking wet panties off of her. He threw them on the floor like a dishrag and then helped Helen into Sara's dry ski pants.

They did the same with her top, and a minute later Helen lay there in reasonably dry ski pants, shirt, and ski jacket. Life was slowly coming back to her, but her teeth were chattering.

"How you feeling?" Sara said.

Helen managed a smile. "W-w-warmer," she said.

"You're gonna be okay," Sara said.

Roger started over to the ladder.

"Where are *you* going?" Sara said.

"We're gonna need some help," he said. "You're standing there in your damn underwear, Sara. You're gonna freeze!"

Sara stood there in a T-shirt and white panties with blue polka dots.

"And if you go up there," Sara said fiercely. "You might not make it back! Don't you leave us here!"

Roger looked torn.

"Well, don't just stand there looking like that," Sara said. "There's gotta be a fireplace in this old of a building. We build a fire. We'll be alright."

Roger shone the beam of light to the darkened hallway beyond the office.

"If there's a fireplace," he said. "It'd be downstairs in a lobby area."

"You've got the Bic?" Sara said.

He held up the navy-blue lighter. He asked, "What about Parker?"

"Maybe he'll come in," Sara said. "Maybe he'll find us."

"He might have made it back to the hotel."

"Help me with Helen," she said. "We can make it downstairs."

• •

They led Helen down a dark hallway inside the library. Roger held her in his arms, and Sara held the flashlight. The beam shone along the darkened walls and the trim, burgundy carpet that covered the floor of what appeared to be an office area inside the library. There was a stairwell up at the end of the hallway, and a shiny silver elevator door.

Sara shone the flashlight's beam against the door, and its light reflected off of the smooth steel.

"Stairwell," Roger said.

Sara turned the beam down the stairs. At the base of the stairs, there was an office with a sliding glass window.

"Looks like library security," Sara said.

"Open that door there," Roger said.

Sara opened the door for him, and Roger carefully passed through the open door with Helen in his arms. Sara followed through and let the door close shut behind them. She flashed the beam up the hallway to the right and saw stacks of bookshelves opening onto two rooms on either side.

"Stacks," Roger said.

Sara flashed the beam to the left and saw a hallway with a glass window along its side. It looked like the window gave onto a view of an open-air inner courtyard area, but the windows were a blank white theater screen. The courtyard was filled with snow.

"What do you think?" Sara said. "You want to try that hallway there?"

"Let's try the stacks first," Roger said. "These old Colorado buildings, most of 'em have fireplaces on each floor."

"We get a fire built—"

"We'll try and thaw out a little bit," Roger said. "Then we figure out how the hell to get back over to the hotel without getting lost in the snow."

"Have you ever seen a storm like this before?" Sara said.

They were walking toward the stacks.

"Never," McAllister said. "I grew up in northern Michigan, Sara, and we had some doozies, but nothing like this. Colorado's a different world, and it's teaching me a respect for Mother Nature like nothing I've ever seen."

They came to the stacks. Helen moaned something about "icicles," and Sara flashed the beam of the flashlight to the left, then the right. There was a hearth over on the right in the corner of the room. To the right of the brick hearth, there was a huge bin with a stack of twenty split logs.

"Okay," Roger said. "Help me with that sofa there."

Sara pulled a sofa up close to the hearth. He carefully put Helen down on the sofa, and then proceeded to take off his jacket. Sara stood there in her polka-dotted panties and her white T-shirt.

"Here," Roger said. "Put this on."

Sara wasn't shy, and she trusted Roger.

"Give it to her," she said. "She needs it more than I do. I'll be fine until we can get a fire started."

Helen croaked, "Take it, Sara. I'll be fine."

"Bullshit!" Sara said.

She took the coat from Roger and knelt down over Helen. She placed the coat around her. Helen smiled up at her. Sara brushed Helen's hair back a little. She sat there on the edge of the sofa. Sara felt Helen's face. It was ice cold.

Sara's warm hands enveloped Helen's bluish hands. Sara worried that it was frostbite.

"You're gonna be okay," she said. "Helen, do you know what happened to Parker?"

Helen's eyes filled with tears. Her lips trembled. "He didn't make it," she said.

Roger built a fire from the split logs and a stack of old newspapers on the left side of the hearth. Both Helen and Sara were amazed to see a bright orange flame burning within minutes. The wood crackled and popped trying to take hold of the flame, and within another five minutes, the icy room was filling with a bright orange glow, warmth, and heat.

Roger knelt down and kissed Helen on the cheek. He tasted a salty tear and brushed back her hair over her right ear. He smiled.

"We're gonna take care of you," he said. "Everything is gonna be okay."

"Maybe I can start in on the books," Sara said, standing.

Helen handed her the coat and said, "Take it."

Sara did. It was large on her, coming down to her thighs. She zipped it up, smiled, and padded with stocking feet over to the stacks.

Roger watched her go, and then leaned forward, kissed Helen's lips and said, "I'm falling in love with you, Helen. We're gonna make it out of here alive."

Helen Richards looked into his blue eyes and believed that they would.

Twenty-Four
Finding Their Friends

Amber Page opened the front door of the Beaumont and saw three feet of snow standing like a little wall where the door had been. She stood there amazed. The trench rose up from the door almost like a tunnel coming up out of the earth, but the "earth" was thirty feet of snow that had buried the hotel and town.

Levine came up behind her in the doorway, and just said, "Oh, man, would you look at that."

Amber turned and looked at her. "Do you think it's safe?"

"We'll have to use the snowshoes," Levine said.

The group had assembled all of their snow equipment by the door. There were two more pairs of snowshoes and another snow shovel. Ski jackets hung from a coat rack, and there was a single pair of cross-country skis that Sara had found earlier in the morning.

"We need to clear away this doorway first," Levine said. "Or it's going to be buried by mid-afternoon."

"I'll start on it," Amber said.

She picked up the red snow shovel and pushed the immediate snow back away from the door.

"I'm gonna get a rope," Levine said. "It's snowing so hard out there, we're gonna need something to guide us back."

"That's a good idea."

Levine went back into the hotel. She'd seen a bright orange climbing rope somewhere.

Amber continued clearing the snow right at the doorway. It was almost a futile effort. By the time she climbed to the top of the trench with her shovel filled with snow, and climbed back down to the door, almost another quarter inch had coated the ground.

On her third trip, she stood at the top of the trench, and looked out into the blizzard. Visibility was about ten meters, but her mind reached much, much farther. She knew that both she and Levine had felt a turning in the Line, and she had even said something to Levine. The other four had been gone for hours.

Something had happened. They were only supposed to be gone an hour or two, but it was past noon now, and neither Amber nor Levine had heard from any of the other four. She *sensed* something.

Was it Parker?

Amber felt a terrible cold that was deeper, something further down inside herself like a scream. Like water. Like ice cracking on a snow-covered lake.

Amber poured the shovel's snow out beyond the trench. She touched the blue stone on the necklace around her neck.

Amber! the voice came to her with blinding force.

"Oh, no," she said.

She knew it was Parker. Parker had fallen into a lake. *Where? Was he still alive?*

Amber rubbed the blue stone with her fingertips. The snow coated her hair and shoulders. Her eyes closed, and her mind reached out to him. Her eyes opened slowly, calmly, and she exhaled deeply.

She had seen his death.

Levine called out, "Amber!"

She was at the bottom of the trench, holding an enormous cord of bright orange climbing rope. Amber shook her head clearing the image from her mind and came back down the trench to the front door.

Levine looked at her, and Amber realized she knew. Levine had felt it, too.

"Is he dead?" Amber said.

"I don't know," Levine said. "It's not good. It's like a tear through the fabric of time and space—"

"—when someone close to you dies."

"Put on your coat," Levine said. "Hand me the goggles. We've got to find them. They're somewhere nearby."

Amber nodded and stepped inside. She tossed Levine the goggles. Levine put them on over her snow cap. Her brown hair spilled out the back of the cap over her dark blue ski jacket. She wore black ski pants, and a pair of black ski gloves was snapped to a latch on her jacket. She tied the rope through a mail slot in the door and pulled the door closed as Amber stepped out into the snow with her.

Amber carried the snowshoes. She herself wore white ski pants and a white jacket with a white cap on her head. She had a pair of reflective blue-lens ski goggles, and she pulled them over her eyes. She trotted up the trench with the snowshoes in hand, and Levine pulled the door fast and checked the tightness of the rope's knot.

At the top of the trench, Amber strapped on her snowshoes. She hoisted up her two ski pools and shuffled out ten feet away from the trench. The falling snow was incredible, but through the shaded lenses of her ski goggles she could almost see as much as fifty feet.

• •

Levine saw that the bright orange rope had paid out about one hundred feet. She had about two hundred feet left with which to work, and she carried it over her left shoulder. She used two ski poles to help keep her balance as she lumbered along in the snowshoes.

Amber was over to her right about ten feet, and they both scanned through the driving snow and saw nothing but endless white around them. Amber—dressed in white—blended in with her surroundings, and she had the hang of the snowshoes, shuffling along quite well with her two shorter poles helping to maintain her balance.

"We've paid out," Levine called through the snow, "about one hundred feet!"

The wind had picked up in the past twenty minutes, and gusts were coming at them upwards of thirty miles per hour. That worried Levine. The temperature had hovered just below twenty degrees all morning, but the wind had stayed reasonable now for twenty-four hours with this storm. With a howling wind kicking up to forty miles per hour though, the wind chill dropped from eighteen degrees *above* zero, to a deadly eighteen below.

It made it difficult to communicate. Amber had not heard her call her through the wind and blinding snow, and continued forward in a direction away from where Levine thought the library was. Levine knew from the maps that the library was no more than three hundred feet from the hotel, and she was certain that it was generally northeast of the hotel. So, even if the town was completely buried under snow, she could pay the rope all the way out to its full three-hundred-foot length and then sweep around in a circumference until she stumbled upon an area where it looked like Sara and the other three had been digging. She'd be sure to find them that way. At least, that was the plan.

But Amber was drifting away from her and was fleeter of foot than Levine. Why didn't she just turn around and see that she was getting away from her?

"*Amber!*" Levine yelled into the roaring wind and snow.

Amber stopped. She was about twenty feet away from Levine and had almost vanished from her sight. Amber looked around and could not see her. Levine lumbered forward with the bright orange rope over her shoulder.

And then she saw it. There was a tiny hole in the snow, only one foot in diameter, and she'd almost stepped into it. She waved for Amber to come back to her.

Amber had passed just a meter to the right of the hole and had not seen it at all, but Levine saw it. She saw the smoke rising from it like some volcanic vent in the earth's crust. A billow of smoke poured up from the hole, before being slammed by the wind above the snow's surface. The wind was so strong and so fast it shredded the smoke quickly, and the smoke vanished into the white blizzard all around them. Levine slowly realized what she was looking at.

"What is it?" Amber yelled over the howling wind.

Levine jabbed a finger at the hole in the snow, the smoke coming off of its surface. Amber was standing right there and could not see it, such was the blinding fury of the wind-swept snow. She saw Levine jabbing at the ground, and her eyes went to the spot.

"It's a chimney!" Amber said over the wind.

Levine nodded her head vigorously up and down.

"That means," Levine shouted, "they're inside. They've built a fire! We're standing on top of the library!"

Amber's eyes shot around looking for any signs of digging. They had to have dug down into the snow to find an opening into the library, and now she and Levine had to find that opening. Visibility was only a few feet, but they knew they were close.

"Take the rope!" Levine called to Amber. "Stand here! I will take a little lead!"—she jabbed at the hole the heat from the chimney made— "But this means we're close!"

"We search from here!" Amber said, the wind carrying her voice away.

Levine nodded her head, gave her a thumbs-up gesture and handed her the remaining coil of bright orange climbing rope. Amber positioned the rope so that she could feed it out to Levine as she walked away.

Levine grabbed her and hugged her.

She said, "I'll be right back, Amber! If I tug three times quick, then follow the rope to me!"

Amber nodded, glanced down at the chimney hole, and then watched Levine vanish into the blinding white blizzard.

Amber held the rope. She drove one ski pole down into the snow and shifted her weight on her snowshoes. She looked at the orange climbing rope. It draped down from her hands onto the surface of the snow, straight out in front of her, vanishing twenty feet away in the blinding white. Amber craned her neck one way then the other trying to see through the blizzard to Levine.

Levine was just beyond her range of vision, but Amber could almost see her, her black ski pants and black and blue jacket moving through the snow. Amber felt the rope in her gloved hands, paying out as Levine moved farther away from her.

Suddenly, the rope rose up, and there were three swift tugs. Amber almost fell forward over her snowshoes, but she tugged back once and kept her balance. She grabbed her ski pole, and she started forward into the blinding fury.

The snow shovel was driven down into the snow. Levine stood beside it, Amber saw, and a drift of snow had buried the bottom third of the shovel. Just the shaft stuck up out of the ground, but it was clearly the shovel Sara had taken with her earlier this morning.

Levine jabbed a ski-gloved finger down into a trench beside the shovel, and both Amber and Levine saw the black hole opening into the roof of the library. More than a foot of snow stood immediately around the hole, which meant they'd been inside for an hour or more. The trench itself was some ten feet down from where Levine and Amber stood, and Levine pumped her fist and started down into the trench.

Down inside the trench, they were a little better protected from the wind, and both Levine and Amber saw Sara, Roger, and Helen's snowshoes stuck in the snow at the base of the trench.

"I don't see Parker's snowshoes," Amber said.

"He might have carried them inside," Levine said. "I'll go in first."

She unlaced the leather straps holding her boots in the snowshoes and climbed down into the hole. Amber followed her in.

Inside, they both saw snow on the floor. Several inches had accumulated on the floor from the opening in the roof.

Levine took off her ski mask, cupped her hand over her mouth and called out into the darkness, "Hello! Anybody here? *Hello!*"

She looked at Amber. They both removed their hoods and stepped away from the snow that fell through the opening in the roof. It was very dark beyond the office, but they could both see two doorways from the room in which they were standing. It looked like there was a hallway.

They walked to the open door, and Levine called out again, "Hello! Sara! Helen! Anybody here?"

And then from deep inside the library, they heard someone answer back.

The voice was muffled through walls: "Did you hear that?" Then a moment later, Sara's voice rang out from down inside the library, "Amy! We're here! We're inside! Where are you?"

Levine smiled at Amber.

"We're up here in the office," Levine called out through the darkness. "It's pitch black up here! Are you guys okay?"

There was a pause, then both Amber and Levine saw a flashlight's beam bouncing along a wall up the hallway as though coming up stairs.

Amber and Levine stepped out into the hallway. Sara's head came up from the stairwell. It was hard to see because she was carrying the flashlight out in front of her, and the light was very bright.

"There's been an accident," Sara said. "Thank God you guys found us!"

She came up to them, and both Amber and Levine saw she was wearing the ski jacket like a mini-dress. It came down almost to her knees. She wore white socks on her feet. She leaned forward and hugged Levine.

"We couldn't find our way back to the hotel," Sara said. "Parker's dead. Helen's thawing out downstairs by a fire."

"Parker's dead?" Levine said.

"I think so," she said. "Helen nearly froze to death out there."

"We've got a line," Levine said. "She pointed back in the office, and Sara saw the rope descending from the opening in the roof. It'll get us back to the hotel."

Sara nodded her head.

"Come downstairs," she said. "You can take a look at Helen. She was in pretty bad shape when we found her."

"What is it?" Amber said.

Sara looked at them both. "The cold got her," she said.

Levine checked her watch, saw that it was a quarter past three, and said, "We only have a couple more hours of daylight."

Amber said, "And that storm doesn't look like it's letting up."

"We may have to stay here tonight," Sara said.

"In the library?" Amber said.

Sara nodded her head worriedly. "We have wood," she said. "And a fire."

"Food?" Levine said.

"We'll have to go back to the hotel."

Levine said, "I found the key, Sara. I think I've pinpointed where we will find the key."

Sara looked at her. "I've found out about the boy," she said. "The one in the photograph. I know who his father is!"

And they started off down the hallway, toward the stairwell, deeper into the library.

"His father was a miner, right?" Levine said.

"How did you know?" Sara said. "He owned the Carbañero Mine, a gold mine, about five miles south of town."

"I pinpointed the key with the Colorado Sequence," Levine said. "The key's inside the Carbañero Mine."

Sara said, "We'll freeze to death if we try to make it there tonight."

Amber glanced back over her shoulder at the darkness behind them, turned, and then saw the dancing shadows of a fire.

"There's not a lot of time left," Amber said.

Both women looked at her.

She said, "I can feel it. There is a shift within the Line."

TWENTY-FIVE
THE SITUATION

Levine inspected Helen's hands under the shine of the flashlight.

"It's not frostbite," she said. "You've got frost*burn*. It's not as severe, which is a good thing. It means if we can get you out of here, you'll probably keep your hands."

"Great," Helen said. She had tears in her eyes, which reflected the glow of firelight.

"Your feet, though," Levine said. "I don't know. They don't look good. We need to get you to a hospital."

Roger said, "How the hell are we supposed to get to a hospital?"

"Roger don't," Helen said.

He turned around and swung at the empty air over the fireplace.

"I knew it," he said. "I should have listened to you back in Durango, Helen. You said it was unwise to come up. This is all my fault."

He walked over toward the library stacks in the darkness. Levine looked at Helen in the flashlight's shine. Sara held the flashlight. Amber stood at the fireplace and watched the women's interactions.

"I'm not a medical doctor," Levine said. "And what experience I have mostly comes from text books. Your hands are gonna be alright. I'm pretty sure."

"We can use the snowmobiles," Sara said feebly. "Once this storm lets up enough, we can use the snowmobiles to get down to Durango."

"*Down* to Durango?" Roger said from the fire's shadows. "Durango's seventy miles with at least two mountain passes above twelve thousand feet. *If* we could follow the road, it would take all day tomorrow to make it down. How much fuel do we have?"

Both Sara and Levine looked at one another.

"Well?" Roger said.

"Might be a quarter tank," Levine said. "In one."

"Quarter tank?" Amber said.

Everyone realized it was not enough fuel to make it seventy miles.

"We could head out to the north," Sara said.

"Everything'll be shut down between here and Montrose," Levine said.

Helen said, "How far is that?"

"Closer to forty," Levine said. "And the elevation is not as bad. You could make Montrose."

"We could siphon off the fuel from the lower tank," Amber said. "Put it all into one."

"What if the storm doesn't let up?" Roger said. "The reports were that this was supposed to get worse all the way through Thursday."

"Well, there's a chance," Sara said. "Even if you didn't make it all the way to Montrose, you might make it to a farm. Somebody. *Something*. We could get a rescue crew up here."

"And you might freeze to death trying," Roger said.

"I'll be fine," Helen said. "We should stay put. Ride the storm out to the weekend. I don't much give a damn as long as I don't lose my hands. Someone's likely to try to make it up here once the storm clears."

"No one knows we're here," Roger said. "And roads into town with that kind of snow may not be plowed for months. The Forest Service has probably closed down all of the land between Durango and Ridgeway, and nobody's gonna be coming up to this elevation for at least two weeks."

"Well, let's say we are pinned up here for two weeks," Levine said. "Do we have enough to live off of?"

"We have an entire town," Sara said. "Only, it's buried."

"But we do have the hotel," Amber said. "There's food and wood, and protection from the elements. But there's something else, something I haven't told you guys."

All eyes went to Amber.

"The world," she said. She looked at Levine. "Things that happen in this world affect the other side. And things on the other side affect this world. The weather is only going to get worse here, as the weather gets worse there."

"What are you saying?" Levine said.

"We have to get that key," Amber said. "We have to go back inside. And we have to get to Kevorak's Needle to restore the balance."

Everyone looked at this young girl, Amber Page.

She said, "Through the red door. We could stay there. It's an option."

"What is she telling us, Levine?" Roger said.

Levine looked from Amber to Roger. "No," Levine said. "When we came through before I noticed that the candle hadn't burned down at all. Time here doesn't pass when we're on the other side."

"The other side of what?" Roger said.

Levine looked into his blue eyes. He looked into Helen's gray-green eyes. She felt Sara's gaze on her. And Amber nodded her head.

Levine said, "The other side of the red door."

Twenty-Six
The Balance

McKenzie, Levine, and Amber Page came up from the trench above the library into a howling wind. Snow swept almost horizontally on a blinding gale that plowed in from the west with no mercy. They all three held onto the bright orange rope that now connected the hotel and the library, and they trudged forward on their snowshoes, packed tight with their high-tech Nordic gear. Even with the gear, none of them wanted to be above ground for more than fifteen minutes in this white fury. A half hour outside in these elements would be death. But they had the rope connecting the buildings, so there was the reasonable assurance that they could make it from one building to the next.

Levine led the way, with Amber next on the rope, and McKenzie bringing up the rear. She and Helen had switched back their gear, and Roger had thrown three more logs on the fire as they left. It looked like Helen would be alright; she may lose her feet, but Helen's clothes were drying by the fire. Amber, McKenzie, and Levine could make it over to the hotel, the plan was to bring back enough blankets, clothes, food and water to make it through the night inside the library.

Levine took one handful of the rope at a time. Her snowshoes lifted up and came down. The wind blasted her from the front, and she had to lean forward into it to maintain her balance. Amber tucked in behind her on the rope, hoping that Levine's presence would shield her from some of the wind, and McKenzie did the same behind Amber, staying close. They made their way along the orange rope, which was frozen hard in their ski-gloved hands.

Levine called out to them in the wind, but her voice was quickly ripped away by the wind. She tried again, yelling as loud as she could, but the wind was so fierce that she couldn't even hear her own voice, and she realized that there was no way that Amber or McKenzie a few feet away could hear her at all.

Forward into the snow. One handful of frozen rope at a time.

Levine looked forward through her blue-lens ski goggles, hoping to see the rope descending down into the trench in front of the hotel, but for the moment there was only blinding white snow. Visibility was less than ten feet. And what little daylight they still had was fading fast. Another thirty minutes and this white fury would be eclipsed by near total darkness as all power and electricity was out in the snow-buried town, and the maelstrom of unmerciful wind and snow continued to pound them.

Suddenly, there was a powerful gust of wind upwards of sixty miles per hour, a hard tug on the rope, and Levine fell over on her side. Her head came up quickly, and she looked around her, grasping blindly around for the rope. Snow had covered her goggles, and she wiped at them with her ski-gloved left hand. It cleared the snow away, but it smeared the lens so badly it was difficult to see.

Her first instinct was to get hold of that rope. They were probably about two-thirds of the way to the hotel, but if she lost the rope, they might spend fifteen minutes searching the blinding snow and wind for it. The rope was their lifeline, and without it they would almost certainly die.

She was on her stomach. The wind swept snow against her so hard it was like she was a rock in a river and the water was roaring all around her, splashing over her head. Only, this water was snow, and right at surface level there was a powerfully steady current of white powder blasting along. Levine climbed up on one knee and looked around her.

She saw Amber seven feet away. Amber was flat on her stomach fighting the wind and snow just as she was. Levine didn't see Sara for a moment, and her body flooded with adrenaline.

She called out, "*Sara!*" as loud as she could but it was like screaming into a 747's jet engine.

Levine leaned forward into the wind, kneeling. She tried to clean her goggles off, but it only smeared the surface worse. She thought she saw the frozen rope a few feet in front of her. She clambered forward on hands and knees, but the snowshoes made it very difficult to crawl that way, and she ended up just falling flat on her stomach and tried shuffling forward to the rope using her elbows and knees. It was just four feet away. Wind-swept snow hit the rope, spraying up several inches into the air.

This was hell. A white snow-death hell.

Levine reached forward and snagged it. She had her hand on the rope, but her ski gloves made it difficult to grip. Her chest was growing cold quickly lying against the snow, but she had her arm on the rope. And she tried to clamber up onto her knees, but it was impossible with the snowshoes on.

She rolled over on her side. It was impossibly difficult, and the roaring wind and snow wasn't making it any easier. She glanced down beyond her feet and saw Amber crawling toward her.

Levine rolled over on her back. The snowshoes made her twist her legs directly to the right, and she could feel the ligaments in her knees straining. She grimaced and glanced over to her left. She saw Sara!

Sara was on her feet, coming toward her in the blasting wind and snow. Levine saw that Sara did not have the rope in her hands, but she saw her leaning forward into the wind.

Levine jabbed a finger toward Amber for Sara to see. She meant for Sara to help the girl. Levine pulled the rope over her and held it in front of her chest. *I'll be damned if I'm gonna let it go, now!*

Levine watched Sara lumbering forward into the wind. She made it over to Amber, and Amber lifted her right hand up to her. Sara took her hand, balanced her legs just beyond shoulder-width apart, and lifted Amber up so that she was standing on her own two feet. Amber looked unsteady for a second, but she managed to get her balance on her snowshoes and both she and Sara came the remaining seven feet to Levine.

Sara roared something down to Levine, but the wind ripped it away and Levine couldn't understand what she was saying. Amber lumbered around to Levine's right and got hold of the rope. Sara was on Levine's left.

Levine rolled over onto her right side, and started to push herself up. But it was just impossible with the snowshoes on. She kicked at the ground, trying to get the sides of her boots to ground level, so she could push herself up from the side. It looked like it was going to work. She got up on her hands and knees, and she just made her mind still.

She glanced at Amber and saw that Amber had her hand out in the air over her. Levine felt something warm inside her legs impossible to describe as anything other than a bright light, and in the mad rush and adrenaline she could not be exactly certain whether it was herself pushing upward off of the ground or whether it was Amber channeling some energy through her, but it felt as if she was floating for a half-second, and suddenly she was up on her feet.

She glanced around, reluctant to believe that everything was okay, but she saw Sara behind her. Sara had the rope in her right hand, and she pumped her left fist enthusiastically. Behind her ski mask, Levine smiled at her friend.

Levine swung her head around and saw Amber, with the rope in *her* hands. Amber nodded sagely and then thrust a ski-gloved index finger forward into the wind. Levine nodded her head vigorously, and they continued forward toward the hotel, each holding onto the rope as though holding onto her own tenuous mortality.

• •

Amber saw that the snowmobiles were buried. There were two large lumps of white snow five feet to the left of the trench into the hotel. Her eyes lit up when she realized that they had made it, and she glanced over her shoulder and saw Levine and McKenzie right behind her. She could tell they were excited, too.

McKenzie shouted something into the wind, pointing to the snowmobiles but neither Levine nor Amber could understand her over the howling wind.

The hotel was buried, all three floors. The trio clomped through the fresh powder that filled the trench, coming down out of the wind. The trench gave them some protection. It felt almost like a tunnel it was so deep down into the snow, now.

All three saw that the front door to the hotel was one-third buried under fresh snow. Two feet of snow swept up at an angle against the door, and this was down inside the safety of a twenty-five-foot-deep trench.

Amber opened the front door and stepped over the little mound of snow.

"Oh, man," she said with relief.

McKenzie and Levine came in behind her, and they quickly removed their ski masks. The quiet inside the hotel was sudden after having walked through such howling wind and snow. Levine closed the door behind her, and saw Amber unlacing the leather straps that held her little boots into the snowshoes.

"You saved my life," Levine said to her.

Amber smiled and stepped out of her snowshoes. "You saved yourself, Dr. Levine," she said. "And your decision to get that rope connected from one building to the next saved us all."

Sara said, "We're gonna need to do something about those snowmobiles, guys."

"What can we do?" Amber said.

"Well, I guess we ought to bring 'em down here into the hotel," Sara said. "Or at least down into the trench."

Levine said, "Amber, I remember seeing several army-green canvas tarps in the store room. Sara and I will bring down one of those snowmobiles—"

"We need both for the fuel," Sara said.

"I think the other tank was empty," Levine said. "We were riding in on fumes."

"We should still *try*."

"We should, and we will. You're right, Sara"—she turned and looked into Amber's eyes—"You get those tarps, Amber. We'll bring the snowmobiles down."

"You got it!" Amber said. And she started off to the store room inside the hotel.

Levine looked at McKenzie. "Well," she said. "You ready?"

"Let's do this thing," McKenzie said.

Levine swung the door open, and they stepped back out into the cold. The wind hollered over the open top of the trench. Snow swept over the opening as in a wind tunnel, some of it just passing right over the top of the trench, other snow getting caught in the downdraft, swirling like a pipeline down onto the floor of the trench.

Levine trudged forward on her snowshoes to the top. The wind started flapping her hood as she came up out of the trench's protection.

She looked to her right and saw the two large mounds of snow where the snowmobiles were buried. She lumbered over to one mound.

She couldn't remember which one had more fuel in it, and they were both buried. She started sweeping snow away from the closer mound. Chunks lifted up and were carried away from her on the howling wind.

Sara squatted down at the front of the snowmobile and began shoveling snow out with her ski-gloved hands. They had it partially cleared in a matter of minutes, but Levine's hands were freezing. And she knew Sara must be feeling the same, too. Even with the gloves on, it was just too cold. The wind chill was like a knife edge, and had to be somewhere beyond the depths of what was safe. These conditions were at the very limit of what the human body could endure.

Sara pushed the snowmobile from the front. Levine was on its left side, pulling with the handlebars. They got the snowmobile backed up enough to point it down into the trench. Levine turned the handlebars, and Sara stumbled around to the back of it, and they began to push it down into the trench.

Sara saw the three girls in the white dresses out of the corner of her eye. They looked like they were sixteen years old. Her head was down over the back end of the snowmobile, and she was pushing the thing forward into the trench. Had it been under any other circumstance or had she been with Helen and Roger just a few days before, she would have noticed them immediately.

Levine was in front of her, guiding the snowmobile's handlebars, and she did not see them at all. But Sara felt and then *saw* three identical girls—like statuesque triplets—wearing identical white dresses, standing on identical bare feet in the same identically blinding wind. And their hair didn't stir at all. Their dresses didn't ruffle at all; if they could be called dresses. They looked almost like robes, or some kind of tunics.

The three girls were just beyond the edge of sight in the blinding white wind and snow, but none of it touched them. They stood there just as peaceful and at ease as if it were a calm and sunny spring afternoon.

All of this Sara saw in a split second before the snowmobile rushed down into the trench, and—a moment later—nosed up against the door of the hotel. Amber opened the door from inside, and they realized they could get the snowmobile inside into the foyer area. The door was just wide enough. They made one final push and got the snowmobile inside the hotel. Amber shut the door behind them, and Levine dropped to the floor, exhausted and all but certain that she'd frozen her fingertips to the point of frostbite.

"Did you see that?" Sara said.

Levine looked up at her from the floor. She was sitting with one arm draped up on the snowmobile, and chunks of ice and snow dropped to the hardwood floor inside the foyer.

"See what?" Levine said.

"I thought I saw something out there."

Levine looked into McKenzie's green eyes. She sensed her fear.

"What did you see?" Levine said.

McKenzie looked at the closed hotel door. Amber stood in front of it. There was a thin line of light around the door's sill, but the inside of the foyer was dark. McKenzie could see young Amber's contours standing in front of that line of light. McKenzie just shook her head lightly back and forth. She couldn't explain it.

"It looked like," she started. She looked from Amber to Levine's eyes. "It looked like—three girls."

Both Amber and Levine said simultaneously, "What?!"

"It might have just been the snow," Sara said. "I don't know."

Levine took her ski gloves off with her teeth and then took them up in one hand. Her legs were lying at an awkward angle because of the snowshoes, and she inspected her fingers. They were bluish at the very tips, almost a dark purple, and they were redder back toward the palms of her hands. She wriggled them to see if she had any movement and was pleased to see that she did.

"We need to get a fire started," she said.

Amber said, "The coals are still glowing. I saw them when I got these."

She held up an army-green canvas tarp. Another was on the floor at her feet, where she'd dropped it when she opened the door.

Levine unlaced the snowshoes and got to her feet.

"Come on," she said. "Let's get this snowmobile over to the side, out of the way."

Sara stood there. "There was something out there, I'm telling you!"

"*What do you want me to do about it?*" Levine snapped.

Sara had never seen her snap before. Amber felt a chill go through the room, and the foyer filled with an uncomfortable silence. In the darkness it looked like Levine was glaring at Sara McKenzie. Sara saw the whites of her eyes. The two women stood there staring at one another.

"Guys," Amber said. "Take it easy. Let's get this snowmobile out of the way. Let's go inside and stoke the fire. We'll warm up, get some food, get all the stuff we need, and get back over to the library before nightfall. Helen and Roger are counting on us."

• •

Sara McKenzie threw another log on the fire and watched the sparks fly up into the chimney. Levine stood just beyond the fire's glow, watching her. Amber had gone back to the kitchen ostensibly to get food and drinks, but actually because the tension coming off of Levine was palpable and unnerving.

Sara refused to look at her, and just reached over in the woodbin to the left of the fireplace, picked up a split log, and threw it on the fire. More sparks exploded up into the darkness of the chimney, and Sara straightened up and held her hands in front of the fire, palms facing the flames.

"You just gonna stand over there in the dark?" Sara said, not turning from the fire.

The wood crackled and popped in the bright orange blaze. It was actually too hot to be standing as close as she was to the fire, but her pride kept her from moving away because she felt if she moved away, Levine would see it as a sign of weakness, some sort of genuflection in her direction and that Levine would feel justified for losing her temper. It was all very childish.

Finally the heat became too intense, and she stepped back from the fireplace, but she stepped away in a turning motion so that her back was facing Levine and she rubbed her hands in front of her. Sara stepped over into the shadows opposite Levine, and stared at the fire's warm glow.

She wanted to look up at her. She could see her just at the edge of her vision, but she was afraid that if she *did* look up and saw Levine staring at her that she would fall all to pieces inside and that Levine would win whatever game it was that they were playing.

"You know you could apologize," Sara said.

Her voice sounded fragile as porcelain as though one swift kick would shatter it, and everything would come out a jumble of anxiety-splintered gibberish.

Levine said nothing, cleared her mind, remained in the shadows.

Sara made a clicking noise with her teeth, tongue and cheeks, and her head turned to the left. She rolled her eyes, and she looked at Levine. Amy Levine's face caught the glow of the fire, and Sara McKenzie saw it all very clearly. Levine wasn't staring *at her*. She was gazing into the fire with something like world-weary remorse straining the lines around her eyes. It was the look of a fighter who's gone the distance and realized no one gives a damn.

Sara stared at her, her lower lip dropping open ever-so-slightly. Her shoulders sagged a little. She stared.

"What do you see?" Levine said.

Sara was so entranced by the silence that she didn't understand the question.

"What do I see?" Sara said.

Nothing but Levine's eyes moved, but they moved to look directly at Sara.

"What do you mean?" Sara asked.

"What do you see?" Levine said. "You're staring at me."

Sara looked away, said something like, "Oh."

Levine's chin came up, and her head turned. She looked squarely at Sara McKenzie. Sara's eyes rose up and looked at Levine tentatively. Sara shrugged her shoulders.

"I see you," she said.

Levine nodded her head lightly and clenched her jaw. Her lips grew agreeably rigid, and she gazed into the fire again.

"I'm tired, Sara," Levine said. "I'm too young to be as tired as I am. There's supposed to be more fight in me than this."

She just shook her head and looked like she wanted to spit.

Amber Page was standing in the hallway, listening to these two women. Her eyes were wide and inquisitive. She held a tray with sandwiches and three glasses of water on it.

"This young girl, this Amber," Levine said. "She has something special"—her eyes went to Sara's eyes—"I've never seen anything like it. You think *my* gifts are strong; wait until she comes into her own. She will cut a swath through the whole of humanity. She has talents no one's ever *dreamed of.*"

"Such as?" Sara said.

"She can move objects," Levine said. "And she can move hearts. She can move minds. She was a born leader before she was even born. She will lead people, and they will follow. And she will pray to the same God that we all in our hearts believe in but cannot put words to, the same—*other*—that men have waged war over for centuries. She will learn to humble herself before that in a way that raises her high in the eyes of man, higher than anyone else has ever scaled."

Amber Page suddenly felt embarrassed at having overheard this. She turned quietly and proceeded back up the hallway toward the kitchen.

Roger stood at a table inside the library thirty feet from Helen. He held a flashlight cocked up in his right hand, and spread out before him on the table were the two dozen newspapers and books through which Sara had been searching. Helen was asleep on the sofa, and the fire's warm glow was burning brightly.

Roger looked up at her asleep on the sofa, smiled warmly (if worriedly) with his eyes, and turned his attention to the book in the center of the table. It was pretty simple investigative work really. Sara had tracked the license plate via its color to 1973. This was corroborated by the model and condition of the VW Bug in the photograph, and they'd ascertained the simple fact that unless the kid was running out-of-date tags the photo had been taken sometime in late 1973. They'd reasoned it was *late* 1973 because of the color of tree leaves in the background of the photo.

So with that, they'd narrowed the date of the boy's photograph down to fall of 1973. Most likely late September to October.

The next stroke had been a little touch of genius on Sara McKenzie's part. She pulled the obituary section for every day from September 10 through November 10 in 1973's *San Miguel Chronicle*. It was enough to make private detective Roger McAllister envious.

The actual legwork took the longest; that is, just locating the newspapers was actually the most time-consuming aspect of the project because the old Ouray Library still ran on a physical card catalogue, which took some work to figure out. But within an hour, she had located the stacks of old local newspapers and within ten minutes she'd found the obituary for October 24, 1973.

"Millionaire Miner's Son Dies in Tragic Auto Accident," the headline read. Roger looked at the article Sara'd circled with a blue ball-point pen. He read the brief article. The boy's name was Curtis David Toms, son of wealthy miner Carlisle Richard Toms. Carlisle owned several gold and silver mines north of Durango, the largest of which was the Carbañero Mine five miles south of Ouray. The article didn't speculate at his net worth, but only gave the facts regarding the son's tragic accident.

The boy was driving his VW Beatle north from Durango up to the family ranch in Ouray when he hit a deer and skidded off the narrow two-lane road just north of Purgatory Ski Resort. Police officials knew it was a deer because of the blood and dent found on the front of the VW. The deer was still alive when a State Trooper arrived on the scene. It was paralyzed and lying at the side of the road, sitting there eerily cocking its head back and forth. National Forest officials put the animal down that afternoon, but the boy's VW had hurtled down the side of the steep embankment killing him instantly, officials said.

Funeral arrangements were being made, the article went on to state. But Roger stopped reading. It all made sense, and the image of that boy (or was it the boy's ghost?) dying in his arms was just too intense, and he walked over to check on Helen.

She was sleeping soundly, blankets pulled up to her chin. Roger looked at the fire and said a quick prayer for McKenzie, Levine, and Amber that they would make it safely back to the library by nightfall. Outside, the wind screamed over the buried library, the buried town, and Roger felt an equally compelling silence deep within the very fabric of the building as though he was standing in the inside of a tomb that separated the world of the living from the world of the dead.

• •

When Helen Richards woke, she saw Roger over the fire with a poker in his hand. He stirred the coals and tossed another log on the fire. The blaze was bright and its heat was hot, but she could feel the depth of cold in the rest of the library seeping in all around them, and it was as if the fire, the fireplace, the hearth, and the sofa were all a part of a little island of heat, light, and life. Helen's head felt heavy, but her eyes smiled at Roger in the fire's warm glow.

"How long have I been asleep?" she said.

Roger turned and looked at her. She was lying on the sofa with blankets up to her chin. Her eyes looked bright, and her skin shimmered in the firelight. She smiled a little at him.

"It's been a few hours," he said. "How're you feeling?"

"I feel like I've been asleep for three days. My head feels heavy."

"It's only been about three hours," Roger said.

Helen nodded her head.

"Haven't heard from the others," Roger said. He turned and stirred the coals once more, then placed the poker in the fireplace rack to the right of the fire.

"Did they make it?"

"We have no way to know," Roger said. "It's nightfall outside."

"You checked?"

"Just a few minutes ago," he said. "I went upstairs, checked the opening onto the roof. The rope is still there, but the wind is still blowing and the snow"—he just shook his head—"there's enough wood for the fire. We can make it through the night."

"But they may be out there," Helen said.

"If they've been out there this long," Roger said. "They're not coming back. No one could survive in that wind and cold for three hours. For *one* hour."

"Well, then they made it. But maybe something's happened over there, at the hotel. Maybe they can't make it back just yet. We have no way to know from here?"

Roger shook his head.

"We need radios," he said.

"We need a way out of this town," Helen said. "Maybe they got the snowmobiles out of the cold."

"Maybe," Roger said. "Maybe so."

Roger stood in the firelight a few feet from the fire. Helen sat up on the sofa. She glanced at her feet. They did not look good. There was a little bit of twitching movement in her toes, which was good to see, but the color was bad and what movement she had, she could not feel, and that probably meant she had serious nerve damage.

"How do they look?" Roger said.

Helen followed his eyes' focus to her feet.

"Not as bad as I thought they may look," she said. "A few hours ago. There's a little bit of movement."

He came over and sat on the edge of the table in front of the sofa. He looked at her gray-green eyes in the firelight.

"Come here," she said, curling her index finger for him to come toward her.

He leaned in close, and her eyes closed. They kissed just right. Roger's hand came up to her left cheek, and he felt the warmth and life flowing through her. He caressed her cheek and swept a strand of hair back over her left ear. He leaned back a little, their faces just a few inches away from one another, and a little smile rose up at the corners of her lips. Helen was cute, adorable, the kind of woman he wanted to cuddle with by a warm fire when the weather outside was brutal and cold. She had love in her heart, and Roger felt it. He knew it. He knew it the way he knew an answer to a certain question seven words into the question's asking. It just clicked in his mind like a metronome.

"I love you, Helen," he said.

"I know," Helen said. "I can tell it here"—she pointed to her heart—"And I can see it here"—she pointed to her temple.

"Do you?" Roger started.

"You know I do," Helen said. "Something's happened these past few days. I've never felt anything like this. I guess this is what we mean when we talk about love."

TWENTY-EIGHT
SAFETY

Levine led the assault carrying a powerful flashlight through the blizzard. Amber and McKenzie were behind her on the rope. The wind screamed, a terrifying fifty-mile-per-hour wail that beat at them with snow and ice and needles of cold. But they were bundled, and they'd faced this storm once already today. Each woman focused on her feet, her snowshoes, each little step forward into the storm. Each woman carried a flashlight, and from a few feet away it looked like three lights flickering forward into the bright white darkness, a soundless scream like the inside of a jet engine. The white fury surrounded them, but they knew its promise was death, and they were prepared for it.

Levine, Amber, and McKenzie carried large packs on their backs, and they held strong to the rope refusing to stumble and refusing to let go. A sudden gust of wind roared up to sixty miles an hour, but they braced themselves into the wind and wall of ice the wind hurled at them. They paused for a few seconds, but they kept their balance. And eventually the wind died down (back to just thirty-five), and Levine, Amber, and McKenzie carried on.

There was no sight around them at all. Only pain and death and fear and cold, and an unremitting world that wouldn't stop until all three were dead and forgotten. But not tonight. Tonight was theirs, and they refused to give into the ceaseless cry around them.

They wore their high-tech Nordic gear, ski masks, and goggles, and they carried packs on their backs. Levine had simply attached herself to the rope with a carabiner, which was attached to her jacket. With her free hand, she used a polished steel ski pole to help her keep her balance. Her flashlight shone forward into thick and blinding white, just a few feet, far enough to see the rope in front of her, the rope that would carry them back to the library. One snow-shoed footstep at a time. Up and then down, right and then left. Forward. Forward. Forward. Into the blizzard.

They reached the trench on the library's roof in less than ten minutes, which was all they had to spare. With darkness came impossibly cold temperatures and a wind chill comparable to the coldest places on Earth. It might have been minus seventy or minus eighty, but they weren't stopping to take measurements. One shot—from hotel to library.

They saw the handle of the snow shovel sticking up above the snow, and Levine was somewhat surprised to see that not much more snow had accumulated around it. She shone her flashlight on the handle which rose from the snow like the remains of a street sign after a hurricane. She glanced once over her shoulder, saw that Amber and McKenzie were there, and then all three climbed down into the trench.

They removed their snowshoes at the hole, threw them down inside the roof's opening, and then climbed single-file down into the library.

Neither said a word until all three were safely standing on the office floor inside the building.

"Everybody okay?" Levine said.

Amber and McKenzie nodded. They removed their ski masks and started down into the library to Helen and Roger.

• •

"Hello!" Levine called. "Roger! Helen! *Hellooo!*"

Her voice echoed down inside the library, past the security desk, up the hallway to Helen and Roger on the sofa.

Roger called back, "We're here! Down by the fire."

He and Helen looked up and saw the band of three coming up the hallway with flashlights. Roger saw that they had backpacks on their backs, and they were removing their first layer of Nordic gear.

"We were beginning to worry," Roger said.

He stood up and came to them. He helped Levine with her pack. Sara was helping Amber with hers. And they all gathered at the table some twenty feet from the fire.

Levine said, "We ran into a little bit of trouble on the way over there."

"Had to dry off," Sara said.

"The wind chill outside is probably minus-seventy," Amber said.

"How are you feeling?" Levine said to Helen.

Helen smiled at her from the sofa, and Levine came around to her in the firelight.

Helen said, "I think I'm gonna be alright. There's a little bit of movement in my feet."

"That's *great* news," Sara said.

Amber said to Roger, "We've got noodles and rice, chicken broth, bottles of water, cans of soup, crackers, peanut butter, macaroni and cheese. We brought enough food to last a couple days if need be."

"That's great," Roger said.

"And blankets," Amber said. She opened up her pack. "We've got sleeping bags for everyone."

Roger said, "Here, let's spread those out by the fire."

Amber and Roger began to set up the sleeping bags and bedrolls over to the right side of the fire. Levine stayed close to Helen, and Sara warmed herself by the fire.

"We're thinking," Levine said. "That we should hold out here overnight and see if the weather let's up at all by the morning."

Sara said, "There's enough fuel in the snowmobile. We could make it up to the mine. See if we can find that key. The mine's only five miles outside of town."

"What if we can't get into the mine?" Helen said.

"Well, there's not going to be snow inside the mine," Levine said. "The whole town is buried underneath this blizzard, but the mine is carved into the side of a mountain. It's a natural barrier."

"Is the key *inside* the mine?" Roger said.

"It looks like it," Levine said. "I checked the Colorado Sequence one more time before we left the hotel. The coordinates don't show up on the topographical surface maps, but there's something about keys in the literature on that mine."

"On keys?" Helen said.

"There's a Key Room," Sara said.

"A Key Room?"

"It's in the mine," Levine said. "If the weather allows it, we'll find out tomorrow."

"A Key Room," Roger said to himself, considering the idea.

TWENTY-NINE
NIGHTFALL

Outside the library, a multitude of young women in white robes came down out of the mountains surrounding the town of Ouray. None were older than eighteen. The wind continued to scream, but the precipitation had let up. The town was an icy barren desert in a snow-white windstorm, and as the evening hours wore on, the temperatures plunged. The wind stayed steady above thirty miles an hour, and occasional gusts blustered upwards of sixty and seventy. In that kind of cold, no matter how bundled people were, they would be dead in a matter of minutes.

The girls were barefooted, and their hair fell down gently around their shoulders. They were beautiful, peaceful, serene, and angelic. They looked identical, but they were not. One young woman leading a particular group had gray eyes and a light smile on her lips. Her straight brown hair fell down perfectly over her shoulders as though not a strand was out of place. The wind howled around her, but she came forward calmly, even inquisitively, looking at the five girls gathered closest to her, looking curiously at the barren landscape of the snow-buried town.

Another young woman toward the front of another group had cobalt blue eyes and straight red hair. She seemed sterner of face with a calm assurance driving each step forward down out of the mountains. The girls closest to her smiled, and she pointed forward, indicating the town. They nodded their heads and continued down into town.

From a distance, the girls seemed to glow. On a mountain range rising just east of town, it looked like a mass of lights moving calmly down the mountain, each woman radiating a glowing white aura. Altogether, there must have been close to ten thousand young women descending from the steep mountains surrounding town, converging on a single spot towards the center of town very near to the snow-buried library.

• •

Amber's sleep was uneasy. She was curled up inside her sleeping bag, and the fire's embers glowed warmly toward the center of the room. The whole gang was gathered in one area just a few feet away from the fireplace, and they slept together. Little snores emitted from Sara's nose and from Helen's throat. Levine whispered every few seconds as though talking to someone in her sleep. Then she rolled over, her arm draping accidentally over Roger's chest.

Amber dreamed she was surrounded by glowing lights, little patches of white amorphous light in a sea of foam. She felt like she was floating, carried on gently rocking waves. The patches of light were composed of hundreds and hundreds of golden points of light which opened and closed, expanded and narrowed, beating like the beat of a strong pulse. The patches surrounded her body, and carried her. She saw that the patches were themselves swirling around and around, composed of the golden points of light which orbited inside the patches at a steady tidal pace.

Amber saw her father there in the distance, and the feeling filled her with a sense of dread. But it was a dread born of guilt at never having said the right things to her father, at never having understood him while he was alive. The dream was filled with a regret that squeezed at her chest like a thumb on a bird's breast. And she clutched at the pressure with her hands, trying to peel away the regret, trying to reach out to a father who had always been too afraid to reach out to her.

In her dream, her father was playing hop-scotch. He was focused and alert and enjoying himself. And he was sober. Something she rarely ever saw, if at all, in real life. The fear and the pressures of failure were just too much for him. And the fear of failure was at little things, not necessarily huge life-altering decisions, but the simple things like choosing the right words to say to convey true love for his daughter, at encouraging her just the right way. He was so afraid of not succeeding that the fear itself ruined any chance for his success.

She saw her mother in the dream, driving a school bus. Her mom was a school bus driver, and she was driving that school bus up the little tunnel of light in Amber's dream. She was heading for her father who stood right out in the middle of the tunnel with his back to the school bus. In the dream, Amber couldn't tell for certain whether her mom realized her dad was standing there in the middle of the tunnel, but the bus roared onward, its powerful diesel engine belching out a black cloud of smoke.

Amber's dad was waving to her, his back to the school bus, and Amber started to scream, started to shout, "Look out! Look out, Dad!" But he only bent over and picked up the hop-scotch rock and continued on through the squares, smiling merrily at Amber. Amber screamed louder, watching the tragedy playing out in front of her, the school bus closing on her father, and then Amber was hit with a gnawing sense that her mother *did* know he was standing there. And at the last second, Amber saw the look in her mother's eyes. Amber saw through the front window of the school bus and saw Donna's face, saw the scrunched lip and the gleam in her eyes. Amber saw that her mother had both hands on the steering wheel and was leaning forward in the seat, as though racing to run her father over.

Amber screamed.

She screamed so loud at the moment when the bus hit her father that it pulled her up out of sleep. At the moment of impact, there was a blinding flash of light, and Amber shot bolt-upright in her sleeping bag. She woke with a scream that woke everyone else up around her, and then from somewhere upstairs there was a loud crash.

It sounded like the roof had caved in.

Everyone was up on their feet stumbling around in the dark.

"What was that?" Sara McKenzie said.

"Somebody's breaking in," Roger said.

He went over to the fireplace and lifted a poker from the rack.

Amber was awake, but trapped in her sleeping bag and she was so disoriented she thought she was drowning.

She cried out, "Help!"

Levine grabbed a flashlight and shone it on her. She knelt down and said, "It's okay, Amber. Everything's gonna be okay."

Levine put a calming hand on Amber's forehead.

Sara knelt down, too, and she said, "Everything's gonna be alright, sweetie."

She helped her out of her sleeping bag, and Amber stood up and embraced Sara like a little child. For the first time since they'd met, Sara was struck with the fact that Amber Page was a kid, a young girl. She may be destined to grow up to do all sorts of wonderful things, but at that moment, Sara just held her tight and said, "Everything's gonna be okay, Amber. I promise."

· ·

Sara, Helen, and Amber stayed by the fire while Roger and Levine went to check out what had made the crashing sound upstairs. Roger carried the fire poker, and Levine carried the flashlight. They turned left at the library security office and headed up the stairs. The flashlight beam shone up the stairwell in front of them. There were two handrails on either side of the hallway, and Levine went first.

"How you doing back there?" Levine said.

"Feels cold," Roger said.

They reached the top of the stairs, where they had to stop. Levine shone the light forward. The roof had caved in. There was snow everywhere. The crossties from the ceiling had fallen in near the doorway into that last office, the office with their opening out onto the roof. Levine crouched and looked around with the flashlight. It looked like a tornado had hit it. Everything was overturned. A cold breeze rustled through the debris.

"It looks like the roof just gave," Roger said.

"Too much weight," Levine said.

"Is there a way out'a here?"

Levine shone the light. "Not through that," she said.

Roger looked at Levine's brown and blue eyes. She looked at the mess of the caved-in roof. She was inspecting it for any openings.

Roger said, "That means we're trapped."

"Maybe we could clear away some of this stuff."

"Yeah?"

"Problem is," Levine said, "if you start pulling stuff out'a the way, more will fall down."

"We could get buried."

Levine shone the light up at the roof. There was a loud cracking sound. Levine screamed. Roger fell backwards down the stairwell. Everything faded to black a second.

Roger shook his head and looked up the stairwell. He'd fallen down the stairs, but he saw that Levine was up at the top. A central ceiling beam had broken, and more of the roof had caved in on them. Levine lay at the top of the stairs. She wasn't moving.

"Amy!" Roger called out.

The flashlight lay four steps down from her. It was shining at the wall, but Roger could see Levine.

She groaned.

Roger ran up the stairs to her. His back throbbed in pain. Levine had a cut up above her hairline, and blood was coming down her forehead.

"God," Roger said.

He knelt beside her. Levine was dazed. He glanced up and realized more of the roof may cave in at any second. He lifted Amy Levine up in his arms and managed to grab the flashlight with his right hand. Levine moaned something about "the clouds."

Roger pulled back an eyelid and saw that her pupil was dilated. She'd taken a knock on the head, but she was going to be alright. Roger threw open the door from the security office and came back up the hallway toward the rest of the gang.

Sara came to him.

"Oh, my God," she said. "What happened?"

Roger held Levine in his arms.

"The roof caved in," he said. "She took it on the head."

Sara came up beside him and looked at Levine.

Levine said, "My head hurts."

Helen stepped out away from the fire. She walked as though she wasn't sure her feet would hold her. *God*, Roger thought. *We're falling all to pieces, here.*

"Clear the sofa," he said. "Amy took a blow to the head."

They cleared the stuff away from the sofa, and Roger placed her gently. Amber handed Sara a clean white cloth.

"We need to stop the bleeding," Amber said.

"That's a pretty nasty cut," Roger said.

He stepped back and let Sara in close. Sara knelt over the sofa and swabbed up the blood from Levine's forehead with the white washcloth.

"How bad does it look?" Helen said.

Sara leaned in close and inspected the cut.

"Shine that light over here," she said to Roger.

The flashlight came up, and Sara began feeling around the cut. Her head was damp with blood, and Sara felt a rock of a knot forming on her head.

"That's a pretty wicked bump," Sara said.

Levine said, "Ow!" Her face grimaced in pain. She was coming to, but the pain was pushing her back into unconsciousness.

"You're gonna be alright," Sara said to her. "Just lie still."

They all started at the sound of another huge crash from upstairs. It was a wood-splintering *crrrack!* followed by the tumbling crash of debris.

"The whole building's gonna fall in on us," Helen said.

They all seemed to consider this for a second.

And then Amber said with a conviction that unsettled them all, "We need to get out of here. This building's going to collapse."

Sara looked at her in the firelight. "Are you sure?"

"Yes."

"We can't get out," Roger said. "There's too much debris."

"And it must be minus-seventy outside," Helen said.

"We have to get out," Amber said, "or we're all going to die."

Thirty
Attempt at Escape

Sara McKenzie helped Levine into her cold weather gear. Levine's head was clearing, but she had a grimace on her face. Her eyes looked like they were squeezing shut against some pain inside her head that was excruciating. She pulled her jacket over her shoulders and kept dabbing at her head with the white washcloth to stanch the bleeding.

"There's another door over here," Helen said.

Helen was across the room. She used one of the fireplace pokers as a cane to help her keep her balance on her nerve-damaged feet. She held the door open.

"It looks like stairs up to the same office," Helen said. "But from a different side."

Roger said, "The whole office up there has caved in."

"Well, maybe we can find an opening out onto the roof."

"Our snowshoes!" Roger said. "They were right above where the roof crashed in. How're we gonna get back to the hotel without snowshoes?"

No one had an answer for this, but they were all finishing up with their cold weather gear.

"Come on," Sara said. "Helen's right. We'll try this door."

Roger looked at Sara worriedly.

"Come on big man," Sara jibed. "You're supposed to be fearless."

Amber said, "A man is always afraid of doing what a woman knows has to be done."

The three older women looked at young Amber with something like amusement in their eyes.

Amber nudged Roger in the ribs. "Come on, Roger," she said. "Don't want to be shown up by a little girl, do you?"

And then they were up and through the doorway, climbing up the stairs. Sara and Helen reached the top of the stairwell first. They shone their two flashlights ahead and saw all the crashed debris of the roof.

Snow lay all over the floor. They could see through the debris to the other side of the hallway, the side they'd all been using earlier.

"There's one section over there," Helen said, pointing with her flashlight.

They all saw what she meant. There was one slab of wood about four feet wide that rose up from the hallway floor in a sixty-degree slant. It was white and covered with snow.

"It looks like it just climbs out on top of all that mess," Levine said.

There was a terrible wrenching metal sound from up the hallway, a thunderous crash, and they were blasted with white powder. Everyone winced, but a few seconds later, the snow began to settle. They glanced around and realized that everyone was okay. The whole building shook.

They looked at one another the way a group of kids might look at one another if they were out on a frozen lake and suddenly realized that the ice was breaking.

Roger said, "We need to get out'a here!"

Sara said, "Levine, you and Amber go first. Helen and Roger next. I'll go last."

Everyone started to protest her selflessness, but suddenly the whole building shook again, and *everything* just rose up and lurched about seven feet to the right. They all screamed and were knocked to the floor.

The flat hallway floor now jutted up like a slide. Debris and snow rolled past them, and they all clung to the floor.

"Look out!" Levine shouted.

A desk rolled down the sloped hallway toward them. It was right in the center of the hallway, and they all rolled quickly to the sides. The desk rushed past them, hit the doorway at the back of the hallway, and then fell for twenty or thirty feet until it crashed into a floor.

They were all lying there, clinging to the floor, which was sloped about as steep as a schoolyard slide. The floor was damp, icy, and coated with a thin layer of snow.

"Okay," Sara said. "Levine! Amber! Come on!"

They had about twenty feet up to the slab that rose up out of the roof. It was impossible to tell what would come next, even if the snow-covered slab did support their weight. But they were running out of options.

Levine tried to stand up, leaning forward into the slanted hallway. She kind of went forward on hands and feet, climbing up the slick floor. Amber stayed low and made it to the slab just ahead of Levine.

Behind them, Roger and Helen started climbing up the hallway.

Levine could see the bright orange climbing rope. It was dangling over the wall of white snow that rose sheer up from the top of the slab.

"What you need to do, Amber," she said, "is climb to the top of this slab. At the top there, you can see that the snow wall rises up ten feet, straight up. Just climb that wall and get out on the surface of the snow. You can use the rope to guide you. You know the rope carries us back to the hotel."

Amber nodded her head, smiled, and said to Levine, "We can do it. We make a good team!"

"You bet'cha!" Levine said. "Now, go. And go carefully."

Amber started climbing the slab. The floor of the hallway was now jutting up at a forty-degree angle, and the snow-covered slab itself rose up at sixty degrees. It was at a level of steepness that required climbing just as much as crawling, and one errant step would bring them sliding straight back down to the hallway.

There was a horrible wrenching sound from somewhere deep inside the building. Everyone held on, but the building just groaned. A blast of air came up from inside the building and washed over them. Amber was almost to the top of the slab.

She reached her hands forward and touched the snow wall. It was flat at the very top, but she was hesitant to just stand up. She knelt on her knees and dug her hands into the snow wall.

"I can't climb this," she called back down to Levine.

Levine was midway up the slab behind her. Levine glanced behind her and saw that Helen and Roger had reached the bottom of the slab. Sara was back in the shadows of the hallway.

Levine looked up at Amber ahead of her. "Sure you can, sweetie," she said.

Levine watched Amber rise up slowly on her feet. Amber was measuring the wall above her. It was a sheer ninety-degree wall. It was about ten feet high, and it was made of pure snow and ice. Levine saw the bright orange rope dangling from the wall about ten feet to the right of Amber. She couldn't reach it from where she was. It would require her to leap through the air to grab it, and there was nothing up there holding the rope.

"You've gotta climb it, Amber," Levine said. "It's just a few feet."

Amber didn't even turn around to acknowledge this. She'd found her line on the wall, and she started climbing. She dug her hands into the snow, then her boot, and she formed her own little rock wall crevices as she climbed.

The wind was really kicking up toward the surface, Levine realized. She looked up and saw a good twenty-mile-an-hour gust ruffling Amber's jacket and ski pants as she clung to the white snow wall. Amber was midway to the top. It was dark outside.

Levine reached the top of the slab. She crouched and glanced back at Helen and Roger. They were both about midway up the slab, and Levine saw Sara now at the bottom.

Sara looked up and her face caught some unnaturally bright light, and Levine saw the focused expression on her face. Levine's head came around, curious to see what had caused the bright light, but she saw nothing. Amber had her arms over the ledge at the top and was pulling herself over onto the surface of the snow beyond the wall.

Levine glanced back and saw Sara beginning to climb the slab. Whatever had caused that glowing light was no longer shining, and Levine felt the dampness of blood on her head and thought that maybe it was just her imagination. She'd taken a good knock on the head and was likely to be seeing shiny lights and all kinds of luminescence. She turned and started to climb the snow wall. She saw Amber hoist her legs over the top. She made it! Amber was safe!

Behind her, Roger and Helen reached the top of the slab. Levine was midway up the wall. She glanced to her right and saw the bright orange rope dangling against the wall just a few feet to her right. She looked above her and saw that she only had a few more feet to the top of the snow wall. Amber's head appeared over the edge. She looked down at Levine, her hair falling all around her.

"Three more feet, Dr. Levine," Amber said calmly. "You've got it now."

Amber disappeared back beyond the edge, and Levine concentrated on the last three steps. She got her hand up over the top. She wind was really moving up on the surface of the snow. It was cold, and it ruffled her hair, her ski jacket, and her black ski pants. Her head felt dizzy, but she threw one arm over the edge, then the other, and she shimmied up over the edge. She made it!

She saw what had made the glowing light. Levine was on her back in the snow, but she rolled over quickly and saw an entire congregation of glowing young women in white robes. The wind gusted at a steady twenty miles an hour, snow rolling along the surface, but these girls stood there peacefully surrounding them at a distance of about fifty feet. There were hundreds of them, Levine saw, maybe even thousands.

"*Oh, my God*," she said under her breath.

The whole town was aglow. Levine looked around her in every direction. These beautiful girls stood there in the distance some fifty feet away, and they were watching them.

Helen came up over the edge, looked around, and said, "*Oh, my.*"

Roger crested the edge and pulled himself over from the snow wall. He saw them, too, and his mouth just dropped open. His eyes moved around the snow-buried town. The whole town was aglow with hundreds and hundreds of girls. He'd seen girls just like these just a few days before, but they weren't friendly, then.

Helen stared around at them, too. The last time she'd seen girls like these they put her into shock, and now their numbers had multiplied by a hundred. There were literally thousands of girls watching them.

"Guys, can I get a little help!" Sara's voice came from down on the slab.

Amber and Levine crouched down and looked over the edge. Sara looked up at them. She had ten feet to climb.

Levine started to say, "Just follow the foot holes there on the wall," but she got to the word "foot," and the slab fell out from Sara. She screamed.

There was a loud crack from down inside the building, and the whole shelf they were standing on rumbled. It sounded like the whole massive snow stack that stood around the library was about to cave in.

Sara had less than a half second to decide. All her weight shifted to the right, and the wooden slab just fell out from under her. She saw that bright orange climbing rope hanging seven feet away, and she just leapt.

She was in the air.

The entire building caved in and dropped down about ten feet. The sound was enormous. There was a shift in the snow shelf, and it knocked Helen and Roger to their feet.

Sara hit the side of the wall, clutching at the rope and managed to get her hands around it. For a moment, it held, and Sara hung onto the side of a snow wall that had just gone from ten to twenty feet tall. She swung a little from right to left, and then her momentum carried her back to the right. She got both hands around the rope and just held on.

Levine's eyes shot forward and saw that the rope had snagged on the snow shovel that someone had driven down into the snow earlier. That snow shovel's handle was all that was holding the rope from falling out completely. And the snow shovel was right at the edge of the snow wall.

Levine leapt up and lunged ten feet toward the rope wrapped around that snow shovel's handle. She could hear Sara wailing down on the side of the snow wall.

"*Help!*" she cried.

Sara McKenzie looked straight down and saw the remains of the roof twenty feet below her. The fall probably wouldn't kill her, she realized, but if she fell onto that unstable debris, it would cause the rest of the building to collapse in, and the building would crush her under all its weight.

She clung to the rope with both hands, and she tried to squeeze her legs around it, too.

"I've got it!" Levine said.

Levine held the rope back behind the snow shovel, but the shovel's handle was actually holding most of Sara's body weight. Levine glanced down at the shovel right in front of her. She saw that it was bending forward, and that if it bent forward far enough the rope would take off, whickering out into the air. Levine glanced around her.

Roger was pushing Helen and Amber back.

"The whole shelf's gonna go!" he shouted at them.

"We've got to help them!" Helen cried.

"It'll kill us all!" Roger said. "Back! Away from the edge!"

Roger was pushing them back away from the edge in the direction of the courthouse's cupola, which rose just above the surface. The wind had died down to a stiff breeze, but Roger pushed Helen and Amber back away from the library area. The whole thing was about to cave in like a snowy sinkhole.

Levine held the rope in one hand. The shovel acted as a temporary stanchion between her and Sara, but Levine didn't have the strength in her to pull Sara up from the snow wall.

She lay flat on her stomach and held the rope in both hands, but her head was dizzy and spinning, and her arms felt weak. She slid toward the edge, and suddenly found herself staring over the edge, down the snow wall at Sara McKenzie. She was only about ten feet down.

"Dig your feet into the wall!" Levine croaked. "It'll take some of the weight off this rope!"

Sara kicked forward at the wall, and the front of her right boot sunk into the hard-packed ice and snow.

"Now the other!" Levine said.

Sara kicked forward with her other foot and sunk it into the wall. The snow shovel creaked and lurched forward. Sara screamed and fell out away from the wall.

"Oh, my God!" she cried.

Levine was pulled half over the edge, and the realization went through her mind that she was going to die. The shovel wasn't going to hold that weight more than a few more seconds, and her traction on the ice and snow was insufficient at best. She would be pulled over the side, and both she and Sara would plunge into the debris twenty feet below.

Sara looked up at her hanging over the edge.

She said, "Just let me go."

Levine grimaced, gripping the rope. Her head throbbed, the snow was beyond any cold she'd ever felt.

"Save yourself, Amy," Sara said. "You can't save me."

"No!" Levine roared.

She started to pull as hard as she could, but her exertion forced the snow to wash out from under her. There was a horrible metallic *twang!* Levine saw the shovel break free and whicker out into the air.

Suddenly the weight she'd been holding was three times as heavy, and she was going over the edge with Sara on one end of the rope and with her on the other; they'd plummet to the bottom. It would be twenty feet straight down onto building debris, and then they'd be swallowed whole by the crushed library.

It was all happening right before her. Levine's mind was just at the brink of letting go of the rope in order to save herself when she heard from back behind her, "Hold on, kids!"

Roger grabbed hold of Levine's ankles and plunked down like a tug-of-war anchorman into the snow.

Levine was over the edge, folded at her midsection, but she held onto the rope. Ten feet below her, Sara dangled back and forth grazing the side of the snow wall.

Slowly, one careful handful at a time, Roger McAllister started to pull Levine back from the edge. He got her up so that her shoulders were back from the edge and only her arms were over the side. She felt the rope burning in her hands. A few inches slipped out of her grip.

Sara screamed.

Levine gasped, "*The rope!*"

Roger said, "Hold on!"

He heard footsteps padding behind him in the snow. And then Amber was there at his side. She went flat on her stomach beside Levine and reached forward and got her two hands around the rope. Levine looked at her. Amber's and her eyes met.

Amber said, "Come on."

She looked back at the rope. She started pulling. Snow trickled down over the side, straight down the wall, over Sara McKenzie and down onto the crushed building's roof far below them.

Roger grunted and pulled as hard as he could. He got Levine back a few more inches. His face turned bright red, and the veins on his neck bulged out. They just didn't have enough strength and traction to pull McKenzie up.

Then they heard more footsteps padding through the snow, and Helen lay down on Levine's other side.

"Come on, guys," Helen said. "Let's get her out'a there!"

She reached forward and got the rope in her hands, and it was just the strength they needed. Sara started to climb up the snow wall. Amber saw that the rope was fraying.

She said, "The rope's going to break."

Roger said, "What?"

Levine called down to Sara, "Dig into the wall! The rope's going to break!"

Sara was in tears, clinging to the rope. She didn't really comprehend what Levine was telling her.

Helen screamed, "The *rope!* It's going to break!"

Sara dug her right foot into the wall and at just that moment there was a wiry *perrk!* as the rope broke into two pieces and fell out into the air away from the snow wall.

Everybody up on the surface fell backward. Levine scrambled to her knees and crawled back over to the edge. Sara clung to the wall just five feet below them.

"Come on, Sara," Levine said. "You've got five feet to go! Just take one step at a time!"

Sara's face was flush against the snow wall. Below her, the rope hit the debris with a light sound. Levine reached her right arm over the edge. Their hands were only two feet apart.

Roger, Helen, and Amber grabbed Levine's legs and anchored themselves into position.

Somebody let out a sound like "Whooooa!"

And slowly, one handful of ski pant at a time, they began to pull Levine and Sara up over the edge.

"We got you, Sara!" Levine said.

Sara clutched at the wall as she came up over the edge. They all saw the tension in her green eyes. The glowing light from all the robed girls lit up her face. She smiled at them worriedly, and she threw her arm over the side and hoisted herself up. She got her right leg over the edge, then her left. She rolled over on her back, clear of the edge. And they all five fell back and let out a sigh of relief.

They stayed there for a few seconds.

Helen said, "We made it."

Everyone seemed to agree. Levine started to climb up onto one knee, and *that* was when they all heard the earth giving out from underneath them.

"The whole thing's gonna go!" Roger shouted.

They were all up, sprinting away from the library. There was an earth-shattering *crack!* as the snow shelf broke.

They ran in the direction of the hotel, and their feet padded over the packed snow that their snowshoes had made earlier. The snow was packed just hard enough where they'd gone back and forth between library and hotel to support their weight.

Sara was out front, followed by Roger. Amber was right behind Roger, then Levine, and Helen brought up the rear, hobbling on her bad feet.

They were all running over the field of white snow toward the hotel. They were about thirty meters from the library when they were all knocked to their faces on the snow. Behind them, it looked like the earth was swallowing everything.

Levine saw the bright orange rope trailing ahead of them, and she knew it led to the hotel.

"Run!" she shouted. "Follow the rope!"

They all scrambled to their feet. Back behind them, there were huge explosive sounds as gas mains inside the library exploded. Fire exploded up into the air, causing an enormous sound like an earthquake.

Levine glanced once behind her and saw a giant black hole where the library had been. It was about two hundred feet across, and flames licked up from the center of the hole. Sparks exploded up into the air, fireball shrapnel lighting the night sky like bright orange fireworks. The group of five just ran.

Snow sprayed up under their boots as they ran, and it looked like they were clear. Sara saw the trench down into the hotel up ahead. She glanced back once, herself, and saw the same thing Levine saw: a giant pit where the library had just collapsed under thirty plus feet of snow.

"Run!" she shouted. "Inside the hotel!"

Roger went down into the trench first, then Amber, Helen, Levine and Sara. Bright orange fireballs exploded up into the sky, and the group hit the door to the hotel and plowed inside, out of breath, but alive and safe.

THIRTY-ONE
SLEEPLESS NIGHT

No one slept in the hotel. Levine and Sara made a pot of coffee at three in the morning when it became clear that they'd be up all night. Roger and Helen explained the story of the white-robed girls to the other three. He told them how a girl not unlike the ones they'd all seen outside in the town had run up into his arms out of the rain. Helen explained how she'd leaned over the bed to listen to the girl, and how she'd almost lost her life because of it.

"The girl looked just like those girls out there?" Levine asked.

"Pretty much," Roger said.

"They didn't seem threatening to me," Sara said.

Sara stood by the fire, sleepless, with a cup of fresh coffee in her hands listening to Roger and Helen on the sofa.

"They just watched us," she said.

"Like observers," Levine said.

Neither Roger nor Helen said anything for a second. "I'm just telling you what I saw the other day," Roger finally said.

"Did they seem threatening to you?" Sara asked them.

"These outside?" Roger said.

"Yeah."

Roger shook his head.

Helen said, "I agree. It looked like they were just watching us. If they wanted us, if they meant us harm, they would have broken in here to this hotel by now. Something's happened. Something's changed."

"What is it?" Levine said.

There was no easy answer to this.

"Well, we've got you here, Dr. Levine," Roger said. "And Amber. Maybe they saw us—Helen and I—as a threat. We were carrying your sequence, the Colorado Sequence. Maybe they wanted that. Maybe you're supposed to go into this world, to do good, to get the key to this Needle."

"Or maybe they're just waiting for the right moment to kill us all," Sara said.

"Well, yeah maybe," Roger said.

• •

The hours wore on. They jumped at every little sound inside the hotel. There were noises in the ceiling like mice scurrying, and it was driving them crazy.

"Maybe we should go out there and see what they want?" Sara said, sometime around four-fifty A.M.

"I feel terrible," Helen said.

No one had slept much at all. Amber had finally dozed off a little after four o'clock, but the adults were uneasy and awake. They all remained in the lobby area and kept a steady fire going in the fireplace.

Helen sat in a leather chair. Levine was sitting on the brick hearth with her back to the fire. Her face was in her hands, and her elbows were propped up on her knees. She looked exhausted. Roger sat on the floor with his hands wrapped around the fronts of his knees. His back hurt, and he didn't believe he'd had a clear thought in his head in hours. Sara sat against one wall only slightly in the shadows.

Amber was asleep on the sofa.

"How does she do that?" Helen said.

Roger said, "When you're that age, you can sleep through an earthquake."

"Well, let's hope *that* doesn't happen," Levine said.

"An earthquake?" Roger said.

"Yeah," Levine said.

They all chuckled very lightly. They were tired.

"Do you think there's enough fuel," Helen asked Levine and McKenzie, "to get that snowmobile up to the mine?"

"Should be," Levine said. "We were lucky to grab the right one."

Sara said, "What would it do to an engine if you put kerosene in it?"

"What do you mean?" Levine said.

"It'd kill it," Roger said. "You're thinking the same thing I was thinking, Sara."

"I saw a couple dozen ten-gallon tanks of kerosene in the store room. If we could put fuel in those things," Sara said. "We could double up and ride right out of these mountains. Get down to low country. Food. A hot tub."

"Screw a hot tub," Helen said. "Just give me a bed and twelve hours of uninterrupted sleep."

"I'd sleep like a log," Roger said.

They smiled at the thought.

Roger said, "But, no, kerosene would kill a snowmobile engine."

They fell silent for a few minutes. They sat there in the firelight listening to the wood in the fireplace crackle and pop. The heat from the fire was warm, but if they left the lobby area the rest of the hotel was frigid. Levine had gone up to the kitchen once and was amazed to see her breath on the cold air *inside* the hotel.

"You hear that?" Levine said.

They all looked up. Their eyes went to Levine's, and then they all craned their necks and listened. There was nothing, only the sound of the wood crackling in the fireplace.

"What?" Helen said.

"The wind," Levine said. "It sounds like the wind has died down."

They all listened.

They could hear nothing beyond the lobby area. There were occasional noises inside the hotel. Water flushing through a pipe, a creak and crack of the building settling under colder and colder temperatures. But they could hear nothing beyond that.

"Maybe we've caught a break," Levine said.

"The weather?" Roger said.

Helen said, "The forecast was for another storm by the weekend. Coming in from the West."

"But maybe we'll have one day of clear weather," Levine said. "Or just one morning."

Sara leaned forward. "We could make it up to the mine," she said excitedly. "Find this key, haul butt back down here to town!"

"What if you can't find the key when you get up there?" Helen said.

"There was one book that I found," Sara said. "It said the mine was famous for its Key Room."

"What *is* that?" Roger said. "A Key Room?"

"I've never heard of a Key Room," Helen said.

"Neither have I," Sara said. "But it was there in the book. The clues all fit. We'll get up there to the Carbañero Mine, hit this Key Room, find our key, and get back down here to town."

"How far is it?" Helen said.

"Five miles," Levine said. "We have just enough gas in the one snowmobile to make it."

Sara said, "Why not use that snowmobile to get down to Durango?"

"Durango's fifty miles," Levine said. "We have enough gas for ten miles but not enough for fifty."

They were silent a moment, listening.

Amber mumbled something in her sleep and rolled over on the sofa. Her eyes opened, and she glanced around the room at all of them.

"What time is it?" she said.

"It's early, hon," Levine said. "Just try and go back to sleep."

Amber smiled and pulled the blankets up around her chin. She rolled over on her side, and in another minute, she was asleep again.

"So," Roger said, after a minute, his voice lowered. "Who's gonna do it?"

They all looked at him.

"Who's gonna take the snowmobile out there," he said. "Who's gonna try to make it up to the mine?"

Levine stood up and crossed the room.

"I've got these topo maps," she said.

She grabbed a map from the check-in counter and returned to the fireplace. They all gathered around her on the floor right in front of the fire. She spread out the map. There were elevation gradations marked on the map.

"We're here," she said, marking one spot on the map with a red felt-tip pin. "You can see the building markings here. That's the courthouse there."

"And that's the library," Helen said.

"*Was* the library," Roger said.

"The mine is up here." Levine pointed to a spot far on the left side of the map.

"That looks like a long way," Helen said.

"With the map scale," Roger said, "an inch is like a quarter mile."

He pointed to the scale at the bottom left-hand corner.

"Yeah," Levine said. "It's really not that far. It's just that the mine is remote."

"And the elevation," Sara said.

"Yeah, it's much higher," Levine said. "You can see the thirteen here."

"Thirteen thousand?" Roger said.

Helen said, "As in feet?"

Levine said, "It's at thirteen-two."

They looked around at one another.

Roger said, "Who's going to go?"

Levine said, "You and Helen should stay here with Amber. Sara and I have been at altitude for awhile now. We crossed up to thirteen on the pass over here the other night."

"Thirteen's not a problem," Sara said. "You start pushing it up to seventeen, eighteen, and nineteen—that's a different story. We'll be fine."

"Is that cool with you two?" Levine asked Helen and Roger.

Roger said, "The snowmobile only rides two?"

"It really only rides *one*," Levine said. "But we can fit two on the seat."

THIRTY-TWO
THE OPTIONS

McKenzie and Levine opened the front door of the hotel prepared to retreat quickly back inside. The earliest shades of daylight were quietly stealing day from night. Everything was white. There was no wind, only a gentle breeze, and the air was crisp and cold. Levine stepped out into the snow, her boots crunching in the hardened powder, her breath steaming out from her mouth in ragged, excited puffs. She smiled at McKenzie.

"There's no wind," McKenzie said.

Roger closed the door behind them, and he stepped out onto the porch. He held a cup of coffee in his hand, and though his eyes looked as though he hadn't slept in days, he smiled at the scene. Levine and McKenzie walked up the trench to the surface and looked around.

"*Holy*," Sara said.

They stood there at the top of the trench gazing at a white desert. To the south, east, and west sides of town, towering mountains climbed up into an early morning sky. The mountains were white, completely white. Everything was white.

They could see that there was a town around them, but it was utterly buried in snow. The landscape was smooth, fresh, unadulterated, white powder. There were a few signs of a town lying underneath: the courthouse cupola, a church spire at St. Daniels Church, the upper half of a satellite dish atop the third floor of the Ouray Elementary School. A U.S. flag was frozen stiff and rose from the snow as though planted on the ground of a white moonscape; Levine knew that the entire city hall was buried underneath that flag in snow that must have been at least thirty feet deep.

Other than those few signs, the entire valley was one smooth white field four miles across, and six miles from end to end.

"Wish I had my skis," Levine said.

Sara smiled. They didn't see any sign of the white-robed young women. A falcon was up in the sky, circling slowly, surfing the updrafts

263

rolling in from the peaks to the south. There were patches of long thin clouds in the western sky. Roger came up the trench to join them. He looked around and was stunned.

"*Oh, my*," he said.

What was clear was the simple fact that no one would be coming into or going out of town for a good long while.

"You joke about the skis," Sara said. "That may end up being the only way we can get out of here."

"An all-out expedition," Levine said.

"No one knows we're here," Roger said. "Phone lines are down. Power is out. And everything is—*buried*."

"And the forecast is for another storm?" Levine said.

"That's what the weatherman said the other day," Roger said. "He said a completely separate system would be moving in from the West, from the Sierra Nevada Range."

"Here's what we need to do, Roger," Levine said. "Sara and I will take one shot at this gold mine. We've got enough fuel for maybe ten miles. That gets us up to the mine and back down. Nothing more. Sara's right; we may have to trek out of these mountains."

"What's the nearest town?" Roger said.

"Montrose to the north," Levine said. "That's forty miles."

"That's a heck of a hike," Sara said, "through this kind'a snow."

"I know it is," Levine said. "We're talking multiple days. Two at the fastest in this kind of snow. But we're probably looking at a three-day hike to the nearest civilization. And that's if the weather holds."

"What are our options?" Roger said.

"There's one other thing we can try," Levine said.

"What?" Roger said.

"This is a town," Levine said. "Somewhere buried underneath all this snow is a service station. I know there was a Texaco at the north end of town, three or four miles that way."

Levine pointed for Roger, and they all three looked but there was nothing but an enormous white field all around them.

"The pumps would still be on," Levine said, "at a gas station."

"*What* gas station?" Roger said.

"And there may be a general store," Levine said, ignoring the question, "with a pump out front, somewhere underneath all of this snow. Roger, if we could pinpoint where to dig, we could probably dig out a pump in a single day."

"Fuel," Sara said, "for the snowmobiles."

"With all five of us digging," Levine said. "It's an option."

"We could do it," Roger said. "We'd have to dig a thirty foot hole, but it could be done."

"Well," Levine said. "Snow levels are at thirty feet right now. Maybe a little deeper. But if this other system moves in later this afternoon, or tonight, it may prove easier to cross-country ski north to Montrose."

"Forty miles?" Roger said.

"It looks like those are our options," Levine said. "We don't have enough fuel in the snowmobile to get us one-quarter of the way to Montrose, and the snowmobile will only carry two people, but there's gotta be a gas station buried under all this snow. We've got the other snowmobile; it's tank is empty, but we have it. So Roger, while Sara and I head up to the mine, you, Helen, and Amber see if you can pinpoint where that service station is."

"How?"

"Check the maps," Levine said. "You may be able to find something in the hotel's library. We'd need a compass and some kind of landmark to know where to dig."

"And shovels," Roger said.

"Yeah," Levine said. "Check the store room, the room with all that kerosene, any place you can think of inside the hotel. Right now, we have the hotel. We could live for a few weeks off of the food in the hotel."

"That's an option, too," Sara said, "to just wait."

"It *is* an option," Levine said. "But we could be waiting a long time. I say we take a couple of active choices. One: see if we can dig out a fuel pump at a gas station. And two: plan for a three-day expedition out of the mountains. If neither of those works, we can always just wait it out."

Levine looked from Sara to Roger.

"It sounds like what we have to do," Roger said.

"I agree," Sara said. "But I'm not against waiting some time. If an airplane flies overhead we could signal them from the ground, and we do have enough food in the hotel to last a few days."

"Right," Levine said.

They stood there looking at one another, and the realization that they were truly cut off began to sink in. Under normal conditions, a drive to Montrose would take sixty minutes, an hour and a half tops. But they'd found themselves snowbound in the worst snow storm in Colorado history. And the way the clouds were building to the west, it looked like they were in for yet another storm.

"What do you think?" Levine said. She looked from Roger to Sara. "What should we do?"

Roger's eyes narrowed, focused. He realized the peril of their situation, their isolation.

"I'm with you, Dr. Levine," he said. "I think we try and see if we can dig out a fuel pump, but if we can't dig it out—if we get even more snow tonight—I think we have to begin thinking about some kind of expedition out of here. We could be trapped up here all winter, and we don't have the supplies for that."

Sara looked from Roger to Levine. Then, her eyes caught the clouds rolling in from the west. The air was cold, probably in the low twenties, but the sun crested the mountains to the east. For a moment, everything was bright, almost blindingly so because of the snow. Sara pulled her sunglasses down over her eyes.

She said, "I say we get this snowmobile up to that mine, get this key, and get back down here. If this kid really is all that special, we may have more to deal with than the worst snow storm in Colorado history. We may be dealing with forces far beyond that. And I, for one, want to make certain that we're ready."

THIRTY-THREE
THE MINE

Amy Levine steered the snowmobile, and Sara rode on the back. Snowshoes were strapped to the sides like saddlebags, and they were both bundled from head to foot in cold-weather gear. The snowmobile raced over the endless white landscape toward the peaks to the south.

Levine knew to look for landmarks like Old Man's Chin, a rocky outcropping that resembled the lower lip and chin of an old man; and Gobbler's Noggin, a peak on one mountain that resembled a turkey's head; she knew most of the peaks by sight, but she had never been to the Carbañero Mine, and everything was buried in deep white snow.

She knew that it was five miles to the entrance of the mine, and that it was five miles back down to town. But all paths and all trails and all clearings through trees were buried, the snowmobile itself riding atop thirty to forty feet of snow. She gripped the accelerator and Sara gripped her waist, and the snowmobile raced over the white landscape, climbing higher and higher into the mountains.

The clouds from the west had rolled in over the mountains, and by the time they reached the mine, both McKenzie and Levine realized that they were in for another devastating storm. Sunlight passed through patches of clouds above the highest jagged peaks. The air was so thin and so cold that they felt they had left the Earth, had arrived on some deserted distant planet or moon where the ground was covered with ice and snow, and the cold was a cold like nothing anyone else had ever known.

There was a building at the entrance to the mine. It was built on such a steep grade that no large amount of snow had been able to accumulate on the ground. The roof of the building was covered with snow, but a steady deadly wind swept the snow off the top of the building like a barber's sheer.

Levine looked around the moonscape of land. She had to calm herself to breathe well, the air was so thin. She could feel Sara on the snowmobile seat behind her. Levine could tell Sara was looking around the scene, too.

To the east it looked like one final range climbed up above fourteen thousand feet. They had to balance themselves on the snowmobile because the grades were so severe. They looked out to the north and felt their stomachs rise up into their chests. Behind them, there was an endless white field of snow that must have descended four miles, dropping nearly three thousand feet in elevation.

There was a sense that if they started to fall, they would fall a long, long way—perhaps for several minutes. These were the kinds of snowfields that created the world's great avalanches, avalanches on a scale of four, five, and six miles wide. There was nothing to obstruct it. Just an endless field of snow descending far down into the valley.

"We should walk up from here," McKenzie said, over the whine of the snowmobile engine and through her ski mask.

Levine nodded her head, pulled the snowmobile over to as level a spot as she could find, and then killed the engine.

"I don't like being out on these snowfields," Levine said, "on a snowmobile."

"Don't even mention the word avalanche," McKenzie said.

They sat against the side of the snowmobile and laced on their snowshoes. McKenzie's pair had clasps and she had gotten used to the ones with the leather straps (the ones now buried with the library way down in town), so it took her a minute to find the right fit.

The wind was steady but bearable. McKenzie removed her ski mask, and lifted her goggles up over her ski jacket's hood. Levine stepped out away from the snowmobile on her snowshoes and looked around her.

"Feels like we're standing on the edge of the Earth," Levine said. She looked out to the north. From here, they could see all the way to Montrose; they could probably see all the way to Delta, Colorado, but all of Colorado was buried under snow. It was huge. It was like looking at a moonscape from the highest peak on the moon. For more than a hundred miles in any direction to the north, they saw nothing but white. The jagged mountain peaks that formed all around them opened onto the western Colorado plain some twenty to thirty miles in the distance, and snow filled the plain all the way to the horizon some one hundred to one hundred and twenty miles to the west and to the north.

At that distance the sky was the same color of the snow-white Earth, and the feeling was so disorienting that for a moment, Sara McKenzie felt like she was upside down, floating in an airplane that was racing upside down toward the Earth.

"Man," she said. "The air's thin up here!"

The sound of their feet crunching over the snow was so tiny in correlation to the vast sound from one hundred miles around them, it was almost surreal.

They turned and looked up at the building at the entrance to the mine. It looked like an old hotel. There was a deck out front of the place, and there was a swinging chair hung on the deck. The deck was forty feet by sixty and sheltered, but snow had blown up under most of the open-air area.

There were two wings on either side of the central area to the building, two stories high with windows along either wing.

"That thing is built on such a slope," Levine said, "it looks like it's just hanging from the side of the mountain."

"Why would they build it that way?"

"Well, one reason is clear."

"What's that?" McKenzie asked. She was out of breath and had to stop.

"You don't get snow accumulation built on a rock face like that."

Levine stopped and looked at McKenzie. Though they'd only walked a minute or so, the snowmobile back behind them already looked tiny in the distance. She could see their trail through the fresh powder.

McKenzie was bent over with her hands on her knees.

"My head feels dishy," she slurred.

She rose up and started walking forward, but her gait staggered like a drunk's, and she giggled.

"Altitude," Levine said under her breath.

She breathed calmly, evenly, allowing what little oxygen there was to pass over her lungs.

"Just take even steps," Levine said. "Everything must be in balance. Don't overexert yourself."

Sara nodded her head and continued up to Levine.

"How you doing?" Levine said. She smiled at her friend.

"I feel lightheaded," Sara said. "My mouth is dry. I feel dizzy. Not good."

Levine stopped, stood there on the snowpack, and said, "Should we go back down?"

"No," Sara said. "Let's see what's in that lodge? Where's the mine, like the actual entrance?"

"All the maps show that it's somewhere inside the building."

"Inside?" Sara said.

"Yep."

"It looks like we can go up those steps there." Sara pointed to a series of zigzagging wooden steps that climbed up to the front deck. The steps were covered with snow, but they were built almost like a ladder and the constant wind kept the snow on each step trimmed down to just a few feet.

They continued up the snowfield.

"What causes an avalanche?" Sara said. "Do you know?"

"Well," Levine said. "Snow avalanches happen most often after or during really intense snow storms."

"Great."

"Yeah," Levine said. "There's a layer way down underneath all this snow."

"A layer of what?"

"A layer of ice," Levine said. "And all this snow just sits right on top of it. Sometimes there are multiple layers of ice, but what happens is all this snow accumulates on top of a big icy layer."

"Slick," Sara said.

"Exactly," Levine said. "Eventually once enough snow accumulates, the law of physics takes over and the whole thing begins sliding atop the ice layer. And once it gets going, there's nothing in this world that can stop it."

"How do you know if you're in danger?"

"Well, that's a big part of the problem," Levine said. "Forest Service personnel often break up the ice layer; they'll detonate small avalanches to avoid huge ones."

"So, this is a real risk?"

Levine glanced over her shoulder at McKenzie. Her eyes wanted to draw down to the enormous field straight down from them, but she stared hard into McKenzie's eyes.

"It's a real risk," she said.

They reached the steps up to the miner's lodge, and Levine took off her snowshoes.

"Come on," she said. "Let's make this quick."

•   •

They were out of breath as they climbed the steps. McKenzie kept looking out to the north. They views were stunning. She glanced up the stairwell ahead of them. She was careful on the snow, using both hands on the railing, and they reached the deck out in front of the lodge a moment later.

"What is this," Sara said, "some kind of bunkhouse?"

"During the summer," Levine said, "some of mineworkers stay up here. A lot live down in town, but a few live up here. This is where they sleep."

They looked in the windows along the front deck. Each window was curtained with frost and ice, but they could see just well enough inside to see that there was some kind of dining area over to the left. There was a fireplace inside to the right. Levine tried the front door, but it was locked.

"We're gonna have to break in," she said.

McKenzie hit a small square pane of glass with her ski-gloved fist, and the glass fell inside in three large pieces that hit the hardwood floor and shattered into a million. She reached her hand inside the window and tried to flip the lock, but she couldn't do it with her gloved hand.

"Here," Levine said. She'd already removed her ski glove. McKenzie stepped back, and Levine reached up inside and turned the latch. "That's got it."

She pushed up the window. Her hands slipped, and she said, "Damn, that's cold." But she got it open on the second try.

"There you go," McKenzie said.

McKenzie suddenly looked up and around her like she was worried that someone was watching her, but then she saw the northern horizon some one hundred and twenty miles from where she stood and she realized how absurd the idea was. They were so completely alone it was beyond frightening, to the point that it actually filled her with comfort at the knowledge. She followed Levine in through the window.

The inside of the lodge smelled of old wood and dust. Somewhere beyond that smell was the odor of carpet deodorizer, an almost equal blend with the fragrance of old fires in the fireplace, a sort of sooty, woodsy stink that was not wholly unpleasant.

"Well, where do we start?" McKenzie said.

"Let's head up to the left," Levine said. "Forward and to the left. What's back down that way?"

"Your guess is as good as mine."

They started up a hallway toward the center of the lodge. A minute later they opened a door at the back of the building and saw the opening of the mine. It was across a swinging bridge about fifty meters long back behind the lodge house. There were little railway cars and tracks at the entrance to the mine, a gaping black hole about twenty feet tall from floor to ceiling. It was almost twice that wide.

Sara said "Well, you can see how it's protected from the wind and snow. The whole thing's built into the side of the mountain."

"Looks like granite walls," Levine said.

"What's that down there at the bottom?"

They stepped up to the swinging bridge and looked down inside the chasm it crossed.

"Looks like ice," Levine said.

One hundred meters straight down under the swinging bridge, the mountain formed a kind of natural cup, and it looked like water had filled, then frozen there. The frozen lake was only about fifty meters across, and they both looked up at the bridge before them. It was held together with steel cables, and there was a thin layer of snow and ice atop its planks. It looked stable for a swinging bridge, and both Levine and McKenzie could tell that the mining car tracks on the other side of the chasm wheeled out around the mountain in the direction where they had parked the snowmobile.

"What do you think?" Sara said.

"I think the bridge looks slick but stable," Levine said. "And it looks like we could go at the mine from around that side, over there, where the railway tracks are."

"But?"

"But the bridge looks fine to me," Levine said. "We'll just have to watch our footing."

They stepped out onto the bridge, Levine holding to the cable railing on the right side, McKenzie holding to the cable railing on the left. The planks were icy and slick, and they moved under their bodyweight. They sloped downward in a light curve that bottomed out twenty-five meters ahead. McKenzie slipped and almost fell down.

"Damn!" she said.

Levine grabbed her right arm and helped her to stand.

"It *may be* easier," Sara said, "to go around to the tracks way over there."

She looked at Levine, but they both continued forward toward the middle of the swinging bridge.

Sara said, "It'd take twenty minutes to walk all the way around there, though."

"We'll be alright," Levine said, "just watch your footing."

The two friends continued forward carefully. Levine was just noticing how peaceful it was out in the middle of the chasm, when a strong gust swept into the indentation in the mountain like a comet horseshoeing around the sun. The gust swirled around them, and their pants and jackets ruffled in the stiff wind. They both held tight to the steel cable on their respective side, and they balanced their feet.

The wind died down, and they continued forward, more than half way across the bridge.

Suddenly, they stopped. Both McKenzie and Levine looked up and saw a hole in the bridge where four planks were missing. The hole created an opening about four feet across that they would have to pass over. McKenzie held to the cable on the left, and Levine held to the one on the right. They both stepped up to the hole and glanced down at the frozen lake far beneath them.

The cables were in place at either side of the hole; it was just missing the wooden planks. Levine thought she saw one of the boards lying atop the frozen lake.

"They must have fallen through," she said.

"The wind," Sara said. "What do you want to do?"

"I say we just jump over it."

McKenzie's pulse picked up, and she felt her heart beginning to beat in her chest. Ordinarily, leaping four feet would be an easy enough proposition, but when they factored in the ice and light dusting of snow on the boards that they would be jumping to, and the fact that if they fell they'd fall a hundred meters straight down, like falling off a ten story building, that made leaping four feet a little more tricky.

"There's no way to get traction," Sara said.

She held the cable in her left hand and shuffled her boots a little on the icy boards beneath her feet. This stirred up a little snow that fell down inside the hole. She watched as the snow fell down toward the frozen lake. It seemed to fall a long time before it hit the frozen surface with a silent *plump!*

Sara gulped and looked up at the icy boards on the other side of the hole.

"I guess it'd be pretty easy," she said.

"Well, we could walk along the cables there," Levine said. "But our footing may be more difficult that way."

Levine turned and worked through that idea in her mind. She put both hands on the steel cable on the right side. She reached out her left boot and placed it on the cable running along the base. It seemed to hold her weight pretty well, but the steel looked icy and slick.

"Just shuffle along the cable?" Sara said.

"I don't know," Levine said. "Might be easier just to jump across. It's only about four feet."

"Or we could just go back," Sara said. "And walk all the way around."

"That's an option, too."

Sara started to lose heart. "We don't even know for sure that the Key Room is up there," she said.

"True."

"And I mean, so what if we don't get this key, or whatever."

Levine looked into Sara's green eyes.

"I mean, all we've got is this kid's story," Sara said.

"Amber's story."

"She says we need this key," Sara said.

"She said it is written in the Oracle."

"And what is that?"

"She said it was an ancient book," Levine said. "An epic book of twelve shorter books."

Sara made an expression with her eyes that made Levine laugh. Sara looked into her friend's brown-blue eyes and smiled.

"This is gonna sound silly," Sara said. "But would you give me a hug?"

"Come here," Levine said.

Standing there on the swinging bridge, the two friends hugged one another.

"I just get scared sometimes," Sara said, stepping back a little now.

"We all do." Levine smiled.

They both looked into one another's eyes a moment longer, then Sara turned and looked at the hole.

"I'll go first," she said.

"You sure?"

Sara stared at the board on the other side of the hole. She nodded her head.

"Okay, stand back," she said.

Levine stepped over to the side of the bridge as far back as she could go. Sara stepped back about six steps and crouched down like a wide receiver getting ready to run a fly. She licked her lips. She looked at the boards at her feet. She looked at the hole, and then at the boards on the other side. She crossed her chest, blinked her eyes, and took off. Levine leaned back, and Sara passed right in front of her, leapt, and was in the air.

She hit the boards on the other side of the hole, slipped, and fell backward down onto the bridge hard. It knocked the wind out of her, and the whole bridge shook. But she made it across.

"Shoot," she said.

She rolled over, and Levine saw an expression on her face that indicated that she was surprised to have made it across.

"You okay?" Levine said.

"Yeah," Sara said. She stood up slowly and dusted herself off. "Not the most graceful move in my life."

"I think I'll just try my cable idea," Levine said.

Sara stood there on the other side of the hole. She glanced down at the frozen lake underneath them, and then her focus went to that steel cable. She stepped up to the edge. Levine was opposite her. They could almost reach out and touch one another across the hole in the bridge.

Sara positioned herself well on her side with her left hand holding the cable in front of her and her right hand free.

"If you can just make it a couple of steps," Sara said, "I can grab hold of you."

Levine nodded her head, but she was studying the cable. There was a little clutch on the underside of her hiking boots, and she positioned her boots such that the cable was filling the clutch. She held both hands on the cable in front of her, and she began to shuffle across that way, sliding her boots very carefully along, moving from right to left.

She made it across without incident, and Sara helped her onto the other side. Levine sighed a deep sigh of relief. They both looked up and saw the opening to the mine twenty meters ahead.

"It looks like a map up there on the wall," Levine said.

It was a map!

They stepped off of the bridge onto the gravelly ground at the entrance to the mine. They both glanced down into the blackness inside the mountain.

"How're we gonna see?" Sara said.

"That car there has a light on the front."

They both saw one of the mining cars. It had two detachable lanterns; one on front, one on back. The lanterns were wired to large six-volt batteries. Levine crouched down and hit an orange switch on top of one light. The light came on, shining brightly down into the darkness of the mine.

"It's good," Levine said. From her crouched position, she looked up at Sara.

"What about the other one?"

Levine reached around and flipped its switch. It came on, but it shone out into daylight.

"Looks like it works," Levine said.

They both turned their attention to the map on the wall. It was positioned in a glass-case bulletin board. There was a lock on the front of the glass so that someone could open and close the glass case and change the fliers inside.

The map showed a series of elevation gradations and tunnels inside the mine. It was shaped in a three-dimensional schematic that rendered depth inside the mine. There was one central image of the whole mine and a half dozen cross-sections that gave a more detailed view of several specific areas.

There was one main shaft right down the center of the mine, but there were literally hundreds of intersecting and divergent cross cuts, winzes, drifts and manways, tunnels branching off from the main central mine shaft. There were names for many of the mine shafts, and numbers correlated with those without names. The central mine shaft was denoted simply "Carbañero Main," but there was "Cobalt 1" through "Cobalt 23" and tunnels with names like "Hastings Shaft" and "Gulchmoore." There were hundreds of ore passes and skips indicated on the map and exactly one hundred and forty-seven decks inside the mine.

They both saw "KEY ROOM" at the exact same moment. It was at the base of Deck 147.

"There it is!" Levine said.

"Yep!"

"That is far down inside."

"What's the map scale?" Sara said, looking for the measurements.

"That's a quarter mile there." Levine saw from the legend. "So, wow, that room is over a mile and half down inside the earth. You can tell each deck is about the same depth down into the mine, and there are numbers for each one. Looks like the Key Room is at the very bottom. Deck 147."

"What in the world would they put a Key Room that deep inside the mine for?"

"The guy that originally built this mine, Carlisle Richard Toms, was an eccentric."

"How much you think he was worth?"

"He owned nearly every gold and silver mine between Montrose and Durango," Levine said. "Extremely wealthy folks like that do some pretty strange things."

"Like build a Key Room at the very bottom of your richest mine?"

Levine shrugged. "Guess so," she said.

Sara looked up inside the mine. There was a red-letter sign that read "Carbañero Main."

"I guess we take the main shaft all the way down," Sara said.

There were several tunnels on Deck 147.

Sara said, "You think we'll be able to find it from memory?"

"Better carry the map with us," Levine said.

She slid the glass case door back and brought the map down from the pushpin bulletin board. Sara was already over at the mining car. She was checking it out.

"How does this thing work?" Sara said.

She reached forward and grabbed the lever. It was rigid in her hands, but then she popped her boot up on the side of the mining car, kicked a steel pinion up, and pulled the lever with both hands. The mining car's brakes clicked loudly, and it started to roll towards her. She leapt into the little car.

"Wait up!" Levine said, running after her.

Sara pulled the lever back, the brakes squealed, and the car came to a stop. Levine climbed in, and Sara turned and smiled.

"You ready?" she said.

Levine said, "I hope you know what you're doing."

The car took off swiftly down inside the mine.

••

The mining car's light shone into the darkness, and the little steel wheels clicked speedily along the track. Sara controlled the car's speed with the lever, and they rolled along swiftly through the darkness for several minutes.

"It's warmer inside the mine," Levine said, "than it was outside."

Sara said from the front of the car, "Underground temperature stays constant and cool. Seems like I read somewhere that underground temperature remains constant at the yearly average of the surrounding area outside."

"How so?" Levine said.

"Well, if the average annual temperature outside the mine is forty-three degrees then that is roughly what the underground temperature remains at all year round inside the mine."

"I've never heard that," Levine said. "But I'd say it feels about that warm inside here."

They both looked forward into the darkness. The headlight shone for about forty feet right in front of the car, lighting up the tracks. The tunnel remained about forty feet wide, and the ceiling was some twenty feet overhead.

Levine caught a sign on one wall that read DECK 27. It flashed by them, and she realized they were moving along at a pretty good clip, about golf-cart speed. Sara had to apply the brake every ten seconds or so to keep them from going too fast. A few seconds later they saw a sign that read DECK 28.

"These decks are huge," Sara said.

"Huge chunks of earth," Levine said.

"The downward grade of the tracks is so slight it doesn't even feel like we're moving down inside the mine at all."

"You're right," Levine agreed. "It seems flat."

They listened to the click of the wheels on the tracks.

Sara asked, "How do we get back up?"

Levine reached back behind the mining car and removed the lantern from the back. She switched it on, and the powerful beam shone brightly on the map.

"According to this," she said. "There are a number of sumps at the bottom of the mine. See?" She pointed at the map, which ruffled in the breeze caused by their movement along the tracks.

"What's that, an elevator?" Sara said.

"Sort of," Levine said. "They're skips. They're used to carry stuff up and down the winding shafts here"—she pointed at a vertical shaft, which descended deep down inside the mine.

"What's that there?" Sara said.

"That," Levine said with a smile, "is an elevator."

"It doesn't go all the way down to the bottom?"

Levine frowned. "No," she said. "It looks like they've only extended the elevator down to Deck 135."

"And it doesn't start right at the top either," Sara said.

Levine said, "That's why we didn't see it at the entrance. Looks like it starts up at Deck 2, near the top."

Levine folded up the map and placed it inside one of her jacket pockets. They cruised along in the darkness for a couple more minutes.

"Deck 78," Sara said, when she saw the sign.

She applied the brake a little, and the cart slowed down. It felt like they were on a steeper grade now, farther inside the mine, and she had to use the brake more and more frequently. Also, it felt like the main shaft inside the mine was winding as it went along. Levine glanced back behind the cart and saw nothing but darkness.

She held up the lantern and shone it behind her, and she could see that it did, in fact, look as though the tunnel was curving around as it went deeper into the earth. Generally though, the trip down into the earth was uneventful. They passed adjacent tunnels and shafts almost constantly, and the sound fluctuated between barren walls and open caverns, the sound of the mining car on the tracks *whooshing* along as it passed openings on either side.

"Deck 117," Levine said.

They both saw the sign on the wall. The lettering was written in a smart plain font, the individual letters each about two feet high. They started to recognize patterns; there were branching shafts on the right and on the left about ten feet past each new deck.

"They're almost like hallways," Levine said.

"What's that?" Sara didn't understand.

"The tunnels," Levine said. "At each deck. They branch off right after we pass the new signs for each deck. One on the left; one on the right. See, watch. . ."

They passed the sign that read DECK 123, and Sara saw that Levine was right. There was a tunnel branching off to the right side of the central mine shaft and another branching off on the left side.

Sara nodded her head at the realization. "Yep," she said. "Like floors inside a department store."

"A really *big* department store."

"Like a mountain," Sara said.

The wheels on the track clicked and clacked along. Sara shivered.

"It's kind'a spooky," she said.

"How so?"

"Just being this far down inside," Sara said. "Feels like we're really deep, isolated. Pinned down somehow. I don't know. It'll be a heck of a trip back up to the top."

Their eyes met, and Levine didn't like where she was going with the conversation.

"We should be fine," Levine said. "We hit this Key Room, find the key, make for the elevator up on Deck 135, and then we're home free."

Sara stared into the shine of the mining car's headlight in front of them. "I hope you're right," she said.

• •

There were reflective yellow signs announcing the end of the mine some one thousand feet before the actual end. The mining car's light shone up ahead, lighting up these signs, and McKenzie braked the car evenly to a halt.

"There it is," McKenzie said. "Right up there."

They both looked forward to the main shaft's end. There were square black-and-white signs that reflected the light's shine. They could see that the tracks ended against a wooden barrier about hip height, but the mine continued forward out into the blackness beyond the headlight's shine. McKenzie brought the cart to a stop a few feet from the barrier, and they both climbed out onto the hard gravelly floor.

"Well, if we had to," Levine said. "We could walk all the way back to the surface. That was what, about ten minutes?"

Sara checked her wristwatch. "Right about nine," she said.

"At ten miles per hour," Levine said.

"Just like the map said. It's about a mile and a half down. It'd take us about thirty minutes to walk. Maybe more because it's uphill. Like forty maybe."

Levine pointed to a sign that read DECK 147.

"We could make it up to 135," she said, "in a minute or so."

"Which way do we go?" Sara said, looking around the cavernous darkness.

She reached down and lifted the lantern from the front of the mining car, and she swung it around. Their voices echoed as though they were inside a very wide cavern. Sara's light shone enough for her to reach one wall over on the right side of the tracks (the wall with the deck sign). But out beyond the barrier, the light just showed endless blackness. She could tell that the mine opened up far beyond the end of the tracks, perhaps a hundred meters or more, but it was difficult to tell exactly.

She called out, "Hello!" And her voice traveled out in that direction for some time before reaching a wall and echoing back to them.

"They're probably mining deeper than this map shows," Levine said. She inspected the map for some kind of printing date. "This map is probably a few years old."

Sara walked over to the right side of the tracks, toward the sign. She shone her light along the wall.

"There's a tunnel over here," she said.

Levine glanced up from the map. She looked at McKenzie in the darkness. Sara shone the light forward so Levine saw her from behind, and her contours stood out in dark relief because of the light out in front of her. Levine held her light cattycornered because she was trying to also hold the map between her two hands in order to locate where they were.

Sara turned and saw Levine behind the map. Her light was shining haphazardly through the paper of the map, and it cast Levine's face in a dimmer, soothing, brown color.

"What do you think, Dr. Levine?"

"It's hard to tell from the map. It's on a larger scale. Too large. But it looks like the Key Room is on the left side of the tracks."

Sara turned and looked at her. "Are you sure?"

"Well, take a look at this."

She came back and looked at the map with Levine. Levine laid it out atop one side of the mining car. They both looked down at the map. Sara looked at Levine's face for a moment and studied her expression. Levine was studying the map.

"See, it looks like here there are two tunnels." Levine looked up from the map in the direction that Sara had been standing over near the wall. "There's that one over there. But it looks like to me, from the map, that the Key Room is over here on this side. You see?"

McKenzie studied the map. It was difficult to tell, and the flashlights were very bright. It hurt her eyes to go from looking into the darkness to looking at the brightly lit map. But she concentrated and really studied the map.

"Okay," she said. "I think you're right. It must be over there." She nodded in the opposite direction from which she had initially thought. Levine raised her flashlight and shone it over that way. They could see the cavernous roof of the mine and the gravelly floor, but the depth was total blackness beyond the flashlight's reach. "There must be a tunnel over there on that side," Sara said.

Levine nodded her head. "Well," she said. "Let's check it out."

She folded the map up and glanced down inside the mining car. She saw dirt and dust, and the metal looked as though it was rusting. There were wet spots where their boots had left signs of snow, and Levine realized that for it to melt like that it was indeed much warmer inside the mine than it was outside.

Sara had taken off across the tracks, and Levine trotted after her, the flashlight bouncing up and down.

• •

"What is it?" Levine said.

Sara was fifteen feet ahead of her and was standing still, shining her flashlight into the darkness. Levine came up beside her and looked from her fierce green eyes to the direction in which she was staring.

Levine saw it, too.

There was a sign on the wall. It was a wooden sign. Both Levine and McKenzie could see that the arrow painted at the bottom of the sign pointed forward into the darkness, and they could both see that there was a tunnel up ahead.

Painted on the sign in smart auburn paint was an old-timey, round key ring with seven old-fashioned keys hanging evenly from it. The words KEY ROOM were painted just above the image of the ring and keys.

"That's it," Levine said.

She stared at the sign. Sara looked at Levine's eyes, and she saw her glance forward into the darkness. Sara's focus went to the tunnel in front of them, too. They both stood there shining their flashlights into the tunnel.

The walls were about eight feet apart, and the roof was ten feet above the ceiling. It felt cavernous, damp, and cool, and their breath steamed out in front of them in even little puffs.

"What do you think?" Sara said.

Levine looked at her. "I think that's the way to the Key Room," she said.

They both looked forward into the darkness, but neither one of them moved. There was something in the air, some smell like coins and moisture, and something underneath that: a smell like algae and fungal growth on the walls of the mine. It made them pause.

Levine looked at McKenzie. "Do you smell that?"

McKenzie nodded her head. "Smells like death," she said. "Like something up there has died. After you, Dr. Levine?"

Levine glanced at McKenzie's green eyes, looked deadly serious a moment, and then started up the tunnel deep inside the mine.

Her flashlight beam moved slowly along the tunnel walls. She pointed it straight out in front of them, and it shone straight out into darkness. They could hear their crunching footfalls on the gravel floor echoing up the hallway. And they could smell that decaying scent growing stronger and stronger.

"What is that?" McKenzie said, shining her flashlight beam forward.

At the edge of the flashlight's reach something was lying on the floor. It looked like a bundle of cloth about the size of a sack of potatoes.

McKenzie and Levine drew a few steps closer, and they both realized that the "bundle" was a dead body.

"Oh, my God," McKenzie said.

They stopped in their tracks. The body was on the floor twenty feet in front of them. They could tell that the tunnel opened up into an inner chamber forty feet on each side with a ceiling some twenty feet overhead. There was a green-and-white marble door on the far side of the room. There was an elaborate golden door handle on the door. *It was shaped like a key.* And both McKenzie and Levine saw that the chamber in front of them was filled with skeletons and dead bodies!

Levine gasped.

McKenzie winced and turned away.

Levine turned and saw McKenzie over to the side. Her hands were on her knees, and she was bent over making terrible gagging sounds as though she was about to vomit.

Levine turned back toward the chamber and held her nose. The smell was putrefying. Most of the bodies were fully decomposed skeletons, but a few around the room were still rotting. There were more than forty bodies and skeletons in the chamber. It smelled so putrid it was difficult to breathe without vomiting, and indeed, *vomiting* was exactly what Sara McKenzie was doing.

Levine turned and saw fluid pouring out of her mouth in the shine of the flashlight's glow. She just wanted to run, somewhere, anywhere to where the air was cleaner, fresher, less filled with the sickening smell of rotting bodies.

"Oh, my God," Levine finally said. "I'm gonna be sick."

She coughed and steeled her stomach and kept it all down, but the odor was horrible. She held her jacket sleeve up to her face and looked over her arm. McKenzie spat and sputtered, and then heaved another terrible spray onto the ground in front of her. Levine listened to the reflexive gagging sound coming from McKenzie and wanted to be anywhere other than where she was. She turned and shone her flashlight across the room at the white-and-green marble door.

Her flashlight's shine caught something glittering on the door. It was high up, centered, on the door, but Levine was almost certain that something was *written* there. Holding her mouth and nose behind the arm of her jacket sleeve, she passed through the chamber. She had to sidestep a few tatter-clothed skeletons, but she made her way up to the marble door.

She glanced at the golden key door handle, and then her focus rose up to the glittering silvery words etched into the marble door.

She who enters must choose the
correct key, or she shall never leave.

With her free hand, Levine turned the golden key door handle. The bolt clicked, and there was a rush of air and a whispering sound as though a hundred voices were all whispering at once. It came from whatever room the marble door opened onto. It passed over Levine, and then the door creaked slowly open into the room.

The shine of light from inside the room blinded her.

With her mouth and nose buried behind her jacket sleeve, Levine said, "*Holy mother. . .*"

The room shone so brightly that Levine squinted and then covered her eyes with her hand until they began to adjust to the light. The room was warm. Levine glanced back over her left shoulder. McKenzie was across the dead-body chamber, straightening up, wiping her mouth off. She coughed twice more but looked up at Levine across the chamber. The light pouring out of the room filled the death chamber, and Sara's eyes widened.

The inner room was filled with gold.

It was huge, more than one hundred meters from front to back and perhaps twice that from side to side, and there were drifts of gold coins in some areas piled twenty and twenty-five feet high, like swells on a sea.

A glowing light source came from the walls and high ceiling inside the room. The room seemed to shine with white and golden light. McKenzie passed through the dead bodies and approached Levine. She saw the gold coins.

A white marble foyer lay just beyond the door. In the center of the marble foyer, the emblem of the keys and key chain was etched in gold some four feet from one end to the next. And beyond the foyer, there was a virtual sea of gold coins.

McKenzie's mouth dropped open. Both she and Levine stared into the room.

It was enchanting, and McKenzie started to step forward onto the marble foyer. Levine raised her arm and stopped her. McKenzie just stared into the room. Levine pointed at the writing on the door.

McKenzie read it aloud, "'She who enters must choose the correct key, or she shall never leave.' What does that mean?"

Levine cast a glance at all the skeletons in the death chamber.

"It means," Levine said. "That these guys didn't choose the correct key."

Sara McKenzie looked into the gold room. It really was amazing, maybe the single most amazing thing she'd ever seen in her life.

The room was as large as four football fields laid side by side by side by side, and at no place in the room was the height of gold coins less than six or seven feet. In most places the drifts were over ten feet high, and in a few places, the peaks were more than twenty-five feet high, as large as houses.

Far on the other side of the room, a wide white marble stairwell rose from the sea of gold coins up to a little wooden door fixed into the wall.

"*The Key Room*," McKenzie gasped.

Again, she started into the room, but Levine stopped her once more.

She looked into Levine's brown and blue eyes.

Levine said, "If we step foot in this room, we can never go back."

"Unless we find the right key," Sara said.

"Look how many people have found the *wrong* key," Levine said. They both glanced at the skeletons in the death chamber. "What makes you think we'll end up any differently. What makes you think we'll find the right key?"

McKenzie shrugged her shoulders. "Well," she said matter-of-factly. "I believe in you."

"You *believe* in me?"

"Yeah, I believe in you."

"Just a few months ago," Levine said. "Your agency was going to *kill* me. You were one of them. You would have seen me die. Sara, you might have leant a hand in my death."

The image of that interview, so many months ago, filled both their minds. Indeed, Sara McKenzie had doubted every story she'd been told about Dr. Amy Levine's "powers." Sara had stood there in a room with two other operatives who were questioning Levine in order to decide her fate: whether she would live or whether she would die. And at her heart, Sara had thought all the stories about Amy Levine were bunk, that she was some sort of pseudo-religious con artist, hell bent on robbing troubled people who'd lost their way. And now, they were standing one hundred meters from a room that could change their fate, and Sara was entrusting that same Dr. Amy Levine with her life.

"People make mistakes, Amy. I was wrong for believing other people's stories about you. In life, no one is what other people say they are. We're something altogether different, genuine, and true. We're something that no words can ever define, though we should always seek the truth in one another."

"What are you saying?" Levine asked.

"I'm saying I was wrong. I was wrong to form such a negative opinion about you. I was skeptical of you. I saw you as the enemy."

"Why?" Levine said. "What caused you to change?"

"Trust," Sara said.

"Trust?"

"And time," Sara said. "I've seen for myself the truth that is within you. You have a gift. Something that I don't understand. A way of seeing the world like no other person before you. You know things before they happen. In a lesser mind, we would call that madness. But tempered with humility and with faith, I would call it genius."

Levine smiled as warm and pure a smile as she had ever smiled in her entire life. She looked into McKenzie's bright green eyes.

"After you," she said, with a hand toward the foyer.

Sara smiled, nodded her head, and stepped onto the white marble foyer. Levine followed after her.

They both stepped out onto the golden keys and key ring emblem in the middle of the marble floor. There was a light tinkling sound like wind chimes, and the marble door creaked shut and sealed behind them like a vault. The room was warm and bright, and they stared across the sea of gold coins.

They both removed their ski jackets and lay them on a stack of gold coins that rose in front of the marble foyer, and they began the ascent up a steep hill of coins right in front of them.

Footing was difficult on the gold coins. The first hill was steep, and the coins slid underfoot; so they kept falling forward. It was like walking up a massive pile of marbles, and though the coins were hard enough and substantial enough that they didn't sink (as into snow), it was still difficult to climb that first hill.

Levine reached the top of the hill first, and she looked out around her at the sea of coins. McKenzie stepped up beside her, a little out of breath. She dropped her hands to her hips akimbo and just stood there trying to take in all that she saw.

She sighed.

"It's a lotta money," Levine said with a chuckle.

"It's a lotta *gold*."

"Come on," Levine said.

And she started off down the hill. Sara knelt down and touched the coins at her feet. They were real. She stirred them around with her hands, smiling wildly. They clinked and clanked together. She picked up a handful in front of her, holding her palm out. There were twenty or more gold coins in her hand. It was very heavy, and she let them fall back down to the ground.

Levine had reached the bottom of the trough in front of her, and was starting up the next hill. She turned around and saw Sara still standing up there.

"What are you doing?" Levine called.

Sara just looked around her, wild-eyed.

She whispered as though to herself, "*They're real!*"

"The Key Room," Levine said. "Come on, Sara."

"They're real!" Her head pivoted around wildly. "It's all real! Real gold!"

Levine felt something like an electrical current flow up through the coins at her feet. She lifted her legs and looked down at the coins. *Was it just her own mind*, or had some electrical current flowed through her? It made her uneasy.

"Sara!" Levine said. "Come on!"

Sara stood up at the top of the hill. She wasn't listening to Levine at all. She was looking wildly around the enormous room and the sea of gold coins. She knelt down and started picking up coins. She started stuffing her pockets, filling them with coins.

Levine definitely felt something stirring in the room, and she heard something, too. It was like a whisper, a hundred voices whispering all at once from down inside the coins. Levine followed the sound. It climbed up the hill toward Sara.

It was making the coins shine as it moved along. Levine looked up and realized it was headed right for Sara McKenzie.

"Sara!" she cried. "Look out!"

But Sara was frantically filling every pocket she had on her ski pants. Levine started running back down the hill, through the trough, and back up the hill atop which Sara stood.

"Drop the coins!" Levine yelled. "Sara, get rid of the coins!"

The little shiny patch moved about ten feet in front of Levine. It whispered fiercely and moved quickly toward Sara.

"Throw the coins down, Sara! Get them out of your pockets! Leave them! They're no good!"

Sara looked up and saw Levine coming toward her. She had forgotten all about her friend, and she stood there with gold in her hands and a crazed gleam in her wide eyes. All of her pockets were packed with coins, and yet she wanted to put the coins that she had in her hands somewhere on her person, too.

Suddenly, the shiny patch hit Sara. She shook. She shook as though a shark down inside the sea of coins beneath her had taken a nibble at her foot. She looked around her at the coins at her feet, and panic rocked her. Her lungs seized up, and her blood pressure skyrocketed. They were all shining, the coins were, and then she heard the hundred whispering voices frantically encircling her. She saw faces in the coins' shine, impressions of faces rising up as from an impression board. There were many faces—thirty or forty—and they were all moving around in the gold coin shine that surrounded her. She had started to sink down into the coins, and she realized that the coins were swallowing her. She screamed.

Levine reached Sara as her ankles and shins dropped below the surface. Levine started grabbing at her pockets, ripping the coins away and throwing them on the ground.

"Get 'em off!" Sara screamed.

The voices were like electrical bugs, and they were all over her face and body. Sara was clawing at them and sinking down deeper into the coins. She was up to her knees.

Levine just ripped open one pocket on the front of her pants, and all the coins poured down onto the ground. She tried the same with another pocket, but the stitching was strong.

"Sara!" Levine screamed. "Give me a hand! You've got to get every coin off of you!"

Sara looked around her wildly like she was seeing something before her eyes that no one else could ever see.

She just screamed, "Get them off of me! They're crawling all over me! *Get them off!!*"

Tears filled Levine's eyes. Sara was buried up to her thighs. Levine screamed at her, but the madness had overtaken Sara McKenzie. Levine realized she was losing her friend. She ripped at the pockets on her shirt. Some coins spilled away, but Sara had filled pockets in her pants that were now underneath the surface. Levine reached down inside the coins and tried desperately to grab at them, but she was too late.

Levine screamed, "*Nooo!!! God, no!!!*"

Sara was up to her chest.

Levine grabbed her hand and tried to stand, pulling her back, but the force from down inside the coins was too strong.

Sara was up to her chin. Her head pivoted around. She grasped at Levine. She was coming out of the madness, and she looked into Levine's eyes.

"Don't let me die!" she pleaded. "Amy, please, don't let me die!"

Levine screamed.

She watched as her best friend's eyes looked into hers. Levine gripped her hand, pulled with all of her strength, and McKenzie looked into her eyes with something like expectant fear. Her head vanished below the gold coins, and Levine continued to grip her hand. She gripped it until her own hand turned white and red from all the pressure, but it started to pull her under. And still Levine wouldn't let go.

"God, not Sara," she gasped. "It's not her time! It's not her *time!*"

Levine's forearm descended below the surface. She was on her hands and knees, her right arm being pulled into the coins. Levine roared fiercely, her whole arm being pulled under, her face coming down closer and closer to the surface of the gold coins.

Spittle came out of her clenched mouth. Tears streamed down her face. Her face reddened and began to shake as though she was trying to dead lift four hundred pounds. She felt her right cheek touch the gold coins and heard the whispering. And she screamed one last time as her best friend's grip slipped from hers, down inside the sea of gold.

Levine cried, *"Nooooo!!!"*

THIRTY-FOUR
THE VISION

Amber knew that McKenzie was dead.

She stood in the Beaumont's library with Helen and Roger when her body seized up. Helen and Roger were at a table in the center of the room looking at a geodetic map. They were trying to pinpoint the location of the service station buried underneath all the snow.

Amber walked over toward the spiral staircase that she knew led back to the red door. She felt something stirring in the room like an electrical current, could almost smell an electrical burning odor like cooked wires, and then it just hit her.

"Ahhh!" she cried out in pain.

Both Helen and Roger swung around.

"What is it?" Helen gasped.

The blinding white sharp pain was gone, but Amber stood there a few feet from the spiral staircase up to that peculiar little door in the wall.

"It's McKenzie," Amber said. Her eyes were wide.

"What?" Helen said.

"What're you talking about?" Roger said.

Amber looked at them. Her mouth was open a little. She stared at them. She said, "Something just took her, grabbed her. There was a scream within the Line."

Roger and Helen exchanged glances.

"It sounded like a hundred voices," Amber said. "Whispering frantically. They just descended on her."

"Amber, honey," Helen said. "I'm sure it's just your imagination. It's been a long couple of days. We probably just need some sunshine, some rest."

"No," Amber said. "She's no longer with us. Not on this side of the Line."

Helen and Roger stared at the young girl, and neither one of them could bring themselves to say that she was wrong.

"It's too late," Amber said. "She tried to save her. Levine tried to save her. Something about gold. Something about gold coins. It swallowed her like the sea."

Thirty-Five
The Key Room

Amy Levine lay on her back atop the hill of gold coins. She stared at the bright amorphous ceiling high overhead. The tears streaming down either side of her face had dried, and she just lay there blinking slowly, calmly, her mind so perfectly clear it was like a mountain stream whose clear water sparkles and shines in sunlight as it moves over, through, around, and with smooth dark stones that lie in its bed.

She watched the ceiling. It shimmered and moved around as though it was alive, as though it was a living, breathing life force itself with only the vaguest comprehension that Levine lay some thirty or forty feet underneath it, alive and aware that the ceiling was there at all. It moved in patches of white and gold, the patches constantly shifting and changing places and dimensions.

Levine's eyes went to one white patch that was roughly ten feet in diameter; it was shaped like a cloud—a cloud of light—moving around in the otherwise golden ceiling. There was depth to the patch, but it was difficult to tell how much or how deep it was. It moved to the right, changing shape as it did so, and it pulsed a beautiful violet color every few seconds.

Why was the fact of death the cause of such fantasy?
Why did we even care?

Levine rolled over and looked at the wall on her far left. She felt the shift of the gold coins underneath her, and she glanced at the spot where Sara had been swallowed alive.

Sometimes life just seemed like an endless fight between living and dying, being and becoming. Levine believed that defining life as simply free will versus fate was too simplistic, and that it was really a combination of the two, but most of that logic she'd long since decided was circular and wasteful, so she just tried to fix her eyes on the concrete, the real. There was hope, though. There was something beyond. There were voices that spoke to her when her soul was quiet, and regardless of what other people would say, she would carry the belief with her to the grave that the grave was only the beginning.

She just missed her friend. And she hated herself for not having done more to ensure their safety, their survival, their sisterhood within the whole balance of the universe, the order that undergirded the very source of reality.

If only I had warned her, Levine thought. *If only I could see more things before they happen. If only I had said something to her, anything—to not touch the gold. I should have seen it coming.*

Then an even deeper, guilty thought leaked into her mind like carbon monoxide filling a bedroom at night.

I did see it coming. I had to have. I was just too naive to react to the signs.

. .

Eventually, Levine heard something. It was like wind chimes, but the wind chimes were people singing, their voices pleasant, melodious, and distant. She sat up and looked around her. The sound seemed to be coming from the walls and the ceiling, but it was very gentle and comforting. She looked across the high drifts of gold coins like sand dunes between her and the little wooden door far across the room.

The stairwell up to the little wooden door was shining and bright, and it seemed as though the greatest concentration of voices was coming from that stairwell and the wall around the little wooden door.

She looked at the spot where Sara had vanished underneath the surface, and she glanced at the gold coins.

They sparkled and shone and seemed to have a voice of their own, their own singing, but it was a mysterious chorus and the feeling that filled Levine's mind as she sat there atop the hill of gold coins was that the gold was mostly empty. She stood up and started down the hill in the direction of the little wooden door across the room.

It took her a minute to reach the stairwell.

She stopped at the foot of the stairs. It was a wide stairwell made of white marble. There were beautiful marble balusters along either side, and the stairwell came together at the top where it was ten feet wide. At the base it was forty feet wide. And at the very top, there was a peculiar little door.

The door was only three feet high, and there was a little bell fashioned into the door. Levine studied the stairwell, reached out with her mind, and felt that it was safe. She placed one foot forward and started up the stairwell. With each step, there was a sound like wind chimes as her feet touched down. She glanced around her and smiled curiously at the pleasant sound.

Levine counted twenty-one steps up from the gold coins to a marble landing. The landing was ten feet from front to back and ten feet from side to side. The marble tiles were arranged in little squares, and each was a twelve-inch square in which there were nine juxtaposed squares like gold and white inlaid parquet. In the center of the landing, there was a circle of pure light that poured down from the ceiling like sunlight from a clear glass window, and the light shone a perfect circle around a three-foot-diameter emblem of the key ring and seven keys.

Levine looked at the little wooden door.

It was only three feet tall and perhaps that wide at its base. The top of the door was shaped in a semicircular arch, and Levine realized she would have to crouch down to enter the door. She saw that there was a little golden bell in the door.

A nook was carved into the wood, and the little bell hung inside the nook. The bell was small enough that she could hold it in her hand.

Levine saw that carved into the golden bell was the emblem of the key ring and seven keys. The emblem was not much larger than a coin, and Levine reached out and touched it with her index finger.

The little bell jingled.

Levine smiled curiously. The door handle was a simple, modest little handle, and it looked like it was made of wood. The wood of the door was a dark brown color, and Levine reached forward and took the door handle in her hand.

She turned the handle and opened the door. Because the door was so short she could not see inside the room well at first, but she knelt down and looked.

"Oh, my," she said.

There were three windows inside the room. One was on the far wall, one on the right side, and one on the left side of the room. The image through each of the windows was the exact same, as though the windows were themselves three large identical paintings. The image through each of the windows was that of a small lake not more than a half kilometer across. In the distance, stone gray bald mountains towered very high, but around the lake everything was green and fertile.

Levine could see there was a footpath around the lake, and she saw on the far side of the lake an old black man fishing from the bank with a cane pole. He had a corn cob pipe in his mouth, which gave him a rustic appearance, but he wore a pair of sleek, black sunglasses. He had a shiny silver beard that descended six inches below his chin. Every few seconds, he stroked his white beard as though deep in thought.

The image was the exact same from either side of the room as though the windows were just three identical paintings, but Levine could see the grass along the lake's bank rustling in the light breeze, and the old fisherman moved around a little, toking on his pipe, adjusting his cane pole every few seconds.

Levine's eyes began to take in the thousands of keys inside the room itself.

There were four main tables inside the room, and the tables were covered with keys. There were glass cases along the three walls inside the room, and inside the glass cases there were hundreds and hundreds of keys. There were keys that hung down from the ceiling and keys hanging from one of four posts inside the room that rose from the floor to the ceiling as support. The ceiling was only six feet high, and though Levine was not six feet tall the closeness of the ceiling filled her with a sense that she had to crouch down a little inside the room.

The room was not designed for an adult.

She went to one of the windows, the window on the left side of the room. She looked at the image and reached her hand forward to touch the glass. It was not hard and impenetrable like glass but smooth and inviting as water. Ripples whirled out from where her finger touched the window, and the sensation was like that when she had opened the red door inside the Beaumont.

She looked around and saw that the ripples had occurred in the other two windows, though she had not touched them, and Levine realized that though there were three images (indeed three windows), they were in fact one and the same, somehow interconnected by forces beyond her comprehension.

She looked back at the little wooden door, which had remained open, and she saw the gold coin room beyond. And then her eyes went around the Key Room.

There were literally thousands of keys inside the room. The room was only twenty feet by twenty feet, and Levine started to go around the room inspecting some of them.

She approached the glass case on the far side of the room from the little wooden door. Inside the case there were some three hundred keys, and atop the case there were perhaps one hundred. Many of the keys had little paper tags attached them, and there was something written on each of the tags. She picked up one particular key.

It looked like a common, ordinary house key. She read the writing on the little paper tag attached to the key. She saw the name "Jonathan Reginald Smith," and she turned the key over and saw that the name was written on either side of the piece of paper. She placed the key back on the glass case and picked up another. The name "The Clines" and "Windsor, South Dakota" and "Patty, Chuck, Dawn, and Little Charlie" was written on the paper tag.

Levine turned and approached one of the four tables gathered in the center of the room. There were hundreds of keys atop the table. They were piled almost a foot high toward the center. Levine took one at random from the pile, and she looked at the little paper tag. "Marlon and Beatrice Bruin" was written on the paper tag and "Jacksonville, Florida." She placed it lightly back on the pile and took another key. Its tag read "Jin and Sayuri Nagura" and "Kyoto, Japan." And underneath this were the names "Sakura, Ren, Nozomi, and Nami." *Four girls*, Levine realized with a smile.

She placed it back on the pile and took up another whose tag read "Taahir and Radhiyaa Abdul-qadir" and "Damascus, Syria." Levine gathered that the names listed beneath them were their children's names: "Thaabit, Zakiy, and Amani."

And yet another read "Mathavan and Charumatee Maharaj" from "Kanpur, India." Levine saw on the tag that their children's names were "Akaash, Maya, and Jafar." She placed the key back and stood in middle of the room.

There were Chinese names and Zimbabwean names, Colombian names and Portuguese names, Russian names and South African names. Some with families, others that lived alone. Individual names and couple's names. There were Hindu names, Buddhist names, Islamic, Taoist, and Christian names. All the great religions—and the great regions—of the world were represented. Each was represented with honor, joy, and with love. Each was represented with equality.

Levine went around the room looking at all the keys in the Key Room, fascinated by the diversity, her imagination reaching out to them, wondering about the stories behind each family. And then the realization began to awaken in her soul that she had to find the correct key. Levine glanced nervously around the room. She had to find one key, one single key, the correct key. Or she would never be allowed to leave.

There were so many keys.

• •

Levine cleared her mind, breathed deeply, shook her arms out a little and walked around the room. She genuinely calmed her mind as though there was nothing in the room, as though she herself was not there, but her mind was aware and alert. It was like she was letting her subconscious guide each little step as she casually moved around the room. She could feel it coming, the right place to stand, but she wasn't even thinking about that. She was actually thinking about how good it felt to take the right step—literally—with each foot being guided by a level of her mind that she dipped down into like a hand scooping into a pail of water.

She stayed there in that state and felt it all around her like warm light. Her focus moved around the room, and she saw each of the keys, but she was seeing them in a way like she never had before. Everything was clear, and she felt no guilt or anxiety while looking around the room. In its own way, it was like seeing the Key Room through new lenses, clearer lenses, and she picked up things that she hadn't seen before. The more relaxed she was, the more details she saw: the shape of a certain pane in the window, the chipped corner on one particular table, a fingerprint—no, a *palm* print—on the side of a glass case.

It was a fundamental premise of her life's work. She had seen it in dates, numbers, strange coincidences, moments of intuition. It was like reality—everything around her in time and space—was an elaborate super-multi-dimensional window *and* a mirror, and how at peace her mind was determined how much of the reflection she saw. It was part of why her math—her Colorado Sequence—was so innovative.

Most humans looked at the world around them as though it was a window: they saw a tree, a park bench, a statue and an apple, and those objects were "out there." And their perception of it is as through a window. But Levine's work had realized that when people look at reality (a tree, a park bench, a statue, an apple) there were points of light like mirror reflections that indicated a return awareness at their standing there seeing the green grass on the lawn, the park bench, the red apple sitting atop the park bench.

Einstein had once said that God does not play dice with the universe, but Amy Levine's work had shown that God *did* play dice with the universe but that the dice were often loaded.

It occurred to her that she was standing in the center of a triangle formed by the three windows in the Key Room. Her mind quickly calculated the feet and meters from where she was standing to each window, and she felt as certain as she had ever felt in her entire life that she was standing in the perfect center of a triangle.

There was one key on a little round table three feet in front of her. Without leaning at all, she reached forward and found the key was exactly at arm's distance. She picked it up and looked at it.

The word "McDonald" was etched into the metal. *The manufacturer?* Levine thought. And then Levine looked at the tag attached to the key. The name written on it was peculiar, not like any other names around the room, and she recognized it immediately. Levine read aloud, "Gamma Cephei B."

Her eyes widened.

She knew exactly what it was. She knew Gamma Cephei B was a star in a binary system, which was part of the constellation Cepheus. It was one of only three binary star systems in which scientists had discovered a planet. She knew the system pretty well, had spent several years studying multiple star systems, and she even knew the lead astrophysicist on the team who had first discovered evidence of Gamma Cephei's Jupiter-like planet. His name was William Cochran. Dr. William Cochran. *The University of Texas at Austin?* Levine thought.

She was pretty sure he was still there, a Senior Research Scientist, at the—

"*McDonald Observatory*," Levine gasped, holding the key up so that it shone in the light coming in from the windows. She pulled the key up closer and looked very closely at the name "McDonald" etched into the key. She touched the paper tag with her fingertips.

She said the name aloud, "Gamma Cephei."

There was a sound. She looked up at the windows. There was a sound like a key turning over in a lock, the click of the bolt turning, and then a creaking sound like a door opening. The sound was coming from the windows in a tri-stereo effect. And for a moment of time, she knew beyond a shadow of a doubt that she was holding the correct key in her hand.

The image at each window rippled. Levine turned, and in the turning, she caught the image of a golden key in each of the windows. It was a transitory image like that of passing a window and seeing the reflection of someone she recognized in the window only to turn and see that the person had rounded a corner and vanished out of sight.

She turned her body back the opposite way to see if she could see the image again. And there was nothing, just the image of the old man fishing by the side of the lake. She held the key up in her hand and made the same turning motion. She realized that the key had passed right through the very center of the triangle formed by the three windows and at equidistance between the floor and the ceiling.

She waved the key through that space again. And she astonished to see an image of a single golden key appear in all three windows. But it vanished as soon as the key in her hand had passed just a few inches beyond the center of the triangle, and the image returned to that of the old man fishing by the side of the lake. He stroked his silver beard and contemplated the water.

She swept the key through the space again, but she must have passed it a few inches too low because the image in the windows was only fragmentary. But she had figured it out. And she moved the key more precisely close to the center, and was amazed to see the image of that golden key appear in all three windows as the key in her hand lit up.

She looked at the key in her hand. It was lit up as from a small but very bright stage light. Levine held the key between her thumb and forefinger and watched the light hit it. She looked at the ceiling for the source of the light and saw nothing. She glanced quickly at the floor, and saw no source there either. She passed her other hand through the space and was surprised to see that no light shone on her hand at all.

It was as though a little one-cubic-inch sphere of space at the exact center of an invisible triangle formed by the three windows and exactly equidistant height between floor and ceiling *recognized* this particular key.

She waved her empty hand back and forth through the space, and no light shone on her hand. The image in the three windows stayed that of the mountain lake with the old black man fishing along its bank. She waved her right elbow through the space, and still nothing changed.

She picked up another key from a nearby table and ran it through the same space. Nothing happened. Neither the images in the windows nor the little light amidst the triangle shone. She made another pass through with the Gamma Cephei B key, and the image on the three windows changed to that golden key standing against a white background. And the light shone on the key.

She tried the other key—saw the name "Paul H. Winters" from "Quebec, Ontario" on the key's tag—but nothing happened.

She reached for yet another key and tried it. Again, nothing happened. She tried several more keys, and each time the result was the same. The center of the triangle only reacted to the Gamma Cephei Key with the name Gamma Cephei B written on the tag.

Fascinating.

It was as much a sign as she could have hoped for. In fact, it was such a clear sign, she was skeptical at first and was reluctant to leave the key room.

She'd seen what had happened to those bodies back in the death chamber. She'd seen so vividly with Sara in the Gold Room that there were forces at work far beyond what she could comprehend. And she thought that maybe it was just a trick. Maybe the Gamma Cephei B key was a misdirection, and she'd gobbled it up hook, line, and sinker.

She went to the window at the back of the room and called through to the fisherman: "Hello?" But her voice hit the surface of the image flatly, and she realized that her voice had not traveled into the image.

She reached her left hand forward and touched the window. Again, it was cool and inviting like water. She pocketed the key in her right front pants pocket and reached both hands through the window.

The sensation was pleasurable yet strange because it raced through her fingertips and hands, up her arms and then deep within her body. She retracted her hands, and everything returned to normal.

She eased her head through the window, climbed through, and tumbled onto the grass atop the lake's bank. The old man flicked his cane pole around, the line switching atop the water.

"Dr. Levine," the man called across the glassy lake surface.

Levine climbed to her feet and waved to the old man.

He looked at her from across the corner of the lake. He wore sunglasses, and he raised that corn-cob pipe up to his lips and took in a couple of tokes before drawing in and exhaling deeply through his nose. At that moment, the old man looked vaguely dragon-like, his shades reptilian, and the smoke came from his nose.

He stroked his silver beard and smiled.

"Do we know each other?" Levine said.

She walked around the edge of the lake, found the footpath, and approached the old man. Levine saw traces of snow high atop the stone-gray bald peaks in the distance, but her eyes came back to the old man sitting in the lotus position on the green grassy bank. As she drew nearer, she saw that his cane pole was positioned in a little metal stand beside the woven mat on which he sat. He wore loose white p'ao-style pants, a black belt, and a white p'ao-style top. He was barefooted.

"Everyone knows one another, Dr. Levine," the old man said. "It is the degree of our awareness that is in flux."

The old man toked on his pipe and looked through his shades at Levine. There was a little ceramic dish on the left front corner of his mat. He placed his pipe there and then lifted the cane pole from its stand on his right. He flicked the line around a little on the gunmetal water, then placed the pole back in its metal stand.

He reached for his pipe, and Levine saw a beautiful blue, yellow, and white flower imprint in the center of the ceramic bowl. The old man raised the pipe stem to his lips, toked on the gently burning herb, and then drew in another breath of smoke. When he exhaled, the smell was pungent, pleasant, and flavorful. He gazed out across the reflective surface of the lake.

"You know my name," Levine said.

The old man nodded.

He said, "It is so."

"Do you know of the Key Room?" Levine said. "What is your name?"

The old man's head jerked a little, came round to her poised, and his shaded eyes took her in.

"Samuel," he said. "And, yes, I know of the Key Room."

Levine removed the key from her pocket. She held it up for him to see.

"Is this the correct key?" Levine said.

"What is the 'correct' key?"

"The one that gets me out of the mine alive."

Samuel nodded and looked out at the lake. He reached to his right and took the cane pole in his hand. He flicked the line around atop the water, and both he and Levine looked at the bright orange bobber on the surface.

"Do you know about the Oracle?" Levine said. "Do you know about Amber Page?"

Levine could see his eyes widen a little behind his shades.

"The Virgo Warrior," Samuel said.

"Yes."

"She has come of age, no?"

Levine nodded, and her eyebrows rose up. She said, "She's still young. She is eleven."

Samuel made a sound like "Hmmm" and gazed at the reflection of the mountains on the lake's glassy surface.

"You must take that key to the Needle," Samuel said.

"Kevorak's Needle," Levine said. "So, this is the correct key. . ."

"The desert world of the Randa has not had rain in a hundred years," Samuel said. "That key will unlock Kevorak's Soul, and you must find a way to release the Needle once inside the Soul. Only then will rain reach the parched land. Only then will the balance be restored."

"The balance?" Levine said.

"The balance of the Line."

Levine looked at Samuel. "You could help us?" she said. "You could come with me? With us?"

"I can not leave this place."

"You are lonely," Levine said. "I can feel your loneliness. Come with us. Come with me."

Samuel cast a glance at Levine. He smiled lightly, if enigmatically.

"You are afraid of your destiny," he said.

"I am afraid of the responsibility," she said. "I am afraid of the mistakes that I will make."

"But your strength grows strong within the Line," he said. "I can feel your powers intensifying. You will fight, and you will fight well."

"I don't know how to fight!" Levine said.

And all at once, Samuel shot his left leg forward and spun like lightning three times around. On instinct, Levine leapt up into the air missing his sweeping kick by just microseconds. His feet made a metallic *whooshing* sound, and he popped up into a deft little stance. Levine stood there two meters from him.

"I do not want to fight," Levine said.

The old man looked into her eyes. "You will have no choice once inside the Line," he said.

And he came at her, his hands a flurry of chopping movements. Levine dodged left, and Samuel pivoted off of her, spinning around once, and ended up higher on the bank. Levine stumbled down the bank, ending up close to the lake. She stood there at the bottom of the bank near the water.

"Your enemy is not your enemy," he said. "Your enemy is yourself. Your enemy is fear."

Samuel somersaulted down the bank and landed on the water ten meters from the shore. Levine turned. Samuel stood on the surface of the lake.

"You must make unreality your reality," he said. "Your enemy is that which you do not know, that which you do not understand."

"I don't understand many things," Levine said, popping up on the balls of her feet. "But I have no enemies."

"Then you understand less than you think you understand."

"An enemy is a creation of the mind," she said. "It is not in nature."

"It is not in nature to hate," he said. "But many will hate you. What will you do?"

"Love," Levine said. "And live truthfully."

"Love is to hatred as water is to fire," he said. "You must fight!"

The old man came across the surface of the lake and leapt into the air. He lunged at Levine. She ducked right, pivoted, and connected her right hand behind the small of his back. She threw him to the ground. The old man hit the grassy bank and vanished into the tall reeds.

Levine craned her head either way trying to see him in the tall grasses.

Levine heard his voice, but she did not see him. "You must make the rocks your hands. The wind must flow through you. The grass must be your fingers."

Levine looked either way trying to spot him.

Suddenly a half dozen little Samuels formed out of the grass. They were all as green as the grass itself, and they came at Levine. She caught one across the head with a kick and retreated back up the hillside. The grass all around her rustled, and suddenly she was fighting the grass, kicking, pivoting, ducking, swinging, leaping. She flipped a double somersault backwards and landed atop a large squat boulder that rose four feet up from the ground.

She rotated around, watching the little green Samuels trying to get at her. They couldn't ascend the rock. She watched them come together. They merged into one, and Samuel resumed his original appearance.

His arms were folded together in his sleeves in front of him. His head was tilted to the ground. He seemed completely relaxed, almost asleep, standing there.

Levine leapt down lightly from the rock. She eyed him.

"I am not a fighter," she said. "The girl is a fighter. I am a scientist! It is not my destiny to fight."

"You know your destiny?" Samuel said.

"I know my strengths," she said. "And I know my weaknesses. And I know that combat is not my strength."

Samuel's head came up slowly. His eyes looked through the shades at her. There was a flash of light from behind his shades. His arms came from the folds of his sleeves. Levine saw the smooth brown flesh of his hands, and he looked into Levine's brown and blue eyes.

"Then, you will die," he said.

Levine glanced across the lake at the portal through which she'd come from the Key Room. It was surreal, just a window-sized blinding white light. They could not see through it into the Key Room. It was just a square of light positioned in free space about thirty meters up from the lake.

"Be that as it may," Levine said.

Samuel looked at her. "You take your own mortality so lightly?"

Levine looked at him. "I have this key," she said. "From what I've been told, from what I've read, this key will return fertility and life to a place that has been a desert for far too long. It will restore the balance on Earth. It will provide a way of life for farmers in that region. I have a responsibility to follow through with this, to get this key to its rightful place. I will do that. I will succeed. And I will help this young girl, Amber Page, to realize her destiny. Our lives are intertwined, but they are not entangled. I have seen too many people die to believe that I will somehow avoid death. My time and my place have been fixed within the order and balance of life, and I only pray that when my time comes, I will meet my fate—my destiny—with courage and with honor."

The old man stood looking at her for some time. He frowned thoughtfully. He nodded his head, and his gaze swept out to the lake, its glassy surface reflecting the mountains in the distance.

"It is the way of things," he said.

Levine said, "So, be it."

Samuel's shaded eyes came back to hers.

"Come here," he said.

Levine stood motionless a second, but then she sensed his goodness and came forward. Samuel reached his right hand forward and touched her left shoulder. He made an arch over her head, and touched her right shoulder. He withdrew his hand, and then moved his fingertips forward and touched her forehead with the fingertips of his index, middle, and ring finger.

Her eyes followed each of his hand gestures, and at the end she felt a warm glow pulse through her.

"You are a seer," he said. "In ancient times, you would have been called a prophet, Amy Levine."

"I am a scientist, a mathematician, and most people think I'm crazy. I wonder myself sometimes."

The old man smiled warmly.

"We know better," he said. "You help this child, this young warrior, and your strength within the Line will grow."

"Can you see," Levine said. "Can you see what will happen?"

"You will help the Randa. You will reach Kevorak's Needle. There will be many obstacles. The young girl will emerge triumphant, a hero."

"And me," she said. "Will I live?"

The old man's brow furrowed over. Levine could see that his eyes were frightened by what his mind saw. He winced and retracted his hand from her head. He looked into her eyes as though at something he hadn't realized before, something he hadn't realized until now, and was now seeing with new eyes.

"What?" Levine said. "What is it? What did you see?"

He smiled at her.

"*What?*" she said.

"I see two futures, two paths," he said. "Your life will take one of these."

"What are they?" she said. "What did you see?"

"One path," he said with a smile. "Leads to love. I see you with a man. You are walking on a beach, holding hands. He leans and kisses you. He understands you. He makes you laugh and makes you cry. But your tears are tears of joy, not of sadness. He loves you, and you love him. It is a perfect match."

Levine's eyes brightened at the thought. She smiled.

"And the other?" she said. "The other path? What do you see there?"

The old man shook his head. "It is dark, unclear."

Levine sensed he was withholding the truth. "What do you see?" she said.

Suddenly a look of horror filled his eyes. His left hand rose to his mouth, which fell open gaping at whatever terrible image his mind had seen.

"Oh, my God," Levine said. "What is it?"

The old man shook his head and looked at her, his eyes wide.

Levine said, "I think I'll take the first one. The guy on the beach. That sounds nice to me."

THIRTY-SIX
THE SEARCH

Roger and Amber came up from the hotel first. Helen closed the door behind them and looked up the trench. Amber reached the top; Roger was close behind. He turned and waved for Helen to come on up. They were all wearing snowshoes.

"It looks like we may have a few hours," Roger said.

Helen came up to the edge of the trench and looked out at the white field all around them. Amber had trotted out from the trench some thirty feet on her snowshoes. Helen saw the massive hole where the library had caved in on itself the night before. They'd barely gotten away with their lives, and now Helen stood there looking at it all with wonder and awe.

"How are we supposed to spot this gas station?" Helen said.

"According to the maps," Roger said, "and the measurements we took from them, we should be able to position ourselves with landmarks."

Helen almost laughed but she realized Roger was serious, and so she forced herself to look out at the white field which stretched some six miles to the north.

"What landmarks?" she said, staring at one rocky outcropping two miles to the northeast.

Roger said nothing, and Helen's eyes came back to meet his.

"Well," he said, shrugging. "I think that knob up there"—he pointed at the rocky outcropping—"is Widow's Peak."

"Yes," Helen said.

"If the maps are right," Roger said, "the service station at the north end of town is almost exactly six hundred meters south, southwest of that outcropping."

Helen looked at him with grave doubt.

"Within a hundred meters or so," he said. "Give or take a hundred meters."

"Within a hundred meters?" Helen said.

"Should be."

"And if we start digging a hundred meters west of the right spot?"

"Probably wouldn't see it."

"And a hundred meters east?" Helen asked.

"Wouldn't see it."

Helen nodded her head. She glanced at Amber who was doing figure eights on her snowshoes about one hundred meters away from the opening of the trench.

"Same for north and south?" Helen said.

"Yes, Helen," Roger said. "We have to find the right spot."

"How're you gonna measure six hundred meters?" Helen said.

Roger's face looked stony.

"I mean," she said. "Let's say that that rocky outcropping *is* Widow's Peak, how're you gonna measure exactly six hundred meters from that outcropping to the spot where the gas station is buried?"

"We have a compass," he said, touching his jacket pocket.

"Compass measures north, south, right?" Helen said. "East, west. Sure we can find the location in degrees from the outcropping, which is brilliant, Roger, but how do we measure six hundred meters from that outcropping?"

Roger smiled weakly. "I thought we could eye it," he said, finally.

"Eye it?" Helen said, as though the two words were foreign.

"We can judge," Roger said, "by looking at the outcropping, measuring with the compass, and making a reasonable estimate of distance with our eyes."

Helen made a thoughtful frown with her lips and nodded her head up and down lightly.

"If we're wrong, we're wrong," Roger said. "But we have to give it a shot, Helen."

"And if it doesn't work?"

"We use our other options."

"Such as?"

Roger said, "We trek out of here on cross-country skis. We'll have to camp at least one night, maybe two, but we could be up to Montrose in a two-to-three day hike."

Helen seemed to appreciate this.

"But first we see if we can find some gasoline," Roger said. "There's a gas station, right here, in town. We just gotta find where it's buried under all this snow. If we find the gasoline, we got two snowmobiles that'll haul us up to Montrose in a few hours."

"*One* snowmobile," Helen said. "The other's with Levine and McKenzie."

"They'll make it back down," Roger said.

"If they're still alive."

"They're still alive."

"Amber doesn't think Sara is," Helen said, looking at Amber.

Amber looked up and realized Helen and Roger were arguing.

She called, "Come on, guys! We've only got a couple hours before the snow flies again."

Roger smiled at Amber, and he raised an affirmative hand for her to see. He glanced at Helen. Helen spied the peaks to the south and the thick heavy gray clouds forming to the west.

"Jeez," she said. "How much more can it snow?"

Roger tried out his snowshoes, walking a few feet from the trench toward Amber who was a good distance away now. He turned and looked at Helen. Helen stood there with desperation straining her eyes.

"This is Colorado," Roger said. "It could snow all winter."

Helen could think of nothing to say. Roger looked into her gray-green eyes. The lines around his eyes crinkled up like crow's feet.

"Come on," he said. "We need to find this gas station."

He turned and started down the hill toward Amber. Helen glanced back down the trench and looked at the door into the hotel.

She shook away the thought and saw that Roger had caught up with the girl. She glanced at her snowshoes. They were in pretty good shape. *Come on, girl*, Helen thought to herself. *Pull yourself together*. She lifted one foot first, then the other, and she started down the snow-white hill toward Roger and Amber. *I'm lucky to even have these two feet.*

· ·

Amber noticed that Roger had broken a sweat, and they had only gone a few hundred meters. She had taken to the snowshoes quickly and was moving well over the snow. Roger was struggling to keep his balance every few steps, and he found the snowshoes cumbersome and each step a task. He was breathing heavily in the thin mountain air, but he judged his distance well and he kept eying the rocky outcropping that they believed was Widow's Peak. It only occurred to him after they had walked a half mile that they could not see the trench into the hotel up the hill.

Everything blended into a white field, and with the exception of a few signs of the town, it was difficult to follow their trail. He stopped and looked back in the direction from which they had come.

"What is it?" Helen asked. She could see the nervousness in his eyes.

"Can you see the hotel?" he said.

Both Amber and Helen looked back up the hill. They could see their tracks in the snow, but beyond fifty meters everything just looked white and flat.

"No," Helen said. "But we can just follow our tracks through the snow to get back."

Roger looked doubtful a moment.

"I don't know, Helen," he said. "Maybe you were right. Maybe we should just stay put at the hotel. Wait for Levine and McKenzie to get back from the mine."

"They asked us to see if we could find this gas station," Amber said. "Eventually we're gonna have to find a way out of these mountains. The snowmobiles may be our best option."

The two adults looked at Amber. She seemed to glow with self-confidence, so much so that there seemed an inner peace about her. Her voice was calm and assured.

"Like Helen said," Amber said, "we can follow our tracks back through the snow."

Roger dropped his hands to his knees and breathed heavily. Helen was a little out of breath, too, but she'd unzipped her jacket and had found her rhythm. She was competent if not graceful moving along in her snowshoes over the snow. Amber smiled at them both.

"You can do it," she said.

Roger's head popped up, his hands on his knees. He had a curious smile on his face, and he just looked at Amber for a second trying to figure her out. She looked into his blue eyes, nodded her head, and smiled.

"Come on, Roger," she said. "Don't wimp out on us, now."

Roger looked at Helen with that same curious smile on his face. Helen's face relaxed. Her cheeks were rosy. She looked into Roger's eyes. She started to shrug her shoulders, thought better of it, and just held her gaze looking into his eyes.

"No, you're right," he said, turning to look at Amber. He held a snow shovel in his hand. "Lead the way, kiddo."

She smiled, turned, and continued down the hill. Helen patted Roger on the shoulder and took up her stride right behind Amber. Roger looked up at the clouds to the west and to the south and realized they were only an hour or two from the start of another snowfall.

Well, at least we got a couple hours break from the snow, he thought. And though the image of falling snow entered his mind, he pushed it away and started after Amber and Helen, his snowshoes clomping and whooshing over the fresh white powder.

Amy Levine stood ten feet from a window of light. The intensity of the light's brightness was like nothing she'd ever seen, and it stood three feet above the grass at window height. It was a square window, the one through which she had crawled from the Key Room, but from the side on which she now stood by the lake, she could not see inside the Key Room; it was only a stunningly bright light. She turned and looked at Samuel.

"Well," she said. "I must go."

Samuel nodded his head. "Yes," he said.

"Thank you for your kindness," she said. "Thank you for your inspiration."

Samuel looked into Levine's brown and blue eyes and smiled warmly. He reached a hand forward and touched her shoulder. She felt a warm pulse of energy flow through her. She looked from his hand to his eyes. She smiled tentatively and then came forward and gave him a hug.

"You're sure," she said, "you won't join us?"

Samuel patted her back lightly. "I will be with you, Amy. My spirit will be with you."

Levine leaned back and looked into his eyes once more. She nodded her head, and then turned and climbed into the light. Everything was warm and bright, and then she fell through onto the floor inside the Key Room. There was a rippling water sound, and she climbed to her feet and looked back through the window.

The image in the window rippled outward from the center where she'd come through, and she could see Samuel standing just a few feet away on the other side. She waved to him, realizing that he could not see through from his side of the window. He smiled as though at a pleasant thought, turned, and walked back around the lake toward his fishing spot.

Inside the Key Room, Levine turned and checked to make sure the Gamma Cephei Key was still in her pocket. She felt the outside of her pants pocket and was terrified for a split second because she couldn't feel the key. But then she reached her hand inside her pocket and felt the key at her fingertips. She pulled the key out and held it up in front of her. It shone.

She walked to the front of the Key Room, knelt down, and crawled through the little doorway. She closed the small wooden door behind her and looked down from the marble landing out at the sea of gold coins inside the enormous room. She stared at the hill of gold coins on which she'd lost Sara, and then she saw the green door on the far side of the room.

She started across the landing, down the marble stairwell, and then out onto the gold coins. She was across the room in thirty or forty seconds, and she stepped down onto the marble foyer with the white and gold key and key ring emblem in its center.

If only I had saved Sara, Levine thought, gazing back at the gold coin hill.

The door stood still, but when she stepped out into the key ring emblem there was a wind chime sound, and the massive marble door creaked slowly open like a vault. Levine saw through the doorway into the death chamber. She patted the key through the outside of her pocket. She turned and picked up her ski jacket, gloves, and the flashlight from the pile to the right of the foyer.

She stepped up to the open doorway and saw all the skeletons on the other side. Her body flooded with adrenaline. This was it. The moment of truth. She was certain she had the right key, but that certainty seemed to crumble into doubt as she stood in the doorway just outside of the death chamber, the memory of her friend's death vivid in her mind. She stepped right up to the opening of the doorway and just stood there a moment.

She reached in her pocket and removed the key. Perhaps her intuition had served her incorrectly. Perhaps she'd step through the doorway only to have her body seize up with some supernatural death grip. She looked at the words on the now-open marble door.

She who enters must choose the
correct key, or she shall never leave.

She looked at the key in her hand. All of a sudden, her faith faltered, and every weakness she had ever been wont to give into flooded her mind. All the greed, all the evil. It hit her, and she felt weak inside. She wasn't a hero. She was just a screwed up woman who had lived her whole life trying to prove herself to the dead parents she had hardly even known.

Levine held the key in front of her. It looked wholly unremarkable. She put it through the doorway and felt nothing. She looked back over her shoulder into the gold room. She saw the wooden door far across the room. She saw the spot on that first hill where Sara had been taken by the gold coins. She wondered at the terrible beauty that was her life, and she said a quick prayer and crossed herself. She closed her eyes and stepped—one foot first, then the other—into the death chamber.

Nothing happened.

The mine was immediately colder, but that was a natural response. The putrefying smell was awful, but again, that was a natural response. She took a few more steps out into the center of the room. She continued on through the room, back toward the tunnel that led up to the main mine shaft.

She stopped at the edge of the room, turned and looked back at all the dead bodies on the floor. She was filled with pity at all the lives that had been lost before Sara's, and she was filled with an emptiness like denial at the thought that Sara was dead. *I must do this for Sara*, Levine thought, *for her courage, her resolve, and her trust.*

She kissed the key with her lips as though it was a rosary, and she turned on her flashlight and continued up the tunnel.

• •

She reached the main mine shaft in less than a minute, and she realized that she was going to be alright. The ground was rocky and gravelly under Levine's feet, and she shone the flashlight across the mining car tracks to the far side of the main mine shaft. The DECK 147 sign caught the flashlight's shine, and she saw the barricade at the end of the tracks. She saw the mining car right where they had left it.

Levine trotted over to the car and looked inside it. The moisture from her and Sara's footprints was still there on the rusty floor of the mining car. How long had she been down here? A couple of hours? Moisture of that kind indicated that she'd only been gone a few minutes.

Levine shone the flashlight out beyond the barricade at the end of the tracks. The light shone out into endless darkness.

"Hello!" she called, and her voice traveled out into the cavern for three or four seconds before it started echoing back to her.

She walked over to the barricade with its black-and-white reflective signs, and she stood there with her flashlight. It was as though the mine opened out onto a huge underground world, and she was tempted to hop over the barricade in order to check it out. But she remembered the key in her pocket, and she remembered the face of Amber Page. And suddenly Levine realized that she was alive, that she'd made it out from the death chamber, and the realization that she *had* the right key filled her with relief and with joy.

She turned and shone her flashlight up the main mine shaft. She could see that the ground sloped upward climbing up a hill, and she started walking in that direction.

It was cold and damp inside the mine, but the climb was uphill and her exertion kept her warm enough that she wanted to keep her jacket unzipped and open, so as to stay cool. It took her about five minutes to reach Deck 135. The mining car tracks continued on up the hill into darkness, and Levine saw three forking tunnels on the left side of the main shaft and three forking tunnels on the right side of the main shaft.

There was a little rectangular sign standing atop a three-foot-high wooden post over on the left side. The word ELEVATOR was painted on it, and to the right of the word, there was a very clearly marked arrow pointing to the right. The post and sign stood right out in the center of the three branching tunnels, and there was no mistaking that the sign indicated the tunnel farthest on the right as the route to take.

Levine shone her flashlight up the other two tunnels. From the tunnel on the left she heard water dripping in the distance. From the tunnel in the middle, she heard some kind of low growling sound. She tilted her head a little and quieted herself so as to hear better.

Sure enough, there was some kind of low mechanical growling, a curious blend of machine parts and an animal that sounded like it was dying. Out of sheer curiosity, she almost started up that middle tunnel toward the growling sound, but she bumped into the little elevator sign atop the picket post.

She could see that the sign had been hammered into the post with a single nail. She grabbed the sign with her hand and was able to rotate it around so that the word ELEVATOR was upside down and the arrow was pointing to the left. There could be no mistaking that the elevator was up the tunnel all the way to the right. Levine glanced back out into the main shaft, shining her flashlight and then turned and headed up the tunnel on the far right.

She walked for more than a minute. There were a series of a dozen smaller tunnels branching off from this tunnel, and Levine came to a point where she realized that if she had to turn around, she might very well not find her way back to the main mine shaft. Everything was pitch black except for her flashlight, and she kept hoping for another sign indicating that she was on the right path to the elevator.

Heaven help me if this flashlight goes out, she thought.

She glanced around her and felt a sickening fear that the walls and ceiling were closing in on her. She continued walking, but it was quite clear that the width of the tunnel was shrinking and the height of the ceiling was lowering.

"Where is this elevator?" she said aloud.

She continued on up the tunnel, shining the flashlight out in front of her, but eventually she had to crouch down a little because the ceiling had reached a height only an inch or two above her head. The walls on either side were now only a foot or two wider than herself, and she finally stopped. She turned around and shone the flashlight back in the direction from which she'd just come. She saw four tunnels branching off, and she couldn't be certain which one was hers.

She swung back around and shone her flashlight on up the tunnel. Up ahead, it looked like the ceiling was no more than four feet high, and the walls narrowed so that the space between them was less than a half meter wide.

And then she saw the little red eye. It was glowing.

It was up ahead on one wall just beyond her flashlight's reach. It was down near floor level, and at first she thought it might just be the darkness playing tricks on her eyes, but she took a couple of steps up the tunnel toward it and realized that it was no trick of light (or darkness) at all. She had to crouch down considerably because the ceiling was only a meter high, but the little red glowing eye made her curious, and she wanted to see what it was.

She had to drop to her hands and knees, but she continued to crawl, holding the flashlight as best she could. She heard that mechanical growling sound she had heard earlier, and suddenly she found herself pinned into a space along the tunnel that was so narrow that she had no way to turn around.

She was on her hands and knees, and the ceiling was less than two feet high. The walls had narrowed to less than two feet wide, and she had the sensation of being inside an industrial pipe. Still, she saw that little red eye up ahead, and she heard the mechanical growling sound.

"Hello!" she called up the tunnel.

There was no reply. The mechanical sound shifted, clanked, and then whirred.

"*The elevator,*" she said under her breath. "I must have taken a wrong turn somewhere, but I'll bet that's it up there. Somehow I looped around."

She drew nearer to the little red eye and realized it was not an "eye" at all, but a red laser light. It shone from one side of the tunnel to the other, a single red beam of light. She realized it must be some kind of sensor. She was only five feet away from it. She crawled closer to it.

"I wonder what happens if I pass through it?" she said aloud.

She reached her hand forward toward the beam of light. Her fingertips were only inches away, when she realized that it might be some kind of trap. She retracted her hand without touching the ray of red light, and tried to see farther up the tunnel with the flashlight.

She couldn't see much, but that mechanical growling sound had grown louder. It sounded like it was only twenty feet away. Almost by accident, she switched the light off on the flashlight. She lay down flat on her stomach inside the narrow tunnel. She looked at the red beam of light.

Her eyes slowly adjusted to the darkness, and she gradually realized there was a light ahead.

She craned her head one way then the other trying to see better, and she squinted her eyes in the darkness. There was definitely some kind of light source up ahead, almost a golden light, a low golden light pouring forth from up ahead around a bend in the tunnel. She glanced at the little red beam of light crossing the tunnel right in front of her.

Maybe I can climb over it, she thought.

She got up on her hands and knees and slowly put one hand over the beam of red light, then the other. She was in a sort of push-up position with her hands forward over the sensor light. Her head and back were touching the ceiling, and her wavy brown hair fell down around her. She tucked it up behind her neck and crawled over the red sensor light. She had made it almost completely over the sensor light when she looked down and saw her left hiking boot pass right through the light. It was just the tip of the boot, but it passed through.

There was a terrible wrenching metallic sound, and suddenly the walls started closing in on her.

"Oh, no!" she cried, and she started shuffling forward up the narrow space.

The ceiling grinded closer and closer, the walls compressing around her. It would squeeze her to death. She screamed and crawled as best she could forward toward the golden light. She dropped the flashlight but didn't stop shuffling up the tunnel. She was being pinned.

Suddenly, she saw an open room out in front of her, and she fell through the final opening down onto the floor of the room. She rolled over and saw that the little hole that she'd just crawled through closed like a constricting arteriole in the wall, and the surface where the hole had been was just smooth wall.

She jerked her head around and saw the source of the golden light.

In the middle of the room, there stood a freestanding brass elevator and from the ceiling above the elevator a bright light shone down like a stage's spotlight. It was a fancy, antique elevator, the kind found inside a posh 1920s hotel. There was a little semi-circular placard above the door to the elevator, and a black arrow rested all the way over to the left near the "135." There was a number for every ten floors on the placard (130, 120, 110, 100, 90, etc.) except for the last one which was 135.

There was nothing else in the room, the rest of which was dark. Levine approached the elevator and looked inside. The door was open, and the carpet inside the elevator was red with little blue palm-sized diamonds interwoven with straight white lines. The red was rich crimson, and Levine poked her head inside and saw the pushbutton panel. There were one hundred and thirty-four pushbuttons from "135" to "2." There was a "TD" and a "BD" as well as "Bell" and "Emergency Stop."

What a strange elevator, she thought.

She leaned back and looked around the rest of the room. The room was dark, and there were three tunnels leading away from the room at three different sides of the room. She partially shielded her eyes and looked up at the light source coming from the ceiling. It was so bright it was actually warm standing right beside the elevator, and she could only look at it for a moment. She winced from the blinding light and then stepped into the elevator.

She turned and looked at the pushbutton panel. She reached forward and pressed "2." The door immediately shut. There was a mechanical growling sound, and the elevator took off, climbing very quickly upward. She watched a lighted panel above the door. The number on the far left was 135, and the farthest on the right was 2. "115" glowed for two seconds, then "114," then "113." The numbers looked like they were made of white plastic, and they lit up from inside, and the elevator emitted a pleasant little chime at each floor.

It took about four minutes to reach the top, and a gentle female voice said through the elevator's speaker, "You have reached the top floor."

A chime sounded, and the door opened. There was only faint light, but Levine stepped out away from the elevator door. The elevator chimed again, and the door closed. Levine looked to the right and saw a tunnel, on the floor of which there glowed the faint silver light of daylight.

Levine was startled when the elevator took off deep down into the earth. There was a flash of light, and she stepped over to the hole in the floor through which the elevator vanished. She saw the top of the elevator inside the shaft, vanishing into the darkness.

She looked to her right and headed for the tunnel. She had to climb one final set of stairs, but she could see an opening out of the mine up ahead. It was still daylight outside!

The light was so bright after having been in the mine, it took a minute to adjust. She stepped out of the mouth of the mine and saw the swinging bridge and the miner's lodge across the chasm.

She'd made it! She was out of the mine!

The sky overhead was clouded over with thick snow clouds, and a gentle flurry had begun. Levine zipped up her jacket and looked back down into the darkness of the main mine shaft. She saw the mining car tracks, and she checked the key in her pocket.

She still had it.

She looked out across the chasm at the miner's lodge. There was a trail around the left side of the chasm, and there were mining tracks along the trail. It looked like the trail led the long way around the chasm back to the miner's lodge, but it came out closer to where she and Sara had left the snowmobile.

She pocketed the key and started along the tracks. It took her a minute to get around the chasm, but she came out onto the massive snowfield about one hundred meters left of the lodge. Clouds had rolled in from the west and the view was limited because of the snow, but she saw the snowmobile, a black dot several hundred meters away.

She glanced back at the mine and thought again of Sara.

She started across the snowfield toward the snowmobile. It was easier going downhill than up, but she didn't have her snowshoes with her and so she kept sinking down into the snow. She glanced up at the lodge and saw hers and Sara's snowshoes sticking up from the snow at the base of that little stairwell up onto the porch.

She kept dropping down to her thighs in the snow, and was having to practically crawl over the surface, so she just rolled over on her back and sledded down the hill toward her snowmobile.

When she got to the snowmobile, she checked the fuel level. She saw that the needle was just a hair on the left side of Empty, which meant she had just enough gasoline to make it back down the mountain to Ouray. She'd have to coast some of the way.

Levine straddled the snowmobile, fired up the engine, and revved the throttle. She turned the thing around, got it pointed back down the mountain, and started over the tracks she'd made on the way up from Ouray.

Ten minutes, she thought. *I can make it back down into town in ten minutes.*

She ducked down behind the snowmobile's windshield, her hair flying out behind her, and she raced down the mountain over the white landscape. She only turned back once, and that was when the snowmobile came out on a ridgeline that afforded one final glance back at the miner's lodge. It was just a tiny gray box up on the side of the mountain. Levine said a quick prayer for Sara McKenzie, turned, and started down the next ridgeline into Ouray.

THIRTY-EIGHT
THE DIG

It was an excavation worthy of twenty workers, and time was not on their side. Amber quietly went about her work with a large red snow shovel, and Roger maintained a steady pace with his. For the past five minutes, Helen had taken a break, but she stood up now and joined the other two who were digging down into the deep white snow. Their hole was thirty feet from side to side, and they'd dug down into it chest deep.

"We should start up a pile over here," Roger said, carrying a shovelful of snow to one side of the snow white pit.

Helen said, "I feel like we're digging our own graves here."

Amber looked up and said, "That's no way to think."

Helen looked at her and managed a feeble smile. Amber held her snow shovel like she meant business, and so Helen just continued digging.

Roger stopped for a moment and leaned on his shovel. The snowfall thus far this afternoon had been light and intermittent, but Roger looked to the south of town and to the west and realized that a light snow was not what nature had in store for them tonight. The clouds were thick and gray, as foreboding as an Atlantic hurricane twenty-four hours from landfall. They were so thick and so gray that they looked evil, and Roger began to realize the futility of their work.

"We're gonna get buried tonight," he said, and without looking at either of them, he turned and continued digging, keeping the rest of his thoughts to himself.

Roger was not a deeply intuitive man, but he had more than once experienced things more romantic-minded folks would call "premonitions." And as he quietly went about his digging, his mind filled with dark and panicky thoughts, a little voice that said, *You must get out of here; you're going to die tonight if you don't get out of this town.*

‥

Amber was the first to hear the snowmobile. She was on one side of the pit, building a little stairwell down into the snow. She used her shovel to level off each step and packed the snow down hard so that it didn't crumble under her footsteps. There were seven steps, and she'd climbed up to the top step and was leveling it off, when she heard the sound of the snowmobile engine in the distance.

"Levine," she said.

Both Roger and Helen looked up from inside the pit. The snowfall had begun in earnest, and thick wet flakes fell swiftly down inside the pit.

"You hear something?" Roger said, holding his snow shovel in his right hand.

Helen lifted another shovelful of snow and carried it over to the side of the pit. She dumped it and then came over to Amber on the steps. Both Helen and Roger climbed up the little stairwell. Amber could only see a hundred meters up the hill into the snowfall, but all three heard the sputtering, whining sound of a snowmobile engine riding into town on fumes.

"Come on," Roger said. "They may need our help."

All three put on their snowshoes and started up the hill toward the buried hotel. They followed the tracks they'd made earlier in the snow.

"There they are!" Roger said, pointing forward into the snow.

They saw the snowmobile up ahead. It was coming down the hill toward them. Amber saw that there was only one person.

"She's alone," Helen said.

They reached the trench down into the hotel about the same time. They could see that Levine was alone. The engine sputtered, the snowmobile lurching forward. The engine died, and Levine put it in neutral and coasted the last fifty feet up to the trench.

Everything was silent except for the sound of their breathing and the sound of the snowmobile coasting the last few feet, crunching over the snow. Levine looked up and waved at the three of them.

Roger looked at Helen, then Amber.

He said, "Where's Sara?"

Levine took her goggles off and looked into his eyes.

"She didn't make it."

Helen looked at Amber, and realized that the young girl was right; she'd *known* the moment that Sara McKenzie died. Somehow she knew it. Levine stood in front of the snowmobile feeling guilt and self-loathing so violently juxtaposed, it felt like her mind was tearing in two.

"She died," Levine said. "I was holding onto her hand."

Roger came over and gave her a hug.

"She died?" Helen said. "Sara's dead? How did it happen?"

Levine just shook with tears and emotion. A gloved finger came up and wiped away the tears cumbersomely.

"*I let her die*," she said.

"Shhhh," Roger said. He held her tightly. "It's okay, Amy. Everything's gonna be alright. It's not your fault."

"*She's dead*." Levine staggered away from Roger and just swung at the air. She fell down onto the snow.

Roger, Helen, and Amber stared at her, speechless.

Levine said, "*I let it happen!*"

• •

Helen stirred the vegetable soup with a shiny silver tablespoon. The fire blazed in the fireplace, and Levine was at the table she'd pulled from across the lobby. Amber and Roger leaned over a corner of the coffee table, and Amber drew a map of the Randa region for him with a pen and white piece of paper.

"There's a region to the north," Amber said. "At least a three-day hike."

"The land of the Randa," Roger said. "How well do you know this land?"

"There's not much there," Amber said. Her young eyes met his to see if he understood. Roger raised a contemplative index finger to his lip. He looked at the map she'd drawn.

"It is north of the desert?" Roger said.

From the table, Levine watched this exchange between Roger and Amber. She noticed Roger's blue eyes looking deep into Amber's eleven-year-old brown eyes.

"It's an arid region, too," Amber said. "But there are mountains there. There *are* springs, and the legend goes that the rain is trapped there."

"The legend," he asked, "that's this Oracle that you keep talking about?"

"Correct," Amber said.

"What is that?" Helen said. "The Oracle?"

"It's a book," Amber said. Her brown eyes met Helen's gray-green eyes. "A very old book. It's written in twelve volumes."

"Twelve books?" Roger said.

"And many believe that the Oracle is just the first part of four in a larger book," Amber said. "Some people just think they're myths, stories; others say the stories have a direct bearing on the world in which we all live."

"And this is one of the stories?" Levine said.

"Correct, Dr. Levine," Amber said. "The legend says that the land of the Randa—a farming people—was to be arid and barren for one century."

"And we're to carry this key"—Levine held the key up, and it shone in the firelight—"to Kevorak's Needle."

"Once there," Roger said, "what happens?"

"No one knows," Amber said. "The legend says that one person—the bearer of the key—will enter Kevorak's Soul. And there, this person will unlock the needle that holds the water inside the soil."

Helen said, "Amber, you say that no one knows. How do *we* know it's real?"

"No one has ever returned from Kevorak's Needle alive," she said. "But it is real. Believe me, it is real."

Roger pointed at the key Levine held. He said, "And that thing's supposed to unlock this Kevorak's Needle? It looks like an ordinary house key."

Helen finished her vegetable soup and placed the white ceramic bowl on the coffee table.

"How long do you think it'll take?" Roger said.

"Three days," Amber said.

"If we're gone from this hotel for three days," Roger said, "and we come back, we're liable to not get out until next spring."

Levine spoke up, "It doesn't work like that."

"What do you mean?" Roger said.

"When I went in before," Levine said, "I left a candle burning outside of the red door. I was in the Randa world for a while, but when I came back through, the candle hadn't burned down at all."

"Time on Earth doesn't pass while we're in the Randa world," Amber said. "But we do have provisions there. We could regroup."

"But when we come back, we'd still have to face this storm." Roger looked at Levine. He said, "You've seen this Randa world?"

"The red door is in this hotel," Levine said. "It's beyond the chess room. There's a spiral stairwell that leads to a hallway. I found this ancient book at the end of the hallway."

"Book?" Helen said.

"It had all these names in it."

"What kind of names?" Roger said.

"All kinds of names," Levine said. "Some were very old."

"Here?" Helen said. "In this hotel?"

"There's an old stone stairwell that leads down below the hotel," Levine said. "That's where I saw the red door."

"And this door," Roger said, "it leads to your home?"

Amber said, "It does. It is a portal."

Roger said, "And you have food there?"

Amber nodded her head. Her brown eyes looked from his, to Levine's, to Helen's eyes. "Enough to last us months," she said.

Roger looked at Helen. She shrugged her shoulders.

"Well," he said. "What are we waiting for?"

Thirty-Nine
The Journey

Amber led the way, followed by Levine, Helen, and Roger. Each of the four held a candle, and the candlelight lighted the hotel hallway in front of them. Ahead at the end, they could see a pitch black room. The sound of a powerful wind howled outside through the snow depth that buried the hotel, and the wood inside the walls and hallway floor creaked and moaned as though the building was settling in for a long winter's nap.

"That's the chess room," Levine said, "at the end of the hallway."

"We were up here earlier," Roger said, "when we were searching for maps."

Amber glanced back over her shoulder at Roger, nodded, then turned and continued on up the hallway. She held her candle up a little higher, and Helen caught the fragrance of antique varnished wood, floor polish, dusty age, and the smell of old paperback novels coming from the chess room.

"Here we are," Amber said.

She stepped out into the room. Helen glanced through the sepia-colored candlelight at the chess board atop the table in the room. She spotted a globe in one corner and saw the books on all the bookshelves in the room. Levine started over toward the spiral staircase, and Amber let her lead the way. Roger looked up the spiral staircase at the curious little door built into the wall near the ceiling.

"What an odd looking door," he said.

"This," Levine said, "is the secret passage."

Amber and Levine were at the top of the spiral staircase. Helen and Roger followed closely. Levine opened the door and stepped through into the wall. Amber stepped through and held the door open for Helen and Roger.

"It's a hallway," Helen said.

She glanced back at Roger and then down at the chess room now spread out below them.

From inside the hallway, Levine said, "It's up here."

Helen and Roger stepped from the spiral staircase into that curious little hallway. They both saw the book on a stand at the end. Levine stood over it, holding her candle up so that she could read the book's pages. Levine waited for them, and when they approached the book, she gave them a meaningful look and pointed at the names on the page.

Amber Page, Helen Richards, Roger McAllister, & Dr. Amy Levine

"Oh my goodness," Helen said.

There was no date written beside their names on the column under "Date."

"How did our names get here?" Roger said.

They each looked at one another, but no one had an answer. It made Helen shiver.

"And why is there no date?" Levine said.

"Perhaps, it's because we're in it, right now," Amber said.

"In it?" Levine said.

"In the story," Amber said. "In the book of the Oracle and because our ending is not yet clear."

"You think our names will be here once our story is over?"

Amber shrugged and frowned thoughtfully. "Maybe the date will be here," she said, "once we get back from the other side."

Roger said, "Come on." And he started down the cobblestone stairwell to the right of the book and its stand.

Levine recognized the windows inside the stone-wall stairwell, and the group stayed together making their way down into the earth.

"Feels damp," Helen said.

Levine said, "There's an underground river down here. There are three"—they reached the bottom and saw the three—"tunnels. One to the right, one straight ahead, and one to the left. The underground river's to the right. We want to go to the left, though. To the red door."

Levine again took the lead, followed by Roger, Helen, and Amber. They came to an intersection. Levine recognized the table in the middle of the intersection as the table atop which she'd found the glowing flowers.

She remembered that the hallway straight ahead led to the room with the three doors.

"It's straight ahead," she said.

The group continued onward. Helen saw that the light ahead was brightening, and she let out an audible gasp when they stepped into the room with the three doors. Levine recognized the cobblestone floors and saw the parchment on the floor exactly where she and Amber had left it.

She saw the glowing bundle of flowers on the tabletop in the middle of the room.

"The doors have changed," Amber said.

Levine looked up and realized she was right.

"The red door is in the middle now," Levine said.

"And the numbers have changed," Amber said. "The boar's head door was door number two before. Now, it's door number three."

"Are you sure?" Levine said. "I thought the unicorn door was door number two, and that the boar's head door was number three. Remember it was over here on the right?"

Amber disagreed. "No," she said. "The unicorn door was on the right, the boar's head was in the middle, and the red door was on the left."

"What is this?" Roger said, kneeling to pick up the parchment. "'Two doors giveth unto Death, but the third shall leadeth to Kevorak's Needle. Beware the obvious choice, for it may proveth your last.'"

"What does that mean?" Helen asked.

"It means," Roger said. "That you better choose the correct door."

"But the doors have changed," Levine said.

Helen and Roger looked up at her and Amber.

"I am certain the red door was on the left," Amber said.

"The other doors are much more attractive," Roger said placing the parchment on the table top. He reached forward and started to touch the unicorn's horn.

"Don't!" Levine said.

"Relax," Roger said. "I'm not going to open it."

"Another thing that's changed," Levine said to Amber. "The shining light is only around the red door. Last time, it was the unicorn and boar's head doors from which the light was shining."

All four realized she was right. There was no light shining from the other side of the fancy doors, but around the sill of the cheap looking red door, there glowed a supernaturally bright light.

"I still think it's the red door," Amber said. "It's just in the middle now."

"How do you know for sure?" Helen said.

They looked at the three doors. On the far right, there was the boar's head door with a shiny silver "3" in the middle of it. The red door was in the middle, and it had a cheap tin "2" in the middle of it. The unicorn door was on the left, and it had a shiny silver "1" on it.

"I think it's the unicorn door," Roger said. "The one on the left."

"No," Helen said. "It's the red door. Remember the boy's dying words, Roger? He said 'the red door in the Beaumont.' That's us. That's here. Don't you get it?"

"I'm with Helen," Amber said.

"That makes three of us," Levine said.

"I think the doors change," Amber said. "The numbers and their position left, right, or center. But the red door is the door to choose."

"How do you know?" Roger said. "Maybe the red door is the *wrong* door this time. Maybe you're supposed to go with the position of the doors, and it was the one all the way on the left the last time, you said."

Amber looked at Levine for help.

"The red door was," Helen said. "Now, it's in the middle—"

"And I think we should choose the one on the left," Roger said. "I think it's position, not color."

Helen said, "But why then did the boy tell us to choose the red door?"

"I don't remember him telling us to *choose* the red door," Roger said. "All he said was 'the red door . . . in the Beaumont.' He didn't say anything about *choosing* it or not choosing it."

"No, Roger," Helen said. "He said to 'choose the red door in the Beaumont.' I remember it perfectly."

Roger looked into her eyes.

Helen stood firm. She said, "He said to choose it, Roger."

"He did not, *Helen*."

"Listen guys," Levine said. "We should all just take it easy. We've been stuck here in this hotel a while now. We've got a storm howling outside that may bury this hotel under enough snow that no one will find us until next spring. We need to stay together on this. We need to keep our heads clear."

Roger leaned his head against the unicorn door. He was trying to listen through the door. He looked at the three women. They stared at him.

"I don't know," he said. "Maybe you're right. There's just no margin for error. I want to make sure that we're in this together. I want you to know that I care. I care about each of you, and I want to choose the correct door."

Roger looked at Helen. He looked at Dr. Levine. They each looked at him with sincerity and pure love in their eyes. Roger felt that they loved him as good friends love one another. And he loved them, too.

"Okay," he said. "I'm with you. We choose the red door. My vote is for the red door. If we're going down, we're going down together!"

Helen smiled at him.

She turned and said, "Dr. Levine, would you do the honors?"

Levine smiled, nodded her head, turned and opened the door.

The light was blindingly bright. Desert sand lay before them in all directions. Roger could see bright sunlight and miles and miles of endless pure white desert sand. It looked like the door opened onto some kind of dune, the top of a high hill of sand.

"Wow," he gasped.

They each placed the candles on top of the table. Roger approached the door. He looked to the left and could see forty miles all the way to the horizon. There were mountains far on the horizon, but everything between the door and the distance was nothing but sand, a huge rolling sea of sand.

Roger saw a little building on a hill across from the door. And then the others saw it, too. Amber gasped.

"My home," she said.

It was up on the hill across the way. Smoke rose from its remains. Someone had set fire to it, and it was blackened and charred. Amber's home had been burnt to the ground.

She rushed forward through the doorway into the light and the liquid warmth of her desert world.

Roger stood in the three-door room. He looked at Helen and Dr. Levine. He looked at the ripples wheeling out from where Amber had stepped through, and he saw Amber there, now, on the other side of the doorway, the other side of everything Roger McAllister had ever known. She was running down the desert dune hillside.

"Come on," Levine said. "She's going to need our help!"

FORTY
BEN

Roger McAllister stepped through the doorway out onto warm, shifting sand. He almost fell forward out onto his hands and knees, but he managed to stay on his feet. He turned and saw Helen and Levine follow him through the doorway. As each stepped into the world, there was a bright flash of light and a sound like an electronic gust of wind through digital tree leaves.

"We made it!" Helen said.

She looked around her at the vast desert in all directions, but Dr. Levine was already running down the huge dune, following Amber.

Amber reached the bottom of the dune and started across the narrow valley that led up to the hill on which her smoldering home stood. Roger saw that her home was a low-lying complex about thirty meters from side to side.

There were palm trees around the complex, and a sparkling lotus pond lay in front of the place. Roger realized that from the shade, Amber's view was some one hundred miles from north to south. He looked and saw two moons near the horizon to the north and a third moon mid-high in the sky on the southern side of the horizon.

"Come on!" Helen said, and she reached for Roger's hand.

He took it, and they ran down the hill together. They crossed the valley and started up Amber's hill. Amber was already in the front yard of the home, and they caught up with her and Levine a minute later.

The house was in charred ruins, and Amber fell to her knees in the sand in front of it. Dr. Levine came over to her and knelt down beside her in the sand. She put her arm around Amber's back and tried to comfort her.

Roger looked at the smoldering embers. The front wall of the home was blackened, and the roof above the front doorway had collapsed. There was one large line of smoke over on the back left side of the complex, and a half dozen smaller ones at other areas. All of the smoke came together fifty meters above the home, and it climbed up high as one tall trail into the blue. He realized the smoke could be seen from miles and miles away, and he thought of the pool, thought of the water in the pool, and was hit with the urge to somehow get that water onto the charred house.

Amber knew his thoughts.

"Don't, Roger," she said.

He'd started over toward the pool, but he turned and looked at her.

Amber said, "There's nothing you can do, now."

Roger looked at Helen. They both wanted to help Amber. They wanted to say something reassuring, but they looked at the ruined home and were speechless.

"They've taken my home," Amber said to no one and to everyone. "They took my father. They took my mother *from me*. They've taken everything that I have!"

Kneeling there in the sand, she looked up to the sky.

"What else?" she said. "What else! *What else can you take?!*"

• •

Helen heard the little old man coughing before anyone else did. They were all standing in the front yard of Amber's burnt home. Helen and Roger held one another close, but Helen's ear perked up at the funny sound. It sounded as much like a pleasant little laugh as a pleasant little cough. Her head came up from Roger's shoulder, and she looked over at the corner on the left-hand side of the house.

"*Ahem*," the little old man said.

He came from around the corner of the house. He held a knobby little cane, and he only stood about four feet tall. He seemed preoccupied, talking to himself.

"Dear me," he said. "Dear me. The house is all a mess. Huff, huff."

He shuffled out away from the house, seemingly unaware that all four people were watching him. He kind of waddled when he walked, a little like a penguin. His steps were small, but he was quick. And something about the way he used his cane indicated a hidden strength, and it made Helen smile.

"Dear me, dear me," he said. "What shall I do?"

Dr. Amy Levine looked up and she remembered the mental flash she'd had on Santana's island, when Sara hit her.

"Ben?" Levine called out to him. "Is your name Ben Tovar?"

The man looked up and gave a frightful start at seeing the four people in the front yard.

"Dear me," he said. "Dear me. It is Dr. Amy Levine."

He suddenly looked worried, and he shuffled forward toward the pool. Amy looked at him and smiled curiously. She glanced at Helen and Roger. She looked at Amber Page.

"You know him?" Amber said.

"I think so," she said.

She trotted toward him. Helen and Roger followed behind, and Amber got up out of the sand to see what this was all about. She'd never heard of Ben Tovar. She tried to shrug off the negative feelings about her home, and she managed to smile. She wiped the tears away from her cheeks. The little old man was almost exactly her same height.

He approached a stone bench by the pool. The bench had been overturned, and he raised his hand up over it. Levine saw a distortion in the space between the old man's hand and the bench. The distortion was clear but blurry like looking through a glass of water, and everyone gasped when they saw the bench float up a foot above the ground, righting itself.

The bench settled into place, and the little old man came around in front of it and took a seat.

"A good seat, yes," he said. "Good for the back. Very peaceful."

They all came over and stood near him. Levine knelt close to him and touched his knee. He turned his head as though feigning surprise to see her there.

"Dr. Amy Levine, yes," he said. "You made it away from the pirate. I have been watching you. I knew you would come."

He smiled at her and leaned his hands forward and held his cane between his knees. He looked at the reflection of the desert and the sky on the pool's shiny surface. He looked off to the north, and he breathed deeply and sighed long and to himself.

Levine said, "I thought it all might have been in my head."

"Far from it," Ben said. He looked deeply into Amy's eyes, a connection was made, and then he smiled and said, "Please introduce me to your friends."

Amy looked up at Helen and Roger. Amber stood behind them unusually shy.

"This is Roger," Levine said. "He is a private investigator."

"Roger McAllister," Roger said. "It is nice to meet you, Ben."

"McAllister," Ben said. "A good name."

Roger smiled and nodded his head.

"And Helen," Levine said. "Helen Richards. Helen is my property manager."

"It's nice to meet you," Helen said.

"Helen." Ben smiled pleasantly.

"And the shy one is Amber," Levine said. "Amber Page."

At this, Ben's eyebrows rose up, and he glanced at the young girl. Amber just nodded.

"Ah, yes," Ben said. "Amber."

He made a contemplative sound like "hmm."

"You are angry at those who have burnt your home," he said.

Amber frowned.

"Homes can be rebuilt," she said. "Wood and nails—we are all time's captives."

Ben looked deep into Amber's glistening brown eyes and shivered. He saw something there, beyond it all, and it disturbed him.

"Yes, yes," he said. "'Tis true, 'tis true"—and here he looked again deep into Amber's eyes, searching—"but perhaps there is no time at all."

Amber looked into Ben's blue eyes, and she understood him.

"You have something," Ben said, turning to Levine. His eyes widened. "You brought it!"

At first, she didn't understand.

"Your pocket," he said. "Your pocket!"

Everyone except Amber looked surprised when Amy Levine removed the key from her pocket. *How did he know?*

"Yes," he said. "The key. You went to the Key Room"—and then he saw the pain hidden in her eyes, his mind seeing her memory as clearly as his own—"But you lost her. Oh, dear. Your friend, you lost a close friend. Oh, dear. Oh, dear."

Levine started to say, "How do you know these things?"

"*Gold*," he gasped. "She was taken by the gold."

"Is she alive, Ben?" Levine said. "Do you know! Is Sara with us?"

Ben shook his head, straining.

"It is not clear," he said. Then, "She is *not dead*."

"Where?" Levine said. "Where is she?"

"She is peaceful. She is not alone. Many are with her, and it is not all bad."

"Where, Ben? Where?"

Ben looked at Levine. He looked at Helen and Roger, and then at Amber.

"She is at a place that is not quite living," he said. "And it is not quite—dead. She says hello. She says she misses you. She says she is sorry."

"Tell her that I'm sorry," Levine said. "Tell her that I love her, that she is my friend. Tell her, Ben. Tell her!"

"She knows, Amy," Ben said. "She is with you. She is with all of you. She will keep you safe on your journey. There will be many obstacles. Dark forces have gathered near Kevorak's Needle. Shadow Warriors. The time draws near. The journey will be long. Come, come, we must eat. I will take you to my home."

"Where?" Levine said. "Where is your home?"

"To the north," he said. "We will reach it by sunset."

FORTY-ONE
BEN'S HOME

There was a small greenhouse beside Ben Tovar's home. Amber saw corn, tomatoes, pumpkins and squash. Outside of the greenhouse, there was one orange tree with bright round oranges on it and beside that, there was a banana tree. There was a single well at the back of the house, and high atop the well (some forty feet overhead) there was a modern windmill fan, its blades about six feet in diameter.

There was a single rickety wooden ladder that ascended up the side of windmill, and Ben approached the base and lifted a wooden lever, which released the brake on the windmill fan. Everyone squinted and looked up at the fan, high overhead, as the invisible wind caught the blades. It started rotating around. It creaked a little, but once it got going, it kept a steady pace, spinning in the gentle breeze.

Amber looked down at the pump in the ground. The rotating fan powered a steel rod, which descended down into the sandy earth. The rod pumped slowly up and down, and a minute later, crisp, clear water poured out of a spigot into a wooden trough at the side of the windmill.

Ben looked at the group and smiled. He saw the delighted expression in Amber's eyes, and he said, "Watch this!"

The wooden trough filled up with some forty gallons of water, and Ben leaned his cane beside it and then reached forward and opened a floodgate on one side of the wooden trough. The water poured into a narrow runner that was about four feet above the ground.

Amber's eyes quickly followed the runner forward, and she saw that it branched out in several directions near the greenhouse some thirty feet away.

Helen let out an audible "*Wow*" when, a moment later, they saw water inside the greenhouse spraying down like a shower on all the plants inside. Amber could see that the orange tree as well as the banana tree were being watered, too.

Ben said, "I can stop the water in the greenhouse, and direct it toward the house, here"—he pointed to his little adobe complex—"and it provides running water inside for drinking, bathing, and for cleaning."

"That's quite a system," Roger said, genuinely impressed.

"What kind of well reserves do you have?" Amber asked.

Ben looked seriously at her. "Some months it's better than others," he said. "You just have to conserve."

"Has it always been like this?" Helen asked. "They mentioned something about one hundred years?"

"Oh, no," he said. "Yes, in the time of my great grandfather, this valley was fertile. This was farming land. It was very prosperous, and the people lived well and were happy."

"What happened?" Roger said.

Ben smiled a curiously wise little smile.

He said, "The legend says that the people lost sight of the Great Good. They took the land and their lives for granted. The rains stopped, and the farms ceased to grow. It has been a hard time, and the people who used to reside here have moved to the coast. There are cities along the coast, of which Barbuda is the largest, but they are no good. Corruption and lawlessness rule their lives."

"How far is the coast?" Helen said.

"It is far," he said. "Many days travel."

"So, there's a lot of land here?" Roger said.

"There is much land," Ben said. "But it is all arid. It's a desert world. It has *become* a desert world. The land along the coast only makes up one percent of one percent *of* one percent of all the land in this world. There are not many left who believe."

"Believe?" Levine said.

"Believe the old stories," he said. "The virtues with which our forefathers brought this world to peace and order. Most people mock those ideas as quaint or naïve. Most people just don't have time for them."

"So, you live alone?" Levine said.

"Well," he said. "I do have a neighbor."

He looked at Amber, and the lines around his blue eyes wrinkled together in a smile. Everyone looked to the setting sun far on the western horizon. The sky filled with brilliant orange, red, pink, and golden light.

It had been a long day, a long trip to Ben's home, and they were all very tired and very hungry.

"Come inside," Ben said with a friendly gesture. "You can clean up. We'll eat. And then I will show you the maps."

Levine looked at Amber. *The maps?* What did he mean?

He started up toward the front door of his adobe home. Helen and Roger followed after him. Amber and Levine stood outside a few minutes more. They exchanged a few words about the day, about the travel, about Amber's home, and about what lay ahead. And as the sky turned periwinkle and the first stars began to shine, they turned to go inside to enjoy the company of their friends and to eat dinner.

• •

They ate dinner around a stone table whose top stood two feet up from the floor. There was bread and warm soup with potatoes. It was good, and they each filled their bowls a second time and asked for more of the fresh baked bread, which was sweet and tasted of butter.

They drank a soda that Ben called "Blueberry Cola" and indeed it was sky blue and fizzed as soda does, and it tasted sweet like blueberries. And afterward, Ben served them each a plate of "Clear Fountain Cake" with a scoop of a multi-colored "ice cream" whose colors literally glowed and shone like there was some kind of light inside it.

After dinner, everyone leaned back in their chairs around the table, and they all felt full and happy and glad to be together.

Roger asked Ben about the maps, and Amber and Levine cleaned up the dishes and washed them in a sink. There was a line outside the kitchen window, and Ben showed them how to hang up the dishes after they washed them, and the dishes dried in the cool desert breeze.

Everyone gathered in the living room area, and Ben lit a dozen candles around the room. He spread out a large map on the floor in the center of the room. The map was rolled up and made of leathery paper, and it was almost ten feet on each of its sides.

Roger saw the "Delphic Sea" on the right of the map and the "Stony Mountains" to the north. The Radian Desert was to the south and on the far left side of the map was "The Great Unknown." There were fortresses near the mountains and what might have been a city, and Ben began to explain to them about the Shadow Warriors and about some of the dangers through which they would have to pass.

"Kevorak's Needle is far to the north," he said, and he pointed with his cane. There was a spot in the midst of the Stony Mountains, and they all saw the name "Kevorak's Needle" beside one very high peak. "It is in the midst of the great Stony Mountains. Shadow Warriors have gathered there in large numbers, and we will have to slip in past them undetected."

"Or," Amber said. "We will fight them."

"What are Shadow Warriors?" Roger said.

"They ride horses," Amber said. "And they move like ghosts. And they don't care about the Great Good."

"They want to control the water," Ben said. "He who controls the mountains, controls the water. And whoever controls the water will own this world for the next millennium."

"*If* there is water there," Levine said.

"Yes," Ben said. "If there is water there. And if we are able to unlock it from the earth."

"And how do we do that?" Roger said.

"The Oracle's legend says that only one person shall enter Kevorak's Soul," Ben said. "The Bearer of the Key."

"And what is that," Helen said. "Kevorak's Soul?"

"Well, the Soul is inside Kevorak's Needle," Amber said. "And the Needle is a very tall mountain, about six miles around at its base"—Amber looked at Ben, and Ben nodded in agreement—"but it climbs up over two miles, straight up, like a natural skyscraper. There is an entrance to the Needle at the very top, and the story is that the Soul is down inside the mountain."

"But no one's ever returned?" Levine said.

"Correct, Dr. Levine," Ben said.

"And so no one knows for sure?" Roger said.

"Only those who believe the stories," Ben said.

"And you do?" Helen said. "You believe them?"

"I do," Ben said.

Everyone looked at Ben for a few moments. No one doubted that he believed, but whether his belief would prove correct was a matter of which no one could be certain.

"How many?" Roger said.

"How many what?" Amber said.

"How many Shadow Warriors?" Roger said.

Amber did not know and so looked at Ben. Ben rubbed his chin and looked into Roger's blue eyes. His eyes widened a little.

"Many," Ben said. "They have built camps around the Needle's base, and the camps have grown to become forts and fortresses, as large as small cities."

"So, several thousand?" Roger asked politely.

Ben said, "Perhaps tens of thousands. But their sheer size is what has left them vulnerable. We can come and go and blend in with the crowds."

"And all we have to do," Helen said. "Is make it to the top of this Needle, the mountain? Then we can get inside?"

"Correct," Ben said. "And Dr. Levine has the key."

"Well, so," Roger said. "All we have to do is make it past ten thousand Shadow Warriors, climb a mountain, deliver a key to this 'Soul', and hope that Amy is the Bearer of the Key"—he looked around the room at each of his friends—"I think we can do it."

••

Amber was outside under starlight sitting Indian-style on her Darpì pad. A gentle breeze rustled the palm tree branches and the little oval leaves of the orange tree. She could feel the warm glow of lights from inside Ben's home, but her eyes were closed and she pictured the desert valley before her.

At the front of her Darpì pad, the white coral stone floated inside the octagonal glass cylinder. It glowed lightly and spun slowly around in midair inside the cylinder. Amber touched the blue Oracle Stone that hung from the black string necklace around her neck, and she lifted it and pulled it from inside her shirt. Amber removed the necklace from her neck. She detached the blue Oracle Stone from the necklace and then pressed a button on the octagonal glass cylinder.

The cylinder hissed, steamed poured out of the top, and Amber reached down inside and removed the white coral stone. She placed the blue Oracle Stone in the cylinder and pressed a button that closed the lid. The Oracle Stone floated inside the cylinder.

She held the white coral stone in her hand and looked at it. She saw the sparkle of starlight on its surface, and she clipped it onto her black string necklace and then placed the necklace back over head. The coral stone glowed at the front of her chest, pulsing now in rhythm with her life force.

Amber heard Ben cough genially, and she turned and saw him shuffling out of the house toward her. She smiled and waved him over to have a seat near her.

"It is peaceful," he said. "Are you going to sleep outside tonight?"

"I think I will," she said. "The stars are shining brightly."

Ben sighed and took a seat in the sand next to Amber. He looked at the embroidery on her Darpì pad.

"Your Darpì pad," Ben said. "Did you make it yourself?"

"I did," she said.

There were four swans at each side, and they were flying around a wheel in the center of the Darpì pad. The wheel was made of a shiny metallic thread, and inside this, there was an image of a thicket of trees. Inside the thicket, there was a square that represented water. Its lines were wavy and the thread was blue and white. There was a picture of three mountain peaks inside the square, and at the very top of the center peak there was a bright, blazing sun whose thread was pink, yellow, and white. The sun's rays poured out from the very center of the Darpì pad.

"We have a long journey ahead of us," Ben said.

"Yes," Amber said.

Ben eyed the young girl. He asked, "How much of it have you seen?"

Amber looked at him. She looked at his blue eyes, the aged wrinkles around the corners of his eyes, the amiable lines of his face. She wasn't sure how much to trust this old man. Ben seemed to realize that about her, and he smiled.

"What?" Amber said.

"I have something of yours," he said.

"Of mine?" she said. "What is it?"

"Something that will make you very happy!"

Amber smiled. "What?! What is it?"

"First you must tell me what you've seen," he said. "Then, I will give you the surprise."

They both heard Helen and Levine burst out laughing from inside Ben's home. Helen, Levine and Roger were talking excitedly, and then Helen said something, and all three burst out laughing again.

"They're happy," Amber said.

"They're good people, Amber."

"Yes," she said. "They are."

"Is it fair?"

"Fair?" Amber said.

"To bring them into this," Ben said.

"I believe it is destiny," Amber said. "Levine is the Bearer of the Key."

The old man nodded his head and looked out over the starlit desert. The sand was white, but the starlight made everything seem deep, soft blue.

"I have seen it, too," he said. "I think you are right."

"Then, we will succeed?" Amber asked. "She is with us. We just have to get inside the mountain."

"That," he said, "will not be easy."

They were quiet for a while, each sitting still and silent, calm and at peace.

"I see you have switched to your coral stone," Ben said.

"Yes," Amber said.

"Your gifts are strong," he said.

"My strengths," Amber said, "are my greatest weaknesses."

"I had a vision of you and a young man."

"Yes?"

"In love," Ben said.

Amber just shook her head. "No," she said. "Not me."

Ben smiled wisely. "In time, you will learn to trust again. You will learn to love."

"I have no love," she said. "My heart has been taken from me. All I ever think about is striking back at those who have taken so much from me, and those who believe they own me."

"You're young. You can not see how young you are."

"I know my responsibilities," Amber said. "I've seen the Oracle. I know my destiny. One of the Gemini Warriors, a boy, that's who will love me."

"You know the stories," Ben said.

"I know the stories, and I'll tell you now: I won't fall in love with any boy, any Gemini Warrior. I will walk alone. I will roam from city to city. I will sleep in different beds each night, and when I am older, I will love who I *choose* to love."

The old man chuckled good-naturedly, and then he sighed. Amber looked at him.

"You think I'm funny?" she said.

He looked at her, looked deep into her eyes, and said with a conviction that made her shiver inside, "I think you have a heart of gold, young Amber. And I am only afraid that it will be broken into so many pieces that you may never put it back together again. Beware your pride. Remain open, clear, and true. Love will come in its time."

Amber stared at the old man, and she realized that he was quaint, but that his heart was good. She smiled and averted her gaze, looking out into the desert.

"So," he said. "You want to see?"

"The surprise!" Amber said. "Yes, what do you have?"

Ben smiled at her, and climbed up onto his feet. He brushed the sand from his pants and gave her a friendly wave.

"Come," he said. "I will show you."

• •

"Rusty!" Amber cried out.

The horse recognized her immediately and whinnied loudly. She rushed up to him, and he ducked his head down and nuzzled her. She held him close to her and petted his head, feeling the silken hair of his mane.

Ben stood there watching the young girl. He had a fatherly smile on his face, and his blue eyes glistened. The horse kept making whinnying, friendly sounds, and tears filled Amber's eyes. She was so happy to see him.

"Oh, Rusty!" she said. "I thought I'd lost you!"

Ben saw Roger, Helen, and Levine at the kitchen window, and he approached them. They came outside, and Levine looked at Ben.

"He must have come here," Ben said, "after you went back to the hotel."

"He's a smart horse," Helen said. "You can tell."

They stood there watching Amber in the yard with her best friend, Rusty, and they couldn't tell who was happier, Amber or Rusty. Levine smiled and said, "That was very thoughtful of you, Ben, to take care of him."

"It was nothing," he said. "I'm glad to see she's happy."

"Come here, Rusty," Amber said. "I want you to meet my friends."

FORTY-TWO
LADIES OF THE LIGHT

They got underway four hours before sunrise, when the desert was cool with starlight, and the only sound was wind sweeping over fine grains of sand on the dunes. Their faces were cheerful, if tired, but there was a curious air of optimism and hope that seemed to fill the sparkle and shine in their eyes like a strong steady wind fills a ship's sails. Each was quiet, solemn, and focused on the task at hand. Each was aware of what was at risk. Each was aware that they were putting their lives and their trust in one another and, perhaps, in something far greater than all of them combined.

Ben quietly made certain that Helen was comfortable, and Roger stayed close to Rusty and Amber. Levine seemed to have accepted her fate—good, bad, or otherwise—and she walked as a person who has walked many miles before, who believes she will walk many miles more, but who expects nothing more than to walk each step as each step comes to her.

The sand was cool underfoot, and they came down a long wide hill into a desert valley filled with shadows and noises that seemed to creep up out of nowhere.

An owl screeched through the moonlight, and Rusty shook his mane and made a quiet, determined sound, breathing air through his powerful nostrils. His eyes were calm and alert, and he listened to the gentle rhythms of the feet of each member in the group as it met with sand, lifted, glided swiftly through air, and met with sand once again. One step at a time.

They came to a wooden bridge, and they could see mountains far beyond, waiting for this little band of travelers.

"It is a half mile across the bridge," Ben said.

Amber guided Rusty out onto the wooden bridge, his hooves clomping on the planks.

"I'll lead us across," she said. "Everyone, keep your eyes open and be aware. Keep your minds clear and alert. Once we cross this bridge, we will start to climb into the mountains."

Amber felt vulnerable crossing the bridge, but they made it across in a matter of minutes, breathing nervously toward the end. The sandy path that they'd been following became a more clearly worn rocky, dirt road that winded up the hillside in front of them.

There were boulders at either side of the road, and the hills climbed to the north, west, and east.

Suddenly, they heard hooves galloping onto the bridge far behind them. They turned and saw six dark figures on horses. Shadow Warriors. It was the first band that they had met, and they were nervous and tired. Ben quickly took control of the group and said, "To the hills!"

He raised his cane and pointed up along a path that climbed away from the road. There were large boulders all along the sides of the path, some as tall as thirty feet. The group wound along the path, climbing quickly up the hill between the tall rocks. Their view of the bridge was blocked for a minute, and they could not see whether the Shadow Warriors had seen them. The path narrowed to only a few feet, winding between the enormous boulders.

Each member was alert and moved swiftly up the hill. A wind swept up from the valley and howled through the narrow passages between the boulders. The group climbed and climbed and climbed. They were out of breath but afraid to breathe too loudly for fear that the Shadow Warriors would hear them.

They came out onto a ridge and looked back down the hill below them. The six Shadow Warriors crossed the bridge, their black horses breathing fire, their evil eyes glowing red. Helen and Roger saw that the Shadow Warriors wore flowing black robes that flapped powerfully in the wind like sails.

"Did they see us?" Roger said.

No one said a word, but they watched the black Shadow Warriors gallop from the bridge on up the main road. They came to the spot where Ben had led Amber, Roger, Helen, and Levine up into the boulder-strewn hillside. The Shadow Warriors stopped. The powerful horses pawed at the ground, and the hooded heads of the Warriors looked left from the main road, then right.

Amber saw one particular Shadow Warrior whose glowing red eyes seemed to look straight up the hill and into her soul, but none of the Shadow Warriors made a move toward them, and Amber breathed a deep sigh when she saw them begin to move forward on the main road, slowly at first, but then building back up to a powerful gallop, fire pouring from the black horses' nostrils.

Amber, Ben, Helen, Roger, and Dr. Levine watched the six Shadow Warriors continue up into the hills, into the mountains, until they vanished over the crest of a hill a mile to the north. Amber gazed around the boulder-strewn hillside. There were thousands and thousands of these tall massive rocks, a sea of wind erosion and time, coming together to create natural protection and camouflage for Amber and her friends.

"Perhaps we should stay in the hills," she suggested.

"Off of the main road," Levine said.

"Yes," Ben said. "I believe you are right."

"The boulders are like organ pipes," Amber said. "We can wind our way through them, on up into the mountains."

"Lead the way," Helen said.

Rusty whinnied, and the group began again, heading north amongst the boulders, keeping the main road down the hill from them in sight.

• •

They walked for two hours, and the air grew cooler. The desert gave way to desert mountains, and they emerged from the boulders and eventually saw little trees that only grew on the desert mountains one mile above sea level.

"Jojub trees," Ben said. "We're drawing closer to Kevorak's Needle."

"There's water in these hills," Amber said.

"Buried under the ground," Ben agreed. "The roots of jojub trees can penetrate deep into the soil. They can tap the moisture far below the surface."

Roger thought that the trees looked funny and said so to Helen. Helen nodded and smiled and said that she agreed. The jojub trees were a curious blend of tree and bush; they looked whimsical yet hardy. The group came down off of the hillside and started out onto the main road.

"Is it safe?" Roger said. "Do you think?"

No one answered Roger's question, but they climbed to the top of the hill and were stunned to see the view of Kevorak's Needle.

It was thirty miles away, to the north, and there was an enormous high country valley between where they stood and where the jagged peaks that surrounded Kevorak's Needle began. The Needle stood there firm in the middle of the mountains. It rose up tall and strong, a single column stretching high into the early morning sky, thousands of feet higher than the sea of mountains all around it. The sky filled with life, and stars gave way to an ever-brightening blue.

Amber saw a whisk of cloud brushing over the summit. And she saw a low lying cloud of smoke at the base of Kevorak's Needle. They all realized that the troops—indeed, the *legions* of Shadow Warriors—were gathered there among the hills at the base of Kevorak's Needle. It looked like a city, a battalion camp of fortresses and towers and thousands upon thousands of black-cloaked Shadow Warriors.

"How in the world," Roger started to say.

"Are we going to get past that?" Helen continued for him.

Roger looked into Helen's gray-green eyes; his own eyes filled with worry and dread. Helen shook her head.

"There must be forty thousand troops," he said.

He looked at Ben, but Ben walked calmly to the side of the road. There was a little rock at the side of road. It was about two feet high by three feet on each of its sides. He walked up to it and tapped it with his cane. Roger felt like he had been brushed off.

"Ben?" he said. But Ben said nothing; he shuffled around the rock, tapping it lightly with his cane as though feeling for an opening. Roger said, "Ben, how are we going to make it past that many troops?"

Roger started to feel desperate and ignored, and so he started toward Ben forcefully, when suddenly a little light poured out from the top of the rock. It stood two feet tall, and Amber smiled with curiosity when she saw three little figures form there in the light. They each wore white dresses, and Helen and Roger gasped. These three ladies were dressed like the white-robed girls.

Ben shuffled around to the front of the rock. The three ladies looked from one to the other, and then they gazed out from the light at Ben. The three girls looked at the other travelers, but their eyes came back to Ben.

Ben stamped his little wooden cane lightly on the ground, drew himself up, and said, "We have come, dear Ladies of the Light."

"Yes," said one.

"It is so," said another.

"It is with great joy," said the third, "that we welcome you here."

"Where is here?" Roger said.

One of the Ladies of the Light looked at him. "And who are you?" she asked politely.

"My name is Roger," he said. "And I've encountered your kind before. A woman dressed like you tried to kill Helen and I."

He nodded in Helen's direction, and the three women looked quizzically at one another, and then the first spoke up.

"We are the Ladies of the Light," she said. "And we are many. We have many sisters in many forms, but our goal is to guide you, to protect you, and to keep you from harm."

"If your heart is good," said the second.

"If your intention is true," said the third, "we will always help you."

Roger gave a significant look to Helen.

Helen spoke up, "But why then did you chase us? One of your kind turned into a monster and chased us out into the desert. Why?"

"You carried a satchel?" the first finally asked.

Roger's lips scrunched up, and he looked hard at Helen and then at the girls in the light.

"A satchel?" Roger said.

"A leather satchel," the first said clearly. "There were papers inside, yes?"

Roger could think of no response.

The second little lady said, "Those papers were a map—a mathematical map—through which Dr. Amy Levine uncovered a secret that connects your world with ours. And through that secret, through the vision that it caused, Dr. Levine found the Key Room in the Carbañero Mine."

The third spoke up, "We were defending those papers. And we were guiding you."

"Guiding?" Roger said. "You nearly killed us!"

"Fear," the first said. "Is a motivating factor."

"A motivating factor!" Roger snapped. He started at the three girls atop the rock. "I'll give you a motivating factor!"

Ben suddenly turned swiftly. He ducked nimbly to his right, and shot his cane behind Roger's arms, under his shoulders, clutching Roger in a kind of full nelson hold. Roger barked at the three Ladies of the Light, but then yelped out in pain.

"Silence!" Ben said. "Stop your quarreling!"

Roger tried to reach backward toward Ben, but Ben had him firmly in place. Ben brought Roger down onto his knees.

"Now, apologize to these girls," Ben said. "Your lack of tact is appalling!"

"Tact?" Roger said. "These three girls and their kind have haunted me and dogged me. They nearly killed me! *They chased us out into the desert!* Helen, tell him. Tell him what happened. A lady just like one of these turned into a horrible monster."

"You fool," Ben said. "Do you know who you are talking to? Show some respect! These ladies tried to guide you."

"Guide?!" Roger choked. The cane's brunt force bore down on his shoulder blades. Roger doubled over. He cried out in pain. "Let up, old man! You're breaking my back!"

"Show them your respect!" Ben said.

Roger's face turned red as much from physical pain as from emotional embarrassment. Helen stood there watching, a look of horror on her face. A shaking hand came up and covered her mouth. Her eyes filled with tears of pity for Roger.

"Ben stop!" she cried. "Let him go! He means no harm."

Ben said quite calmly but firmly, "Apologize to them."

Roger looked once over his shoulder. He could just see Ben behind his right shoulder. The old man's eyes were filled with life, and for a second, Roger grew intensely angry at what he felt was a deception on the part of the old man, at an entire system of events that had led to him kneeling before these three hologram ladies with a cane bearing down on his back.

"I'm sorry!" he cried out. "I apologize."

Tears filled Roger's eyes, but he refused to cry. He felt the tug of tears welling up inside his chest at what he felt was the most unjust moment of his life, but somewhere deeper still, he caught a flash of light in his mind's eye like hope. And further, he felt a twinge of truth at the fact that they *were* right. Ben was right. The three Ladies of the Light were right. He had done wrong; he had lashed out in anger and frustration when he should have been more understanding. He lacked compassion and calm; it was a weakness.

He said, "I am sorry. Truly, I am. I should have listened more carefully. I should have respected you more. I am sorry for being selfish and for giving into anger. It is a weakness of mine. Can you forgive me?"

The three Ladies of the Light looked at him with sober judgment in their eyes.

"We are to blame, too," one of the Ladies said. "We accept your apology. Perhaps, you can find it in your heart to understand that our motives were good, even if our actions were questionable. In that respect, we apologize to you. Let him go, Ben. Let him go."

And with that, Ben released the cane from Roger's back. Roger slumped forward onto the ground, feeling the pain breaking up in his shoulders, and he climbed up from all fours, then to his knees, and slowly he stood up on his feet. He dusted himself off, and everyone felt awkward for a moment, waiting for someone to speak.

"Their forces look strong," Roger said. He stepped away from the group for a moment, and he looked at the mountains in the brightening morning sky. "We will need to stand together."

The first of the three Ladies of the Light stepped over to one side of the rock. She looked across the great distance to Kevorak's Needle.

She said, "There are at least two options. We can call together our sisters to fight. Or, it may prove more prudent for you to try and pass through the Shadow Warriors' legions undetected."

Roger stepped back out of the way, and he looked solemnly at Helen, Amber, Levine, and Ben.

Levine spoke up, "How many sisters do you have? How many of you are there?"

The three Ladies of the Light looked from one to the other.

"Enough to fight," the first one said.

"Enough to fight well," said the second.

"We could create a diversion," the third said. "So that you may pass into the mountain with the key. You *do* have the key?"

Levine took the key from her pocket and showed it to them all.

"I do," she said. "I have the key."

The three Ladies all nodded at this affirmation, and they looked at one another.

"Then we will fight," the first said. "We will call together our sisters, and we will fight these Shadow Warriors. You will go into Kevorak's Needle."

The second looked at Roger standing there alone.

"Roger, will you help us fight?" she asked him. "Can we come together?"

Roger said, "I will stand with you. We will fight these Shadow Warriors together."

Helen, Roger, Amber, Levine, and Ben came together at the rock and reached their hands forward so that the three Ladies of the Light could touch their hands, too. Rusty the horse stood just a few feet away and whinnied with conviction.

Everyone said, "Together!"

FORTY-THREE
PREPARATION

The three Ladies of the Light led the band across the high country valley all morning and afternoon. By four that afternoon, they reached the top of a hill from which they could see the armies of Shadow Warriors quite well. Their sheer number was astonishing. The armies lay along the base of Kevorak's Needle like ants around an anthill. The height of Kevorak's Needle was breathtaking from this distance, climbing straight up into the sky some two miles from where the armies were encamped. The Needle was only six miles around at its base, so it rose up like a giant natural skyscraper more than ten thousand feet.

There were clouds near the top, but they were thin, and they were surrounded by an endless sea of blue. Two moons were in the sky at different angles, and they were visible while looking at the Needle. The third moon was far on the western horizon, thirty degrees east of a sun that was driving toward the horizon.

"How are we going to climb that thing?" Helen said.

Ben spoke up, "There are trails up from where the armies are encamped."

The first Lady of the Light said, "They are navigable to one kilometer, at which point the steepness of the grade becomes severe."

"What do we do then?" Roger asked.

"There is a single trail," the second Lady said, "that winds around the mountain. It is slow going from there to the top, and the trail is treacherous, but it can be ascended in just a few hours."

"And once we make it to the top?" Amber asked.

"There is a single opening," the third Lady said, "one hundred meters across. We will find a stairwell there that winds down inside the Needle, deep into the mountain, all the way to Kevorak's Soul."

"And once we reach the Soul?" Levine said.

"They key which you have," the first Lady said, "should unlock Kevorak's Soul. Only then, may one person—the Bearer of the Key—enter the Soul."

"And that is Levine?" Roger said, looking around the group.

No one said anything. Finally Ben spoke up, "There is an inscription above the Soul that should make clear who the Bearer of the Key is."

Roger nodded his head. Everyone looked around at one another solemnly.

"And once inside the Soul," Levine said, "how do you release the water?"

The first Lady of the Light said, "No one knows what is inside the Soul. No one's ever been there."

• •

With darkness, there came an unease and anxiety. Ben gathered together roots, berries, and leaves and quietly went about making a stew so that everyone could eat. Amber and Levine sparred together, practicing karate-style moves. Amber showed Levine that through her coral stone, she could create a green staff—her Fenwan—and Levine watched the young girl rotating that staff, wielding it and spinning it well.

Amber was intense and quiet, but occasionally she would crack a smile and she and Levine would laugh at one another, before growing serious again and commencing with another round of sparring. Amber's moves were smooth and fluid, deft, and Levine realized that she was very glad that Amber was on *their* side, and not the other way around.

Helen and Roger walked over to the edge of their little camp and held one another's hands. They watched the Shadow Warriors' fires a mile away in the distance, and Helen quietly prayed and tried to think encouraging and positive thoughts. The three Ladies of the Light helped Ben prepare the stew. They made bowls out of jojub leaves placed inside a nest of twigs wound tight as a straw basket.

"When will your sisters come?" Levine asked.

She came up to the little group. She had broken a sweat. Behind her, Amber continued practicing her moves with her green Fenwan light staff. She ducked and kicked, and she swept the Fenwan around through the air.

The first Lady of the Light said, "They will come before dawn."

Levine nodded and looked at the line of fires around the base of Kevorak's Needle. The orange fires glowed in the darkness like a ring around the base of the mountain. There were terrible trumpet sounds and the slow steady beating of drums. The noise was intimidating, and once darkness settled over the mountains, they could not see exactly how many Shadow Warriors there were. The sound coming from the camps filled everyone's mind though, with the impressions of thousands of black-cloaked warriors.

• •

"I never really knew my parents," Levine said, "and yet I've always been filled with this gift, an intuition, that I believe comes from them. And when I'm open to it and my mind is clear, it enables me to dip down into that world—our sixth sense—and to see things that will happen before they actually happen."

They were all sitting in a circle. Each had eaten a bowl of Ben's stew, and they were comfortable and alert. The sound of the Shadow Warriors' war drums continued ominously in the distance, but this small group gathered on a hillside just a mile away seemed focused and engaged with one another.

"You think it comes from them, your parents?" Helen said.

"I think that they're connected to it somehow, yes," Levine said. "For a long time, people just wrote it off as crazy. The scientific method has gone a long way toward annihilating belief in the acausal, non-linear aspects of our universe."

"How do you mean?" Roger said.

"The scientific method which has so dominated the twentieth century only allows for that which can be proven, and *repeatedly* proven. It's a very simple method that precludes randomness, insight, moments of acausal action. The problem is that much of our lives is shaped and formed by intuition, by moments of synchronicity, by completely random behavior, even at its most fundamental level."

"How do you mean?" Amber asked.

"At its most fundamental level, reality exhibits a large degree of random behavior. This is what is so strange about quantum mechanics, the idea that quanta of light behave as though they are aware of their own being. The idea is so radical that even a century after its discovery most people still view the world around them largely as an action-reaction universe. We want to believe that we can control our destinies."

"But you're saying that we *can't?*" Roger said.

Levine said, "I believe that the next level of human awareness will take into account that randomness occurs. Right now, there's not even an ideological system by which science can understand the inner workings of the mind. It may be fair to think of human thought as three parts causal, to one part acausal; that twenty-five percent of human thought is completely creative, original, and not a result of prior experience. It's just the way the mind works, but there's no system by which to approach that part of our nature. In terms of our ability to harness the human brain's capabilities, seven hundred years from now, the twentieth century will very likely be viewed as having been a mental 'dark ages' where primitive psychologists asked us about our childhood experiences as a means of clearing the mind of its depressions and neuroses."

"But what does that have to do with your parents?" Roger asked sincerely.

Everyone chuckled.

"*Every*thing," Levine said with a smile. "Parental behavior is like a blue-print for how we construct our individual approaches to life. Only, I didn't really know my parents. They died when I was very young. So, what I did was probe very deeply into my mind for answers to who I am, and to why I am here. It's why I went so far into that world. I wanted answers. And I wanted them, in part, because the basic blue-print for how to live my life was not readily available. I had to create my own behavior and my own system for *constructing* that behavior."

"But even that," Helen said, "you had to have learned from somewhere, the confidence to let yourself dip into that world, to go so deeply into the human mind *for* answers. Where did you learn that from?"

"I learned it largely through failure," Levine said. "And I learned it because our society doesn't give up on people like me. My life could have turned out very differently. I could have been a troubled teen who went a step too far in the wrong direction. But I had a good education, good foster homes, a good support system, and I believe it to the very core of my being: this world is what you make of it. Your life is only as good as the goodness you see in your fellow human beings."

All during this, Amber had remained quiet except for the one terse question. She had an intense look on her face, and she kept rubbing her eyes and then trying to smile. Levine interpreted this as her willingness to try and understand, even if her independent soul was driving her in another direction. Levine sensed the good in young Amber, but she sensed a deep and profound internal conflict, too. But another part of her realized that Amber's course was set, that the dice were in mid-air, and she could only hope that the outcome would be good.

"What do you think?" Levine said, looking at Amber.

High overhead, stars filled the night sky. The war drums continued to pound. A gentle breeze swept up over the hill, and all eyes in the group went to Amber.

The young girl sat there in the darkness, Indian-style, with her right hand on her right knee and her left hand on her left knee. She looked around the group at each of them. The white coral stone on the black string necklace glowed lightly. Her eyes held Heaven and Earth in their balance.

"I think it will be a good day for a battle," she said.

The group fell silent.

FORTY-FOUR
THE BATTLE

The chorus was sung as a chant, an ominous throng of seven hundred thousand young women singing in unison. It sounded like ancient Latin.

Helen woke, rolled over, and gazed around her in shock and awe. As far as she could see—thirty miles—there was a wide band of white light encircling Kevorak's Needle and the forty thousand Shadow Warriors gathered at its base. That white band of light, Helen realized, was some seven hundred thousand young women dressed in white robes that glowed in the darkness one hour before daybreak.

Helen saw Amber standing thirty meters away from their camp where everyone had fallen asleep. Amber stood on the hill, gazing down at the Shadow Warriors' dying fires. Dr. Amy Levine stood on Amber's right side. Ben stood on Amber's left side with his cane held firmly in front of him.

"What in the world?" Roger said.

He woke, looked at Helen, and then looked around them at the thirty-mile-wide circle of light that ringed the mountains surrounding Kevorak's Needle. The girls' chorus continued on, a multitude of voices preparing for war.

"What are they singing?" Roger said.

Helen said, "I think it's Latin."

Roger climbed to his feet and trotted up to Amber and Levine. They were actually inside the circle of white-robed girls; that is, the enormous band was some seven miles behind them at its closest, and on the far side of the valley, on the other side of Kevorak's Needle, it was some eight miles in the distance.

Helen looked down at the ring of fires around Kevorak's Needle. The forty thousand Shadow Warriors looked like a small band in the center of this multitude of light. The seven hundred thousand voices singing together was louder than thunder; it was the single loudest thing that Helen had ever heard. It was ominous, powerful, chilling, and beautiful. Helen stared with wonder, then conviction.

"This is going to be a slaughter," she said.

The multitude marched in unison, their feet and each step a resounding clap of thunder. With each step, they drew closer and closer to the pocket of evil surrounding Kevorak's Needle. And they continued with that chorus, a multitude of beautiful voices rising to the sky, rising to right centuries of wrong.

There was a pause for two hours. The multitude was so large that it took them two hours to come together within one mile of Kevorak's Needle. During this time, Amber conferred with the three little Ladies of the Light. They ate a light breakfast of berries and roots, and they watched the sunrise over the Shadow Warriors. All during this two hours, the seven hundred thousand young women marched in unison, their feet a continuous thunderclap, their chorus angelic.

"Will they even fight?" Roger asked.

Ben stood on the hillside in the early morning light. He said, "Shadow Warriors have no comprehension of life's value. They will fight. They will fight until every last one of them is destroyed. That is their way."

• •

The first attack came from a quadrant of Shadow Warriors on the southwest side of Kevorak's Needle. The initial charge was comprised of about seven thousand horsemen and foot soldiers, and from their vantage on the hill a mile away, Helen and Roger watched the little pocket moving out toward the massive band of white-robed young women. It looked like an eye-dropper of black water dropped into a ten-gallon bucket of sand.

Amber (on Rusty), Levine, and the three little Ladies of the Light joined with the front ranks of the others in descending down their hill into the valley. From the valley, they marched forward for five minutes before fire was lobbed their way.

Ben, Roger, and Helen remained on the hill, but the sheer number of white-robed young women that passed by them on the hill held them in its midst for more than twenty minutes. Eventually the ranks cleared enough that they could see down the hill, across the valley, to the base of Kevorak's Needle.

••

Amber saw a cavalry charge of black-cloaked horsemen coming toward her across the valley floor. She looked to her right and left. The sheer number of young women was impressive. She looked down at Amy Levine who was on foot. Levine was focused and intent.

Most of the young women carried white Fenwan staffs of glowing light, most six feet in length. Many carried clear shields that glowed white around their edges. Many more carried shorter Fenwans like swords. For every ten foot soldiers, there was one white-robed young woman on a white horse. And for every thirty foot soldiers, there was a white-robed young woman behind a white horse and golden chariot.

Amber touched her coral stone. There was a flash of bright light, and the Fenwan formed in her hand. She trotted Rusty forward and got out in front of the line by about thirty meters. She slowly rotated her Fenwan round and round. Ahead, there was a line of Shadow Warriors about two hundred meters from east to west. They galloped powerfully toward her.

Fire bombs came from the fortresses at the base of Kevorak's Needle. They struck near the front ranks, and several girls cried out and fell. A barrage of arrows flew over Amber's head and found their mark in the ranks behind her. More girls fell to the ground. And then a barrage of fire bombs flew through the air, more than one hundred in a matter of seconds, arcing across the sky. There was the strong odor of smoke, fire, and burning tar.

The horsemen were only fifty meters away from her now. Amber spun her Fenwan on her right side and held her position. Rusty's nostrils flared. His eyes filled with fright, but Amber heeled him into holding still. She rotated her Fenwan round and round. The shadow warriors were twenty meters away, and Amber kicked Rusty and yelled, *"Ride!"*

Rusty took off toward the line of Shadow Warriors. And a moment later, they were in their midst.

• •

Amber found her mark with her Fenwan staff and struck a Shadow Warrior hard in its chest. The Shadow Warrior lifted up in the air, off of its saddle, flew over Amber, then slammed to the rocky earth, and was immediately trampled over by his fellow Shadow Warriors' horses' hooves.

Amber spun around on Rusty's saddle and found her next mark. She swung her Fenwan staff around furiously and took this warrior's head clean off of his shoulders. Another Shadow Warrior plowed into Rusty's left front side, and Rusty reared up on his hind two legs. Amber held on, and in a brief flash she was above the fray and saw all around her in every direction the fierce fighting that was now underway.

Behind her, the line of white-robed young women clashed with the Shadow Warriors, their bright white Fenwan staffs, clashing and flashing. Overhead, fireball missiles arced through the sky coming from the direction of Kevorak's Needle. There were cries of agony and of rage, but Amber was so in the moment that she didn't hear any of it. Rusty came back down on all four hooves, and Amber was immediately thrown back into the fighting.

She saw one pair of glowing red eyes inside a black cloak coming at her. She pivoted Rusty around, and she swung her Fenwan powerfully. It whickered through the air and struck the black-cloaked horseman powerfully on his left shoulder.

Another Shadow Warrior barreled into Rusty's hindquarter. The horse kicked, but something hot came down on Amber's left shoulder. She was so charged with adrenaline and rage that she didn't even feel the pain. She pivoted around to her right and thrust the Fenwan straight into the Shadow Warrior's chest.

She quickly removed the Fenwan from the thing's chest and got Rusty moving forward into the fray, faster and faster. Everything was a blur for a moment, and Rusty galloped through the battalions of Shadow Warriors. Amber kept low on the horse, swinging her glowing green Fenwan staff from one side of her horse to the other, taking out one Shadow Warrior after the next.

She could see Kevorak's Needle in front of her, towering high overhead. She was only four hundred meters from one Shadow Warrior tower at its base. Suddenly, there was an explosion in front of her, and Rusty went down. Amber was in midair but caught her balance, landed on her feet, and then stumbled forward hitting the ground hard.

She shook her head dazedly and leapt up onto her feet. Her Fenwan was on the ground thirty feet away from her, and a Shadow Warrior horseman had caught sight of her and charged. He was twenty feet away. Amber focused on her Fenwan and channeled all of her psychic energies through the Line to her staff. The energy grabbed the staff, and her Fenwan flew through the air. Amber caught it in her hand, leapt up into the air, spinning furiously, and struck the horseman squarely across the face.

Her staff went right through him, and the Shadow Warrior toppled over backwards off of his horse. Amber landed on her feet in a kneeling, crouched position. She glanced back and saw Rusty struggling to get to his feet.

"Come Rusty!" Amber cried, and she started running toward her horse.

She glanced up at the hill where Roger, Helen, and Ben had been standing, and she saw they were coming down the hill to join in the fighting. She glanced back at the fighting. It was fierce, but it was already clear that the young women were subduing the Shadow Warriors. Amber looked at Rusty. Rusty was still trying to stand, and Amber realized that something had happened to his front legs. He could not place any weight on them, and he fell back forward on his knees and then rolled over on his side.

"Rusty!" Amber cried. "No, Rusty! *Nooo!*"

Tears of rage filled her eyes, and she lifted her Fenwan up in her hand. Her face turned crimson with hatred and vengeance, and, on foot, she charged a Shadow Warrior horseman. The horseman turned and saw the young girl running at him.

He pivoted his horse around, but Amber leapt up into the air. She spun her green Fenwan furiously. The Shadow Warrior's head, then left arm fell to the ground, and Amber came down onto the ground on the other side of its horse, bringing the whole warrior down onto the ground. She drove her Fenwan into the dead Shadow Warrior's chest.

••

The most intense fighting lasted an hour, but the Shadow Warriors would not stop until every last one of them was dead, such was their destructive drive and their zealous pride. But the power of good was too great, and the moment of time had come that their dark clutch on this world would be no more.

Levine saw Amber kneeling with Rusty, and she went over to her. Amber whispered into Rusty's ear and petted his shoulder and neck. Levine came closer and heard that Amber was singing to Rusty as he lay dying. It was a warm tune, slow and soothing, and young Amber sang it with such hopefulness that it broke Dr. Amy Levine's heart.

Helen ran up to Levine, and both women stood thirty feet away from Amber and her fallen horse. Amber sang to him, and he made slow breathing noises and tried to look into her eyes. She caressed his neck and when the song was done she said, "You're going to a better place, my friend. A place where there isn't all this fighting. And evil doesn't exist. I will come to you. I will come to you again."

Helen looked at Levine, and Levine saw her gray-green eyes tremble with worry and pity, and yet they were strong with pride at seeing a young girl so brave and possessing such dignity.

Smoke climbed from the Shadow Warriors' burning towers to the northeast. Black-cloaked figures lay fallen on the battlefield. The white-robed young women were covering their own with white sheets. There was crying and tears, but even the eldest of them would later say that they had rarely seen such a clear victory.

The battle was all but done, and now the final journey lay ahead of them.

Roger and Ben came to Helen and Dr. Levine. All four stood watching Amber and her horse. The mountain loomed high overhead, but none of them looked at it. They all watched Amber singing quietly to a best friend who was no longer with them. No one said a word.

FORTY-FIVE
KEVORAK'S NEEDLE

They began the climb quietly. Helen, Roger, and Ben led the way, and Dr. Levine stayed close to Amber who looked up the thin mountainous trail with a single-minded determination. That Amber's best friend was dead and that she was continuing on with a task that seemed to pale in significance to that death created an energy and intensity inside her mind and inside her young soul that would not allow her to be stopped.

They climbed the trail in silence for forty-five minutes. Amber said, "Two hours."

Levine looked at her. Amber's brown eyes were filled with life; her shoulder was badly cut. Her face was dirty, and there was someone else's blood in her hair.

"Yes," Dr. Levine said. "Maybe less, if we are lucky."

Amber looked at her, and she saw worry in Levine's eyes. Levine tried to smile, but it was an awkward smile, and so Amber just reached out and touched her arm warmly.

"Everything will be okay," Amber said. "The grief will pass. I'll just need some time. Right now, we have one objective."

Levine nodded her head in agreement, and they continued up the thin trail. They were a couple thousand feet above the surrounding battlefield. The number of black-cloaked Shadow Warriors fallen on the ground was great. Forty thousand dead; they lay three miles east to west, two miles to the south, and this was only on the south side of Kevorak's Needle. They'd not made it around the mountain far enough to see the carnage on the north side.

Stupidity, Amber thought. *The enemy's sheer stupidity.*

She shook her head, resisted the urge to spit her disgust on the ground, and continued on up the trail.

••

By early afternoon, they reached a section of trail that was only a few feet wide. It wound around Kevorak's Needle like a massive spiral staircase, and with every little ridge that they came around, they saw more and more of the aftermath far below. Fallen evil lay around Kevorak's Needle in every direction spreading some two miles outward from the mountain's base. Small pockets of smoke continued to rise from the Shadow Warriors' burning towers, which now looked tiny, five thousand feet below them.

"The Dolphins' Rock," Ben said, pointing his cane straight ahead. "It marks the half-way point!"

Everyone looked up. Fifty meters ahead on the trail, there was a small clearing and a stone table with two stone benches on either side. The clearing was cut away some twenty feet into the mountain, and fifteen feet overhead inside the clearing, there were three dolphins carved into the granite. The statues were tall, each dolphin about seven feet.

"The ancients believed that dolphins once ruled the world," Ben said. "That they lived together in peace and harmony in the great seas that covered the earth. They ruled through love and generosity, and everyone was happy. But greed to control the waters came over evil creatures, and in their pursuit to control the water, the natural balance of life was upset. Many believe the Oracle's story that dolphins will one day lead the world again."

"Their eyes are blue," Helen said

"Sapphire," Ben said. "They're the six largest sapphire stones known to exist. Each is seven inches in diameter."

"Wouldn't someone be tempted to steal them?" Roger said.

Ben smiled and shook his head. "Many have tried," he said. "And those who have tried did not live to tell about it. The dolphins' eyes are protected by powers no one can fathom."

They looked at the statues for a moment. The dolphins were beautiful, and their beautiful blue eyes sparkled in the sunlight.

"We should continue," Ben said.

Everyone lingered a moment more, and then they began again up the trail. The trail was only a couple feet wide, and it was very rocky, but they were high above the desert valley below Kevorak's Needle. At this height, everything below seemed smooth and flat, reaching several miles to the surrounding mountains. The group reached a level where they began to see over the surrounding peaks, and they could see very far into the distance, more than one hundred miles. There was no sound at this height other than the wind, and it was deeply peaceful and relaxing.

The winding narrow trail continued around Kevorak's Needle, climbing higher and higher with each step. Soon the air was noticeably cooler, and it was more difficult to breathe. Their steps grew more cautious, and occasionally smaller rocks slipped away and tumbled down the steep inclines. The sun was bright and warm on them, but the air was much cooler, and there were bizarre plants that glowed different colors. It reminded Dr. Levine of the flowers she's seen back inside the Beaumont Hotel.

"Is that the sunlight," Helen said, "the way the light is glowing?"

"These are Dōkum trees," Ben said. "At night they light these darkened slopes high atop Kevorak's Needle. They are friendly trees."

"They make me happy," Roger said.

"They are very pretty," Dr. Levine said.

The Dōkum trees grew straight out from the rock wall above the trail and then rose up about six feet. They looked like large glowing wall lamps, and they were each evenly spaced about seven feet apart as they continued up the trail. Higher and higher, they climbed.

"We are not far away, now," Ben said, "from the top."

Ahead, they could see that the narrow trail began to widen. The curve around Kevorak's Needle grew less severe and began to level out. They continued on up the trail, and they could tell they were no longer walking on the outermost perimeter of the Needle. The wider trail climbed inward toward the center of the six-mile-diameter Needle, and they glanced back and saw the edge of the mountain behind them, and then the vast views beyond, perhaps one hundred and twenty miles all the way to the farthest horizon where the earth met the sky in a seamless band.

The rocky ground that they walked through grew moist. There was a low-lying mist that covered the ground, and there was actually green grass as they drew closer to the center on the top of Kevorak's Needle.

"It's wet up here," Amber said.

Ben nodded his head and pointed his cane to one little pool about twenty-five meters left of the trail. The pond was about the size of a football field, and at just that moment, a fish snapped up above the surface and splashed back down into the water. Everyone grew excited and said, "Did you see that? Did you see that? It was a fish!"

Ben said, "That is Gardner's Lake."

He continued up the trail. They were now on top of Kevorak's Needle, and the top was relatively flat.

"You could build a house up here," Roger said. "There's water and fish, and trees for wood." He pointed ahead to a thicket of tall pine trees. The trail continued into the woods.

"It is a sacred mountain, though," Helen said.

"I'm just sayin'—"

Ben broke in, "Shhhh." He held up his hand for them to stop.

Everyone stopped. They had taken a few steps into the woods, and they all heard the wind rustling through the treetops. It was very cool at this elevation, and they all leaned their heads so as to hear up the trail that continued into the woods. They heard something faint and distant coming to them through the trees.

"What is that?" Dr. Levine said.

Helen said, "It sounds like—"

"Water!" Amber said. They all started trotting up the trail through the stand of tall pine trees. The trail was clear, and a minute later, they came to the edge of the trees. Everyone stopped and looked out in front of them at the giant hole down into the mountain.

"*Oh, my goodness*," Helen gasped.

They stood on the edge of the hole. It was enormous and roughly circular. They could see all the way around the rim of it. They must have been on a slightly higher side of the rim because they could see out above the forest on the opposite side of the hole. The hole itself was about one hundred meters in diameter, and there was a pine tree forest all around it. But, Levine realized, they *were* on a higher side of the rim because they *could* see over the trees on the opposite side of the opening. Across the hole, the treetops looked like a field of green before the abrupt drop-off that must have been the edge of Kevorak's Needle on the opposite side from which they had come. Beyond the edge, they could see all the way to the horizon, perhaps two hundred miles in the distance.

It looked like the trail continued around the rim.

"It's like a volcano," Roger said.

They all looked down inside the hole. Nearer to the rim, the sunlight allowed them to see just fine, but the farther down inside the hole they looked the darker it became. They could see the thin band of trail went to their left, and then it began to wind down inside the mountain, deeper inside the hole.

"How far down is it?" Levine asked.

"No one knows for sure," Ben said. "But our best guess from the ancient Oracle texts is that it is about two miles from here to Kevorak's Soul."

They looked down inside the mountain and saw what they had all heard a few minutes before. All the way around the inside of the mountain about four hundred meters below the rim, there was a curtain of shimmering water that poured into the darkness. It was a giant circular waterfall.

"Where is the water coming from?" Roger asked.

They all looked inside the hole for the water's source. Amber was the first to see it. She pointed and said, "There!"

Down inside the mountain, there was a stream that flowed in a circle around the inside of the hole. It looked like it was about ten feet wide, and it must have been built on a shelf along the wall. At a number of places along the stream, there were openings that allowed the water to pour out from the wall. The water splashed along the inside walls.

"Come on!" Amber said. "Let's follow the trail!"

They started down inside the rim along the thin trail, down into the darkness.

• •

The shelf was about twenty feet wide, and it descended in a counter-clockwise direction. The initial descent down inside the mountain had been clockwise, but once they reached the shelf, there was a switchback, and the trail continued down inside Kevorak's Needle alongside the stream in a counter-clockwise direction.

Amber looked up in front of her and followed the stream around the inside of the round chasm with her eyes. There were a number of places where the water poured out to the left of the stream, forming waterfalls down inside the mountain, and the sound of rushing water was quite loud.

"We may have to pass underneath these falls," she said loudly. "Eventually."

They continued down along the trail, deeper into the mountain, all the while keeping the stream about five feet on their left side. On the other side of the stream, they could see down into the endless darkness. Overhead, they could see the rim on which they'd been standing just a few minutes before. It was now about four hundred meters above them, and they continued along the trail deeper into the mountain.

"What's that?" Levine said. She pointed up the curved trail in front of them.

"Looks like a handrail," Helen said.

They continued up to the handrail. There was a little stone stairwell along the wall inside the mountain. The incline of the trail was steeper, as was the rushing water in the stream on their left side. They walked down the stone stairwell, using the handrail to keep from slipping on the moist stone steps.

They saw the end of the stream up ahead. There was a sharp curve out to the left, and the water poured from the curve as from a slide. The water pressure was intense at this last slide, and it poured out into the air a few feet away from the wall. The stone stairwell continued on ahead of them, and they kept on walking.

They reached a point along the trail where the water from overhead began to spray them with a fine mist. Ben raised up his cane and pointed ahead of them. They could see that they had come full circle, all the way around inside the mountain, and they were going to walk underneath the shelf on which they'd stood just a few minutes before. The waterfall poured out above them, but the stone stairwell carved deeper into the wall so that they were not soaked.

A minute later, they were walking down the stairwell, and twenty-five feet to their left there was a thick curtain of water. They had made it back behind the circular waterfall!

The ground was vry damp, and the air was thick with moisture, but the stairwell was not directly hit by the water, so they stayed relatively dry. The stone stairwell continued downward, sloping along the wall, deeper inside the mountain.

It was kind of dark behind the waterfall, but light reflected and refracted through the water and they could see well enough to stay with the trail. Gradually the waterfall began to dissipate and at one last section, they came out on the trail from inside of the wall, and they looked up above them and were amazed to see just how far they had come.

The opening into the mountain was now a wide round circle of blue up above them. The waterfalls had blended into the rock wall, and they reasoned that they were about eight hundred meters down inside Kevorak's Needle.

"The blue line!" Ben gasped. He pointed ahead of them, and everyone looked up and saw a blue line on the wall. It came out of the stairwell, but as the trail descended the blue line grew taller. "That mark means we're a half mile inside the mountain."

"It's a level circle?" Levine asked.

"Yes," Ben said. "It wraps all the way around the mountain on the wall, exactly one half mile down from the rim."

"What're those?" Amber asked.

Everyone looked up the trail. It looked like there was some kind of light coming from the wall. Ben shook his head, and they all approached the light.

About five feet above the stairwell, fixed into the wall, there were round portholes of light. Levine looked up and realized that the portholes continued around the entire inside of the mountain along the trail.

"They're about shoulder height," she said.

The effect was like seeing several rows of lights wrapping around along the wall. Far across the chasm, they could see the row of lights descending down along the trail. Then they saw it. Way down at the bottom of the chasm, they could see a faint light in the darkness. It was too far out in the center of the hole to be anything but the floor. And the light must have been very bright because they realized it was more than a mile farther down inside the mountain.

"Come on, guys!" Amber said.

They began to hurry down the steps.

The porthole lights along the wall were otherworldly bright, and their rays poured out from the wall into the open darkness of the chamber on their left side. There was a porthole for about every twenty steps along the stone stairwell, and each light was about seven feet above ground and pointed toward the center of the chasm.

The group hustled down the stone stairwell, and the light at the very bottom grew more and more clear. Levine glanced back overhead once and was surprised to see that the round disc of blue sky that was the opening into the mountain looked small. They were more than a mile from the rim, and everyone was growing excited.

"What *is* that?" Helen gasped.

Their voices echoed out into the open chasm, but they could see the floor now about a quarter mile further down. They continued to run down the stone stairwell along the wall. The group was spread out a little more than Levine might have liked. Amber was about one hundred meters ahead of them. Roger was not far behind her. Helen and Levine were close to one another, but Ben was way behind them almost on the opposite side of the chasm and beyond sight. He was struggling down the steps with his cane, but everyone was so excited to be reaching the bottom that they just hurried onward.

"Amber!" Levine called out, and her voice echoed through the open space. Amber turned and waved for them to hurry, and Levine looked down and saw the source of the light at the center of the floor.

In the middle of the darkness, there was a vivid circle of light. It looked like a spotlight shining on the floor, but it was large, perhaps thirty meters in diameter. And at the center of light, there was a clear cylinder.

It immediately reminded Levine of RK-81 on Santana's Island.

She and Helen ran down the final few stairs and stepped out onto the floor at the bottom of Kevorak's Needle. Roger and Amber were standing in the light, near the clear tube. Roger was bent over on his hands and knees, trying to catch his breath. Amber circled around the cylinder.

Helen gave Levine a look, and the two women approached the thing.

It was a seamless, clear cylinder about nine feet tall, and it was large enough that three people might fit inside it if they squeezed together. The top was dome shaped, and the whole unit stood in the middle of the circle of light.

"What in the world is it?" Roger said.

Amber circled it.

"There's no way to get inside," she said.

They all looked at it and realized she was right. While it was shaped like a tall phone booth, there was no door. It just looked like a large glass tube with a dome-shaped top, and it was seamless. Everyone heard Ben reach the floor from the stairwell behind them, and they waited to hear his opinion regarding this thing.

Amber reached forward and touched the cylinder's surface.

"Whoa," she said.

Everyone looked at her.

"What?" Levine said.

They watched her reach forward again. Her fingertips touched the surface and then appeared to penetrate into it, into the surface! Had she not touched it, they would have all thought it was hard glass, but it was clearly giving way underneath her touch.

"It's like water," Amber said.

They each approached the clear tube. Ben raised his cane and touched the side of the tube. The surface rippled outward from where his cane touched.

"Hmmm," he said.

He pushed his cane inside it further, but the surface appeared to stretch with his cane. He pushed it all the way through the open space inside the clear cylinder until it touched the opposite side and began pushing outward from the other side. The surface simply stretched to accommodate the cane.

"Amazing," Roger said.

"It appears to be hard glass," Ben said, "but it is actually quite pliable."

He removed his cane from inside the cylinder, and the cylinder resumed its original shape.

"How far could you stretch it?" Helen asked.

Ben tapped the side with his cane again, and everyone started when a bright light flashed from Amber's chest. She had touched her coral stone and formed her Fenwan staff in her hand. Everyone stepped back and watched her.

She held her Fenwan out in front of her like a long sword, and touched the surface of the cylinder. There was an electrically static-filled sound, and little flashes of electric current surrounded the tip of her Fenwan, where it was touching the outside of the cylinder. She thrust her staff into the cylinder. There was more bright electrical static, but neither the staff nor the cylinder seemed to be harming the other.

She rowed her Fenwan around so as to pull the "water-like" material outward away from the cylinder. It stretched out from the surface, and Amber carefully backed up with it held on the end of her Fenwan. She took two, then three steps, and the material continued to stretch outward from the cylinder. She got about ten feet away from the cylinder when the whole thing slipped off of the end of her Fenwan staff and sprung back into the cylinder, taking its original form. It wobbled for a second or two, but a moment later the whole nine-foot-tall, clear tube resumed its original shape.

"Fascinating," Amber said.

"It looks like you could get inside it," Levine said.

"It does," Helen said.

Roger said, "Maybe you should try your key, Dr. Levine."

"How so?" Levine said.

She removed the key from her pocket.

"Just try and touch it," Ben said.

Levine reached forward with the Gamma Cephei Key, but just as she was about to touch the key to the surface of the cylinder, the water-like surface bent away from the key. Everyone's eyes widened.

The other objects they'd stuck inside the thing had actually touched the surface, but the key seemed to repel the surface, and an indentation formed, moving away from the key. She pushed the key in further, and everyone watched as it appeared to form a bubble inside the cylinder.

Roger asked, "What would happen if you stepped inside the thing with the key in your hand?"

Levine looked at him, nodded her head, and then stepped into the cylinder. She was immediately sucked into the cylinder, and everyone gasped in horror. For the moment, it looked like she was trapped inside the cylinder. A bubble had formed all around her, but Dr. Levine was standing right in the middle of the cylinder with the key in her hand.

The surface of the cylinder had resealed around her, and she appeared trapped inside.

"Can you breathe?" Ben asked excitedly.

Levine's mouth formed the word "yes." She said something else, but they could not hear her at all. She was inside the cylinder.

Amber reached forward and eased her hand into the tube. Her hand went through the surface, and she tried to reach through to the bubble in which Levine was now standing. But her hand couldn't penetrate the surface of the bubble inside the cylinder.

Amber stepped into the cylinder, but like lightning, she was pushed around the little bubble in which Levine stood and was "spat out" the other side. She was thrust out with such force that she stumbled and fell to the ground.

She laughed, stood up, and brushed herself off.

"Guess it doesn't want us both in there at the same time."

Levine tried to exit, but it was difficult, and her bubble stretched against the outer surface of the cylinder. Finally, she pushed hard enough, and she too "sprung" out from the cylinder, stumbled, and fell to the ground. She quickly climbed to her feet, brushed herself off, and looked around the group.

"I could hear you inside," she said. "It was like listening through water."

"We couldn't hear you at all," Helen said.

They all just stood there looking at this thing. It was a nine-foot-tall clear tube, about three feet in diameter with a dome-shaped top. They were all puzzled.

FORTY-SIX
THE MIRROR

Amber was the first to realize that the floor was not what it seemed to be. She walked over to the edge of the circle of light in the center of the room. She stepped one foot out into the darkness, and she looked up overhead for the source of the light. They were so far down inside the mountain that the opening high overhead was a blue disc. She glanced around her beyond the light at floor level, and she touched her coral stone and brought her bright green Fenwan staff to life.

Using the Fenwan like a glowing torch, she walked out into the darkness. She was looking for a wall. Everyone else remained near the clear cylinder in the center of the room, but Amber moved out toward the perimeter.

To everyone standing in the center, Amber was lighted by her green Fenwan, and they watched her walking fifty meters away.

"Check this out!" she said.

Everyone looked up. Amber held up her Fenwan staff, and they saw that she had reached the surrounding wall. About ten feet overhead fixed into the wall, there was a rectangular box. The wall around the box was dark cavernous stone, but the box caught the reflection of Amber's Fenwan, and they saw the light glint off of its metallic surface.

"What is that?" Levine said, coming to her through the darkness.

Levine stepped up beside Amber and looked up at the rectangular box affixed into the wall. It was about a foot tall and two meters long. Levine realized the shiny metallic glint had come from the outer rim around the "box," but she saw that the surface was a dark red color. She looked at Amber.

"It looks like numbers," Amber said.

They both looked at the surface of the box, and indeed, it did look like there were numbers etched into the box's surface. Amber moved her Fenwan around to get a better view of the box, but it was just too high to see clearly.

Helen, Roger, and Ben came up behind them.

"What is it?" Roger said.

"Some kind of box," Levine said.

"Hold the light over here," Roger said.

Amber moved her staff as he asked.

"That's not a box," Roger said.

Levine and Amber looked at him.

"Here, Helen," Roger said. "Stand up on my shoulders."

Roger knelt down, and Helen climbed up awkwardly on his shoulders. Her feet kept slipping at first, but she found a good hold, and Roger slowly stood. She leaned forward against the wall, and her head came up right in front of the "box."

Everyone looked at her and waited for her response.

"Hmmm," she said, peering into it. She touched the surface with her fingertips.

"What is it?" Amber said.

"Let me see your staff," Helen said.

Amber handed her the staff and said, "Be careful. You have to hold it here, or it will burn through your hand."

Helen took the staff where Amber indicated and held it up to the box so that she could see it better.

"It's some kind of timer," Helen said.

"*What?*" Levine and Amber said simultaneously.

Roger adjusted his stance and re-braced his hands around her ankles. Helen touched the surface of the box with her fingertips.

"Like a clock," she said.

"A clock?" Ben said. "Very interesting."

Helen handed the Fenwan down to Amber, and Roger helped her back to the floor. She stood there, looked around at them, and glanced back at the box on the wall.

She said, "Like a digital clock. The numbers aren't lighted obviously, but that's what it looks like. Like a digital timer."

"Why would there be a timer here?" Roger said.

No one had an answer.

"And another thing," Helen said. "How is this circle of light, here? What is its source?"

Levine said, "I think I figured that one out."

She led them back into the light and pointed up high overhead.

"The angle of the light reflecting from the waterfalls up there," she said, "is mathematically aligned with the light here on the floor."

"How do you mean?" Helen asked.

"Well, if the only source of light came from the opening, it wouldn't shine down this way."

"You mean it wouldn't be this bright?" Roger said.

"Exactly," Levine said. "But this entire mountain—at least inside—is mathematically precise."

"How so?" Amber said.

"The ambient light coming in through the opening reflects off of the water—the circular waterfall—and shines here like a giant magnifying glass capturing the light near the Needle's rim. There may be some way that it's trapped in the wall, too, which would account for the lights along the stairwell. This entire chasm is designed like the ancient pyramids; it is mathematically perfect. There are probably clues hidden all around us, just beyond the surface of what we see—"

"Look at this!" Amber said.

Everyone looked at her. She was rubbing the toe of her shoe into the floor. The ground appeared to be loose sandy rock, but they all caught something reflecting from the floor where Amber had cleared away a space. She dropped down to her knees and started brushing the sand away from the floor with her hands.

Suddenly a bright light shone up from the floor.

"What in the world?" Roger said.

Amber cleared away about one square foot of space on the floor, and they all realized that the floor was shiny underneath the sand.

"Like a mirror," Levine said.

She dropped down beside Amber and started brushing away the sand, too. In a minute they had cleared away a five-foot-square area, and everyone realized that underneath the sand at their feet, there was a giant mirror hidden just below the surface.

"Would you look at that," Roger said in awe.

Everyone looked in the direction he was pointing. Far across the room, there was now a five-foot-diameter patch of light shining on the wall. They realized that the patch of light was coming from the reflection on the floor. Amber and Levine kept sweeping the sand away from the floor, revealing more and more of the mirror that was hidden just beneath the surface. And the more they cleared away, the more light shone through the room and onto the surrounding wall.

"There's something drawn on the wall!" Helen gasped.

Everyone looked up and realized she was right. The light shining from the floor was bright on the wall. There was a ten-foot-by-ten-foot patch of wall clearly visible now, and they could all see that something was painted on the wall. It looked like a large round circle with lines and something brown and fine above the circle.

"What in the world?" Roger said awestruck.

He dropped to his knees and started helping Amber and Levine, and then Helen joined in and they kept pulling sand away from the center of the room, revealing more and more of the mirror buried underneath the sand. The more sand they cleared away, the more light shone on the mirrored floor and then onto the wall.

They all looked up and realized that the image on the wall was something that they all recognized.

"An ear!" Levine said.

"I think you're right," Roger said.

Ben walked over to the wall and pointed with his cane.

There on the wall in the fifteen-foot-square section was the image of a beautifully shaped human ear.

There was brown hair sweeping down over the back of the ear, but it was clear that someone had drawn a massive painting on the wall around them. They were seeing one little piece of it, like three connecting pieces in a hundred-piece puzzle set.

"It's a human ear," Helen said.

"It looks like a painting," Roger said.

"I think you're right," Levine said. "The more sand we clear away from the floor, the more light shines on the wall."

"And the more light that shines on the wall," Helen said, "the more of the painting we can see."

"It must surround the whole chamber," Amber said.

Ben shuffled around along the wall, directing them with his cane. On the floor near the center of the room, Helen, Roger, Amber, and

Levine continued sweeping sand back away from the center, revealing more and more of the mirror hidden just beneath the surface of the floor.

As the light filled the room, they realized that the room was round and that it was a hundred meters in diameter. After twenty minutes, sweaty and exhausted, they revealed about one fifth of the floor in the room. The sand they swept back was collected in little piles almost three feet tall. There were four such mounds, and a good portion of the mirrored floor was now cleared enough to see quite well around the whole chamber.

The painting on the wall was large. The light reflecting from the floor up onto the wall revealed the side of a woman's head. It was more than forty feet tall, and they could see that the woman had brown hair. The more sand they cleared away, the more they thought they knew who it was.

"It looks a little like Dr. Levine," Helen said at one point.

They all looked up. It was difficult to tell for certain, but it did look a little like Dr. Levine. It was definitely someone with brown hair, and they could tell by the angle of the left lower cheek that it was probably a woman. But the image was slow in revealing itself to them, and the more they cleared away, the more excited they became.

"Try a piece over here," Helen said. "Maybe it'll shine on a different section."

She and Roger crossed the room and started clearing away sand from the floor. Immediately, light shone up on the wall. But Helen had been right; this piece of light shone on another section of the darkened wall. Helen squinted and craned her head to see better. She brushed back sweat from her brow with the back of her hand.

"It almost looks blue," she said.

Roger looked at the image on the wall, but he couldn't tell. They kept pulling back sand away from the floor, and the image on the wall grew brighter and more clear.

"It's brown," Roger said, pointing with a sandy hand. "See here, and over here."

"It's kind'a round," Helen said.

The point at which the light was shining was high up on the wall about thirty feet.

"It's an eye," Roger said.

"That's not just any eye," Helen said.

Everyone looked up. High on the wall was a single round disc about six feet in diameter. At the center of it was a black iris about a foot wide. And around the iris, there was a small sea of brown, and everyone looked beyond the brown and saw the thin trail of blue speckled around the edges.

It was as clear as a fingerprint to a forensic specialist. There on the wall buried way the heck down inside this mountain was the unmistakable brown and blue of Dr. Amy Levine's eyes.

They all stood up and stepped toward the center of the room. They looked around them and pieced together the space from ear to cheek, the lower left side of her chin, the brown hair, and proportional with everything else, was the Dr. Amy Levine's left eye.

She looked like she was smiling.

• •

"What is that on your head?" Roger asked.

Levine looked at him.

"I don't know that it *is* me," Levine said.

In the past forty-five minutes, they had revealed more and more of the mural on the wall. To everyone but Levine, there was no mistaking that it was Levine, but how a giant painting of her came to be on this wall, no one could explain. Something about the image was disorienting.

They had revealed enough of the painting to realize that she was wearing some kind of royal blue cape. There was an elaborate broach holding the cape together just below her neck, and they were just now realizing that she wore something on her head.

"It looks like a helmet," Helen said.

They continued sweeping away more and more of the sand.

"It's a Viking helmet!" Amber said.

Everyone looked up and realized that she may be right. The image, which was about sixty percent revealed, was quite romantic and beautiful. The woman looked very much like Dr. Levine, but her clothing indicated she was from a different era and a different place.

The headpiece was shiny silver, and Levine's wavy brown hair flowed down from it. Gathered around the base of the helmet, there was beautiful piece of Royal Blue cloth like a Saxon veil. It swept down around the right side of her head and neck and met with the broach and the cape.

The expression of the mural Levine's eyes was pleasantly enigmatic. She, at once, looked bold and charming. But there was something in the way her lips rose up ever so slightly on the right side of her mouth that gave her expression a suggestion of true confidence, as though she had just learned something of great value and was now looking to the distant horizon with hope and optimism and with determination.

"You look like a Viking," Amber said, and everyone smiled.

She *did* look like a Viking.

"What does it mean, though?" Dr. Levine said. "I just don't understand what this all means."

"Look here!" Ben said.

He shuffled quickly over to one side of the wall. It was directly below the rectangular box they had inspected ninety minutes earlier. Something was painted on the wall. It looked like a wooden box. Ben waved his cane excitedly.

"Please clear away that section right there," he said to Amber.

Amber swept more of the sand away from the floor, and the light shone up onto the wall near Ben. There was a wooden box painted on the wall. Ben was shuffling excitedly around it.

"*This is it*," he whispered to himself. He was ecstatic. "*This is the box!*"

"What is it, Ben?" Amber said.

Ben stared at the box.

"The key box," he said. "This will open Kevorak's Soul!"

Everyone dropped what they were doing, and they came to him.

There on the wall was a simple wooden box. There was a gold ribbon banner just above the box. There were words written on the banner.

Ben read them aloud, "'The Bearer of the Key must insert the Gamma Cephei Key into the lock to open Kevorak's Soul. Beware the time that passes, for once the Soul is opened, you have ninety minutes to complete your task.'"

"What task?" Levine said.

"You have to turn the water on," Roger said.

"What water?" Levine said. "How do I do it?"

"Maybe it'll become clear," Helen said, "after you insert the key."

"And maybe we'll all be trapped down here," Levine said, "at the bottom of this mountain."

They looked at the wooden box painted on the wall. There was a single black hole on the front of the box's lock.

"But it's a painting," Levine said.

"The keyhole is real," Amber said.

Amber reached her fingers up to the keyhole. The wooden box and its lock was nothing but paint on rock, but there was a little keyhole where a key could be inserted at the front of the box. She put her finger in it.

"It's not a painting," Amber said. "Or the keyhole isn't anyways. The box is a painting, but the keyhole is real."

Levine removed the key from her pocket. She held it up in front of her. It glinted in the bright light coming from the center of the room. She reached the key forward to insert it into the keyhole.

Immediately, the floor underneath their feet began to move. Everyone staggered backward away from the wall and toward the center of the room. They glanced down around them at the floor.

"Oh, my God!" Helen cried. "We're going to be trapped down here!"

The floor was rising up along the perimeter near the wall. At the center of the room it stayed the same, and so the effect was that a slide was created. Everything was sliding toward the center of the room, toward the clear cylinder.

"The clock!" Roger shouted.

Everyone looked up and saw that the digital clock had lighted up and was now counting backward.

1:29:53.9

"One hour and twenty-nine minutes!" Amber said. The seconds clicked relentlessly backward forty-nine, forty-eight, forty-seven, forty-six. "We have an hour and half to figure this thing out!"

The floor continued to rise higher and higher near the wall. The room was turning into a bowl, and all the sand poured down toward the clear cylinder in the center of the room. They had to lean against the slope with their hands, but the slope was getting so severe that even on hands and knees they started sliding toward the center of the room. The outer end of the floor was now ten feet higher than the center of the room, and they all slid down the slick mirrored surface toward the clear cylinder. It was intensely bright now that all the sand had piled around the cylinder, and the giant mirror was completely revealed.

Helen screamed and clung flat to the surface of the floor. The outer end of the floor was now thirty feet higher than the center of the room, and still the floor was sloping more and more. Ben sat down and slid toward the center of the room, holding his cane above his head. Levine looked up at the clock with its digital red numbers.

1:27:17.8

She looked at the giant painting on the wall and realized that the lighting change caused by the mirrored floor's moving had completely changed the image on the wall. It must have been some kind of paint that showed different images at different intensities of brightness, like the bend and movement of the hologram playing cards of her childhood. Before she had time to realize what the new painting was, she lost her footing and started sliding toward the center of the room.

Ben and Helen were already at the middle of the room. All of the sand had piled there—some six feet high by ten feet in thickness—a huge mound gathered around the cylinder in the very center. Ben was trying to get up on top of the mound of sand.

1:26:47.2

Suddenly, the floor stopped moving. Everyone had slid down to the mound of sand in the center of the room. Levine was buried up to her knees and was trying to free herself. Helen was in tears. Her hands and face were covered with sand. Roger braced to fight the floor if it continued to close up, squeezing them at the center like a conical trash compactor. Amber was up on top of the mound with her Fenwan drawn, and Ben tried to keep his balance on the ever-squeezing sand.

They looked around and realized that the floor had stopped moving. They looked at one another. They were prepared for the worst.

But suddenly, the floor started declining. It was leveling back out, flattening. All the sand in the room had poured to the center, but now the floor was flattening out again and the whole mirror was revealed. The light shining down from above reflected off of it so brightly that it was difficult to see without squinting. Still the floor continued to flatten out, more and more.

They all stepped down from the sand mound, and they were able to walk out onto the mirror. The light was bright, white, and blinding. The floor leveled out more and more, until it was only about five feet higher along the outermost perimeter than it was at the center, and everyone looked up and saw that the painting on the surrounding wall had changed. The light shone up from the mirrored floor, and everyone stared open-mouthed at what could be nothing other than a pictorial representation of the universe.

All along the wall, stars glimmered and twinkled. There were giant swirls of galaxies seen from great distances. There were fantastic nebulae and weirdly bright quasars. There were spaces along the wall blacker than anything imaginable and other places as bright and beautiful and perfect as anything the greatest creative minds on planet Earth could collectively imagine at a single moment of total clarity. It sparkled and shone and stood there silently peaceful and enigmatic at once, and all the years that Amy Levine had spent alone in isolation praying for an answer to life's simplest and greatest questions became perfectly clear to her.

It was all around her: life.

It was a teeming symphony of being and choices and freedom and love. It was as ethereal as the air she breathed and as concrete as a gravestone, and it flowed through her and her friends, and she stood there on the brink of all that she would ever know, tears of wonder and joy filling her eyes, tears of sublime power, tears that could only come from something far greater than anything she could possibly imagine, and she fell to her knees in absolute wonder and awe at the beauty that was her life.

"What causes it to sparkle like that?" Helen said.

Roger staggered up the mirror toward the edge, toward the wall. There were shining red colors and shining blue colors and towering orange and golden colors, and glittering white and empty darkness.

"I think they're jewels," Roger said. He leaned up and touched the wall, and hidden there in what had just a few minutes before been a giant painting of Dr. Amy Levine in Viking clothes were billions and billions of speckled jewels: rubies, sapphires, topaz, and onyx; diamonds and more diamonds and more diamonds still. It had all been elaborately constructed, sculpted, pieced together, one painstaking square inch at a time, and the total cumulative effect was a hundred-meter diameter room that climbed up higher than they could see; jewels shimmered, shone, and reflected the light to create a clear representation of the universe.

1:23:12.3

"Eighty-three minutes, Dr. Levine!" Amber said. She pointed at the clock.

Everyone looked up and realized she was right; nearly seven minutes had clicked off of the clock, and they weren't even certain what the countdown was counting down to.

"Maybe we should just get out," Roger said. "We could make it back out of this mountain in plenty of time, if we go now!"

They seemed undecided, but Roger's suggestion was a very real possibility. It would only take fifteen or twenty minutes at top speed to make it to the top of the mountain, to the rim, and then out and to safety.

"It'll take us an hour at least to make it back down the mountain," Amber said.

Roger said, "That's twenty minutes to the top, and then an hour down. If we go now, we could make it off of this mountain safely."

"But we don't know what it's counting down to," Levine said.

"Well, it can't be *good*," Roger said.

"Could be," Levine said, "this thing will count all the way down to zero, and a box of flowers will spring up out of the floor."

"I don't think it's that kind of timer," Roger said. "I think it's counting down to some kind of destruction!"

Everyone wanted to trust one another's judgment, but the clock *was* ticking and they were worried.

"What about it, Ben?" Roger said. "What should we do?"

Ben looked at him. He looked at each of them. "I think you're right, Roger. I don't think it's going to be a box of flowers. I think that timer's counting down to the end."

"The end?!" Levine said.

"The end of our time allowed here inside this mountain," Ben said, "inside Kevorak's Needle."

"Then, we should go?" Roger said. "We should go, right?"

Ben shook his head. "No," Ben said. "I think we should figure out how to get Levine into into Kevorak's Soul."

Everyone's eyes went to that nine-foot-tall clear cylinder standing in the middle of the room. There was a giant pile of sand now gathered around it, but it looked largely unchanged. The cylinder stood silent and enigmatic. It was some kind of tool, everyone realized, but figuring it out and understanding how to use it had thus far proved all but impossible.

"*Is* that the Soul?" Helen asked, "Kevorak's Soul?"

"It is," Ben said. "And understanding its secrets stands between us and the future of everything we will ever know. We must find a way to get inside it! We must find a way to understand!"

1:18:59.9

FORTY-EIGHT
THE RIDDLE OF THE SOUL

"What is that?" Helen said, pointing at the clear cylinder in the center of the room.

Everyone looked at the cylinder. About seven feet up, near where the top started to curve inward in its dome shape, there was a ring of words within the surface. The words wrapped around the cylinder, and by looking through the cylinder, everyone could see the backside of the words as well as the front. The words were written in a sky blue color inside the clear surface, and they were somewhat transparent, such that everyone could read them as well as see through them.

IS THE SOUND OF A DOOR OPENING
SEPARATE FROM AN OPENING DOOR?

"What does it mean?" Amber said.

"It's a riddle," Dr. Levine said.

Suddenly, the words on the cylinder changed.

HE WHO ANSWERS THIS RIDDLE CORRECTLY
WILL GAIN ENTRANCE TO THE SOUL.

Ben read the words aloud chuckling. He looked at each of them and said, "It wants to test our merit."

"The cylinder does?" Helen said.

Again the words changed, returning to the riddle. Everyone looked perplexedly at the words. They circled the cylinder, each reading the words quietly to himself. There was suddenly the sense that anyone could enter the soul, if they could come up with the correct answer. The group seemed to realize this at the same time, and they became charged with competitive energy.

"What do you think it means, Ben?" Helen said.

The words changed again.

Levine read the new words, "'Each person may answer one time by touching the cylinder while giving your answer.'"

"Hmmm," Amber said with a grin. "We each get to answer."

And again the words changed back to the riddle.

"I guess so," Levine said.

"What do we do, just step up to it and touch it?" Helen asked.

"And then give your answer," Roger said. "It seems pretty clear to me. Touch the cylinder and give your answer."

"I wonder what happens if you answer incorrectly," Amber said.

They all considered this possibility, and they didn't like where the possibilities led them.

"Maybe we shouldn't answer it at all," Helen said.

"Maybe we should just get out of here," Roger said.

"Or maybe we should face our destiny," Ben said. "Maybe we should face the responsibility of our being here."

Everyone looked up at the sky blue words.

IS THE SOUND OF A DOOR OPENING
SEPARATE FROM AN OPENING DOOR?

"I'm thinking 'no'," Roger said.

He looked at his friends, but no one either encouraged or discouraged this probe.

"They're one in the same," he said.

"Yeah," Helen said, "but what if a door opened in a vacuum?"

"Like in space," Amber said.

"Right," Helen said. "A door on the exterior of a space shuttle, say."

"There's no sound in space?" Roger asked.

"You *know that*," Helen said.

"I just never understood it," Roger said. "So like if there's an explosion in space, there's no sound?"

Helen just gave him a look, her lips furling downward in a frown, her shoulders rising up slightly, her head tilting to one side. It was as if to say "Don't be a moron, Roger."

"What?!" Roger asked feigning innocence.

"Well, then," Amber said, "the door would still open."

"In space," Helen said.

"Yeah."

Levine said, "So, a door doesn't need sound to be an opening door?"

Ben said, "But that's not what the riddle's asking."

"If it *is* a riddle," Levine said.

Ben looked at her. "What do you mean?" he asked.

"Well, it reads like a riddle," Levine said. "But it sounds like a koan."

"A cone?" Helen said.

"*Ko-an*," Levine said. "It's the Eastern version of a riddle. Usually a Zen koan is a paradoxical statement or question, which a master will ask a novice. The point is not to answer the question by logic or will, but to meditate on the question until the analytical part of your mind gives way to intuition and creative insight. They're mental exercises, kind of like anagrams or crossword puzzles, maybe a little deeper."

Everyone looked at the words again. Each of them circled the cylinder. Helen whispered the words aloud, reading them intensely.

"Well, it sounds like a riddle to me," Roger said. "The thing said, 'He who answers the *riddle* correctly'. It seems pretty clear to me; it ain't no Zen cone, pine cone, traffic cone, or any other cone. The thing's a riddle, and the answer's probably as obvious as the air you breathe."

A few meters away, the digital clock continued counting backwards. Amber glanced at it and was surprised to see just how much time had elapsed.

1:03:19.7

She realized that even if they left right this moment, they would not have enough time to climb all the way to the rim and then down to the base of the mountain, and that realization flooded her with adrenaline and panic.

"Guys," she said. "We may just need to book it out'a here. We're getting near sixty minutes."

Everyone looked at the clock. They looked up at the long stairwell wrapping around inside the mountain. They saw the small disc of blue sky way up at the top of the mountain, and they realized Amber was right. They may not have enough to time to get away from the mountain safely, but it was a crucial moment because if they went now, and they went fast, they may still have a chance to get away. But with every minute that clicked off of the clock, the possibility of getting away safely deteriorated more and more, stretching further into infinity.

"We should go," Roger said. "We can still get away."

"I think I know the answer," Helen said.

Everyone looked at her. She was standing before the clear cylinder. She looked up at it and felt life flowing through it, its surface, inside its clear chamber. There seemed to be an electrical current flowing through the room.

"Can I give my answer?" Helen asked the group.

No one said anything a moment.

Roger stepped forward and said, "I don't think it's wise."

Amber said, "If she wants to give an answer, I believe she has the right to give an answer."

"And what if she gives the wrong answer?" Roger said. "What if it traps us all inside this mountain? Does she have that right, too?"

"You would rather run, Roger?" Helen asked.

"I would rather be smart," he said. "I say we clear out of here and come back better prepared. In time, we could build an elevator in and out of this mountain. Or a tunnel. We could come and go with more safety. It may take weeks. It may take months. But if we all die here today, then all of this will have been for nothing. Are you truly willing to risk that, Helen?"

"Perhaps we should put it to a vote," Helen said.

Roger glanced at Ben, Levine, and then Amber. He was gauging what their vote would be.

"I don't think that's fair," he said. "It's clear that you all want to test fate."

"I think a vote is fair," Levine said.

She looked at Ben and Amber, then at Helen and Roger. The clock continued its unremitting countdown.

"Well, then, let's do it," Roger said. "And let's be quick about it."

"A vote," Ben said.

"A vote," Amber said.

Ben grabbed a handful of sand and poured it flat on one piece of floor twenty feet from the group. In the sand he wrote "Yes" and "No," and he drew a line between the two. He stood up and looked at the group.

"We'll each vote," he said, "by making a marking under 'Yes' if you want to stay and answer the riddle or by making a mark under 'No' if you think we should go."

"'Yes' to stay," Roger said, "and 'No' to go."

Everyone walked over and looked at what he had done, and they agreed that it was fair.

"Helen should go first," Levine said, "and then Roger."

They stepped back away from the sand so that each person would have privacy while making a decision.

"Okay," Roger said.

"Okay," Helen said.

Helen walked over to the sand, knelt down, and made a mark in the sand. She stood up and came back to the group. Roger nodded solemnly, and then he walked over to the little pile of sand. He knelt down and made a mark in one of the columns. He stood up and came back to the group.

"Who's next?" Amber said.

"Ben," Levine said. "You should go."

Ben said, "Yes," and he walked over to the little pile. He knelt down and made a mark in the sand. He stood up and came back to the group.

"I'll go next," Levine said, and she crossed to the little pile, knelt down, made a mark, and then stood and returned to the group.

Amber looked at each of them, and then she approached the pile of sand. What she saw when she knelt down to consider her vote surprised her.

YES | NO

| | | |

That meant that either Levine or Ben had cast a "no" vote against Helen. Amber almost looked back over her shoulder with surprise, but she steeled her will and realized that her vote would determine their fate. Hers was the deciding vote. She glanced up at the giant clear cylinder. It stood silent, clear, and inanimate, yet Amber felt its presence as though there *was* life inside the chamber. And for a moment, she was almost certain that it was aware of her. She heard Helen clear her throat, and she turned, looked at the sand, and made her decision. She reached forward, marked the sand, then stood up, and came back to the group.

"Ben," Helen said, "should tell us the result."

Levine started to say something, but she glanced at Amber and realized that Amber knew the result, too, and Ben had already shuffled over to the pile.

"The vote is clear," he said. "Three to two. We stay and answer the riddle."

Roger made a slight groaning noise and stepped a few feet away from the group. He looked back at the clear cylinder and shook his head. *We're all going to die*, he thought. *None of us are going to make it out of here alive.*

53:52.3

Helen stepped up to the clear cylinder and outstretched her right hand, palm facing the surface. She felt a tickling electrical current flow through her hand, and then her hand stuck to the surface, and she filled with panic. She tried to take her hand back from the surface of the cylinder, but it would not let her go.

"It's got me!" she said.

Roger ran up to her and tried to help her remove her hand from the surface, but he could see that it was not going to let her go. He tried to pry his fingertips in between her palm and the cylinder's surface, but it was impossible. Her hand and the surface of the cylinder were one. The cylinder was not flexing and liquid-like the way that it had been a few minutes before. The surface felt rubbery, but it was hard rubber, and it did not give much at all.

Everyone else came up and saw her hand was attached to the surface.

"Does it hurt?" Levine asked.

"No," Helen said. "Only when I try to pull it away, it hurts in my wrist."

"Well, then don't fight it," Ben said. "Give the cylinder your answer."

"But what if it's the wrong answer?" she said.

"I don't think you have a choice," Roger said, "not now. But you could answer correctly. You could be right. Give it your answer and pray that it's right."

Everyone stepped back down the mound of sand. Helen stood there at the top, her outstretched hand above her attached to the cylinder's surface. The riddle's words were still there: Is the sound of a door opening separate from an opening door?

Helen said, "My answer is 'no'. They are one in the same."

Everyone waited for something to happen. Something started moving in the sand, deep down under the surface of the mound. It looked like some sort of shoebox-sized creature was burrowing just below the surface, and then it hit Helen's feet and pulled her six inches down into the sand. Helen screamed, and in her shock she didn't realize that her hand had come free from the cylinder.

Suddenly, she was moving away from the cylinder down the mound. She flailed her arms all around and cried to her friends for help, but it was like she was moving on a conveyor belt six inches below the sand mound's surface. She moved ten feet away from the cylinder and then stopped. She swung around trying to see what it was, what had happened. Her feet were buried in a little pile of sand up to her shins, and she could not move her feet at all. She was like a fly stuck to flypaper. She pivoted around and looked at everyone, and she reached down and pawed at the sand, but it was clear that her feet were locked down and that she wasn't going anywhere.

High up on the cylinder was a single word consisting of nine red letters:

INCORRECT

In pure anger, Roger ran up to the cylinder, slapped his hand to the surface, and shouted, "Then my answer is 'yes'. They are separate! The sound and the door are separate!"

There was a pause, and then everyone saw that same burrowing movement underneath the surface of sand. It struck Roger's feet, and he dipped down six inches.

"Hey!" he shouted.

And he, too, moved away from the cylinder. The sand positioned him at the same distance from the cylinder as Helen, but he was fifteen feet to her left.

Ben, Amber, and Levine watched all of this with shock and horror. Roger swung all around, cursing, and yelling, but his feet were cemented inside a little pile of sand that came up to his shins.

Amber ran up to the cylinder, pressed her hand against the surface, and said, "It's neither. It's not separate or the same. A sound is a sound, and a door is a door. Sometimes they're separate, and sometimes they're not. They're both, and they're neither!"

Everyone watched as the lump rose up from inside the sand.

"No!" Amber shouted.

It struck her feet and pulled her down inside the sand, and then she was sliding away from the cylinder, ten feet away. It stopped with her fifteen feet to Roger's left, so that she, Roger, and Helen were each on different sides of the cylinder.

She brought her Fenwan to life and struck at the sand pile around her feet, but her light staff hit the sand and sputtered, its light flickering out. She tried to lift her feet, but it was as though they were cemented to the floor.

Helen, Roger, and Amber looked at Levine and Ben, and they realized that the whole thing was some horrible trap. They'd been lured into believing that the riddle *was* a riddle, and as such that it could be solved. Helen cried and said, "I'm sorry." Roger pivoted around futilely, his feet cemented to the floor.

"What in the world?" Amber said. She looked at the cylinder. "It's a simple 'yes or no' question," she said. "And we answered 'yes' and we answered 'no'. And we answered 'both' and 'neither'! What else could it be?" She read the words aloud, "'Is the sound of a door opening separate from an opening door?'"

She looked at Dr. Amy Levine.

"I don't understand," Amber said. "We answered it every way you could answer it."

Everyone looked at Levine. She was quietly nodding her head. She started to saunter silently around the cylinder. She looked at the sand mound, and she looked at the cylinder and the sky blue words. She fed the words of the riddle through her mind over and over and over, until she wasn't even "reading" them per se but was contemplating them, their form, their structure, their sound—inside her mind.

A contemplative index finger came up and tapped her lower lip.

Suddenly, she looked up across the room to where she had inserted the key nearly forty-five minutes earlier. The key was still there, but she could not see it. It was hidden in the jeweled wall. Levine squinted, deep in thought. And then her eyes went back to the cylinder and the sky blue words.

Everyone watched her. They could see she was getting her mind around the riddle like water surrounding an island, like a cheek surrounding a teardrop. She was digging down inside the words, seeing what they looked like from the other side. She looked at the words backwards. She sounded them out in her mind from back to front, then front to back.

She broke them down into individual units: twelve words, one question mark, exactly fifty characters. She listened to the sound they made as she spoke them in her mind, but she only made it halfway through the sentence before she lost herself inside the sentence and inside the *sound* of the words.

She sat down on the floor, cross-legged, and she placed her hands on her knees. The trouble was, she realized, she was trying to understand the sentence logically, and true insight only came when the mind was free from logic's convincing forcefulness. It *was* like a Zen koan, and she had to free herself from the will to find the answer before a true answer would come.

Is the sound of a door opening separate from an opening door?

Levine realized that it could not be answered by the will, but that the will to answer it was the only motivation *to* answer it. Quite literally, it was a mental exercise meant to exhaust her mind to the point of desperation; only once beyond desperation could she begin to understand it. Only once her mind was broken could she begin to build it anew. Only once confronted with nothing could she begin to understand anything.

The riddle *was* that there was a riddle.

Levine exhaled deeply and understood.

There were no bright and shining lights, no twinkling bulbs or bells or whistles; there was just the certainty that comes from true understanding. It was total calm, freedom and awareness. Her eyes blinked and were filled with life.

She rose and approached the cylinder. She climbed the mound of sand and reached her hand forward. Her fingertips stretched, and her hand came forward. She touched the cylinder.

And she was no more.

43:57.9

FIFTY
THE DECISION

Levine stood on the banks of a pond filled with lotus flowers. Her eyes were closed, and she could hear her breathing. She felt as though she were waking. She opened her eyes.

The pond was exactly one acre, and there was nothing beyond the water except white light. There were water lilies scattered around the pond, and one hundred white lotus flowers rose up from the water and stood at various heights. The tallest stems rose nearly two meters above the water's surface, and the broadest flowers were nine inches in diameter. Some of the flowers had broken off from their stems and floated on the water's surface.

Levine looked down at the water just a few feet from where she stood. The water was clear, and she could see that some lilies were submerged beneath the surface of the water. Some were very deep below the surface. Others were closer to the surface, and many floated *on* the water's surface. Others hung from the lotus flowers' stems several feet above the water.

She looked up and saw Noah Johnston coming to her around the pond. He wore a white robe, and his hands were folded together in the sleeves at the front of his robe.

"You have done well," Johnston said.

Levine heard his voice all around her. It was a calm and pleasant voice, filled with confidence and with love.

"*Johnston?*" Levine said. "Noah Johnston?"

Her voice was not only audible, but it was perfectly clear, as though separate from and united with a deeper silence that surrounded her. Everything was contradictory, paradoxical, and yet it was completely at peace. Her lips formed the words, but it was as though her senses had changed roles. She physically *felt* the words, even *tasted* and *saw* the words, rather than simply hearing them. As strange as it might have been to comprehend before entering the Soul, she knew the words before she even thought them. And she knew what would come after them. It was as though there were literally no time; only freedom. Her awareness had been heightened.

"The pond is in a garden," Johnston said. "Search around you to open the windows."

Levine's head pivoted around, but she saw only white light around her in every direction except for the pond. She squinted her eyes and knelt down. She was looking at nothing but white, the pond now over her right shoulder, and she thought she saw very fine gold threads floating around her. They were transparent and were so fine that they were almost invisible, but Levine reached her hand forward and took hold of one thread between her thumb and forefinger. It moved.

She heard the sound of a woman laughing.

It made Levine smile, and she looked up and saw Johnston standing there now, just a few feet from her. He smiled.

Levine brought her other hand forward and held the thread between the fingers of her right hand and the fingers of her left. She twisted the thread around and realized that she could peel it apart. When she peeled it apart, a window was created in the whiteness, and she could see through it. The further she spread it open, the larger the window was.

An old woman with white hair sat in a blue recliner. One leg was propped up over the arm of the chair, and the woman held a phone in her right hand. She was talking to someone else, and she seemed very happy. Though she looked to be in her late seventies, she was as happy as a child of seven.

"What is this?" Levine asked.

"Each thread opens a window into your world, Dr. Levine."

Levine let go of the thread, the window closed quickly, and the golden thread floated back to its original position within the whiteness. Levine nodded her head and started to walk around the lotus pond. She could see the threads all around her in the white space that surrounded the pond. They were very fine and almost completely transparent, and they appeared to vibrate. She looked at Johnston and was amazed.

She realized that many of the threads were overlapping and interwoven as though it was the stitching that held together the seemingly infinite space surrounding the pond.

Levine reached out and took hold of another thread. She held it between her hands and pulled it apart as she had done before, and it began to open a window in the white space.

She saw a wife and husband standing near their home on a rolling arid hillside. The home consisted of several straw mats interwoven in a dome-shape over a dozen strong sticks. It was a nomadic tent, and Levine reasoned by the woman's clothing, which covered her arms, legs, and head, that they were from a Muslim nation in Africa. Only her face was visible, but she wore a playful smile, and she seemed very happy. The man wore a white tunic, a white cap, reddish-brown pants, and he wore no shoes. The ground was sandy and arid, and there were little desert trees on the rolling hillside behind their camp.

The wife said something that made her husband smile. She turned and shooed him away, and he laughed good-naturedly and jumped away from her playfully. Then he leaned over and picked up a white ceramic plate that sat atop a tin pan beside their home. He handed her the plate, and Levine saw her say "Merci beaucoup." He looked at her with true love, and Levine realized they were very happy.

"Where is this?" Levine asked.

"That is a farm one hundred kilometers north of Ndjamena," Johnston said, "in the Republic of Chad. They are happy, yes?"

"They are," Levine said, and she nodded her head as though she were beginning to understand this place. She asked, "So, each of these threads opens a window into our world?"

"Yes, they are like windows into your world on Earth."

Levine looked at Johnston. "And what about you?" she asked. "How long have you been here?"

"I don't know," he said. "We don't measure time here. There is no time. I do not remember my being before I entered the Line."

"You don't remember Santana's island?"

"It seems like a dream," Johnston said. "I think I've come to realize that what most people consider life, what most people consider reality, is only a passage."

Levine let the string go, and the window closed. She walked a little farther around the lotus pond.

"I don't understand," Levine said.

"People's souls enter life at birth," Johnston said, "and when they die, they come here."

"Their souls?"

"Until it is time to be born again," he said.

Levine took another thread in hand, and she opened another window. A woman stood right in front of her, the lower half of her body buried underneath a thick green field of tea plants. The woman had dark skin and a star-shaped ring on her right nostril, and she wore a sarong and a white headdress. Attached to the headdress were straps that led down to a light woven basket on her back. She was at work on a green hillside, so rich and fertile it made Levine's eyes shine.

"India?" she asked.

"Sri Lanka," Noah replied. "A tea estate in the highlands of Sri Lanka."

There was another tea-picker about twenty meters behind the first woman, but instead of a woven basket, she wore a tan sack on her back. The first woman was singing in Sinhalese, and Levine caught the words "Irida," "Sanduda," "Badada," and "Sikurada." She realized that the woman was singing about the days of the week, and Levine thought that her voice was beautiful and noble. They were at work, and they seemed very happy.

"It is good," Noah said.

Levine let the thread go, and the window closed.

"Yes," she said. "It is very peaceful here."

Levine opened another window, and she saw the smiling round face of a young Chinese girl. The girl held a ceramic bowl filled with steaming soup in one hand and chopsticks in her other hand. She wore a blue winter coat, a blue scarf, and a blue wool hat on her head. She was standing outside of some kind of tent. A bright red tapestry hung down from the tent, and a group of seven people were standing at a table at the front of the tent waiting to get their soup.

The cook looked very happy, and his assistant smiled at the young girl. There was a giant steaming kettle of soup beside the table, and Levine realized that it was snowing lightly on the group. The soup looked hot, plentiful, and good, and everyone seemed eager and happy. The cook said something to one man at the front of the hungry group, and he waved his ladle at him. Everyone burst out laughing, and the cook smiled warmly at the man. He took the man's bowl benevolently, and he filled it to the brim. The man nodded, seemed to say thank you, and stepped away from the group with his soup bowl filled. He looked very happy.

"What is all this?" Levine asked. She let the thread go, and the window closed. "What am I to understand?"

"You have come here by choice and by destiny, Dr. Levine. You were not supposed to be born. You were not supposed to accomplish anything of substance in your lifetime. And yet, you have arrived here with faith and humility. You have earned this right, and the Great Good is pleased with you. I am to offer you an answer to any question."

"A question?" Levine said.

"Any question," Noah said.

"Will we make it?" Levine asked. "Will humanity survive? What is our future?"

"There will be a period of great prosperity for humanity," Noah Johnston said. "There *will* be cells of violence, but humanity stands at the dawn of one thousand years of peace and prosperity. But it is a peace that requires respect and love from one human being to another. Patience, Dr. Levine, may prove to be humanity's greatest gift. Patience, love, and respect."

"What about those who are destructive?" Levine asked.

"In time," Noah said, "destruction will consume itself. In time, evil will subside. Most people only want their families to be happy and content. The family is the most important unit on Earth. Through the family, love grows. And love will overcome evil. You must believe that, Amy."

"I want to believe that," Levine said. "I do."

Tears streamed down her cheeks. She stood in this infinite space of whiteness, talking to a voice that filled her with confidence and love, and she only wanted to live a right and good life. She only wanted to contribute love and harmony to life. She was not perfect, but she could adapt and change and *listen* to other people. She could learn, compromise, and admit when she needed to grow, when she did not understand. She could be willing to try to learn from her misunderstandings and her mistakes. She could be honest with herself, know herself, listen to others, and simply let others be free to be who they were: unique, beautiful, creations of life.

She wanted to cry out her love. There was such beauty in the world it staggered her imagination to fathom why anyone would want to kill or maim or destroy another *gift*. Another *life!*

"All we *are* is the sum total of our being," she said.

"It is so," Noah said.

Levine wiped the tears away from her face, and she walked farther around the pond. Johnston stayed by her side. She reached out at random and took another thread in her hand. She pulled it apart and opened up a very large window five meters high by ten meters wide.

"I know this city," Levine said.

The view was high over the rooftops of a European city.

"This clock tower is in Poland," Levine said, pointing to a clock tower that rose some twenty stories above the city's other buildings. "It is the city of Gdansk. Hitler demanded this city be given to him, but the Polish refused. He used it as provocation to invade Poland on September 1, 1939."

"Four forty-five A.M., September 1st, 1939," Noah said. "You know your history, Dr. Levine."

Far below, there was an open air mall—the Stare Miasto—and people strolled along the mall between the buildings.

"How do I go in closer?" Levine asked.

"Reach into the window."

Levine looked forward into the window. She raised her left hand and eased it into the window. She felt the cold air of Gdansk, Poland on her hand, and she grabbed at the air and pulled the image closer to her.

People walking along the mall looked up and saw a beautiful burst of sunlight through the clouds high over the city, and then, momentarily, a cloud formation that resembled a woman's hand, grasping at the air above their city.

Levine removed her hand from the window, and from their perspective walking along the streets of Gdansk, the few people that even noticed the cloud formation saw it dissipate, and they thought nothing more of it. But Levine's view was much closer now, and she could see the people walking along the mall.

"Can I affect things?" Levine asked.

"Within reason," Noah said. "From here, you can."

Levine saw one particular gentleman standing on a street corner, facing toward her from across the street. He wore a business suit and a fedora, and he glanced at his watch and started walking toward the pedestrian crossing. From her heightened perspective, Levine could see a taxi on an adjacent street was speeding along, but she realized that the man in the fedora had no way of knowing.

Quickly, she reached into the window, stretching her arm at full length, and grabbed the man. Her hand hit the man as a powerful gust of wind, and he shivered and shook and staggered backward away from the street. Everyone standing nearby braced themselves in the powerful gust of wind. The man regained his footing and braced into the strong cold wind, but the moment had given him pause, and he started to step out onto the pedestrian crossing into the strong wind. The taxi swerved around the corner. The man leapt back away from the street, slipped, and stumbled backward up onto the sidewalk.

The taxi's horn blared at him, but it continued racing around the corner, tires squealing, and continued on up the street that the man had been about to cross. Levine removed her hand, and inside the window, the wind died down.

Several other pedestrians looked at the man who had fallen. He was cursing the taxi driver, and one or two people realized that he'd just missed being hit by the taxi by a matter of inches. Had he been one meter farther out into the crosswalk, he would have been completely run down by the car.

A lady came over, knelt down beside the man, and appeared to ask him if he was alright. The man was embarrassed and angry, but he was alive, and he tried to thank the woman for her concern. He even seemed somewhat amused and amazed by his good luck at not having been hit, and he smiled at the woman and said as much. He stood up and began brushing himself off. The woman handed him his fedora, which had fallen onto the sidewalk.

"They will fall in love," Noah said.

"What do you mean?" Levine said.

"They work at the same building and know one another by acquaintance. They will have one daughter, and she will marry a young man from Vaduz, Liechtenstein, who hasn't even been born yet. You just affected the course of history."

Levine looked at her hand, now removed from the window. She pulled the window closed, and it snapped back into a single thread floating in infinite white space. She didn't know whether to be proud of herself or afraid of the power that she had just exercised. She felt good that the man was alive.

The thought made her think of her friends and the timer counting down back inside Kevorak's Needle.

"My friends!" she said. "Are they okay?"

"You are now inside the Line, Dr. Levine," Noah said. "And here time does not exist as it does outside of the Line."

"But what about those things I've just seen," Levine said. "That seemed like normal time to me."

"Those actions will not occur until you are back on Earth," Noah said. "They are glimpses of what will come."

"But that man will live?" Levine asked.

"Everything you have seen here through these strings will happen as soon as you step back inside the hotel."

"What if I stayed here?" Levine asked, "saving people's lives?"

"Then that would be your fate for all eternity," Noah said. "But you have not made that decision, not yet. And if you do make that decision, then you can stay here and use these powers, and you will never age."

"But my friends," Levine said, "will they be safe if I stay here?"

"No," Noah said, "because they have already answered the riddle incorrectly. You can not change what has already been done. You can only affect the future. If you decide to stay here, the clock would continue for them."

"And they would be trapped?" Levine asked.

"All except Ben," Noah said. "Ben did not answer the riddle incorrectly."

"But Amber, Helen, and Roger?" Levine said to Noah Johnston.

"They have already chosen their fates by hastily answering the riddle. From here, you can not guide them or tell them what to do."

Levine looked out over the pond. She saw the lotus flowers swaying in a gentle breeze.

"But if I decided to go," Levine said, "to leave this place?"

"Then you could save your friends," Noah said. "You could directly guide them."

"And the world of the Randa?" Levine said. "How do I unlock the water? Can I unlock the water if I leave?"

Noah looked out at the lotus pond. He said, "One drop of water from this pond is all that is needed to set the rains in motion."

"So the question is," Levine said, "do I stay here where I can affect millions of lives for the good for all eternity, or do I save my friends?"

"That is the question."

"Can I ever come back?" Levine said. "Could I save my friends and then come back?"

"No, you can not," Noah said. "It is an ethical question that stands before you now. If you stay here, in time, you will save millions and millions of lives. You will contribute great peace and harmony to humanity."

"Yes, but my friends die," Levine said. "And I don't know this place. I feel lonely here."

"Your friends will never know the decision you make," Noah said. "And you have only seen one drop in an ocean that is the Line. There are many others here, Amy. There are mountains and cities. There is no suffering, and the farther you come, the freer you will be of negative emotions, such as guilt and anger."

"Yeah, but my friends die," Levine said.

"If you leave," Noah said, "many people such as the man you just saved will step out into their own crosswalks. The decision is yours, Dr. Levine. What will you do?"

"That's a heavy decision," Levine said. "I need to think on it."

"That would be wise."

Levine sat down cross-legged beside the lotus pond. She placed her hands on her knees, and she breathed deeply and exhaled.

"If you choose to save your friends," Noah said, "simply reach your hand into the lotus pond and take one scoop of water. You will return to Kevorak's Needle, and that scoop of water will unlock the hidden reservoir within the Randa World."

"I understand," Levine said.

"I will leave you so that you may consider your decision in peace."

Levine watched Noah Johnston walk around the pond away from her. He walked further into the white space until he vanished.

Levine sat there and thought about the decision.

It all came down to one choice: should she save her friends, or should she help save the lives of millions of strangers? In saving her friends, she would also save the Randa World. However, the positive change that she could affect by staying within the Line was unprecedented. Eternity was a long time, and humanity could use her help from within the Line. She would be like an angel, helping people for the rest of time.

The question, Levine thought, *is how to best be.*

There was silence while Levine thought through the dilemma. She visualized Amber, rotating her Fenwan. In the image Levine saw, Amber had a confident, eager smile and bright, alert eyes. The Fenwan rotated around and around. The girl held so much promise, that the choice was clear. Levine nodded her head and exhaled deeply.

And she made her decision.

To Helen, Roger, Amber, and Ben it looked like Levine passed right through the cylinder. She had stepped right up to it, outstretched her hand, and touched the cylinder. There was a burst of light that lasted exactly three seconds, and Levine emerged out of the other side of the cylinder, and the flash of light inside the chamber vanished.

Levine held her hands cupped together as though they held something, and she staggered down the sand mound. She quickly glanced around and saw Amber, Roger, and Helen still cemented in place to the floor. She glanced up at the clock.

43:54.9

"You made it!" Ben said.

"What happened?" Helen said.

"Did you go somewhere?" Roger asked.

Ben shuffled around and looked at her, and he knew. He knew she had entered the Line. He could see it in her eyes and in her expression. She was filled with such calmness and such clarity that it awed him, and he bowed his head before her and said a prayer.

"What do I do?" Levine said to him.

When Ben looked up, Levine stood in front of him, and he saw the water in her hands.

"What is it?" he said.

"It's water from a pond," she said, "from a lotus pond. I don't have time to explain. What do I do with it?"

Ben did not know what she was supposed to do with it, but randomness and destiny answered them both in a single drop of water that seeped between her fingers, hung for a moment, and then dropped like a tiny missile three feet to the floor.

The ground shook and moved. Everyone screamed. And then a torrent of water started pouring from the walls around the base of

Kevorak's Needle. It poured from openings ten feet above the floor, and it quickly started coursing across the floor, pooling together in some spots. Little creeks formed pools in indentations and permutations on the floor, and then from high overhead it started to rain on everyone.

Levine looked up and realized that the waterfalls they had passed through earlier, almost a mile up inside the mountain, must have increased their pressure. Their water was now reaching them as a fine rainy mist. Ten seconds later, the fine rainy mist turned into a heavy downpour and in less than a minute, everyone was soaked.

"I guess that did it," Levine said to Ben.

She let the rest of the water in her hand drop to the floor, which was already several inches deep with water. It was filling very quickly. She and Ben looked at Amber, Roger, and Helen.

"It's still got us!" Roger shouted, pivoting around.

The sound of water pouring from the walls was thunderous.

Levine and Ben waded over to him, the water now shin deep. Levine ducked her hands under the water and felt the sand encased around his feet. She brought her hands up from the water, and the sand poured from them. He was still fixed to the floor somehow. She reached down and grabbed more sand, trying to shovel it away from his feet, but she saw through the water that it was immediately replaced by more sand. The sand seemed to come up from within the mound that encased his feet. It was endless.

The water was nearly up to his knees.

Levine glanced quickly around and saw Amber flailing around wildly. On her, the water was up to her thighs. Roger shouted something and pointed up at the cylinder.

"Look!" he said. "There's something new on the cylinder!"

Levine looked up and saw that the sky blue words on the cylinder had changed to a transparent green phrase.

YOU MUST DEPOSIT THE KEY
INTO THE SOUL TO BE FREE.

Levine's eyes rose to the wall where she had inserted the key. It was still there in the painted wooden box and painted padlock. She saw the end of the key gleam, and she took off across the room to it.

By the time she reached the wall, the water was nearly up to her waist, and she was not able to move very well. She grabbed the key, turned it, and removed it from the wall. She started back toward the center of the room, but she was having to bounce and swim along.

She saw that Amber was underwater up to her chin. Amber craned her head to keep it above the surface, but she could only stretch so far.

"Hurry, Dr. Levine!" she cried, and then her mouth was underwater.

By the time Levine reached the cylinder, the water in the room was five feet deep, quickly filling up to six. Helen was almost underwater, now, and Ben was treading water.

Levine ducked down underneath the surface and swam toward the cylinder. Holding her breath, she held her eyes open, and she reached the key out toward the cylinder. The cylinder glowed light blue underneath the water, and Levine touched the key to the cylinder's surface and winced backward at the bright flash of light.

Both the key and the cylinder vanished, and Levine came up to the surface of the water gasping for air. She looked across the surface of the water and saw Amber floating lifelessly on the surface.

Roger and Helen came up choking, but they regained their composure and swam toward Ben. All three were heading toward the stairwell that rose from the water along the far wall.

Levine reached Amber, hitched her arm around her, and swam for the stairwell. Amber didn't move.

Roger, Helen, and Ben saw Amber's pale face tinted a horrifying blue. Roger dragged her up onto the stairs and tried to lay her body flat. Everyone stared at him and just held their breath.

He applied several pumps of pressure just below her sternum, then rolled Amber over and hit her three times hard on her back. Amber made a retching sound, and all the water came up from her. She coughed and gagged and sputtered, and tears of joy filled Levine's eyes.

She glanced back and saw the water was still rising.

"Move her up a few more stairs," she said, and everyone climbed up about ten more steps above the water.

Levine saw the clock on the far wall was about to go under, and she was horrified to see the time on it.

27:38.4

Amber was getting to her feet. She held her throat as though it hurt, but the color had returned to her cheeks. She coughed a few more times and spat on the ground, clearing her windpipe.

Her voice was raspy, but she said, "Come on, guys! Let's go!"

Levine quickly punched the numbers from the digital clock into her wristwatch and started her watch timer. Amber began up the stairwell, followed quickly by Roger, Helen, Ben, and Levine.

• •

They were four hundred meters below the rim, and their legs ached almost as badly as their lungs. Roger and Helen were far ahead of Amy and Amber, and it looked for certain that they would be out of the mountain before it erupted. But Ben was struggling, and Amber and Levine kept slowing down to help him along. It was a lot harder going up the stairs than it had been going down.

"Come on, Ben!" Amber said.

The old man struggled along with his cane. They'd just come up from behind the waterfalls, and Amber could see the torrent pouring out from the walls. Levine's thighs ached, and she glanced down at her wristwatch.

9:12.7

Ben came up to her on the steps, and though his aged lungs were completely out of breath, he could tell by her expression that they were running out of time.

"How much time's left?" he gasped.

"Nine minutes," she said. "Come on!"

The three turned and looked up the remaining flight of stairs. The sky was late-afternoon blue overhead. They saw Roger and Helen had reached the end of the stairwell and were starting up the dirt path just inside the rim.

Levine, Amber, and Ben hurried on up the little cobblestone stairwell beside the creek, which was now splashing over its sides. Water poured both into the wide chasm from the creek and up onto the cobblestones. It made footing much more difficult.

And then all at once, the ground shook violently as in an earthquake. Amber screamed. Levine and Ben staggered forward up the stairwell. Everything was shaking so violently that she couldn't get a fix on Roger and Helen, and they just struggled to stay on her feet. Parts of the interior wall of the mountain started giving away. Huge chunks fell out into the chasm.

Levine glanced at her wristwatch.

5:19.2

"Five minutes!" Levine shouted. The noise inside the mountain was deafening.

They were near the end of the stairwell, and from there, it was a straight shot up the dirt path to the top of the rim.

"Hurry, Ben!" Amber shouted.

Ben struggled along as quickly as he could, and they reached the end of the stairwell. They could see pine trees up ahead on the inner slope of the rim. The ground continued to shake. Levine glanced down once to see how much water had already filled the chasm, but it was just blackness down inside the mountain.

They hurried up the dirt path. Levine didn't see Roger and Helen at all in front of them, so they must have made it away from the opening. Her legs ached. Sweat poured from her body. Her mind swirled with exhaustion. Her lungs swallowed huge gulps of air.

Another two hundred meters, and they would be away from the opening to the mountain.

"Come on!" she said. "We're almost there!"

"How much time?" Amber shouted over all the noise.

Levine glanced at her wristwatch.

3:47.2

"Less than four minutes!" she shouted.

Footing on the dirt path on the inner side of the rim was difficult. The earth continued to lurch and sway underneath them, and they staggered forward up the mountain.

There were slides of dirt on the path, coming down from higher up on the rim. Some of the pine trees scattered along the rim shook and swayed from the dirt and the trembling earth.

Ben stumbled and fell to the ground. Levine turned around and quickly helped him to his feet. Amber ran on up the trail thirty meters in front of them.

Hot, wet blasts of wind and misty water came up from inside the mountain. The wind gusted thirty miles per hour from down inside the mountain. Amber shouted something at Levine and Ben, and she waved her hand for them to hurry up.

Levine glanced at her watch.

57.9

"Less than a minute, Ben!" she shouted, but her voice was ripped away on a powerful blast of wind that came up from inside the mountain with a force that knocked her forward onto her hands and knees. She staggered up to her feet as best she could, and Ben pushed her forward with a firm hand.

Amber reached the rim. She was only fifty meters in front of them. Levine roared at her and told her to go, waving her hand forward, but Amber stood there a moment more. She looked torn between running for clearer safety and staying there to help Levine and Ben on their last few steps to the top.

They were only thirty meters from the rim's lip. It was late afternoon, and golden sunlight slanted across the sky at them. The sky to the west was brightening for sunset.

All around them, the mountain shook. Earth slid down the rim. Trees splintered and cracked. A powerful hundred-mile-per-hour wind rushed up from the depths of the mountain. They only had ten meters to go. A tree splintered right in front of them, started to fall, and Levine grabbed Ben's hand and dove forward. They both hit the ground hard. The tree fell behind them, and the farthest edges of the tree's branches hit their legs.

Levine grabbed Ben and pulled him to his feet. In that turning motion, she saw the numbers on her wristwatch.

12.2

"Come on!" Amber shouted.

Levine yelled, "Go!"

Amber hesitated a few seconds more and then turned and ran.

Levine and Ben crested the rim of the mountain. Levine saw Amber ahead of her, running on the level tan path atop Kevorak's Needle. She headed forward into the forest of trees.

Would it be enough? Would they be safe?

Ben hurried along as best he could. They entered the thicket of ponderosa pines.

Was it fifty meters to Gardner's Lake? Would that be far enough away from the opening?

Levine looked at her watch, saw that there was only four seconds left, and took off, running as hard as she could over the path through the trees. She thought she saw the glimmer of the mountaintop lake up ahead, through the trees.

The blast of wind that preceded the eruption was over five hundred miles per hour directly in the center of the chasm. It was caused by the rush of water pushing the wind forward up through the mountain. The "stream" of air was one hundred meters in diameter, the width of the opening into the mountain.

It was like a giant firehose had been turned on, and Levine felt, and then heard the blast of wind and water from deep inside the mountain.

She was far enough away and the jet of wind and water was concentrated enough, that the wind that blasted her from behind was only about one hundred and twenty miles per hour. It was enough that the pine trees all bent over, away from the center of the mountain, some snapping and cracking in a horrific cacophony of sound. Levine rushed out of the stand of trees, saw Gardner's Lake up to her right, saw Amber forty meters ahead of her on the trail, and she dove to the ground and covered her head.

The initial blast and the ensuing minute afterwards was the most violent period. Rocks and debris blasted up into the air and then came down. Levine was covered in dirt and gravel before the water started pouring down from the sky.

The jet of water blasting up from inside the mountain reached up into the sky some nine miles directly above Kevorak's Needle. From ten miles away, it looked like a giant fountain shooting water straight up into the sky.

It was at once violent and the single most beautiful thing Levine had ever seen. She lay there covering her neck and head for two minutes, until she heard Ben over her. She rolled over and looked up at the old man.

Ben was dancing a jig, and rain poured down on them.

Gardner's Lake was far enough away from the immediate center of the mountain that the residual wind died down to a steady thirty miles per hour, still strong, and many of the trees had been bent or laid out flat in the initial blast. But now there was just a steady stream, a *river* filling the sky high overhead.

It was raining!

Levine smiled at Ben and climbed to her feet. Amber came running back up the trail to them through the wind, and then Levine saw Helen and Roger. Everyone came together near Gardner's Lake.

The sky overhead was already darkening with moisture and with pockets of clouds, and everyone shouted excitedly at one another. Everyone smiled. They were soaking wet, and they were alive, and they were together on top of a mountain in the single greatest moment of their lives.

• •

The rains did not stop for four weeks, by which time, the mountains in the northern Randa lands flowed with rivers and creeks and ponds and lakes. The water flowed down out of the mountains and met with the parched desert land to the south. There, the earth soaked up the water for three days like an enormous geologic sponge. The group reached Ben's home in three days, by which time the ground was so saturated that it could not hold the water any more, and lakes formed in giant ten and twenty-mile-wide permutations on the desert plains.

As the rains continued, lakes overflowed their natural banks and joined with other lakes, forming even larger lakes, some as large as one hundred miles across.

And still, the rains continued.

It was a fortunate circumstance that no one lived in the desert because the shifts in land, in hills, in dunes were on a scale like nothing anyone had ever seen.

The largest of the lakes flooded over into other large lakes, and by the third week, there were three seas to the west, north, and east of where Ben and Amber had once lived.

The immediate reaction had been jubilation and celebration, but as the rains continued on into their fourth week, there began to grow a very real fear that everything would just be washed away, the whole Randa world submerged under a giant ocean.

But then the mountain subsided. The jet coming up from Kevorak's Needle settled, and three days later the skies began to clear. And instead of one giant blanket of cloud, there were patches of white amidst the blue heavens. The three moons continued their daily courses across the sky, and gentle waves rose up from the seas. Everything seemed to find its balance and its rhythm, and the hill that had been Ben's home became a thirty-mile-wide island.

There were other islands poking up from the crystal blue waters, and atop one island far to the south, there was a bright and shining light. It rose from the waters like a beacon, and Levine, Roger, Helen, and Amber knew they had to go home.

Epilogue
An Arizona Wedding

Amy Levine stood in front of the mirror and checked her bridesmaid's dress one last time. The dress was cobalt blue, and her hair was up in a chignon. She looked very pretty, but more importantly, she was happy. She was home.

Helen was up the hallway, and Levine could hear the chatter and nervous laughter coming from the room. The irony that it was the same room in which Helen and Roger had found Levine's leather satchel so many months ago was not lost on her. She appreciated the ironies of life. And besides, there was a practical reason for having the wedding at Levine's cottage: she had a big enough yard to accommodate the seventeen hundred people who were outside in folding chairs, waiting for the bride.

All of Oracle's residents were invited, and almost all were in attendance. Family had flown in from as far north as Maine and as far south as the Florida Keys. A television news crew from Tucson had tried to get up the mountain to Dr. Amy Levine's newly bought cottage and land, but security had politely asked to see their invitations, and they had none. A few photographs were snapped, but the news team went back down the mountain without further incident.

Another news helicopter was circling the mountains, but it was staying far enough away as to keep from annoying the guests too much. The rumor had leaked three days before that it was *Levine* who was being married, and media interest and speculation had escalated to a feverish pitch.

The search and rescue of a small band of friends trapped in a snowbound Colorado town had captured the public's interest the past winter. It was as though people wanted something to believe in, a story to quietly follow in the headlines, a real-life cliffhanger with a happy ending. More than five hundred people had volunteered to help in the search effort, but in the end, Levine and her friends were located by a farming family fifteen miles southwest of Montrose, Colorado.

"I knew 'em as soon as I saw 'em," cattle rancher Donnie Millerton told CNN. "They looked rough, sure, but their photos had been on the television non-stop for three months."

"What were your first words?" the CNN anchor asked Millerton.

Donnie's face widened into a grin. His eyes gleamed. "I said, 'Nice day for a cross-country ski, ain't it?'"—off-camera the news anchor laughed—"And then I invited them down to the house for soup. We got on the horn from there."

Levine walked up the hallway toward Helen's room. She knocked on the door and poked her head in. Everyone inside looked up.

"Wow!" Levine said.

Helen stood in the middle of the room, and her white bridal gown flowed down onto the ground. She was surrounded by her four sisters, who were each dressed in bridesmaids' gowns matching Levine's. Helen smiled nervously.

"Do I look okay?" she said.

Levine stepped into the room. She looked at Helen's sisters and at her mom, who was dressed in a pretty black and gray dress. Helen's mom wore a corsage on her left wrist and a pretty hat on her graying hair.

"Helen, that gown kicks butt," Levine said, and everyone burst out laughing. "Wow."

"How is everything?" Helen said.

"Outside, you mean?"

Helen nodded her head vigorously, and Levine walked back up the hallway and looked through the kitchen, out the kitchen window, into the front yard and down the hill.

She called back, "Looks like a rock concert; except everybody's dressed up and seated in folding chairs."

She turned and smiled at Helen who was now standing in the doorway to the room. Helen's gray-green eyes were bright and eager.

There were upwards of two thousand friends, neighbors, and relatives outside. There were three huge white tents on either side of the outdoor congregation. There was so much love in the air that it felt to Levine that her heart was filled with sunshine, and the feeling was so pure and so true and so *good* that she felt like she might fall all to pieces inside, such was the intensity of her emotions. Helen looked beautiful, and she came up the hallway and gave her friend a hug.

She whispered, "We did it."

Levine couldn't hold it back any longer. She started to cry. She bit her lip and said, "Yeah. We did."

The two friends looked at one another for a long minute, Levine wiping tears away from her face, Helen becoming almost serene with contentment, pride, and joy.

A young girl's voice said, "What's with all the tears?"

Levine and Helen looked back through the kitchen, toward the washer and dryer room. There in the doorway stood Amber Page, dressed in a matching cobalt-blue bridesmaid's dress. She was the most beautiful eleven-year-old that Amy Levine or Helen Richards had ever seen.

"There's a groom out here, waiting for the love of his life," the voice came from the front door.

Helen's father stood in a smart tuxedo. His silver hair was combed back, and his gray eyes took in all the ladies, and he just smiled.

Levine, Amber, and Helen pulled themselves together a moment, looked calm, and then looked at one another and burst out laughing, and all the women in the hallway started laughing, too.

The group sitting closest to the house (at the back of the congregation) heard the laughter, and heads started turning, looking up towards the front door. Helen's father turned, looked at them, and shrugged.

A minute later, the small group went out the front door and down the hill in the front yard. There were more than two hundred rows on either side of the centermost aisle, and a stir went up among the crowd as they made their way toward the stage.

The views to the west were stunning, easily fifty miles down to and past Tucson and more than seventy miles to the north, all the way to Phoenix. The air was a perfect seventy-five degrees, and the late-afternoon sun was cruising toward the mountains on the horizon. By the end of the service, the crowd would be treated to an Arizona sunset from this mile-high terrace.

And then the party was scheduled to go all night under starlight like few had ever seen. Three bands were lined up, and there were decks and pools and hot tubs and caterers and wet bars, a dance floor, go-carts, a merry-go-round, a Ferris wheel, and a fleet of limousines to carry anyone anywhere they wanted to go. In the past five weeks, Levine's little place had been transformed from secluded to included with a blacktop asphalt driveway winding through the newly purchased seven-thousand-acre ranch, ground level lights spaced ten feet apart on both sides of the drive. It was going to be a fun night for everyone in Oracle.

Ten minutes later, the service began, and Helen's father walked her down the aisle. Roger stood at the front looking as cool as a two-dollar bill. Zeb Brudock even looked polished and happy, standing a few feet to Roger's right.

As the music played and Helen made her way down the aisle, Zeb subtly patted his jacket pocket and felt the wedding ring. Roger gave him a friendly wink, and Zeb smiled bashfully.

The service went off without a hitch, and Amber squeezed Levine's hand when the pastor asked Helen if she'd take this man to be her husband.

Helen said, "I do," and more than a few eyes in the audience moistened with tears of joy.

A moment later, Roger McAllister answered the same way to a similar question, and the noble-looking pastor smiled and said that he now pronounced them "husband and wife."

Everyone in the audience began to clap and cheer and whistle, and a few men had to wipe their eyes with white hankies.

Helen and Roger kissed, and to the west, the sun touched the desert mountaintops on the far horizon, casting rays of golden, orange, pink, and red sunlight across the sky.

Helen and Roger held one another's hands and started up the aisle, and everyone started showering them with rice. Roger ducked and smiled, and Helen laughed and led him faster up the aisle.

• •

The manila envelope that Roger handed Levine the next afternoon at one o'clock contained three black-and-white photographs and a letter written on Nano Tech letterhead.

Roger and Levine stood twenty meters from the packed and loaded limousine that would carry Roger and Helen McAllister to the Phoenix Sky Harbor International Airport. From there, it was a direct five-hour flight to the island of Maui.

The envelope was not sealed. Levine took it from Roger and looked up quizzically into his eyes.

"There was a check in that envelope," Roger said, "for a lot of money."

"I don't understand," Levine said.

The photos slid out of the envelope first.

"I'll never have to work another day in my life," Roger said.

Helen burst out laughing at something one of her sisters said to her at the limousine door.

Roger said, "But I can't cash that check in good conscience unless you follow through with what's written on the note."

Levine glanced at the photos. The three photos were of an older man with an academic-looking beard. He had spectacles, and he smiled in a curious way. In the third photo, the man was standing in front of a table at a teak-wood lodge, and Levine could clearly read the name of the lodge on the sign. It read "Portal Peak Lodge."

"He'd like to meet you," Roger said, "according to the letter."

"Who?" Levine said, but her eyes were already reading the letter. They'd already glanced at the name at the bottom of the page.

Tears filled Levine's eyes, and a hand came up to her mouth. The hand was shaking. Levine staggered backward the way someone might stagger if they'd just read that they won the three hundred million dollar jackpot lottery.

The letter was signed "Your father, Oscar Levine."

Levine couldn't bring herself to speak for some time, but when she did, she said, "This has got to be some kind of a joke. A hoax." She looked at Roger, then at the crowd that had gathered around them, as though her whole life was unraveling in front of her.

Roger looked at Levine. She'd built her whole life on the foundation that her parents were dead. Everything she was, was a result of her belief that they were dead, that *both* of her parents were dead, and she was suddenly faced with the possibility that her father had never died. The note said that her mother *was* dead, had died in the plane crash, but that he—her father—was very much alive. It was too much for her to handle.

"Amy," Roger said. "It's no joke. Go to him, or don't go to him. Sleep on it a day, or a month, or a year. The choice is yours. But your father—he's alive."

Whispers rippled through the crowd.

Levine just stood there; she was stunned. She was shaking. Roger crossed to her, embraced her, and kissed her on the cheek.

"Go to him," Roger whispered. "You deserve that much."

Roger leaned back, clasped her shoulders, and looked into her eyes.

Amber stood with the rest of crowd, taking it all in.

"I've found my peace," Roger whispered to Levine. "Now, you find yours."

He smiled, nodded his head, and embraced her one more time. The group began to break up, and everyone began saying their goodbyes. Helen climbed into the back of the limousine, followed by Roger. Everyone was shouting and waving their goodbyes, and Roger smiled one last time, leaned and kissed his wife, and then closed the door.

• •

Three days later, Amy Levine woke at 3:47 A.M. Amber was asleep in the guest room and serious plans about her future were in order. Levine had been unable to sleep well since Roger gave her the manila envelope. She'd occupied herself with cleaning up after the wedding, but it was the third day, and everyone was gone.

She crossed to the kitchen window and looked out at the city lights twinkling down in the valley. She made a pot of coffee. She stood there gazing down at the city until the pot of coffee was done brewing, and then she poured herself a cup.

She opened the manila envelope and looked at the photos again. In her heart, she knew it was her father. He had aged thirty years from the photos by which she remembered him, but there was something in a person's eyes that never aged. It grew weary, but there was *something* there, a shine, a glimmer, a sparkle, something that no words could ever capture.

It was the edge, that division between humanity and the devine, and it was almost always there even in the most desperate of lives, even when all hope was gone. She saw it in her father's eyes, and she knew he was alive.

She crossed to the back of the house and saw Amber sleeping. The young girl looked peaceful, almost angelic in the moonlight that streamed in through the window. Levine crossed to her, shook her shoulder lightly, and woke her up. Amber's eyes opened.

Levine said, "I have to talk to my father."

Even waking from the depths of sleep, Amber perfectly realized the gravity of what Levine was telling her. She too had lost a father, once upon a time. She understood very clearly what Levine was saying.

Amber sat up. "Should I pack?" she asked.

Levine sat there on the bed. She said, "Enough for two nights; we'll know by then."

Amber rubbed sleep from her eyes, nodded, and climbed out of bed.

"How long is the drive?" she asked.

Levine stood up. She said, "Three hours."

And the two friends started to pack enough for two night's stay at the Portal Peak Lodge in Portal, Arizona.

· ·

Ninety minutes southeast of Tucson, Levine's beat-up green '73 Plymouth Fury exited Interstate-10 at Exit 382. They were in the middle of the desert, and there was a 4-K Truck Stop "OPEN 24 Hrs" and not much else. Tumbleweed rolled across the parking lot, and there were three eighteen-wheelers gassing up at the big-rig pumps.

Levine pulled into the parking lot and let the top down on her car. Amber ran inside and used the restroom. She bought a soda and sunflower seeds from a barrel-chested convenience-store clerk who must have weighed two hundred pounds more than her. The man smiled and said, "Have a nice day, young lady."

"You too," Amber said with a smile, and she trotted back out to Levine and the beat-up convertible Plymouth Fury.

Levine got back into the car and pointed them south on the old two-lane state highway. The yellow lines painted down the middle were so aged they weren't intelligible, and the road looked like it hadn't seen work since it was first built back in the late 1940s.

Amber pointed to a green sign up on the side of the road. It read "Portal Road To Paradise 2," but it looked like it was missing a number on the right side of the "2."

She checked the map and said, "It looks like it's about twenty-five miles, but it turns into a dirt road on up ahead."

The sky was brightening, and they could see the Chiricahua Mountains rising to the south and to the west. Portal and then Paradise were perched up on the northeast side of these mountains over seven thousand feet above sea level. The word *was* that they were ghost towns, but a ghost, Levine supposed, was what they were looking to find.

Her pulse beat hard in her chest, and her breath grew shallow and thin. She let her hand hang out the window like a bird in flight. The wind whipped over the open convertible, and she breathed in the cool desert air and felt alive and free.

From the passenger seat, Amber looked at her. There was a hesitation where she didn't know what to think or say. Levine seemed to have passed through whatever roadblocks lay inside her mind. She'd reached some kind of resolution; perhaps some kind of inner peace, for Amber saw it shining in Levine's eyes.

Amber fixed her eyes on the eastern horizon and watched the sunrise. The sky filled with golden reds, oranges, pinks and blues, colors that blended into one another and into the heavens.

A few miles farther, the car hit the dirt road, and a cloud of dust rose up behind it.

THE END

An Afterword by the Author

I loved writing this book. I remember exactly where I was when I began it in May 2003. I remember what I did thirty minutes before I put the first words on the page: I took a walk through the community of Warner Ranch in Tempe, Arizona, and I saw the lawn maintenance guys who inspired the opening chapter.

I remember where I got the image for the house in which Levine is interviewed. It's an actual fourteen-acre compound known as Rock Harbour on the northern end of Man-O-War Cay in the Bahamas. It had been for sale on Christie's Great Estates.

The Colorado Sequence was my fourth novel (*The Band*, *Culpepper*, and *Amber Page* preceded it), and I wrote it at a time of great hope and joy in my life. For over a year, I had been dating an extraordinary gal who would later become my wife, and I had worked out the kinks of a writing process in the first three novels.

The Colorado Sequence was the first novel where I really felt like I knew what I was doing, and I just had a blast writing it. The first draft was completed in January 2004 in Oracle, Arizona. So, it took eight months from start to finish.

After I was done, I gave the manuscript to three readers: my wife Dr. Susan K. Miller-Cochran, Shelley Rodrigo, and Lisa Cahill. These three exceptional readers gave me great feedback, and we workshopped the novel in Scottsdale, Arizona in March 2004.

One of the comments in that session that made it into the revised version was that I should introduce the Black Wraith characters earlier in the novel. They also suggested a major change to the Parker Walcott character. Initially there had been a romantic subplot between Parker and Sara that ended up on the cutting room floor. There were aspects to the Arizona motel room scene that were changed, and the final chapter was trimmed back considerably.

There were dozens of subtle changes like this to improve the manuscript, and I can't say enough how helpful that feedback was. I'd like to take this opportunity to thank all three readers for their time and effort. I believe this novel is better for having been read by them.

I would like to give thanks also to several readers of the previous novel in the series who wrote reviews of *Amber Page and the Legend of the Coral Stone*. Your reviews mean a great deal to me.

Thank you to Becky from England who courageously and compassionately wrote the first review ever of a novel by me. Thank you also to Meredith from Huntersville, North Carolina who wrote a thoughtful and intelligent review of *Amber Page*. Thank you to Mary Lou, whom I met at the airport my first day at WorldCon 2006 and who promised to write a review of *Amber Page*. And did. Thank you as well to Hannah Stone, fellow Lulu author, who wrote a review.

Thanks to Gene Curtis, author of *The Seventh Mountain* who wrote an insightful review and invited me to speak with his writers' group in South Boston, Virginia. I had a blast at the Prizery, folks.

I'd like to thank my mom and dad, too, who have never questioned my career choice in over twelve years. I don't think I've said it until now how important your constant support and love has been to me.

I keep a framed note my mom gave to me during the winter of 2002, when I was absolutely broke, living in Oracle, Arizona, and writing my first novel. Written on that note (which is above my desk as I write this Afterword) is the following by Lisey King:

> Faith is about
> Being in a vulnerable position
> And knowing
> You'll be okay.
>
> It's about
> People telling you
> Certain things
> Aren't possible
> When you know that they are. . . . .

And finally, I would like to say thank you to Susan. This, ladies and gentleman, is a woman who took a chance on a guy who was living in

a remote mountain town in Arizona, a guy who had scant publication credits and said that he was a writer. To me, Susan is proof that there is a God, and that that God cares about us.

Many prayers over many lifetimes led to our meeting.

Thank you.

Stacey Cochran
Raleigh, North Carolina
February 1, 2007

CLAWS

A Suspense Novel by Stacey Cochran

Coming Fall 2008

For more info, visit staceycochran.com

Stacey Cochran was born in 1973. He was selected as a finalist in the 1998 Dell Magazines undergraduate fiction competition, and that gave him the determination he needed to pursue a career as a writer. In 2001, he made his first professional short story sale to *CutBank*. He has since received a Master's degree in English, published two novels and a short story collection, and four times been selected as a quarterfinalist in the Writers of the Future short story competition. In 2004, his novel *Culpepper* was selected as a finalist for the St. Martin's Press/PWA Best First Private Eye Novel Contest. He lives in Raleigh, North Carolina with his wife Dr. Susan Miller-Cochran and their son Sam, and he teaches writing at North Carolina State University.